THE
QUEEN'S
RESISTANCE

ALSO BY REBECCA ROSS

The Queen's Rising

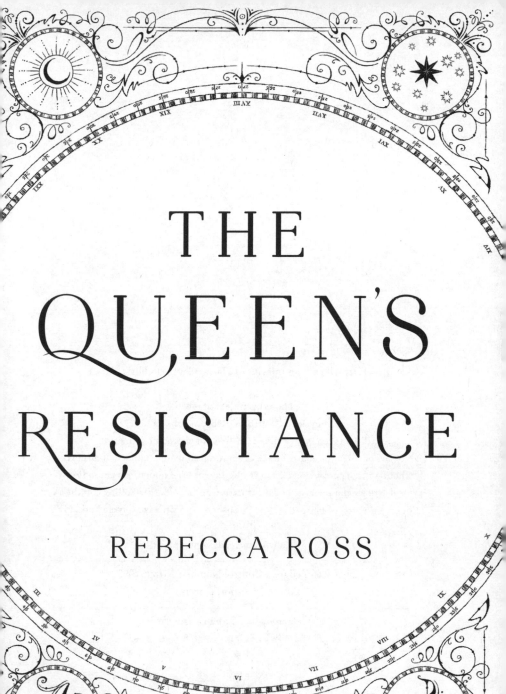

THE
QUEEN'S
RESISTANCE

REBECCA ROSS

HARPER TEEN
An Imprint of HarperCollinsPublishers

HarperTeen is an imprint of HarperCollins Publishers.

Library of Congress Control Number: 2018966092
ISBN 978-0-06-247138-3

Typography by Aurora Parlagreco
19 20 21 22 23 PC/LSCH 10 9 8 7 6 5 4 3 2 1

First Edition

To my grandparents—
Mark and Carol Deaton & John and Barbara Wilson,
who continue to inspire me every day.

TABLE OF CONTENTS

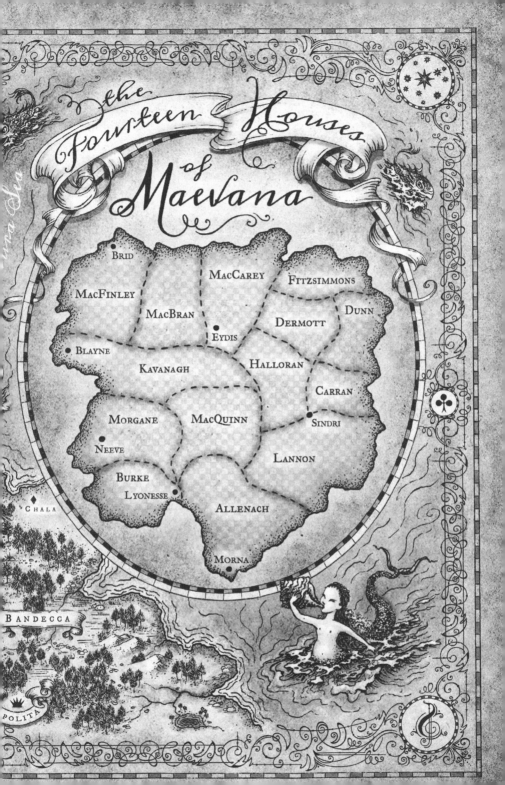

CAST OF CHARACTERS

HOUSE of MacQUINN—*The Steadfast*

Brienna MacQuinn, mistress of knowledge, the lord's adopted daughter

Davin MacQuinn, lord of MacQuinn (formerly Aldéric Jourdain)

Lucas MacQuinn, master of music, the lord's son (formerly Luc Jourdain)

Neeve MacQuinn, weaver

Betha MacQuinn, head weaver

Dillon MacQuinn, groom

Liam O'Brian, thane

Thorn MacQuinn, castle chamberlain

Phillip and Eamon, men-at-arms

Isla MacQuinn, healer

HOUSE of MORGANE—*The Swift*

Aodhan Morgane, master of knowledge, lord of Morgane (formerly Cartier Évariste)

Seamus Morgane, thane

Aileen Morgane, wife of Seamus, castle chamberlain

Derry Morgane, stonemason

HOUSE of KAVANAGH—*The Bright*

Isolde Kavanagh, queen of Maevana (formerly Yseult Laurent)

Braden Kavanagh, father to the queen (formerly Hector Laurent)

HOUSE of LANNON—*The Fierce*

Gilroy Lannon, former king of Maevana

Oona Lannon, wife of Gilroy Lannon

Declan Lannon, son of Gilroy and Oona

Keela Lannon, Declan's daughter

Ewan Lannon, Declan's son

HOUSE of HALLORAN—*The Upright*

Treasa Halloran, lady of Halloran

Pierce Halloran, the lady's youngest son

HOUSE of ALLENACH—*The Shrewd*

Sean Allenach, lord of Allenach, Brienna's half brother

Daley Allenach, the lord's manservant

HOUSE of BURKE—*The Elder*

Derrick Burke, lord of Burke

HOUSE of DERMOTT—*The Loved*

Grainne Dermott, lady of Dermott

Rowan Dermott, husband of Grainne Dermott

OTHERS MENTIONED

Merei Labelle, mistress of music

Oriana DuBois, mistress of art

Tristan Allenach

Tomas Hayden

Fergus Lannon

Patrick Lannon

Ashling Morgane

Líle Morgane

Sive MacQuinn

THE FOURTEEN HOUSES of MAEVANA

Allenach the Shrewd

Kavanagh the Bright

Burke the Elder

Lannon the Fierce

Carran the Courageous

MacBran the Merciful

Dermott the Loved

MacCarey the Just

Dunn the Wise

MacFinley the Pensive

Fitzsimmons the Gentle

MacQuinn the Steadfast

Halloran the Upright

Morgane the Swift

ALLENACH FAMILY

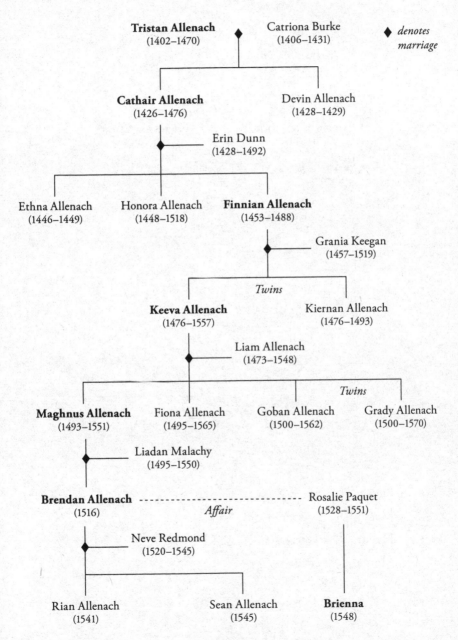

Tristan Allenach
(1402–1470) ♦ Catriona Burke
(1406–1431)

♦ *denotes marriage*

Cathair Allenach
(1426–1476)

Devin Allenach
(1428–1429)

♦ Erin Dunn
(1428–1492)

Ethna Allenach
(1446–1449)

Honora Allenach
(1448–1518)

Finnian Allenach
(1453–1488)

♦ Grania Keegan
(1457–1519)

Twins

Keeva Allenach
(1476–1557)

Kiernan Allenach
(1476–1493)

♦ Liam Allenach
(1473–1548)

Twins

Maghnus Allenach
(1493–1551)

Fiona Allenach
(1495–1565)

Goban Allenach
(1500–1562)

Grady Allenach
(1500–1570)

♦ Liadan Malachy
(1495–1550)

Brendan Allenach
(1516) - - - - - - - - - - - - - - - - *Affair* - - - - - - - - - - - - - - - Rosalie Paquet
(1528–1551)

♦ Neve Redmond
(1520–1545)

Rian Allenach
(1541)

Sean Allenach
(1545)

Brienna
(1548)

MacQuinn Family

Tiernan MacQuinn
(1494–1543)

Isibeal Byrne
(1496–1541)

Davin MacQuinn
(1517)

Bebinn MacQuinn
(1519–1550)

Sive Coghlan
(1520–1541)

Lucas MacQuinn
(1540)

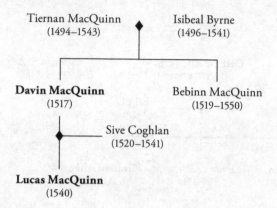

MORGANE FAMILY

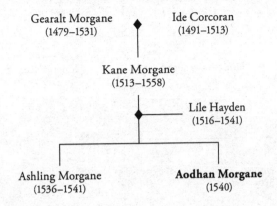

Gearalt Morgane
(1479–1531)

Ide Corcoran
(1491–1513)

Kane Morgane
(1513–1558)

Líle Hayden
(1516–1541)

Ashling Morgane
(1536–1541)

Aodhan Morgane
(1540)

KAVANAGH FAMILY

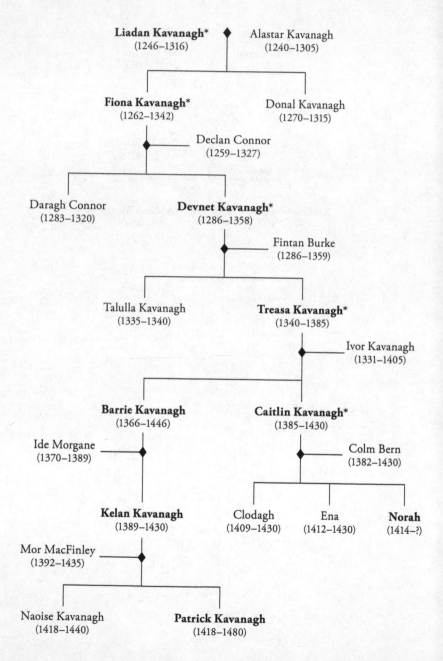

Liadan Kavanagh* (1246–1316) ◆ Alastar Kavanagh (1240–1305)

Fiona Kavanagh* (1262–1342) — Donal Kavanagh (1270–1315)

◆ Declan Connor (1259–1327)

Daragh Connor (1283–1320) — **Devnet Kavanagh*** (1286–1358)

◆ Fintan Burke (1286–1359)

Talulla Kavanagh (1335–1340) — **Treasa Kavanagh*** (1340–1385)

◆ Ivor Kavanagh (1331–1405)

Barrie Kavanagh (1366–1446) — **Caitlin Kavanagh*** (1385–1430)

Ide Morgane (1370–1389) ◆ — ◆ Colm Bern (1382–1430)

Kelan Kavanagh (1389–1430) — Clodagh (1409–1430) — Ena (1412–1430) — **Norah** (1414–?)

Mor MacFinley (1392–1435) ◆

Naoise Kavanagh (1418–1440) — **Patrick Kavanagh** (1418–1480)

KAVANAGH FAMILY
(continued)

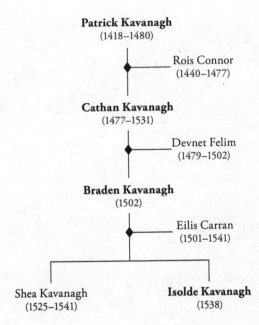

Patrick Kavanagh
(1418–1480)

Rois Connor
(1440–1477)

Cathan Kavanagh
(1477–1531)

Devnet Felim
(1479–1502)

Braden Kavanagh
(1502)

Eilis Carran
(1501–1541)

Shea Kavanagh
(1525–1541)

Isolde Kavanagh
(1538)

PART ONE
THE RETURN
October 1566

⇥ ONE ⇤

THE ENEMY'S DAUGHTER

Lord MacQuinn's Territory, Castle Fionn

Brienna

The castle was brimming with laughter and dinner preparations when Cartier and I entered the hall, blue passion cloaks on our backs, the night breeze tangled in our hair. I came to a stop in the heart of the grand room to admire the hanging tapestries, the high arch of the ceiling that melted into smoky shadows, the mullioned windows on the eastern wall. There was a fire roaring in a glazed hearth, and the women of the castle were setting the best pewter and silver on the trestle tables. They did not take note of me, for I was still a stranger to them, and I watched as a group of young girls decorated the table spines with a current of pine boughs and dark red flowers. A boy was rushing behind them to light a mountain range of candles, his eyes clearly taken with one of the auburn-haired girls.

For a moment, it would almost seem as if this castle and these people had never known the darkness and oppression of the Lannon family's reign. And yet I wondered what wounds remained in their hearts, in their memories after surviving a tyrannical king for twenty-five years.

"Brienna." Cartier came to a gentle stop at my side. He stood a safe distance away from me—a full arm's length—although I could still feel the memory of his touch, I could still taste his lips on mine. We stood together quietly, and I knew he too was soaking in the clamor and rustic beauty of the hall. That he was still trying to adjust to what our lives were about to become now that we had returned home to the queen's realm of Maevana.

I was the adopted daughter of Davin MacQuinn—a fallen lord who had been in hiding for the past twenty-five years—who had finally returned to light his hall and restore his people.

And Cartier, my former instructor, was the lord of the House of Morgane. The lord of the Swift—Aodhan Morgane.

I could hardly find the will to call him by such a name. It was one I would have *never* imagined him possessing throughout all the years I had known him in the southern kingdom of Valenia, when I had been his pupil and he had been my teacher, a master of knowledge.

I thought of how our lives had intertwined, from the very first moment I had met him when I was accepted into the prestigious Magnalia House, a Valenian school for the five passions of life. I had assumed that he was Valenian—he had taken on a Valenian name, was polished in etiquette and passion, and had lived nearly all of his life in the southern kingdom.

And yet he had been far more than that.

"What kept you?"

I startled, Jourdain taking me by surprise as he stepped into my view, his eyes sweeping me from head to toe, as if he expected me to have a scratch. Which almost struck me as humorous, because three days ago, we had ridden into battle with Isolde Kavanagh, Maevana's rightful queen. I had donned armor, streaked blue woad across my face, braided my hair, and wielded a sword in Isolde's name, not knowing if I was going to live through the revolution. But I had fought for her, as had Cartier and Jourdain, and with her to challenge Gilroy Lannon, a man who should *never* have been king of this land. Together, we had brought him and his family down in the span of a morning, a bloody yet victorious sunrise.

And now Jourdain was acting as if I had been darting through battle once more. All because I was late for dinner.

I had to remind myself to be understanding. I was not accustomed to fatherly fussing—I had lived my entire life not knowing who my blood father was. And, oh, how regretfully I knew now who I had descended from; I pushed his name from my mind, focusing instead on the man standing before me, the man who had adopted me as his own months ago, when the two of us joined our knowledge to plot a rebellion against King Lannon.

"Cartier and I had much to talk about. And don't look at me like that, Father. We're back in time," I said, but my cheeks warmed under Jourdain's attentive scrutiny. And when he shifted his eyes to Cartier, I think he knew. Cartier and I had not been merely "talking."

I irresistibly thought back to that moment when I had stood with Cartier in his dilapidated castle on Morgane lands, when he had given me my passion cloak at last.

"Yes, well, I told you to be back before dark, Brienna," Jourdain said, and then he softened his tone when he addressed Cartier. "Morgane. Nice of you to join us for a celebratory feast."

"Thank you for extending the invitation, MacQuinn," Cartier returned with a respectful bow of his head.

It was odd to hear such names spoken aloud, for they didn't align as such within my mind. And while others would begin to address Cartier as Lord Aodhan Morgane, I would always think of him as Cartier.

Then there was Jourdain, my patron-turned-father. When I had met him two months ago, he had introduced himself as Aldéric Jourdain, his Valenian alias. But, like Cartier, he was far more than that. He was Lord Davin MacQuinn the Steadfast. And while others would begin to address him as such, I would call him "Father," and would always think of him as Jourdain.

"Come, the two of you." Jourdain led us up to the dais, where the lord's family was to sit and sup at a long table.

Cartier winked at me when Jourdain's back was angled to us, and I had to swallow a smile of pure joy.

"There you are!" Luc cried as he entered the hall through one of the side doors, his gaze finding me on the dais.

The young girls paused in their pine-and-flower arrangements to giggle and whisper as Luc passed them. His dark brown hair was in disarray, which was a daily occurance, and his eyes were bright with mirth.

He clomped up the dais stairs to sweep me into an embrace, acting as if we had been apart for months although I had seen him earlier that afternoon. He took me by the shoulders and turned me about, so he could see the silver threads stitched upon my passion cloak.

"*Mistress* Brienna," he said. I turned back around and laughed, to finally hear the title linked to my name. "It's a beautiful cloak."

"Yes, well, I waited long enough for it, I should think," I replied, helplessly glancing to Cartier.

"Which constellation is it?" Luc asked. "I fear I am rather horrible with astronomy."

"It is Aviana."

I was a mistress of knowledge now, something I had labored years at Magnalia House to achieve. And in that moment, standing in Jourdain's hall in Maevana, surrounded by family and friends, wearing my passion cloak, with Isolde Kavanagh about to return to the northern throne . . . I could not have been more satisfied.

As we all sat down, I watched Jourdain, a golden chalice in his hands, his face carefully guarded as he surveyed his people entering the hall for dinner. I wondered what he was feeling, to finally come home after being gone for those twenty-five years of terror, to wade back into his role of lord to these people.

I knew the truth of his life, of his Maevan past as well as his Valenian one.

He had been born in this castle as a noble son of Maevana. He had inherited the lands and people of MacQuinn, striving to protect them as he was forced to serve the horrible King Gilroy

Lannon. I knew Jourdain had witnessed terrible things in the king's hall—he had seen hands and feet cut off of men who could not pay the full amount of their taxes, had seen old men lose an eye for looking at the king for too long, had heard women scream from distant chambers as they were beaten, had seen children scourged for making a sound when they should have been quiet. *I watched it*, Jourdain had once confessed to me, pale from the memory. *I watched it, afraid to speak out.*

Until he had finally decided to rebel, to take down Gilroy Lannon and put a rightful queen back upon the northern throne, to snuff out the darkness and the terror that had become the once-glorious Maevana.

Two other Maevan Houses had joined his secret revolution—the Kavanaghs, who had been the one magical House of Maevana and the origin of queens, and the Morganes. But Maevana was a land of fourteen Houses, as diverse as the land, each holding their own strengths and weaknesses. Yet only three dared to defy the king.

I think it was doubt that held most of the lords and ladies back, because two precious artifacts were missing: the Stone of Eventide, which gave the Kavanaghs their magical power, and the Queen's Canon, which was the law that declared no king was to ever sit upon Maevana's throne. Without the stone and the Canon, how was the rebellion ever going to completely overthrow Gilroy Lannon, who was deeply rooted on the throne?

But twenty-five years ago, MacQuinn, Kavanagh, and Morgane had united and stormed the royal castle, prepared to wage war. The success for the coup depended on taking Lannon by surprise, which was spoiled when my biological father, Lord Allenach, learned of the rebellion and ultimately betrayed them.

Gilroy Lannon was waiting for Jourdain and his followers.

He targeted and killed the women of each family, knowing it would take the heart out of the lords.

But what Gilroy Lannon did not anticipate was for three of the children to survive: Luc. Isolde. Aodhan. And because they did, the three defying lords fled with their children to the neighboring country of Valenia.

They took on Valenian names and professions; they discarded their mother tongue of Dairine for the Valenian language of Middle Chantal; they buried their swords and their northern sigils and their anger. And they hid, raising their children to be Valenian.

But what most did not know . . . Jourdain never stopped planning to return and dethrone Lannon. He and the other two fallen lords met once a year, never losing faith that they could rise again and be successful.

They had Isolde Kavanagh, who was destined to become queen.

They had the desire and the courage to revolt once again.

They had the wisdom of years on their side, as well as the painful lesson from the first failure.

And yet they were still missing two things that were vital: the Stone of Eventide and the Queen's Canon.

That was when I joined them, for I had inherited memories from a distant ancestor who had buried the magical stone centuries ago. If I could recover the stone, magic would return to the Kavanaghs, and the other Maevan Houses might join our revolution at last.

And that was exactly what I had done.

All of this had happened mere days and weeks ago, and yet it felt like it had happened very long ago, like I was looking back upon all of it through fractured glass, even though I was still bruised and battered from battle and secrets and betrayals, from discovering the truth of my own Maevan heritage.

I sighed, let my reveries fall away as I continued to regard Jourdain sitting at the table.

His dark auburn hair was pulled back by a ribbon, which made him look Valenian, but a circlet crowned his head, a glimmer of light. He was dressed in simple black breeks and a leather jerkin with a golden falcon stitched over the breast, the proud sigil of his House. There was still a cut on his cheek from the battle, slowly healing. A testament of what we had just endured.

Jourdain glanced down into his chalice, and I finally saw it—the flicker of uncertainty, the doubt in himself, the haunting unworthiness—and I took a goblet of cider and drew out the chair close to his, to sit at his side.

I had grown up in the company of five other ardens at Magnalia House, five girls who had become like sisters to me. Yet these past few months surrounded by men had thoroughly taught me about their natures, or, more important, how fragile their hearts and egos were.

I remained quiet at first, and we watched his people bring

forth steaming platters of food, setting them down on the tables. I began to notice it, though; quite a few of the MacQuinns talked in hushed tones, like they were still afraid to be overheard. Their clothes were clean but threadbare, their faces deeply grooved from years of hard labor, decades absent of smiles. Several of the boys were even sneaking slivers of ham from the platter, stuffing the food in their pockets, as if they were accustomed to being hungry.

And it was going to take time for the fear to fade, for the men and women and children of this land to heal and find restoration.

"Does this all feel like a dream to you, Father?" I eventually whispered to Jourdain, when I felt the weight of our silence.

"Hmm." Jourdain's favorite sound, which meant he was agreeing in half. "Some moments it does. Until I look for Sive and realize she is no longer here. Then it feels like reality."

Sive, his wife.

I could not help but imagine what she had been like, a woman of valor, of bravery, riding into battle all those years ago, sacrificing her life.

"I wish I had known her," I said, sadness filling my heart. I was familiar with such a feeling; I had lived with it for many years, this longing for a mother.

My own mother had been Valenian, having died when I was three. But my father had been Maevan. Sometimes, I felt broken between these two countries: the passion of the south, the sword of the north. I wanted to belong here with Jourdain, with the MacQuinn people, but when I thought of my paternal blood . . . when I remembered that Brendan Allenach, lord as he was traitor, was my blood father . . . I wondered how I could ever be accepted here, in this castle that he had terrorized.

"What does this feel like to you, Brienna?" Jourdain asked.

I thought for a moment, savoring the golden warmth of the firelight and the happiness that swelled in Jourdain's people as they began to gather around the tables. I listened to the music Luc spun on his violin, melodious and sweet, rousing smiles from the men and women and children, and I leaned toward Jourdain, to rest my head upon his shoulder.

And so I gave him the answer that he needed to hear, not the one that I fully felt yet.

"It feels like coming home."

I didn't realize how ravenous I was until the food was set down, platters of roasted meats and herb-sprinkled vegetables, breads softened by butter, pickled fruits, and plates of sliced cheese with different-colored rinds. I piled more food than I could possibly handle onto my plate.

While Jourdain was preoccupied with speaking to the men and women who continually ascended the dais to formally greet him, Luc pulled his chair around so he could face Cartier and me.

"Yes?" I prompted when Luc continued to smile at us.

"I want to know the truth," he said.

"About what, brother?"

Luc cocked his brow. "About how the two of you knew each other! And why you never said anything about it! During our planning meetings . . . how did you not know? As far as the rest of our rebel group went, we all believed you two were strangers."

I kept my eyes on Luc, but I felt Cartier's gaze shift to me.

"We never said anything because we did not know of the other's involvement," I said. "In the planning meetings, you called Cartier *Theo D'Aramitz*. I didn't know who that was. And then you called me *Amadine Jourdain*, and Cartier didn't know who that was." I shrugged, but I could still feel the shock of the revelation, that heady moment when I had realized Cartier was Lord Morgane. "A simple misunderstanding caused by two aliases."

A simple misunderstanding that could have destroyed our entire mission to restore the queen.

Since I had known where my ancestor had buried the Stone of Eventide, I had been sent to Maevana, to seek Lord Allenach's hospitality while I covertly recovered the stone on his lands. In addition, Jourdain's rebel group had planned for Lord Morgane to masquerade as a Valenian noble visiting Castle Damhan for the autumnal hunt. His true mission was to prepare the people for the queen's return.

"And who told you about it?" I asked Luc.

"Merei," my brother said, taking a quick sip of ale to hide how his voice softened when he spoke her name.

Merei, my best friend and roommate at Magnalia, who had passioned in music and had also known Cartier for what I had always believed him to be—a Valenian master of knowledge.

"Mm-hmm," I said, relishing the fact that my brother was now the one to flush beneath my scrutiny.

"What? She offered the truth to me after the battle," Luc

stammered. "Merei said, 'Did you know Lord Morgane taught Brienna at Magnalia? And we had no idea he was a Maevan lord?'"

"And so—" I started, but was cut short by Jourdain, who suddenly rose to his feet. At once, the hall fell quiet, every eye going to him as he held his chalice, gazing over his people for a few moments.

"I wanted to speak a few words, now that I have returned," he began. "I cannot tell you how it feels to be home once more, to be reunited with you. For the past twenty-five years, I have thought of you upon rising, and upon lying down at night. I spoke your names in my mind when I could not sleep, remembering your faces and the sound of your voices, the talents of your hands, the joy of your friendship." Jourdain paused, and I saw the tears in his eyes. "I have done wrong by you, to abandon you as I did that night of the first rising. I should have stayed my ground; I should have been here when Lannon arrived, seeking me. . . ."

A painful lull overcame the hall. There was only the sound of our breaths coming and going, the crackle of the fire burning in the hearth, a child cooing in its mother's arms. I felt my heart quicken, as I had not expected him to say this.

I glanced at Luc, whose face had gone pale. Our eyes met; our thoughts united as we both thought, *What should we do? Should we say something?*

I was one moment away from rising myself when I heard the steady footsteps of a man approaching the dais. It was Liam, one of Jourdain's remaining thanes, who had escaped Maevana years ago to search for his fallen lord and who had eventually found

Jourdain in hiding, joining our revolution.

We could not have fully revolted without Liam's insight. I watched him now ascend the steps and set his hand on Jourdain's shoulder.

"My lord MacQuinn," the thane said. "Words cannot describe what we feel to see you return to this very hall. I speak for all of us when I say that we are overjoyed to be reunited with you. That we thought of *you* every morning upon rising, and every evening as we lay down to sleep. That we dreamt of this very moment. And we knew you would return for us one day."

Jourdain stared at Liam, and I saw the emotion building in my father.

Liam continued. "I remember that dark night. Most of us here do. Coming around you in this very hall after the battle, bringing your lad into your arms." He glanced to Luc, and the love in his eyes nearly stole my breath. "You fled because *we* asked and wanted you to, Lord MacQuinn. You fled to keep your son alive, because we could not bear to lose the both of you."

Luc rose, walking around the table to stand on the other side of Liam. The thane set his right hand upon my brother's shoulder.

"We welcome you both back, my lords," Liam said. "And we are honored to serve you once more."

The hall came alive as everyone stood, holding up their cups of ale and cider. Cartier and I stood as well, and I held my cider up to the light, waiting to drink to my father's and brother's health. "To Lord MacQuinn—" Thane Liam started, but Jourdain abruptly turned to me.

"My daughter," he rasped, extending his hand for me.

I all but froze, surprised, and the hall fell silent as everyone looked at me.

"This is Brienna," Jourdain said. "My adopted daughter. And I could not have returned home without her."

I suddenly was flooded with the fear that the truth from Castle Damhan had spread—*Lord Allenach has a daughter*. Because I had certainly announced myself as Allenach's long-lost daughter last week in his hall. And while I did not know the extent of the terror and brutality that had happened on this soil, to this people, I did know that Brendan Allenach had betrayed Jourdain, and had taken Jourdain's people and lands twenty-five years ago.

I was their enemy's daughter. When they looked at me, did they still see a shade of him? *I am no longer an Allenach. I am a MacQuinn*, I reminded myself.

I stepped to Jourdain's side, let him take my hand and draw me even closer, beneath the warmth of his arm.

Thane Liam smiled at me, an apologetic gleam in his eyes, as if he was sorry to have overlooked my presence. But then he raised his cup and said, "To the MacQuinns."

The toast bloomed throughout the hall, scattering the shadows, soaring as light up to the rafters.

I hesitated for only a moment before I lifted my cider and drank to it.

After the feast, I found myself being ushered by Jourdain with Cartier and Luc up the grand stairs to the room that had once been my father's office. It was a wide chamber with walls carved deep with bookshelves, the stone floors overlaid with furs and rugs to mask our footsteps. An iron chandelier hung above a table set with a beautiful mosaic face, the beryl, topaz, and lapis lazuli squares depicting a falcon in flight. On one wall was a large map of Maevana; I took a moment to admire it before joining the men at the table.

"It's time to plan the second step of our revolution," Jourdain said, and I recognized the same spark that I had seen in him when we had plotted our return to Maevana in the dining room of his Valenian town house. How distant those days felt now, as if that had occurred in another life entirely.

On the surface, it would seem that the hardest leg of our revolution was over. But when I began to think upon all that sprawled before us, exhaustion began to creep up my back, weigh upon my shoulders.

There was plenty that could still go wrong.

"Let's begin by writing down our concerns," Jourdain suggested.

I reached for fresh parchment, a quill, and a stopper of ink, preparing to scribe.

"I'll go first," Luc volunteered. "The Lannons' trial."

I wrote *The Lannons* on the paper, shivering as I did so, as if the mere scratch of the quill's nib could summon them here.

"Their trial is in eleven days," Cartier said.

"So we have eleven days to decide their fate?" Luc asked.

"No," Jourdain replied. "*We* will not decide it. Isolde has already made it known that the people of Maevana will judge them. Publicly."

I wrote that down, remembering that historic event three days ago when Isolde had entered the throne room after battle, splattered with blood, the people standing behind her. She had removed the crown from Gilroy's head, struck him multiple times, and then made him slither down to the floor, to lie prostrate before her. I would never forget that glorious moment, the way my heart had beat with the realization that a queen was about to return to the Maevan throne.

"We arrange a scaffold on the castle green, then, so all may attend," Cartier said. "We bring forth the Lannons one at a time."

"And we have our grievances read aloud," Luc added. "Not just ours, but anyone who wishes to testify against the Lannons' transgressions. We should send word to the other Houses, to bring their grievances to the trial."

"If we do so," Jourdain warned, "the entire Lannon family will most likely face death."

"The entire Lannon family must be held accountable," Cartier said. "That is how it has always been done in the north. The legends call it the 'bitter portions' of justice."

I knew that he was right. He had taught me the history of Maevana. To my Valenian sensibilities, this merciless punishment felt dark and harsh, but I knew this had been done to prevent resentment growing in noble families, to hold those with power in check.

"Lest we forget," Jourdain said, as if he had read my mind,

"Lannon has all but annihilated the Kavanagh House. He has tortured innocent people for *years*. I do not like to assume that Lannon's wife and his son, Declan, supported him in such endeavors—perhaps they were too afraid to speak out. But until we can properly interview them and those around them, I think it is the only way. The Lannon family as a whole must be punished." He fell quiet, deep in thought. "Any public support we can gather for Isolde is vital and needs to happen quickly. While the throne is empty, we are vulnerable."

"The other houses need to publicly swear fealty to her," I said.

"Yes," my father replied. "But even more so, we need to forge new alliances. Breaking an oath is far easier to do than breaking an alliance. Let's sort through the alliances and rivalries we know of—it'll give us an idea of where we need to begin."

I wrote *House Alliances* first, creating a column to fill. With fourteen Houses to consider, I knew this could quickly become a tangled mess. Some of the older alliances were the sort of relationships that had originated when the tribes became Houses and received their blessings from the first queen, Liadan, centuries ago. And they were often alliances forged from marriage and from sharing borders and similar foes. But I also knew that Gilroy Lannon's reign had most likely corrupted some of those alliances, so we could not wholly depend upon historical knowledge.

"Which Houses support Lannon?" I asked.

"Halloran," Jourdain said after a moment.

"Carran," Cartier added.

I wrote those names down, knowing there was one more, one

final House that had fully supported the Lannons during the terror. And yet the men were not going to say it; it would have to come from my own mouth.

"Allenach," I murmured, preparing to add it to the list.

"Wait, Brienna," Cartier said gently. "Yes, Lord Allenach supported Lannon. However, your brother, Sean, has now inherited the House. And your brother joined us in the battle on the green."

"My *half* brother, but yes. Sean Allenach threw his support behind Isolde, even if it was last-minute. Do you want me to persuade Sean to publicly support the Kavanaghs?" I questioned, wondering how I could even go about such a conversation.

"Yes," Jourdain said. "Gaining Sean Allenach's support is vital."

I nodded, eventually writing Allenach off to the side.

We conversed through the remaining alliances that we knew of:

Dunn—Fitzsimmons (through marriage)

MacFinley—MacBran—MacCarey (covers the northern half of Maevana; alliance shared from a common ancestor)

Kavanagh—MacQuinn—Morgane

The Houses of Burke and Dermott were the only freestanding Houses.

"Burke declared his support when he fought with us on the green," I said, remembering how he had brought his men- and women-at-arms just as we were faltering in battle, when I thought we might lose. Lord Burke had changed the tide of the fight, granting us that final burst of strength we needed to overcome Lannon and Allenach.

"I'll speak privately with Lord and Lady Burke," Jourdain

said. "I don't see why they wouldn't swear allegiance to Isolde. I'll also reach out to the other three Mac Houses."

"And I'll extend an invitation to the Dermotts," Cartier offered. "Once I get my House in order."

"And perhaps I can win over the Dunn-Fitzsimmons alliance with a little music, eh?" Luc said, waggling his eyebrows.

I smiled at him, to hide the fact that the Allenachs were left for me to deal with. I would think on it later, when I had a moment alone to sort through the array of emotions it provoked in me.

"Now, on to the rivalries," I said. I knew two of them and took the liberty to write them down:

MacQuinn—Allenach (border dispute, still unresolved)

MacCarey—Fitzsimmons (over access to the bay)

"Who else?" I asked, my quill dripping stars of ink on the paper.

"Halloran and Burke have always been at odds," Jourdain said. "They compete with their steel goods."

I added them to the list. Surely, there had to be more rivalries. Maevana was known for its fierce and stubborn spirit.

I was staring at my list, but from the corner of my eye, Jourdain looked to Cartier, and Cartier shifted minutely in his chair.

"Morgane and Lannon," he said, so quietly I almost didn't hear him.

I raised my eyes to Cartier, but he was not looking at me. His gaze was transfixed on something distant, something that I could not see.

Morgane—Lannon, I wrote.

"I have another concern," Luc said, breaking the awkward silence. "The Kavanaghs' magic has returned now that the Stone of Eventide has been recovered. Is this something we need to be addressing now? Or perhaps later, after Isolde's coronation?"

Magic.

I added it to the list, one little word that held so much possibility. It was evident after the battle that Isolde's gift in magic was healing. I had set the stone about her neck, and she had been able to touch wounds and heal them. I wondered if she was somehow controlling her magic.

"I'm not," she had confessed to me. "I wish I had an instructor, a guidebook . . ."

She had confided in me the day after the battle.

"If my magic goes astray . . . I want you to swear to me that you will take the Stone of Eventide away. I do not desire to wield magic for evil, but for the good of the people," she had whispered, and my gaze had drifted to where the stone rested against her heart, alight with color. "And as of this moment, there is still so much about it I do not know. I do not know what I am capable of. You must promise me, Brienna, that you will hold me in check."

"Your magic will not go astray, Lady," I had whispered in return, but my heart began to ache at her admission.

This had been the *very* reason why the stone had gone missing one hundred and thirty-six years ago. Because my ancestor Tristan Allenach had not only resented the Kavanaghs for being the one House to bear magic, but he had also feared their power, particularly when they wielded it in war. Magic *did* go astray in battle, this much I knew, even though I didn't fully understand it.

I had seen bits and pieces of this filtered through the memories I had inherited from Tristan.

The last memory had been of a magical battle gone terribly wrong. The way the sky had nearly split in two, the dreadful trembling in the earth, the unnatural way weapons had turned on their handlers. It had been terrifying, and I partly understood why Tristan had decided to assassinate the queen and take the stone from her.

And yet . . . I could not envision Isolde becoming a queen whose magic went corrupt, a queen who could not control her gifts and power.

"Brienna?"

I glanced up at Jourdain, unaware of how long I had been sitting at the table, reminiscing. All three men were gazing at me, waiting.

"Do you have any thoughts about Isolde's magic?" my father asked.

I considered sharing that conversation with the queen, but I decided that I would hold her fears privately.

"Isolde's magic favors healing," I said. "I don't think we need to be afraid of it. History has shown us that the Kavanaghs' magic only went astray in battle."

"Yet how vast is the Kavanagh House now?" my brother asked. "How many Kavanaghs are left, and will they all be of the same mind-set as Isolde and her father?"

"Gilroy Lannon was bent upon destroying them, more than any other House," Jourdain said. "He killed a 'Kavanagh a day' at the beginning of his reign, accusing them of false crimes, making a sport of it." He paused, grieved. "I would not be surprised if only a small remnant of the Kavanaghs remained."

The four of us fell silent, and I watched the candlelight trickle over the falcon mosaic, catching the glimmer of the stones.

"Do you think Lannon kept record of their names?" Cartier asked. "They should be read as grievances at the trial. The realm needs to know how many lives he has stolen."

"I do not know," Jourdain responded. "There were always scribes in the throne room, but who knows if Lannon allowed them to record truth."

More silence, as if we could no longer find words to speak. I stared at my list, knowing we had not truly created any solid plans this night, and yet it seemed as if we had at least opened a door.

"I say we meet privately with Isolde when we return to Lyonesse for the trial," my father finally said, breaking the quiet. "We can speak to her more about the magic, and how she would prefer her grievances to be read."

"I agree," Cartier said.

Luc and I nodded our consent.

"I think that is all for tonight," Jourdain said, rising. Cartier, Luc, and I mirrored him, until the four of us stood in a circle, our faces cast half in firelight, half in shadows. "I shall send a letter to Isolde, to let her know our thoughts for the trial so she can begin gathering grievances in Lyonesse. I'll also send missives to the other Houses, to prepare their grievances. The only thing I ask of the three of you now is to remain aware, vigilant. We

TWO

A TRAIL OF BLOOD

Lord Morgane's Territory, Castle Brígh

Cartier

There was a time in my life when I believed I would never return to Maevana. I did not remember the castle I had been born in; I did not remember the lay of the land that had been in my family for generations; I did not remember the people who had sworn fealty to me as my mother held me to her heart. What I did remember was a kingdom of passion and grace and beauty, a kingdom that I later learned was not mine although I yearned for it to be, a kingdom that had held and guarded me for twenty-five years.

Valenia was mine by choice.

But Maevana . . . she was mine by birthright.

I had grown up believing myself to be Theo D'Aramitz; I had

have planned a rebellion before; we should know what to look for, should supporters of Lannon dare to impede our plans to crown Isolde."

"Do you think we will face opposition?" Luc asked with an anxious fidget of his hands.

"Yes."

My heart plummeted at Jourdain's response; I had believed that every Maevan would be thrilled to see the Lannons overturned. But the truth was, there were most likely groups of people who would scheme to disrupt our progress. People with darkened hearts who had loved and served Gilroy Lannon.

"We are one step from returning the queen to the throne," my father continued. "Our greatest opposition will no doubt come in the next few weeks."

"I believe so as well," Cartier said, his hand drifting close to mine. We did not touch, but I felt his warmth. "Isolde's coronation is going to be one of the greatest days this land has ever seen. But wearing the crown is not going to protect her."

Jourdain looked to me, and I knew he was imagining me in her place, not as a queen, but as a woman with a target upon her.

Crowning Isolde Kavanagh as the rightful queen was not the end of our rising. It was merely the beginning.

later defiantly become Cartier Évariste, and both were names to hide beneath, a shield for a man who did not know where he was supposed to live or who he was supposed to be.

I thought of such things as I departed Jourdain's castle well past midnight.

"You should stay the night, Morgane," Jourdain had said to me, after our planning meeting had come to an end. He followed me down the stairs, concerned. "Why ride out so late?"

What he meant to say was, *Why ride back to sleep alone in a crumbling castle?*

And I did not have the courage to tell him that I needed to be on my own lands that night; I needed to sleep where my father and my mother and my sister had once dreamt. I needed to walk the castle I had inherited, dilapidated or not, before my people began to return.

I stopped in the foyer, reaching for my passion cloak, my travel satchel, my sword. Brienna was there, waiting on the threshold, the doors open to the night. I think she knew what I needed, because she looked to Jourdain and murmured, "It'll be all right, Father."

And Jourdain, thankfully, left it at that, clapping me on the arm in a wordless farewell.

It had already been a strange night, I thought, moving to where Brienna waited. I had not expected to hear Jourdain speak his regrets, to witness the first step of healing for the MacQuinns. I felt like an imposter; I felt burdened each time I anticipated my own homecoming and reunion.

But then Brienna smiled up at me, the night breeze playing with her hair.

How did you and I reach this point? I wanted to ask, but held the words captive in my mouth as she caressed my face.

"I shall see you soon," I whispered, not daring to kiss her here, in her father's house, where Jourdain was most likely observing us.

She only nodded, her hand falling away from me.

I departed, fetching my horse from the stables, the sky crowded with stars.

My lands lay to the west of Jourdain's, our castles only several miles apart, which equated to roughly an hour's ride. On the way to Castle Fionn that evening, Brienna and I had found a deer trail connecting the two territories, and we had chosen to take that instead of the road, winding through a forest and over a rill, eventually meandering into the fields.

It was the longer route, beset by thorns and branches, but I chose again to take it that night.

I rode the trail as if I had done so countless times, following moonlight and wind and darkness.

I had already been to my lands once, earlier that day.

I had come alone and taken my time walking through the corridors and the rooms, uprooting weeds and streaking through dust and cutting down gossamer, hoping I could remember something fair about this castle. I had been one year old when my father had fled with me, but I hoped that a fragment of my family, a seed of my memory, had lingered in this place, proving that I deserved to be here, even after twenty-five years of solitude. And when I could remember nothing—I was a stranger within these walls—I had conceded to sit on the dirty floor of my parents' chamber, eaten by grief until I had heard Brienna arrive.

Despite all of that, the castle still took me by surprise.

Once, Castle Brígh had been a beautiful estate. My father had described it to me in perfect detail years ago, when he had finally told me the truth of who I was. But what he had depicted to me did not correspond with how it looked now.

I eased my horse to a trot as we approached, my eyes smarting from the cold as I struggled to see it in full by moonlight.

It was a crumbling sprawl of gray stones; the foothills of the mountains rose steadily behind it, draping shadows on the uppermost floors and turrets. A few slopes of the roof gaped with holes, but the walls were thankfully intact. Most of the windows were shattered, and vines had nearly overtaken the front of the exterior. The courtyard was thick with weeds and saplings. I had never seen a place more forlorn in my life.

I dismounted, standing in waist-high grass, continuing to stare at the castle, feeling as if the castle was leering back at me.

What was I to do with such a broken place? How was I to rebuild it?

I untacked my horse, leaving him hobbled beneath an oak, and began the trek to the courtyard, stopping in the wild heart of it. I stood on vines and thorns and weeds and broken cobbles. All of it mine, the bad as well as the good.

I found that I was not the least bit sleepy although I was bone weary and it had to be drawing nigh to two in the morning. I began to do the first thing that came to mind: pull up the weeds. I worked compulsively until I warmed myself, sweating against autumn's frost, eventually getting on my hands and knees.

That was when I saw it.

My fingers yanked up a tangle of goldenrod, exposing a long cobble with a carving in the stone. I brushed away the lingering roots until I could clearly see the words, gleaming in the starlight.

Declan.

I shifted back to my heels, but my gaze was hooked to that name.

Gilroy Lannon's son. The prince.

He had been here that night, then. The night of the first failed rising, when my mother was slain in battle, when my sister was murdered.

He had been here.

And he had carved his name into the stones of my home, the foundation of my family, as if by doing so, he would always have dominion over me.

I crawled away with a shudder and sat down in a heap, the sword sheathed at my side clattering alongside me, my hands covered in dirt.

Declan Lannon was in chains, held prisoner in the royal dungeons, and he would face trial in eleven days. He would get what he deserved.

Yet there was no comfort in it. My mother and my sister were still dead. My castle was in ruins. My people scattered. Even my father was gone; he had never had the chance to return to his homeland, dying years ago in Valenia.

I was utterly alone.

A sudden sound broke my chain of thoughts. A tumbling of stones from within the castle. My eyes went to the broken windows at once, searching.

Quietly, I rose, drawing my sword. I waded through the weeds to the front doors, which hung broken on their hinges. It rose the hair on my arms to push those oaken doors open further, my fingers tracing their carvings. I peered into the shadows of the foyer. The stones of the floor were cracked and filthy, but by the moonlight that poured in through the shattered windows, I saw the imprint of small, bare feet in the dirt.

The footprints wound into the great hall. I had to strain my eyes in the dim light to follow them back to the kitchen, weaving my way around the abandoned trestle tables, the cold hearth, the walls stripped bare of their heraldic banners and tapestries. Of course, the footprints went to the buttery, to every cupboard in an obvious search for food. Here there were empty casks of ale that still sighed with malt, old herbs hanging in dried batches from the rafters, a family of goblets encrusted with dust-coated jewels, a few broken bottles of wine that left glittering constellations of glass on the floor. A smudge of blood, as if those bare feet had accidentally stepped on a piece of glass.

I knelt, touching the blood. It was fresh.

The trail of blood took me out the back door of the kitchens, into a narrow corridor that emptied into the rear foyer, where the servants' staircase wound in a tight spiral to the second floor. I stepped through a hoard of cobwebs, stifling a shudder when I finally reached the second-floor landing.

Moonlight poured in patches through this hallway, illuminating piles of leaves that had blown in from the broken windows. I continued following the blood, my boots crunching the leaves and finding every loose stone in the floor. I was too exhausted to be stealthy. The owner of the footprints undoubtedly knew I was coming.

They led me right to my parents' chamber. The very place I had stood with Brienna hours ago, when I had given her her passion cloak.

I sighed, finding the door handles. Nudging them open, I peered into the dim light of the chamber. I could still see where Brienna and I had wiped the dust from the floors, to admire the colorful tiles. This room had felt dead until she had stepped within it, as if she belonged here more than I did.

I entered and was promptly assaulted with a handful of pebbles.

I whirled, glaring across the chamber to see a flash of pale limbs and a mop of unkempt hair disappear behind a sagging wardrobe.

"I am not going to hurt you," I called out. "Come. I saw your foot is bleeding. I can help you."

I took a few steps closer but then paused, waiting for the stranger to reappear. When they didn't, I sighed and took another step.

"I am Cartier Évariste." And I winced, to realize my Valenian alias had come out so naturally.

Still no response.

I edged closer, nearly to the shadow behind the wardrobe. . . .

"Who are you? Hello?"

I finally reached the back of the furniture. And I was greeted by more pebbles. The grit went into my eyes, but not before my hand took hold of a skinny arm. There was resistance, an angry grunt, and I hurried to wipe the dust from my eyes to behold a scrawny boy, no more than ten years old, with a splash of freckles on his cheeks and red hair dangling in his eyes.

"What are you doing here?" I asked, trying to subdue my irritation.

The boy spat in my face.

I had to find the last dregs of my patience to wipe the spittle away. I then looked at the boy again.

"Are you alone? Where are your parents?"

The boy prepared to spit again, but I pulled him from the back of the wardrobe, guiding the lad to sit on the saggy bed. His clothes were in tatters, his feet bare, one still bleeding. He couldn't hide the agony on his face when he walked on it.

"Did you hurt yourself today?" I asked, kneeling to gently lift his foot.

The child hissed but eventually let me examine his wound. The glass was still in his foot, weeping a steady trickle of blood.

"Your foot needs stitches," I said. I released his ankle and continued to kneel before him, looking into a pair of worried eyes. "Hmm. I think your mother or father will be missing you. Why don't you tell me where they are? I can take you to them."

The boy glanced away, crossing his lanky arms.

It was as I suspected. An orphan, squatting in the ruins of Brígh.

"Well, lucky for you, I know how to stitch wounds." I stood

and slipped my travel satchel from my shoulder. I found my flint and sparked some of the old candles to life in the chamber, then withdrew a woolen blanket and my medical pouch, which I never traveled without. "Why don't you lie down here and let me tend to that foot?"

The boy was stubborn, but the pain must have worn him down. He settled back on the wool blanket, his eyes going wide when he saw my metal forceps.

I found my small vial of stunning herbs and dumped the remainder into my flask of water.

"Here. Take a drink. It'll help with the pain."

The boy carefully accepted the mixture, sniffing it as if I had sprinkled in poison. Finally, he relented and drank, and I waited patiently for the herbs to begin to work their numbing effect.

"Do you have a name?" I asked, propping up the wounded foot.

He was silent for a beat, and then whispered, "Tomas."

"That's a good, strong name." I began to carefully extract the glass. Tomas winced, but I continued to talk, to distract him from the pain. "When I was a lad, I always wanted to be named after my father. But instead of Kane, I was named Aodhan. An old family name, I suppose."

"I thought you said your name was . . . C-Cartier." Tomas struggled to pronounce the Valenian name, and I finally pulled out the last of the glass.

"So I did. I have two names."

"Why would a man"—Tomas winced again as I began to clean the wound—"need two names?"

"Sometimes it is necessary, to stay alive," I replied, and this answer seemed to appease him, for the boy was quiet as I began to stitch him back together.

When I finished, I gently bound Tomas's foot and found him an apple in my satchel. While he ate, I walked about the chamber, looking for any other scrap of blanket that I might sleep with, for the night's chilled air was flowing into the room through the broken windows.

I passed my parents' bookshelves, which still held a vast number of leather-bound volumes. I paused, remembering my father's love of books. Most of them were moldy now, their covers stiff and rippled from the elements. But one slender book caught my interest. It was drab in comparison to the others, whose covers were exquisitely illuminated, and there was a page sticking out at the top. I had learned that the most unassuming of books typically held the greatest of knowledge, so I slipped it beneath my jerkin before Tomas could see me.

No other blanket could be scrounged up, so I eventually conceded to sit against the wall by one of the candles.

Tomas rolled around in the wool blanket, until he looked more like a caterpillar than a boy, and then sleepily blinked at me.

"Are you going to sleep against the wall?"

"Yes."

"Do you need the blanket?"

"No."

Tomas yawned, scratched his nose. "Are you the lord of this castle?"

I was surprised by how I wanted to lie. My voice sounded odd as I replied, "Yes. I am."

"Are you going to punish me, for hiding here?"

I did not know how to respond to that, my mind hung upon the fact that the boy thought I would punish him for doing all that he could to survive.

"I know I was wrong to throw pebbles in your face, milord," Tomas rambled on, his brow wrinkled in fear. "But please . . . please don't hurt me too badly. I can work for you. I promise I can. I can be your runner, or your cup bearer, or your groom, if you like."

I didn't want him to serve me. I wanted answers from him. I wanted to demand, *Who are you? Who are your parents? Where do you come from?* And yet I had no right to ask such of him. These were answers that would be won by trust and friendship.

"I'm sure I can find a task for you. And as long as you are on my lands, I will protect you, Tomas."

Tomas murmured a sigh of gratitude and closed his eyes. Not a minute passed before he was snoring.

I waited a few moments before withdrawing the book from my jerkin. I gently leafed through the pages, tickled that I had randomly chosen a book of poetry. I wondered if this had been my mother's, if she had held this book and read by the window years ago, when a page fluttered loose from the leafs. It was folded, but there was a shadow of handwriting within it.

I took the parchment, let it unfold in my palm, delicate as wings.

January 12, 1541

Kane,

I know we both thought this would be for the best, but my family cannot be trusted. While you were gone, Oona came to visit us. I think she has grown suspicious of me, of what I have been teaching Declan in his lessons. And then I saw Declan yanking Ashling around by her hair in the courtyard. You should have seen his face as she cried, as if he enjoyed the sound of her pain. I am afraid of what I see in him; I think that I have failed him in some way, and he no longer listens to me. How ardently I wish it were different! And perhaps it would be, if he could live with us instead of being with his parents in Lyonesse. Oona, of course, was not even surprised by his behavior. She watched her son yank our daughter around, refusing to stop him, and said, "He's only a lad of eleven. He'll grow out of such things, I assure you."

I can no longer go through with this—I will not use our daughter as a pawn—and I know you would be in agreement with me. I plan to ride to Lyonesse and break Ashling's betrothal to Declan at dawn, for it is I who must do this, and not you. I'll take Seamus with me.

Yours,
Lile

I had to read it twice before I felt the bite of the words. Kane, my father. Líle, my mother. And Ashling, my sister, betrothed to Declan Lannon. She had only been five then, as this letter was written mere months from the day she was killed. What had my parents been thinking?

I knew the Lannons and the Morganes were rivals.

But I never imagined my parents had been at the origin of it.

My family cannot be trusted, my mother had written.

My family.

I held the letter to the candlelight.

What had she been teaching Declan? What had she seen in him?

My father had never revealed that my mother had come from the Lannon House. I had never learned her lineage. She was beautiful, he had said. She was lovely; she was good; her laughter had filled the rooms with light. The Morgane people had loved her. He had loved her.

I refolded her letter, hiding it in my pocket, but her words lingered, echoed through me.

My mother had been a Lannon. And I could not stop the thought from rising . . .

I am half Lannon.

⇥ THREE ⇤

TO TAKE UP GRIEVANCES

Lord MacQuinn's Territory, Castle Fionn

Brienna

I woke to the sound of banging below in the hall. I lurched out of bed, momentarily dazed. I didn't know where I was— Magnalia? Jourdain's town house? It was the windows, of all things, that reminded me; they were mullioned and narrow, and beyond them was the fog Maevana was notorious for.

I fumbled for the clothes I had worn yesterday and brushed my hair with my fingers on the way down the stairs, servants noticeably quieting as they passed me, their eyes wide as they took me in. *I must look wretched,* I thought, until I heard their whispers follow me.

"Brendan Allenach's daughter."

Those words sunk into my heart like a blade.

Brendan Allenach would have killed me on the battlefield had Jourdain not stopped him. I could still hear Allenach's voice—*I will take back the life I gave her*—as if he was walking in my footsteps, haunting me.

I hurried along, following the noise, realizing the clamor was inspired by Luc's music. My brother was standing on a table playing his violin, rousing hearty claps and cup banging from the MacQuinns.

I watched for a moment before sitting alone at the empty lord's table to eat a bowl of porridge. I could see the love and admiration in the MacQuinns' faces as they looked upon Luc, cheering him onward even as he knocked over a pint of ale. My brother's music spread over them like a healing balm.

Beyond the revelry, on the other side of the hall, I noticed Jourdain standing with his chamberlain, a grouchy old man named Thorn, no doubt discussing the plans for the upcoming day. And I began to think about what my own plans should be now, in this strange time of in-betweens—in between resuming normal life and the trial, in between an empty throne and Isolde's coronation, and perhaps more than anything, my place in between arden and mistress. I had been a student for the past seven years; now it was time for me to decide what to do with my passion.

I felt a wave of homesickness for Valenia.

I thought about the possibility of a passion House in Maevana. There were none here that I knew of, as impassionment was a Valenian sentiment. Most Maevans were familiar with the idea; however, I worried their attitudes toward it fell as cynical or skeptical, and I honestly could not fault them for it. Fathers and mothers had been more concerned about keeping their daughters and sons alive and protected. No one had time to spend years of their life studying music, or art, or even the depth of knowledge.

But all of that would soon change beneath a queen like Isolde. She had a vast appreciation of the study. I knew she desired to reform and enlighten Maevana, to see her people flourish.

And I had my own desires to sow here, one in particular being to start a House of Knowledge and maybe, hopefully, convince my best friend Merei to join me, uniting her passion of music with mine. I could see us filling these castle chambers with music and books, just as we had done at Magnalia as ardens.

I pushed my porridge bowl aside and rose from the table, walking back to my room, still struck with homesickness.

I had chosen an eastern chamber in the castle, and the morning light was just beginning to break through the fog, warming my windows with rosy hues. I walked to my desk, staring down at my writing utensils, which Jourdain had ensured I had an ample supply of.

Write to me whenever you miss me, Merei had said to me days ago, just before she departed Maevana to return to Valenia, to rejoin her patron and her musical consort.

Then I shall write to you every hour of every day, I had replied, and yes, I had been a touch dramatic to make her laugh, because we both had tears in our eyes.

I decided to take Merei's advice.

I sat at my desk and began to write to her. I was halfway

through the letter when Jourdain knocked on my door.

"Who are you writing to?" he asked after I had invited him in.

"Merei. Did you need something?"

"Yes. Walk with me?" And he offered me his arm.

I set my quill down and let him guide me downstairs and out into the courtyard. Castle Fionn was built of white stone in the heart of a meadow, with the mountains looming to the north. The morning light glistened on the castle walls as if they were built of bone, nearly iridescent in the melting frost, and I took a moment to look over my shoulder to admire it before Jourdain led me along one of the meadow paths.

My wolfhound, Nessie, found us not long after that, trotting ahead with her tongue lolling to the side. The fog was finally receding, and I could see the men working in an adjacent field; the wind carried snatches of their hums and the whisk of their sickles as the grain fell.

"I trust my people have been welcoming to you," Jourdain said after a while, as if he had been waiting until we were liberated from the castle before he voiced such a thing.

I smiled and said, "Of course, Father." I remembered the whispers that had chased me to the hall, about whose daughter I truly was. And yet I could not bear to tell Jourdain.

"Good," he replied. We walked farther in silence, until we reached a river beneath the trees. This seemed to be our talking ground. The day before, he had found me here among the moss and currents, revealing that he had secretly married his wife in this lush place, long ago.

"Have you had any more memory shifts, Brienna?" he asked.

I should have expected this question, yet I still felt surprised by it.

"No, I have not," I responded, looking to the river. I thought about the six memories I had inherited from Tristan Allenach.

The first had been brought on by an old book of Cartier's, which happened to have belonged to Tristan over a century ago. I had read the same passage as Tristan had, which had created a bond between us that not even time could break.

I had been so bewildered by the experience, I had not fully understood what was happening to me, and as a result, I told no one about it.

But it had happened again when Merei had played a Maevan-inspired song, the ancient sounds of her music vaguely linking me to Tristan as he had been searching for a place to hide the stone.

His six memories had come to me so randomly, it had taken me a while to finally theorize *how* and *why* this was happening to me. Ancestral memory was not too rare of a phenomenon; Cartier himself had once told me about it, this idea that all of us hold memories from our ancestors but only a select few of us actually experience them manifesting. So once I had acknowledged that I was one of those few people to have the manifestations, I began to understand them better.

There had to be a bond made between me and Tristan through one of the senses. I had to see or feel, hear or taste or smell something he had once experienced.

The bond was the doorway between us. The *how* of it all.

As far as the *why* . . . I came to surmise that all the memories he had passed down to me were centered on the Stone of Eventide, or else I would have most likely inherited more memories from him. Tristan had been the one to steal the stone, to hide it, to begin the decline of the Maevan queens, to be the author of magic's dormancy. And so I was the one destined to find and reclaim the stone, to give it back to the Kavanaghs, to let magic flourish again.

"Do you think you will inherit any more memories from him?" Jourdain asked.

"No," I replied after a moment, looking up from the water to meet his concerned gaze. "All of his memories pertained to the Stone of Eventide. Which has been found and given back to the queen."

But Jourdain did not appear convinced, and to be honest, neither was I.

"Well, let us hope that the memories have come to an end," Jourdain said, clearing his throat. His hand went to his pocket, which I thought was a nervous habit for him until he withdrew a sheathed dirk. "I want you to wear this again," he said, holding the blade out to me.

I recognized it. This was the same small dagger he had given me before I crossed the channel to set our revolution into action.

"You think it necessary?" I asked, accepting it, my thumb touching the buckle that would hold it fast to my thigh.

He sighed. "It would ease my mind if you wore it, Brienna."

I watched him frown—he suddenly appeared so much older

in this light. There were more threads of gray in his russet hair and deeper lines in his brow, and suddenly I was the one to feel worried about losing him when I had just gained him as a father.

"Of course, Father," I said, tucking the dirk away into my pocket.

I thought that was all he needed to say to me, and we would begin to walk back to the castle. But Jourdain continued to stand before me, the sunlight dappling his shoulders, and I sensed the words were caught in his throat.

I braced myself. "Is there something else?"

"Yes. The grievances." He paused and took a breath. "I was informed this morning that a large portion of the MacQuinns, mainly those younger than twenty-five, are illiterate."

"Illiterate?" I echoed, stunned.

Jourdain was quiet, but his eyes remained on mine. And then I realized the cause of it.

"Oh. Brendan Allenach forbid them education?"

He nodded. "It would be of great help to me if you could begin to gather grievances for the trial. I worry that we will run out of time to appropriately collect and sort them. I have asked Luc to approach the men, and I thought perhaps you could scribe for the women. I understand if it is too much to ask of you, and I—"

"It is not too much to ask," I gently interrupted him, sensing his apprehension.

"I made an announcement at breakfast this morning, for my people to begin to think about if they had any grievances, if they wanted them to be made known at the trial. I believe some will remain quiet, but I know others will wish to have them recorded."

I reached out to take his hand. "Whatever I can do to help you, Father."

He raised our hands to kiss the backs of my knuckles, and I was touched by the simple act of affection, something that we had not quite reached yet as father and daughter.

"Thank you," he rasped, tucking my fingers in the crook of his elbow.

We walked side by side back along the path, the castle coming into view. I was comfortable with the silence between us—neither of us were known as avid conversationalists—but Jourdain suddenly pointed to a large building on the eastern edge of the demesne, and I squinted against the sun to see it.

"That's the loom house," he explained, glancing down at me. "Most of the MacQuinn women will be there. That is where I would have you start."

I did as he asked, only returning to the castle to gather my writing tools. My mind was swarming as I walked the path and approached the loom house; the greatest of my thoughts was hung upon the fact that all of the young MacQuinn people were illiterate, and how devastating that was. Here I had hopes and dreams of beginning a House of Knowledge among them, but in truth, I would need to change my tactic. I would need to offer reading and writing lessons before I even attempted to educate on passion.

I stopped in the grass before the loom house. It was a long, rectangular structure built of stone, with a shingled roof and beautiful filigreed windows. The back side offered a sharp view of the valley below, where boys were herding sheep. The front door was cracked open, but it did not feel very inviting to me.

I took a deep breath and roused my courage and stepped into an antechamber. The floors were caked with mud and lined with boots, the walls crowded with hanging scarves and tattered cloaks.

I could hear the women talking farther inside. I followed the threads of their voices down a narrow corridor, nearly reaching the room in which they were working when I heard my name.

"Her name is Bri*enna*, not Bri*anna*," one of the women was saying. I stopped short at the sound, just before the threshold. "I believe she is part Valenian. Her mother's side."

"That explains it, then," said another woman in a rougher tone.

That explains what? I thought, my mouth going dry.

"She's very pretty," a dulcet voice stated.

"Sweet Neeve. You think everyone is pretty."

"But it's truth! I wish I had a cloak like hers."

"That's a passion cloak, love. You would have to go to Valenia and purchase one."

"You don't *purchase* them. You *earn* them."

My face flushed from eavesdropping, but I could hardly move.

"Well, at least she doesn't look like *him*," the rough-hewn voice spoke again, spitting the words out. "I don't think I could bear to look at her if she did."

"I still cannot believe Lord MacQuinn would adopt Allenach's daughter! His enemy! What was he thinking?"

"She fooled him. That's the only explanation."

There was a crash, as if something had accidentally overturned, followed by an exasperated curse. I heard footsteps draw close, and I rushed back down the corridor, leather satchel banging against my leg, through the muddy antechamber, and out the door.

I didn't cry, although my eyes smarted as I hurried back to the castle.

What had I thought? That Jourdain's people would like me at once? That I would fit into the weavings of a place that had suffered while I had flourished on the other side of the channel?

As I stepped into the castle courtyard, I began to wonder if it would be better for me to return to Valenia.

I began to believe that perhaps I truly didn't belong here.

— FOUR —

THE SWIFT ARE BORN FOR THE LONGEST NIGHT

Lord Morgane's Territory, Castle Brígh

Cartier

I woke with a start, a crick in my neck, my hands aching from the cold. I was slumped against the wall, and morning light was pooling on the floor, illuminating the dust on my boots. A few yards away was my wool blanket, wrinkled and empty. I blinked, gradually gaining my bearings.

I was in my parents' bedchamber. And it was freezing.

Rushing my hands over my face, I heard the distant pounding on the front doors. The echo of life moved through the castle like a heart remembering its pattern.

I stumbled to my feet, wondering if Tomas had snuck away in the night, rethinking his offer to stay here. Halfway down the broken stairwell, I heard the lad's voice.

"Are you here to see Lord Aodhan?"

I halted. There, in the crook of the front doors, was Tomas balanced on one foot, speaking to a man standing on the threshold. The light was too bright for me to wholly discern the visitor, but I couldn't breathe in that moment.

"He's sleeping. You'll have to come back later," Tomas stated and began to close the doors, which would not have done much good with how they hung from the hinges.

"I'm here, Tomas," I said, my voice almost unrecognizable. I descended the remainder of the stairs, taking care on the shattered stones.

Tomas begrudgingly relented, swinging the doors wider so that they banged against the wall.

An older man stood in the sun, his white hair knotted in a braid, his face deeply lined, and his clothes ragged. As soon as he met my gaze, astonishment shone in his eyes.

"Seamus Morgane," I said. I knew who he was. He had once held me as a child; he had once knelt before me as he swore his fealty to me. My father had told me of him countless times, this man who had been his most trusted of thanes.

"My lord Aodhan." He knelt before me, among the weeds.

"No, no." I took Seamus's hands, guiding him back to his feet. I embraced him, forgoing formality. I felt the tears rack his body as he clung to me.

"Welcome home, Seamus," I said with a smile.

Seamus composed himself and leaned back, his fingers on my arms as he stared up at me, somewhat agape, like he still could not believe I was standing before him. "I cannot . . . I cannot believe it," he rasped, tightening his hold on me.

"Would you like to come in? I fear I do not have any food or drink, or I would offer you some refreshments."

Before Seamus could respond, there was a cry from the courtyard. I glanced up to see a slim woman, also older, with curly silver hair that rested on her shoulders like a cloud, standing by a wagon overflowing with supplies. She had a corner of her patchwork apron pressed to her mouth, as if she was also trying to wrestle back a sob at the sight of me.

"My lord," Seamus said, shuffling to stand beside me, to hold his hand out to the woman. "This is my wife, Aileen."

"Gods above, look at you! How you've grown!" Aileen burst, dabbing her eyes with her apron. She extended her hands to me, and I crossed the distance, to embrace her. She hardly reached my shoulder in height, and yet she took hold of my arms and gave me a gentle shake, and I could only laugh.

Aileen nudged me back, to peer up at my face, memorizing it.

"Ah, yes," she said, sniffing. "You have Kane's build. But look, Seamus! He has Líle's coloring, Líle's eyes!"

"Yes, love. He is their son," Seamus responded, and Aileen swatted him.

"Aye, I know. And he's the most handsome lad I've ever seen."

I felt my face warm, embarrassed by all the fuss. I was grateful to be saved by Seamus, who directed the conversation to more practical matters. "Are we the first to arrive, my lord?"

I nodded, the crick in my neck protesting. "Yes. I've sent out a call to my people, to return as soon as they are able. But I fear the castle is much worse than I anticipated. I have no food. No blankets. No water. I have nothing to give."

"We didn't expect that you would," Aileen said, indicating the wagon. "This is a gift from Lord Burke. We were made to serve him during the dark years. Thankfully, he was good to us, to your people."

I walked to the wagon, to hide the tangle of my emotions. There were bundles of blankets and yarn, fresh sets of clothing, cast iron to cook in, casks of ale and cider, wheels of cheese, bushels of apples, dried shanks of meat. There was also a collection of buckets to draw water from the well, and paper and ink for letters.

"I owe Lord Burke a great debt, then," I said.

"No, my lord," Seamus spoke, laying a hand on my shoulder. "This is the beginning of Lord Burke's payment, for remaining silent when he should have spoken."

I stared at Seamus, not knowing what to say.

"Come! Let's carry the goods inside and we can begin to tidy the place," Aileen declared, seeming to sense the sorrow of my thoughts.

The three of us began to carry the casks and baskets into the kitchens, and that was when I realized Tomas had disappeared again. I almost called for him when there came another knock on the front doors.

"Lord Aodhan!" A dark-haired young man with a freckled face, whose arms were nearly the size of my waist, greeted me with a broad smile. "I am Derry, your stonemason."

And that was how the morning continued to progress.

As the light strengthened, more of my people returned, bearing whatever gifts they could bring. Two more of my thanes and their wives arrived, followed by the millers, the chandlers, the weavers, the healers, the gardeners, the brewmen, the cooks, the masons, the coopers, the yeomen . . . They returned to me laughing and weeping. Some I had never seen before; others I instantly recognized as the men- and women-at-arms who had rallied to fight with me days ago on the castle green. Only now they brought their families, their children, their grandparents, their livestock. And my mind swelled with their names, and my arms became sore from carrying so many bundles of provisions to the storerooms.

By late afternoon, the women had busied themselves with cleaning and straightening the hall, and the men had begun to clear the weeds and vines from the courtyard, to sweep out the broken glass and splintered furniture from the rooms.

I was carrying out the remains of a chair when I saw Derry standing with his back to me in the courtyard, staring down at the stone bearing Declan's name. Before I could think of something to say, the mason took an iron wedge and viciously uprooted the stone. Holding it facedown, so that the name would not show, he whistled for one of the lads, setting it into his hands.

"Run this to the quagmire, just on the other side of those woods," Derry said. "Don't turn it over, you hear? Give it to the bog just like that, facedown."

The boy nodded and bolted away with a frown, awkwardly holding the stone in his hands.

I forced myself to keep walking before Derry took note of my presence, carrying the splintered chair to the fire pit. And yet I felt a darkness creeping over me, even as I stood in the broad daylight of the meadows.

I paused before the pit, the castle at my back and a mountain of old broken furniture before me, waiting for a flame. But there was a whisper in the wind, cold and sharp from the mountains. And the dark words rose up like a hiss in the rasping of the grass, like a curse in the groaning of the oaks.

Where are you, Aodhan?

I shut my eyes, focused on what was truth, what was real . . . the rhythm of my pulse, the solidness of earth beneath me, the distant sound of my people's voices.

The voice came again, young yet cruel, accompanied by the stench of something burning, the overwhelming smell of refuse.

Where are you, Aodhan?

"Lord Aodhan?"

I opened my eyes and turned, relieved to see Seamus bearing pieces of a stool. I helped him toss the remains into the pit and then together we silently walked back to the courtyard, where Derry had already patched the Declan hole with a new, nameless stone.

"Aileen has been looking for you," Seamus finally said, guiding me back into the foyer.

I noticed how quiet and empty it was, and followed the thane into the hall.

Everyone had already gathered, waiting for me to arrive.

I took one step into the hall and stopped upright, surprised by its transformation.

There was a fire burning in the hearth, and the trestle tables were arranged and set with mismatched pewter and wooden trenchers. Corogan wildflowers had been harvested from the meadows, woven together to make a blue garland for the tables. Candles cast light over the platters of food—most of it was bread and cheese and pickled vegetables, but someone had found the time to roast a couple of lambs—and the floors beneath me gleamed like a burnished coin. But what truly caught my eye was the banner that now hung over the mantel.

The Morgane sigil. It was blue as a midsummer sky, with a gray horse stitched over the center.

I stood among my people in the hall, staring at the symbol I had been born to wear, the symbol my mother and sister had been slain beneath, the symbol I had bled to reawaken.

"The swift are born for the longest night," Seamus began, his voice resounding in the hall. These words were sacred, the motto of our House, and I watched as he turned to me, set a silver chalice of ale into my hands. "For they shall be the first to meet the light."

I held the chalice, held on to those words, for I felt as if I was falling down some long tunnel, and I did not know when I was to meet the bottom.

"To the swift!" Derry shouted, raising his cup.

"To Lord Morgane," Aileen added, standing on one of the benches so she could see me over the crowd.

They held their cups to me, and I held mine to theirs.

For appearances' sake, I appeared calm and joyful, drinking to the health of this hall. But within, I was trembling from the weight of it.

I heard the whisper again, rising from the shadows in the corner. I heard it over the cheers and clamor as dinner began, as I was led to the dais.

Where are you, Aodhan?

Who are you? I inwardly growled back to it, my mind tensing as I sat in my chair.

It faded, as if it had never been. I wondered if I was hearing things, if I was beginning to lose my wits with exhaustion.

But then Aileen set the finest mutton chop on my plate, and I watched the red juices begin to pearl on the plate. And I knew.

Those words had once been spoken in this castle, twenty-five years ago. They had come from the person who had ripped this castle apart, trying to find my sister, trying to find me.

Declan Lannon.

→ FIVE →

CONFESSIONS BY CANDLELIGHT

Lord MacQuinn's Territory, Castle Fionn

Brienna

The last thing I expected was for one of the weavers to come knocking at my door that evening.

I had managed to take down a few grievances among the women-at-arms, those who I had fought alongside during the battle. But after overhearing the conversation at the loom house, I did not approach any others. I spent the remainder of the day trying to appear useful, trying not to compare my scant list of grievances with the great tome that Luc had accumulated.

I was more than ready to retire for bed after dinner.

I sat before the fire with woolen stockings pulled up to my knees and two letters perched on my lap. One letter was from Merei, but the other was from my half brother, Sean, who I was supposed to persuade to alliance with Isolde Kavanagh. Both letters had arrived that afternoon, surprising me; Merei's because she must have written it the day after she departed Maevana, and Sean's because it was entirely unexpected. The question of the Allenachs' allegiance was a constant simmer in the back of my mind, but I had not yet determined a way to address it. So why was Sean writing me, of his own accord?

October 9, 1566
Brienna,

I am sorry to be writing you so soon after the battle, because I know that you are still trying to adjust to your new home and family. But I wanted to thank you—for remaining with me when I was injured, for sitting with me despite what others might have thought of you. Your bravery to defy our father has inspired me in many measures, the first being to do my best to redeem the House of Allenach. I believe there are good people here, but I am overwhelmed with how to begin purging the corruption and cruelty that has been encouraged for decades. I do not think I can do this on my own, and I wondered if you would be willing to at least write to me for now, to pass some ideas and thoughts on how I should begin to right the wrongs committed by this House. . . .

There was a hesitant rap on my door. Startled, I quickly folded my brother's letter and hid it within one of my books.

So the Allenachs, as far as my brother was concerned, would not be too difficult to persuade.

I pushed the relief aside as I opened the door, perplexed to see a young girl.

"Mistress Brienna?" she whispered, and I recognized her voice. It was sweet and musical, the voice that had remarked I was pretty when I eavesdropped on the weavers' hall.

"Yes?"

"May I come in?" She cast a glance down the corridor, as if she was worried she would be discovered here.

I took a step back, wordlessly inviting her inside. I shut the door behind her, and the two of us returned to sit before the fire, awkward and adjacent to each other.

She was wringing her pale hands, her mouth quirked to the side as she stared at the fire, as I tried not to stare at her. She was thin and angular with wispy blond hair, and her face was scarred by the pox—tiny white flecks dotted her cheeks like snow.

Just as I was drawing breath to speak, she brought her eyes to mine and said, "I must apologize for what you overhead today. I saw you through the window leaving in a hurry. And I felt horrible that you had come to us and we were speaking of you in such a way."

"I must be the one to apologize," I said. "I should have announced myself. It was wrong for me to linger at the door without your knowledge."

But the girl shook her head. "No, Mistress. That does not excuse our words."

But you were the only one to speak well of me, and yet you are the one to come and ask for forgiveness, I thought.

"May I ask why you came to see us today?" she inquired.

I hesitated before saying, "Yes, of course. Lord MacQuinn has asked me to help gather grievances of the people. To take to the Lannon trial next week."

"Oh." She sounded surprised. Her hand fluttered up to her hair, and she absently wrapped the ends around her finger, a slight frown on her face. "I am sixteen, so Allenach was the only lord I ever knew. But the other women . . . they remember what it was like before Lord MacQuinn fled. Most of their grievances are held against Lord Allenach, not the Lannons."

I looked to the fire, a poor attempt to hide how much this conversation rattled me.

"But you are not Allenach's daughter," she said, and I had no choice but to meet her gaze. "You are Davin MacQuinn's daughter. I have only thought of you as such."

"I am glad to hear that," I said. "I know that it is difficult for others here to regard me that way."

Again, I was overcome with the cowardly urge to flee, to leave this place, to cross the channel and sink into Valenia, where no one knew whose daughter I was. Forget about establishing a House of Knowledge here; I could easily do such in Valenia.

"My name is Neeve," she said after a moment, extending a beacon of friendship to me.

It nearly brought tears to my eyes. "It is a pleasure to meet you, Neeve."

"I do not have a grievance for you to write down," Neeve said.

"But there is something else. I wanted to see if you could write down a few of my memories from the dark years, so one day I can pass them down to my daughter. I want her to know the history of this land, what it was like before the queen returned."

I smiled. "I would be more than happy to do that for you, Neeve." I rose to gather my supplies, dragging my writing table before the fire. "What would you like me to record?"

"I suppose I should start at the beginning. My name is Neeve MacQuinn. I was born to Lara the weaver and Ian the cooper in the spring of 1550, the year of storms and darkness. . . ."

I began to transcribe, word for word, pressing her memories into ink on the page. I soaked in her stories, for I longed to understand what life had been like during "the dark years," as the people here referred to the time of Jourdain's absence. And I found that I was grieved as well as relieved, for while Neeve was forbidden some things, she was protected from others. Not once had Lord Allenach physically harmed her, or allowed his men to do so. In fact, he never once looked at her or spoke to her. It was the older women and men who were given the harsher punishments, to make them bend and cower and submit, to make them forget MacQuinn.

"I suppose I should stop for now," she said after a while. "I'm sure that is more than enough for you to have written down."

My hand was cramped and my neck was beginning to tighten from stooping over the desk. I realized she had talked beyond an hour, and we had accumulated twenty pages of her life. I set down my quill and bent my fingers back and dared to say, "Neeve?

Would you like to learn how to read and write?"

She blinked, astonished. "Oh, I don't think I would have the time, Mistress."

"We can make time."

She smiled, as if I had lit a flame within her. "Yes, yes, I would like that very much! Only . . ." Her delight faded. "Could we keep the lessons secret? At least for now?"

I couldn't deny that I was saddened by her query, knowing that she would not want others learning of our time together. But I thought again on ways I could prove myself to the MacQuinns— I needed to be patient with them, to let them come into their trust of me in their own time—and I smiled, stacking the pages together, handing them to her. "Why don't we begin tomorrow night? After dinner? And yes, we can keep it a secret."

Neeve nodded. Her eyes widened as she took the pages, as she gazed down at my handwriting, tracing it with her fingertip.

And as I regarded her, I helplessly thought back to what I had overheard that morning. *I believe she is part Valenian*, one of the weavers had said of me. They were seeing me as either southern or as an Allenach. I worried this would always set me apart from the MacQuinns no matter how much I might attempt to prove myself to them.

"Neeve," I said, an idea coming to mind. "Perhaps you can teach me something in return."

She glanced up, shocked. "Oh?"

"I want to know more about the MacQuinns, about your beliefs, your folklore, and your traditions."

I want to become one of you, I almost begged. *Teach me how.*

I already harbored *head* knowledge of the MacQuinn House, courtesy of Cartier and his teachings at Magnalia House. I knew their history, the sort that could be found in an old, dusty tome. They were given the blessing of Steadfast, their sigil was that of a falcon, their colors were lavender and gold, and their people were respected as the most skilled of weavers in all the realm. But what I lacked was knowledge of the *heart*, the social mores of Mac-Quinns. What were their courtships like? Their weddings? Their funerals? What sort of food did they serve at birthdays? Did they harbor superstitions? What was their etiquette?

"I don't know if I am the best one to teach you such things," Neeve said, but I could see how pleased she was that I had asked her.

"Why don't you tell me about one of your favorite MacQuinn traditions?" I offered.

Neeve was quiet for a moment, and then a smile emerged on her lips.

"Did you know that if we decide to marry someone beyond the MacQuinn House, we have to choose them with a ribbon?"

I was instantly intrigued. "A ribbon?"

"Or, perhaps I should say that the *ribbon* chooses for us," Neeve said. "It is a test, so we may determine who is worthy beyond our House."

I settled back in my chair, waiting for more.

"The tradition began a long time ago," Neeve started. "I do not know if you are familiar with our tapestries or not . . ."

"I've heard that the MacQuinns are known to be the best weavers in Maevana."

"Aye. So much so that we began to hide a golden ribbon in the tapestry wefts as we wove. A skilled weaver can make the ribbon melt into the design, so that it is very difficult to find."

"Every MacQuinn tapestry holds a hidden ribbon, then?" I asked, still very confused as to how this corresponded to choosing a mate.

Neeve's smile widened. "Yes. And this is how the tradition began. The first lord of MacQuinn had only one daughter, one that he loved so greatly he did not believe any man—MacQuinn or beyond—would ever be worthy of her. So he had the weavers hide a ribbon within a tapestry they were making, knowing that it would take the most determined, dedicated of men to find it. When the lord's daughter came of age, man after man arrived to the hall, desperate to win her favor. But Lord MacQuinn called forth the tapestry and his daughter challenged the men to bring her the golden ribbon hidden in the wefts. And man after man could not find it. By the time the twentieth man arrived, Lord MacQuinn believed the lad would only last an hour. But the man stood in the hall for one hour searching, and then one hour turned into two, until evening stretched into dawn. By the first light of the sun, the man had pulled the ribbon from the tapestry. He was a Burke, of all people, and yet Lord MacQuinn said he was more than worthy should his daughter choose to marry him."

"And did the daughter choose him?" I asked.

"Of course she did. And that is why to this day we MacQuinns think twice before challenging the Burkes to a competition, because they're a stubborn old lot."

I laughed; the sound provoked Neeve to join me, until we sat before the fire wiping our eyes. I couldn't remember the last time I had felt so lighthearted.

"I think I like that tradition," I eventually said.

"Yes. And you should use it yourself, if you decide to take a mate outside of the MacQuinns," Neeve stated. "Unless, that is, the handsome Lord of Morgane is already your secret beau."

My smile widened, and I felt my cheeks warm. She must have noticed it last night, when Cartier had sat beside me at dinner. Neeve raised her brows at me, waiting.

"Lord Morgane is an old friend of mine," I found myself saying. "He was my instructor in Valenia."

"For the passion?" Neeve asked. "What does that mean, exactly?"

I began to explain it to her, inwardly struck with the worry that she would find the passion study frivolous. But Neeve seemed hungry to hear of it, as I had been to hear of her traditions. I would have kept talking deep into the night had we not heard voices in the hall. The sound seemed to jar her, reminding her that she was here in my chamber secretly, that she had been here for well over an hour.

"I should probably go," Neeve said, hugging the stack of paper to her heart. "Before my absence is noted."

We stood together, nearly the same height.

"Thank you, Mistress, for writing this for me," she whispered.

"You're welcome, Neeve. I shall see you tomorrow night, then?"

She nodded and quietly slipped out into the corridor as if she were nothing more than a shadow.

My body was exhausted, and yet my mind was brimming with what had just happened tonight, with all that Neeve had said to me. I knew if I lay down, sleep would evade me. So I tossed another log on the fire and sat before the hearth, my writing table still before me spread with paper and quill and ink. I found Merei's letter and tore it open gently, the wax seal of a musical note catching beneath my nail.

Dearest Bri,

Yes, I know you'll be surprised by this letter coming to you so soon. But didn't someone vow they would "write me every hour of every day"? (Because I'm still waiting on that mountain of letters you promised me!)

I'm currently sitting at a lopsided table at an old leaky tavern in the city of Isotta, right by the harbor, and it smells of fish and wine and a man's terrible cologne. If you hold your nose to this parchment, you can probably smell it—it's that strong. There's also a one-eyed tabby cat that keeps glaring at me, trying to lick the grease from my dinner. Despite all of this chaos, I have a moment before I'm supposed to meet up with my consort, and I wanted to write you.

I just disembarked from my ship, and it's hard to believe I just left you behind in Maevana as a lord's daughter, that I just saw you yesterday, that the revolution you and Cartier drew me into has done everything you dreamt it would. Ah, Bri! If only we'd known what was to come that night at the summer solstice four months ago, when we were both so worried we would fail our passion! And how long ago that time feels now. I confess, I wish you and I could go back to Magnalia, just for a day.

Old memories aside, I do have a little snippet of news that I think you will find interesting. You know how taverns attract the salt of the earth? Well, I overheard quite a few of them talking about Maevana's revolution, about Queen Isolde returning to the throne and the Lannons being in chains awaiting trial. (It took everything within me to remain quiet and sip my wine.) Quite a few people here think it is marvelous that a queen has taken back the northern crown, but there are a few who are nervous. I think they worry unrest might spread to Valenia, that some here will dare to contemplate a coup against King Phillipe. Valenians are very curious and will be watching the north in the upcoming weeks, eager to hear how things are resolved with the Lannons. I've heard talk center on everything from beheadings to torture to making all of the Lannons walk over flames so that they slowly burn to death. Let me know the truth of what actually happens, and I will have to keep you abreast with such gossip and developments here in the south, but it only makes me miss you more.

I need to wrap this up, and you know I am going to ask these three vital questions (so you had better answer them all!):

First, what does your cloak look like?

Second, how good of a kisser is Cartier?

Third, when can you come visit Valenia?

Write me soon!

Love,

Merei

PS: Oh! I almost forgot. The sheet of music in this letter is for your brother. He asked me to send it to him. Please do pass it on to him, with my regards!—M

I read the letter a second time, my spirits lifting. I reached for my half-written letter I had begun that morning, and then decided to start it over. I asked Merei about her consort, where they were traveling to next, what sort of people and parties had she played her music for. I answered her three "vital" questions with as much grace as I could—*my cloak is beautiful, stitched with the constellation of Aviana; I should hopefully visit Valenia sometime in the next few months when things settle here (prepare for me to bunk with you wherever you are); Cartier is a terribly good kisser*—and then I told her about the grievances: that I was still struggling to fit in here, that I thought about her and Valenia nearly more than I could bear. Before I could hem my worries, I wrote them down, as smoothly as if I were speaking them to her, as if she were sitting in this room with me.

And yet I already knew what she would say to me:

You are a daughter of Maevana. You are made of ancient songs and stars and steel.

I stopped writing, staring at the words until they blurred in my weary sight. And yet I could almost hear the echo of Merei's music, as if she were only playing down the hall, as if I were still at Magnalia with her. I closed my eyes, homesick yet again, but then I listened to the hiss of the fire, to the sounds of laughter drifting down the corridor, the howl of the wind beyond my window, and I thought, *This is my home. This is my family. And one day, I will belong here; one day, I will feel like a daughter of MacQuinn.*

→ SIX ↞

THE LASS
WITH THE BLUE CLOAK

Lord Morgane's Territory, Castle Brígh

Cartier

I've invited Lady and Lord Dermott to stay with us next week," I said to Aileen one morning, the Lannons' trial steadily growing closer by the day.

"*Lady* and *Lord* Dermott?" Aileen repeated, her voice a touch too shrill for my liking. "Here?"

We both glanced around to the broken windows and empty rooms.

I had written to the Dermotts, inviting them to lodge at Castle Brígh on their journey down to the trial. And I thought that I had given myself enough time to finish restoring the castle for proper visitors, as well as to get my plans in place for wooing the Dermotts into a public alliance with the queen. But by the look on Aileen's face . . . I realized I had bitten off more than I could swallow.

"I apologize," I said in a rush. "I realize we are not best suited for visitors at the moment." *But this alliance must be done quickly,* I wanted to add but nipped it before the words could emerge, as Aileen arched her brow at me.

"Does this mean you are positioning me as the castle chamberlain?" she inquired, a faint smile in her eyes.

"Aye, Aileen."

"Then don't worry, Lord Aodhan," she said, touching my arm. "We shall get this castle ready in seven days."

Later that afternoon, I found myself standing in the office with Thane Seamus, both of us trying to decide how we would repair the hole in the roof, when Tomas came hopping into the room, his injured foot cocked back.

"Milord," the boy said, tugging at my sleeve. "There's a—"

"Lad, do *not* tug on the lord's sleeve," Seamus gently scolded, and Tomas's face flushed as he jumped back to put some proper distance between us.

"It's all right," I said, glancing down at Tomas. The boy had made himself scarce the past two days, as if he had been overwhelmed by all the people now gathered in the castle. "Let me finish this, and then you and I can talk."

Tomas nodded and hopped from the room. I watched him go, noticing how his shoulders were stooped.

"My lord Aodhan, you need to instruct young ones like him to respect you," Seamus said with a sigh. "Or else he will constantly be out of line."

"Yes, well, as far as I know, he is an orphan," I said. "And I want him to feel at home with us."

Seamus said nothing. And I wondered if I was wrong to think such—I knew nothing of raising children—but I did not have time to stand and ponder it. I returned to talking about roof repairs, sorting Tomas to the back of my mind.

Half an hour later, Seamus left to begin overseeing repairs to the alehouse, about a fifteen-minute ride but still on the property, after Aileen had admonished that "we cannot have Lady and Lord Dermott here without proper ale." I could not fault her for ranking drink above proper beds and glass windows, and I departed the office in search of Tomas. The boy seemed to disappear at will, slipping into shadows and finding the best hiding places.

I went to the hall first, where some of the women were working at trestle tables around a pot of tea, sewing curtains and quilts for the guest chambers. Their laughter hushed at the sight of me, their gazes softening as they watched me approach.

"Good afternoon. Have you seen Tomas?" I asked. "He's about yea high, with red hair."

"Yes, we saw him, Lord Aodhan," one of the women said, her fingers working a needle through the fabric all the while. "He's with the lass with the blue cloak."

Brienna.

I startled; it was like my heart was on a string, yanking through me at the mere thought of her.

"Thank you," I said and rushed from the hall, the women's whispers chasing my heels as I emerged into the courtyard. From there I hurried to the stables, but there was no trace of Brienna. One of the grooms informed me that she had just been there with Tomas, speaking of honey cakes, and so I returned to the castle through the kitchens, where a tray of honey cakes was cooling on the windowsill, two of them noticeably missing. . . .

I walked back toward the office, my tread quiet on the stone floors; I could hear Brienna's voice drift into the corridor as she talked to Tomas.

"So I began to dig, just beneath the tree."

"With your bare hands?" Tomas eagerly asked.

"No, silly boy. With a spade. I had stowed it away in my pocket, and—"

"Your pocket? *Dresses* have pockets?"

"Of course they do. Don't you think women need a place to hide a thing or two?"

"I suppose so. What happened next?" Tomas insisted.

"I dug until I found the locket."

I gently pushed the door open, almost hesitant to interrupt this moment. The door creaked, as everything in this castle did, alerting them of my arrival, and I stood on the threshold, gazing down at them.

There was no furniture in the office. Brienna and Tomas were seated on the floor in a ring of sunlight, legs outstretched as they leaned back on their hands.

Brienna quieted as she met my gaze.

"I tried to tell you, milord!" Tomas hurried to say, as if he was worried he would be in trouble. "Mistress Brienna arrived, but you sent me away before I could."

"Yes, and I apologize, Tomas," I said, moving to join their circle on the floor. "Next time, I will listen."

"Are you ill, milord?" The boy frowned as he studied me. "You look like you have a fever."

I conceded to chuckle, and wiped my brow again. "No, I am not ill. I merely chased the two of you around the property."

"I brought her back here to you, milord."

"Mm-hmm. I should have waited here, then." My eyes helplessly shifted to Brienna. Her hair spilled over her shoulders and her face was flushed from the ride, her eyes bright. Her cloak was knotted at her collar; the dark blue spread around her, basking in the light.

"I was just telling Tomas the story about how I found the stone," she said, amused.

"What happened next?" Tomas insisted, directing his attention back to her.

"Well, the Stone of Eventide was within the locket," Brienna continued. "And I had to hide it in my . . . ah, in my dress."

"In your pocket, you mean?" Tomas suggested, propping his chin in his palm.

"Yes. Something like that." She glanced back to me with a wry smile.

"What does the stone look like?" he asked.

"Like a large moonstone."

"I've seen a few moonstones," the boy remarked. "What else?"

"The Eventide changes colors. I believe it reads the moods of the one who bears it."

"But only the Kavanaghs can wear it without the locket, right?"

"Yes," Brienna said. "It would burn people like you and me."

Tomas finally became quiet, mulling over what we had told him. My gaze traced Brienna again, and I softly suggested, "Tomas? Why don't you go see if Cook needs another hand in the kitchen?"

Tomas groaned. "But I want to hear the rest of Mistress Brienna's story."

"There will be another day for stories. Go along now."

Tomas huffed to his feet, hobbling his way out.

"You should get him a little crutch before he tears those stitches you gave him," Brienna said. "I had to carry him on my back."

"You *what*?"

"Don't look so surprised, Cartier. The boy's nothing but skin and bones."

The silence stretched between us. I felt pricked by guilt.

"I don't know who he belongs to," I finally said. "I discovered him the other night. I think he had been squatting here."

"Maybe one day he will tell you where he comes from," she responded.

I sighed, leaning back on my hands, regarding her once more. There was an echo of a bang, followed by Cook's distant shouting. I could hear Tomas defiantly shouting back, and I groaned.

"I don't know what I'm doing, Brienna." I closed my eyes, that weight coming over me again. Weight of the land, weight of the people, weight of the Dermott alliance, weight of the impending trial. Months ago, I would have never imagined myself in such a state.

Brienna moved closer to me; I listened to the whisper of her dress, felt her block the sun as she sat before me, her hands on my knees. I opened my eyes to see the light crowning her, and for a moment it was simply her and me and no one else in the world.

"There is no guidebook for this," she said. "But your people have gathered about you, Cartier. They are wonderful and they are dedicated. They don't expect you to have all the answers, or to settle into your role by tonight. It will take some time."

I did not know what to say, but her words reassured me. I took her hands in mine—our palms aligned; our fingers linked. I noticed the ink stains on her right hand.

"You've been busy writing, I see."

She smiled wanly. "Yes. Jourdain asked me to begin gathering grievances."

That took me somewhat by surprise. It felt too soon to be gathering up that darkness; we had just arrived back home, becoming reacquainted with what our lives were supposed to be. But then I reminded myself that the trial was in a matter of days. Of course, I should be gathering up my people's grievances, as well. I should begin penning my own. Which meant I needed to fully confront what had happened in detail that night. Because while I knew some truth, I did not know the whole of it. I did not know who had given the killing blow to my sister, or the full extent of violence that was done to the Morgane people.

And then there was my mother's letter, which I continued to carry around in my pocket, uncertain what to make of it. I had Lannon blood in my veins; did I need to acknowledge this truth or conceal it?

I broke from those thoughts to see Brienna was watching me.

"Have you written many grievances down?" I asked.

"Luc has collected quite a tome."

"And why haven't you?"

She glanced away from me, and a dark suspicion began to cloud my mind.

"Brienna . . . tell me."

"What is there to tell, Cartier?" And she gave me a false smile, one that did not reach her eyes.

"You were never a good dramatic," I reminded her.

"It is truly nothing." She tried to slip her hands from mine, but I tightened my hold on her.

If she would not speak it, then I would. "Jourdain's people have not been welcoming to you."

I knew it was the truth, because there was a flicker of pain in her gaze before she covered it up with irritation.

"What have they said to you, Brienna?" I pressed on, my anger rising at the thought. "Have they been unkind?"

"No. It's what I should have expected," she countered, as if defending them, as if it was her fault, that she could control who she had descended from.

"Does Jourdain know?"

"No. And I would ask you not to tell him, Cartier."

"Don't you think your father should know his people are slighting you? That his people are slighting his *daughter*?"

"They aren't slighting me. And if they were, I would not want Jourdain to know." She freed her hands from mine and rose, turning to face the window. "He has enough on his mind as it is. And I would think you would understand that."

I did understand it. And yet more than anything, I wanted Brienna to feel like she belonged here. It was nearly the shadow of all my other thoughts—for her to be accepted, for her to find happiness. I wanted her to claim her home in Maevana, this wild land that she and I had once spoken of in lessons. Half of her heritage was in this soil, and I did not care which territory it had risen from.

I stood, wiping the dust from my breeks. I approached her slowly, coming to stand just behind her, just as I could feel her warmth. We were quiet, our gazes to the land beyond the broken glass, the meadows and the woods and the hillocks that rose into mountains.

"They see me as Allenach's. Not as MacQuinn's," she said quietly. "They believe I fooled their lord into adopting me."

And it broke me to hear her acknowledge it. I could have said countless things to her in return, the foremost being that I never saw her as an Allenach, that I had only seen her for who she was—a daughter of Maevana and a beloved friend to the queen. But I held the words down.

She finally turned to face me, her gaze lifting to mine.

"They only need a little more time," she whispered. "Time

for my blood father's memory to fade, for me to prove myself to them."

She was right. We all needed time—time to settle, time to heal, time to discover who we were supposed to become.

And all I could say was her name, spoken as if in prayer.

"Brienna."

My hand rose; my fingers traced the edge of her jaw. I wanted to memorize her, to explore her lines and her bends. And yet my fingers stopped at her chin, to tilt her face up, to watch the sunlight dance across her cheeks.

Her breath caught, and I leaned down to draw it from her. I kissed her softly once, twice, until she opened her mouth beneath mine and I discovered that she was just as hungry as I was. I suddenly found my hands in her hair, my fingers tangled in the silk of it, lost in the desire to fully surrender to her.

"Cartier." She tried to speak my name; I drank the sound from her lips. I felt her hands move up my back and take fistfuls of my shirt, tugging. She was warning me, because I could now hear the footsteps scuffing loudly, just beyond the office door.

I struggled to break away from her, my breath shallow as I somehow recovered enough to whisper, "You taste like a stolen honey cake, Brienna MacQuinn."

She smiled, laughter in her eyes. "Does nothing evade the lord of the Swift?"

"Not when it comes to you." I dared to kiss her again, before whoever it was reached the office, but something sharp pressed into my leg. Surprised, I leaned back and traced my hand down to her skirts, to her thigh. There was the hard shape of a dirk beneath the fabric, and I met her gaze, speechless yet deeply pleased she was wearing a concealed blade.

"Yes, well," she all but stammered, her cheeks flushing. "We women can't hide everything in our pockets, now, can we?"

SEVEN

BRING ME THE GOLDEN RIBBON

Lord MacQuinn's Territory, Castle Fionn

Brienna

I planned to skip dinner in the hall that night, to prepare for Neeve's first reading lessons. I was carrying a tray of soup and bread to my chambers, reflecting on how nice the afternoon had been visiting Cartier and his people, when Jourdain loomed before me out of the shadows.

"Saints, Father!" I almost spilled dinner down the front of my dress. "You should know better than to sneak up on me!"

"Where are you going?" he asked, frowning at my tray of food.

"My room," I drawled. "Where else?"

Jourdain took the tray from my hands and passed it to a servant who just so happened to walk by at that moment.

"I was going to eat that."

Jourdain, though, did not seem to hear my exasperation. He waited until the servant disappeared around the bend, and then he took my hand and pulled me along to my bedchamber, shutting the door behind us.

"There's a problem," he finally said, his voice hoarse.

"What sort of problem, Father?" I tried to read the lines in his brow, to prepare myself for anything.

"Tell me all that you know of the House of Halloran, Brienna."

I stood frozen before him. "The Hallorans?" I cleared my throat, still caught off guard by Jourdain's request and trying to remember everything Cartier had taught me. "Queen Liadan gave them the blessing of the Upright. They are known for their orchards and their steel goods—they craft the finest swords in Maevana. Their colors are yellow and navy; their sigil is of an ibex standing in a ring of juniper. Their territory is known as the hinge of Maevana, as it is the only one to touch seven neighboring territories. They historically had a strong alliance with the Dunns and the Fitzsimmonses, which was broken when the Lannons took the throne. Since then, they have pledged their allegiance to the House wielding all the power." I paused, feeling the constraint again of my head knowledge. "I can recite their noble lineage if that is what you are seeking. Even the bastard daughters and sons."

"So the name Pierce Halloran should mean something to you," Jourdain said.

"Yes. Pierce Halloran is the youngest of Lady Halloran's three sons. Why?"

"Because he is here," my father all but growled.

I could not hide my surprise. "Pierce Halloran is *here*, at Fionn? How come?"

But I had a suspicion as to why. The Lannons were our prisoners. The Hallorans' alliance with them had begun to crumble. . . .

"He wants to get a look at you."

"He wants to *look* at me?"

"He wants to present himself as a suitor to you," Jourdain amended, as it would have been phrased in Valenia.

This revelation shocked me at first. But then the shock dissipated as I began to strategize.

"My, he must think he is very clever," I stated, which thankfully loosened the tension that had been building in Jourdain.

"So you see what I see in this?" my father said, his shoulders sagging a bit.

"Of course." I crossed my arms, glancing to the fire. "The Hallorans have been in bed with the Lannons for over a hundred years. And that bed has just been overturned. By us." I felt Jourdain watching me, hanging on to my words. "The Hallorans are scrambling right now, as they should. They are seeking an alliance with the strongest House."

"Aye, aye," Jourdain said, nodding. "And we must tread very carefully, Brienna."

"Yes, I agree."

I took a moment to sort through my thoughts, to weave a plan together, walking about my room, absently touching the braids in my hair. I had decided to start plaiting my hair, as many of the MacQuinn women did. Warrior braids, as I liked to think of them.

When I came to stand before Jourdain once more, I saw a slight smile on his face.

"By the gods," he said, shaking his head at me. "I never thought I would be so happy to see that scheming gleam in your eyes."

I grinned and playfully laid my hand over my heart. "Ah, Father. You wound me. Why wouldn't you be happy to hear of my plans?"

"Because they give me gray hairs, Brienna," he responded with a chuckle.

"Then perhaps you should sit for this."

He obeyed, taking the chair Neeve had graced the night before, and I sat beside him in my favorite armchair, our boots stretched out to the fire.

"All right, Father. Here are my thoughts. The Hallorans are seeking to form an alliance with us through marriage to me. I cannot say that I fault them for their effort. I'm certain they were tools of the Lannons during the past twenty-five years. And the political landscape of Maevana is dramatically shifting. The Hallorans need to rebrand themselves, to win the favor of the queen in some way. Marriage is one of the easiest yet strongest ways to forge a new alliance, hence why Pierce has shown up on our threshold."

"Brienna . . . please do not tell me that you are considering this," Jourdain said, covering his eyes for a moment.

"Of course not!"

He dropped his hand and let out a relieved huff. "Good.

Because I do not know what to think about this! More than anything, I would like to spit on the gifts Pierce brought us, to send him off with a kick to the breeks. But both of us know that we cannot afford to be so rash, Brienna."

"No, we cannot," I agreed. "The Hallorans want to ally with us. Should we let them?"

We were both quiet, contemplating all the possibilities.

I broke the silence first. "We were just discussing alliances, rivalries. The four of us sat down and parsed out Houses to win over for Isolde. We are still trying to decide what to do with the Lannon people, but what about the Carran House, the Halloran House?" I shrugged, betraying my uncertainty. "It nearly makes me ill to think about letting them join our fold. They *thrived* the past twenty-five years while so many of your people suffered. But if we refuse them . . . what sort of ramifications come with that?"

"There is no way to be certain," my father responded. "All I can say now is, I do not want the Hallorans in our alliance. I do *not* trust them."

"You think they would deceive us?"

Jourdain met my gaze. "I *know* that they would."

I tapped my fingers along my knees, anxious. "So we cannot outright deny them. But I still need to give Pierce Halloran an answer."

Jourdain went very still, staring at me. "All I ask—if you would heed me as your father—is that you would *not* play games with him. Do not do anything that would put yourself at risk, daughter."

"I would not assume to play Pierce in a romantic way. But as

I just said, I need to answer him."

"Can you not simply tell him you are with Aodhan Morgane?" Jourdain spouted.

"Cartier needs to appear as a lord with no weakness." It almost sounded harsh, but the words hovered in the air between my father and me as truth; the people we loved were always a weakness. "And the fact that Cartier, essentially, has nothing—no living family, no spouse, no children—sets him higher than us in this game of politics."

I watched Jourdain as his eyes glazed for a moment. I worried that he was thinking of himself, of his wife, Sive, of how he had lost her.

"I simply want for you to be happy, Brienna," he eventually whispered, and his confession nearly wrung my heart.

I reached forward to take his hands in mine. "And I thank you for that, Father. After the trial—after Isolde is crowned and we have a better understanding of how everything is going to settle— Cartier and I will make it known."

Jourdain nodded, looking down at our linked hands. "So, daughter. How will you answer Pierce Halloran tonight?"

"How I will begin to answer every man beyond this House who wishes to earn my favor as a suitor."

Jourdain went still, soaking in my words, slowly understanding. His eyes lifted, meeting mine, and I saw the surprise within him.

"Oh? And how is that?" But he already knew.

A smile warmed my voice. "I will ask Pierce Halloran to bring me the golden ribbon from a tapestry."

Every MacQuinn showed up for dinner that night in the hall.

There was hardly an empty space at the tables, and the great room soon grew stifling from the fire in the hearth, from the inspirations of so many curious people, from the fact that I was sitting beside Pierce Halloran at the lord's table.

He was exactly as I expected: handsome in a sharp, unforgiving way, with eyes that flickered with deceptive languidness. And he liked to set that ruthless gaze on me, I soon found. He traced the braids in my hair, the neckline of my dress, the curves of my body. He was weighing my physical attractiveness, as if that were all to me.

You are a fool, I thought halfway through the meal as I took a steady sip of my ale, his eyes resting on me again. He was too preoccupied to entertain the thought that I might be plotting something detrimental to him.

I smiled into my goblet, just for a moment.

"And what is humoring you, Brienna MacQuinn?" Pierce asked, noticing.

I set down my ale and looked at him. "Oh, I just remembered that the tailor is sewing a new dress for me on the morrow, one with white fur on the trim. I am excited to see its design, of course."

From his place two chairs down, Luc snorted and then hastily tried to cover it up by pounding on his chest, like he was choking. Pierce glanced at my brother, brow arched. Luc finally quieted, waving in apology, and Pierce set his focus on me again, wolfishly grinning.

"I should like to see you in white fur."

To which a second coughing fit began, this time from Jourdain, who was on my other side. Poor Father, I thought, his knuckles white as he gripped his fork.

Jourdain spared me a swift glace, and I saw the spark of warning in his eyes. I was playing Pierce too well, then.

I reached for the plate of bread. Pierce reached for it as well, our fingers bumping.

"Shall I cut you another slice?" he asked with feigned politeness, his eyes, unsurprisingly, on my décolletage.

But my eyes were on something else entirely. His sleeve had ridden slightly up his wrist, and there was a dark tattoo on his pale skin, just over the faint blue shadows of his veins. It looked like a *D* with the center filled in. An odd thing to permanently etch on one's skin.

"Yes, thank you," I said, forcing my gaze to shift before he saw that I noticed his strange mark.

Pierce set a slice of rye bread on my plate, and I knew it was almost time, that I had let this dinner drag on long enough.

"May I ask why you have come to visit us, Pierce Halloran?"

Pierce took a long sip of ale; I saw the gleam of perspiration on his brow, and I tried not to revel in the fact that he was barely concealing his worry and nerves.

"I brought you a gift," he said, setting his goblet down. His hand swept to the other side of the table, where two broad swords sat on the oak, resting in gilded sheaths. They were, perhaps, two of the most beautiful swords I had ever beheld, and it had taken all of my restraint not to touch them, not to unsheathe one of the blades. "I also brought one for your father."

Jourdain made no reply. He was doing a rather poor job of hiding his annoyance with Pierce.

"And why have you brought us such magnanimous gifts?" I inquired, my heart beginning to beat faster. I saw from the corner of my eye that Neeve was rising from the table, a few other weavers following her. They were preparing to bring the tapestry into the hall as we had planned.

Can you find me a tapestry whose golden ribbon can never be found? I had asked Neeve after scheming with Jourdain.

Neeve had looked surprised. *Yes, of course I can. You need the tapestry so soon, then?*

As soon as dinner tonight.

"I hope to win your favor, Brienna," Pierce answered, finally looking me in the eye.

I merely stared at him; that minute dragged on for what felt like a year, and I tried not to squirm with discomfort.

He broke the stare first, because there was a commotion sprouting on the other side of the hall.

I didn't have to look; I knew the weavers were bringing in the tapestry, that the men were aiding them in hanging it up so that both sides could be seen.

"And what is this?" Pierce asked, a sly smile at the corners of his mouth. "A gift for me, Brienna?"

I rose, not realizing that I was trembling until I walked around to the other side of the table, to stand between Pierce and the tapestry on the dais. I swallowed, my mouth suddenly going dry, and the hall grew oppressively quiet. I could feel the weight of all the gazes gathering upon me. The tapestry Neeve had chosen for me was exquisite: a maiden in the thrall of a garden, a sword resting over her knees as she sat among the flowers, her face tilted upward to the sky. She was haloed in light as if the gods were blessing her. Neeve could not have chosen a more suitable depiction.

"Lord Pierce," I began. "First, let me thank you for troubling yourself by coming all the way to Castle Fionn, so soon after battle. You obviously had us on your mind this week."

Pierce was still smiling, but his eyes narrowed on me. "I will make no more pretenses. I have come to seek your hand, Brienna MacQuinn, to win your favor as my wife. Do you accept my gift of the sword?"

He had certainly brought the best of his House, I thought, resisting the urge to admire the swords. And yet how dull his character was in comparison to the steel.

"I will assume that you do not know one of the traditions of our House," I continued.

"What tradition?" Pierce ground out.

"That marrying beyond the MacQuinn House requires a challenge."

He laughed, to cover up his uneasiness. "Very well. I shall play along with your games."

He was making me out to be a child. I hardened myself to his insult, glancing over my shoulder to admire the tapestry.

"Within every MacQuinn tapestry lies a golden ribbon that the weaver has hidden among the wefts." I paused to meet Pierce's cold stare. "Bring me the golden ribbon that hides within this tapestry, and I will accept your sword and give you my favor."

He stood at once, rattling the dishes on the table. By the swagger in his stride, he thought this would be very simple, that he would be able to study the intricate design and find the hidden ribbon.

I cast a glance to my father, to my brother. Jourdain looked like he was carved from stone, his ruddy face caught in a scowl, his hand curled in a fist beside his plate. Luc merely rolled his eyes as Pierce passed, pouring himself another cup of ale and settling in his chair as if preparing for great entertainment.

Pierce stood before the tapestry, his fingers at once going to the halo around the maiden's face and hair, the most obvious place to hide something golden. But his five minutes of study turned into ten, and ten into thirty. Pierce Halloran lasted forty-five minutes before giving up, tossing his hands up in frustration.

"No man could find such a ribbon," he scoffed.

"Then I am sorry, but I cannot accept your sword," I said.

He gaped up at me; the shock morphed into a sneer when there was a sudden gust of applause. Half of the hall—half of the MacQuinns—were cheering, standing for me.

"Very well, then," Pierce said, his voice surprisingly calm. He strode back up the dais, gathering the two swords he had brought. But then he walked over to me, to stand with his face terribly close to mine. I could smell the garlic on his breath; I could see the bloodshot veins in his eyes as he whispered, "You will regret this, Brienna MacQuinn."

I wanted to respond, to whisper a threat back to him. But he turned so quickly he gave me no time, hastily departing the hall, his accompanying guard rising from their tables to follow him.

The excitement broke, and the MacQuinns who had cheered for me sat back down, resuming their dinner. I felt Neeve's gaze; I looked to her, to see that she was grinning in delight. I tried to smile in return, but there was an older woman at her side who was regarding me with such disgust that I felt my relief melt, leaving me cold and worried.

"Well done," Jourdain whispered.

I turned to see my father standing in my shadow; he took my elbow, as if he sensed I was about to drop.

"I greatly offended him," I whispered back, the words scratching up my throat. "I did not realize he would be so angry."

"What did he say to you, just before he left?" Jourdain asked.

"Nothing important," I lied. I didn't wish to repeat Pierce's threat.

"Well, do not let him upset you," my father said, guiding me back to my chair. "He's nothing more than a pup with milk teeth who just had his bone taken away. We are the ones in power here."

I prayed Jourdain was right. Because I did not know if I had just stomped on the serpent's head or its tail.

→ EIGHT →

WHERE ARE YOU, AODHAN?

Lord Morgane's Territory, Castle Brígh

Cartier

I t was time for me to write my grievances of the Lannons, and yet I did not know where to begin.

After dinner, I retreated to my chambers and sat at my mother's desk—one of the few pieces of furniture I had insisted remain during the castle purge—and stared at a blank sheet of parchment, a quill in my hand, a vial of ink open and waiting.

It was freezing in my room; the windows were still broken, as I had chosen to replace the other, more prominent windows first. Even though Derry had boarded up the casements for now, I could hear the wind's endless howl. I could feel the bitterness in the tiled floors, the darkness that seemed to have me by the ankles.

I am half Lannon. How am I to bear these grievances?

"Lord Aodhan."

I turned in my chair, surprised to see Aileen holding a tea tray. I had not even heard her knocking or sensed her entrance.

"I thought you could use something warm," she said, stepping forward to set the tray close by. "It feels like the winter king is overstepping the autumn prince tonight."

"Thank you, Aileen." I watched as she poured me a cup, and that was when I realized she had not just brought one mug but two.

She set my tea beside the blank page, and then poured herself a cup, drawing up a stool to sit. "I won't pretend that I'm ignorant as to what you're trying to compile, my lord."

I gave her a sad smile. "Then you should know why I'm struggling."

She was quiet as she regarded me, anguish lining her brow. "Aye. You were only a baby that night, Aodhan. How could you remember?"

"Since I've returned here, there seem to be a few things coming back to me."

"Oh?"

"I remember smelling something burning. I remember hearing someone call out to me, searching for me." I stared at the wall, at the mortar lines between stones. *"Where are you, Aodhan?"*

Aileen was silent.

When I glanced back to her, I saw the tears in her eyes. Yet she was not going to weep. She was smarting with anger, reliving that horrible night.

"Aileen . . . ," I whispered. "I need you to tell me the Morgane grievances. Tell me what happened the night that everything changed." I took up my quill, rolling the feather in my fingers. "I need to know how my sister died."

"Did your father never tell you, lad?"

Mention of my father brought up another wound. He had been dead for nearly eight years now, and yet I still felt his absence, like there was a hole in my body.

"He told me that my mother was killed by Gilroy Lannon," I began, my voice wavering. "He told me that the king cut off her hand in battle and then dragged her into the throne room. My father was still on the castle green and could not reach her before the king brought out her head on a pike. And yet . . . my father could never tell me how Ashling died. Perhaps he did not know the details. Perhaps he did, and it would have killed him to speak of it."

Aileen was silent for a moment as I dipped my quill in the ink, waiting.

"All of our warriors were gone that night," she said, her voice hoarse. "They were with your father and mother, fighting on the castle green. Seamus was even with your parents. I remained behind at Brígh, to care for you and your sister."

I did not write. Not yet. I sat and stared at the page, afraid to look at her as I listened, as I envisioned her memory.

"We did not have much warning," she continued. "For all I knew, the coup was a success, and your parents and the Morgane warriors would ride home in victory. I was sitting in this very room by the fire; I was holding you in my arms, and you were asleep. That's when I heard the clatter in the courtyard. Lois, one of your mother's women-at-arms, had ridden home. She was alone, battered and bleeding to death, as if it had taken all of her strength to make it back, to warn me. I met her in the foyer, just as she collapsed. *Hide the children*, she whispered to me. *Hide them now.* She died on the floor, leaving me in a cold panic. We must have failed; my lord and lady must have fallen, and the Lannons would now come for you and Ashling.

"Since I had you in my arms, I thought to hide you first. I would have to hide you and your sister separately, in case one of you were discovered, the other would not be. And so I called for one of the other servants to fetch Ashling from her bed. And then I stood there, Lois's blood pooling on the floor, and I looked down at your sleeping face and wondered . . . where could I hide you? What place could I lay you, where the Lannons would never look?"

She paused. My heart was pounding; I had still not written a word, but the ink was dripping onto the page.

"That's when Sorcha met me," Aileen murmured. "Sorcha was a healer. She must have heard Lois's words, for she brought a bundle of herbs and a candle. 'Let him breathe this,' she said, catching the herbs aflame. 'This will keep him asleep for now.' So we drugged you and I took you to the one place I could think of. The stables, to the muck pile. That is where I laid you; I covered you in filth and I hid you there, knowing they would not seek you in such a place."

The odor . . . the smell of refuse . . . I understood now. I rushed my hand over my face, wanting to silence her, dreading to hear the rest of it.

"By the time I hurried back to the courtyard, the Lannons had arrived," Aileen said. "They must have come to us first, before the MacQuinns and the Kavanaghs. There was Gilroy, mounted on his horse with the crown on his despicable head, and all of his men around him, blood on their faces, torches in their hands, steel at their back. And then there was Declan, beside his father. He was just a lad, only eleven years old, and he had been to Castle Brígh countless times before. He had been betrothed to your sister. And so I thought surely, *surely* there would be mercy.

"But Gilroy looked to Declan and said, 'Find them.' And all I could do was stand there on the cobbles, watching as Declan slid off his horse and entered the castle with a group of men, to search for you, for your sister. I stood there, the king's eyes on me. I could not move; all I could do was pray that Ashling had been hidden as well as you. And then the screams and shouts began to rise. But still . . . I could not move."

I could scarcely hear her, her voice was trembling so hard. She set down her tea and I set down my quill, and I moved to kneel before her, to take her hands in mine.

"You do not have to tell me," I whispered, the words like thorns in my throat.

Her cheeks were wet with tears, and Aileen gently touched my hair—I nearly wept at the gentleness of it, to know such hands had hidden me, had kept me alive.

"Declan found your sister," she murmured, closing her eyes,

her fingers still resting in my hair. "I watched as he dragged her out into the courtyard. She was sobbing, terrified. I could not stop myself. I lunged for her, to take her from Declan. One of the Lannons must have struck me. The next thing I knew I was on the ground, dazed, blood on my face. I saw that Gilroy had dismounted, and all of the Morganes had been called out into the courtyard. It was dark, yet I remember all of their faces as we stood, silent and terrified, waiting.

"'Where is Kane?' the king shouted. And that was when I realized . . . your mother had been killed at the rising, but your father had survived. And Gilroy didn't know where he was.

"It gave me hope, just a tiny thread, that we might survive this night. Until the king began to ask about you. 'I already have Kane's daughter,' Gilroy taunted. 'Now bring me his son, and I will be merciful.' None of us for a moment believed him, this king of darkness. 'Where are you hiding his son?' He insisted. No one but I knew where you were. And I would never tell him; he could tear me to pieces, and yet I would never tell him where I had hidden you. So he drew forth your sister, held her before us, and said that he would break each of her bones until one of us revealed where we had hidden you, where Kane was hiding."

She opened her eyes, and now I had to close mine. My strength faded into dust; I leaned forward, to conceal my face, as if I were a boy, as if I could hide again.

"Watching them torture your sister was the most difficult moment of my life," she whispered. "I hated myself, that I had failed her, that I had not hidden her in time. The king made

Declan begin it. I screamed at him. I screamed that Declan did not have to do it. He was just a lad, I kept thinking. How can a lad be so cruel? And yet he did exactly what his father ordered. Declan Lannon took up a mallet and broke your sister's bones, one by one, until she died."

I could no longer fight it. I wept the tears that must have been hiding in me the entirety of my life. That my sister had died so I might live. *If only it had been me*, I thought. If only I had been the one to be found, and she had been the one to survive.

"Aodhan."

Aileen called me up from the darkness. I raised my head; I opened my eyes and looked at her.

"You were my one hope," she said, wiping the tears from my face. "You were the only reason why I lived day after day these past years, that my despair did not kill me. Because I knew you would return. Your father had to sneak back to the castle after the Lannons left that night; I have never seen a man more shattered in my life until I set you in your father's arms and made him swear to me that he would escape with you. I did not care where Kane went or what he did; I said, this child slipped through the Lannons' fingers, and he will be the one to return and crush their reign."

I shook my head to deny that it was me, but Aileen took my face in her hands to hold me steady. There were no more tears in her eyes. No, there was now fire, a burning hatred, and I felt it catch in my own heart.

"I will record all of our grievances for you to take to the trial," she said. "After they are read, I want you to look Declan Lannon in the eye and curse him and his House. I want you to be the beginning of his end, to be your mother's and your sister's vengeance."

I spoke no vow to this. Was not my mother a Lannon? Did I still have distant family among them? I lacked the courage to ask Aileen, to address Líle's letter that I had found. But my compliance, the eagerness to do as she bid, must have been in my eyes.

I was still kneeling on the floor when I heard it again in the howling of the wind.

Where are you, Aodhan?

This time, I answered the darkness.

I am here, Declan. And I am coming for you.

NINE

THE SHARP EDGE OF TRUTH

Lord MacQuinn's Territory, Castle Fionn

Brienna

The next morning, I packed up my writing tools and returned to the loom house.

This time, I emerged on the threshold and knocked on the lintel to announce my presence, my eyes sweeping the vast weaving hall and the women who were already hard at work.

"Good morning," I greeted as cheerfully as I could manage.

After last night, the weavers would undoubtedly talk about me. And I had decided not to hide from such conversations, but to meet them directly.

There were perhaps sixty women in all, working on various tasks. Some were at the looms, coaxing the wefts into tapestries. Others were stationed at a table, drawing the cartoon that would be replicated into tapestry threads. Others were still spinning wool. This is where Neeve was, sitting at a wheel in a stream of morning light that cast her hair into a shade of gold. I noticed that her eyes brightened at the sight of me, and I could tell by the smile tugging on her mouth that she wanted to invite me into the weaving hall. But she didn't move, because at her side was that older woman again, the one who had glared at me last night after Pierce had departed.

"May we help you?" the woman questioned in a careful, yet not very hospitable, voice. She had a large gray streak in her hair and a frown on her angular face. The only movement she made was to place her chapped hand on Neeve's shoulder, as if to keep her in place.

I drew in a deep breath, my hand fiddling with the strap to my leather satchel. "My father has asked me to help gather the MacQuinn grievances, to take to the Lannon trial."

No one spoke, and I began to realize that the woman at Neeve's side was the head weaver, that I could not gain entrance to this place without her blessing.

"Why should we give up our grievances to you?" the woman asked.

For a moment, I was speechless.

"Be gentle to the lass, Betha," another weaver, whose white hair was braided in a crown, spoke from the other side of the hall. "You would be wise to remember that she is Lord MacQuinn's daughter."

"And how did all of that come about, hmm?" Betha asked me. "Did Lord MacQuinn know whose daughter you truly were when he adopted you?"

I stood silent, my heart striking my breast like a fist. I could feel the heat rise in my face; I wanted to give nothing but honesty to the MacQuinn people. And yet to answer Betha's question would make it seem that I had fooled Jourdain. Because he had not known I was Brendan Allenach's daughter when he adopted me, but neither had I known. Yet I knew saying such would only sound hollow to these women.

"I am here to take up grievances, per my father's request," I repeated, my voice strained. "I will sit just beyond the main door. If anyone would like for me to scribe for them, they may come to me there."

I avoided looking at Neeve, worrying my façade might shatter if I did, and I walked back down the corridor, out the antechamber and beyond the main door into the morning light. I found a stump to sit on, just beneath the windows, and there I sat, my boots lost in the long grass.

I don't know how long I waited, the wind nipping my face, my passion cloak drawn close around me, my stack of paper held in place with a rock, my ink and my quill waiting. I could hear the women speaking, their words indecipherable through the glass of the windows. I waited until the shadows grew longer, and I could no longer feel my hands, the truth settling like a barb in my heart.

None of the weavers came to me.

The weavers did not want me to record their grievances, so I was shocked when one of the grooms did.

He found me after dinner, meeting me on the stable path as I took an evening walk with my wolfhound.

"Mistress Brienna?" The groom stood before me, tall and lanky, his long dark hair braided in traditional Maevan plaits. I didn't know why he looked so worried until I realized his gaze was on Nessie, the hound beginning to growl at him.

"Peace, Nessie," I said, and her hackles lowered. She sat at my side, and I looked to the groom once more.

"I know what you are doing for Neeve," he murmured. "I must thank you, for teaching her to read, for writing down her memories."

If he knows about it, Neeve must have decided to tell him.

"Neeve is very smart," I said. "I am happy to teach her as much as I can."

"Would you be willing to write something down for me as well?"

His request caught me off guard. At first, I didn't know what to say, and a cold burst of wind came between us, flirting with the end of my cloak.

"Never mind," he said and began to walk away.

"I would be honored to write for you as well," I stated, and the groom stopped. "But I wonder why you have come to me rather than my brother."

He turned, regarding me again. "I prefer that you scribe for me, Mistress."

His words perplexed me, but I nodded. "Where?"

He pointed farther down the stable wall, rough-hewn stones and mortar, where a narrow door sat between two stall windows.

"That's the little tack room. No one will be in there tonight.

Meet me there in an hour?"

"Very well." We parted ways; he returned to the stables while I continued on to the castle. But I wondered . . . why was he coming to me instead of Luc?

An hour later, night had fallen and I found my way to the little tack room, my writing supplies packed away in my leather satchel. The groom was waiting inside for me, a lantern lit on a lopsided table before him.

He stood when I entered, the door creaking shut behind me.

I set my satchel on the table and sat on the pile of grain sacks he had prepared for me in lieu of a chair, unpacking my paper, my ink, my quill by the trickle of candlelight. When I was ready, I looked across the table at him, breathing in the earthy tang of horse and leather and grain, waiting.

"I don't know where to begin," he said, resuming his seat.

"Perhaps you could begin by giving me your name," I said.

"I'm Dillon. Named after my father."

"Dillon MacQuinn?"

"Yes," he replied. "We've always had the lord's last name as our own."

I wrote down the date, followed by his name. Again, Dillon seemed to be hindered by something. But I held my tongue; I let him sort through his thoughts. After a while, he began to talk. And I began to transcribe.

My name is Dillon MacQuinn. I was born in the first dark year, a year after Lord MacQuinn fled and Lady MacQuinn was slain. I don't remember a time when Allenach wasn't ruling us and our lands. But I've always been in the stables, even before I could walk, and so I heard plenty of gossip, and I knew what Allenach was like.

He was good to those of us who knelt before him, who praised him, who followed his every order. My father was one of those people, the horse master of the stables. When Allenach said to eat, my father ate. When he said to weep, my father wept. When he said to jump, my father jumped. And when he said for my father to hand over his wife, he did that too.

I paused, trying to keep my hand steady. For a moment, my throat grew so narrow I didn't think I could swallow, and I realized I had mistaken my courage. I wanted to help, to write down stories and grievances, to let Jourdain's people purge their minds and hearts from the dark years. But this . . . it only made me despise my blood even more.

"Mistress Brienna," Dillon whispered.

I struggled to meet his gaze, the words on the page rising like smoke to burn my eyes.

"I promise, Mistress, that you will want to hear the end of this tale."

I drew in a deep breath. I had to trust him, that there was something within this story that I needed to hear. Slowly, I dipped my quill into the ink, ready to transcribe again.

My mother was beautiful. She caught Allenach's eye from the beginning, and it all but broke my father to know she was being forced into the lord's bed. I was only three years old; I had no inkling as to why my mother was no longer around as much.

My mother served the lord for two years as his mistress. By the time Allenach realized she was not conceiving, he had her killed, quietly. My father went shortly afterward, a man so shattered there was no chance of healing him.

But in the year 1547 . . . something odd happened. Allenach spent more time at Damhan, on his own lands, and left us be. Our women began to relax, thinking he would not choose them next. For the rumor was that Allenach wanted a daughter, even an illegitimate one. Because all he had were two sons, and a lord without a daughter is considered cursed, indeed.

A different sort of rumor reached us that following autumn. Allenach had a daughter with a Valenian woman, a woman named Rosalie Paquet, and he was planning to eventually reclaim that daughter. But then three years after that, something must have gone wrong with his plans. For he returned to Fionn and chose another woman as his mistress, determined to have a daughter of his own.

He chose the most beautiful of the weavers. It broke all of us to see her taken by him. Lara delivered him a child. Yes, it was a girl, as Allenach so greedily wanted. Yet the little girl contracted the pox when she was one year, which left her face scarred and claimed Lara's life. The little girl should have died, followed Lara to the edge of the realm, but she fought to live. She wanted to live. And when Allenach realized his daughter was not going to die, but wear her scars as a proud banner, he suddenly acted as if the child was not his, leaving her to the weavers to raise as their own.

My hand was shaking. I couldn't write any more, for the tears that blurred my gaze.

But Dillon kept speaking. He spoke for me to listen, not to write.

"The weavers loved her, took her as their own daughter. And they named her Neeve, and decided in that moment they would never reveal to her who her blood father was, that they would tell Neeve her father had been a good cooper.

"And once again, we began to wonder why Allenach left our women alone after that. He didn't touch another one of them after Neeve's birth. But I can now imagine why—our women were protected by the life of someone else, by the promise of the other daughter across the channel."

Dillon rose and leaned over the table, to take my hands. I was weeping as if I had been pierced, like I would never recover from this.

Neeve was my half sister. *My sister.*

"I know they resent you now, Brienna," Dillon whispered. "But one day, when time heals their wounds, they will love you as they love Neeve."

~~✦~ TEN ~✦~~

ORPHAN NO MORE

Lord Morgane's Territory, Castle Brígh

Cartier

Lady and Lord Dermott arrived just before dusk with a guard of seven men. I was not in the best frame of mind that night after Aileen's tale, and yet I had an alliance to seal for the queen. I went through the motions of a lord, hoping it would stir something in me; I washed in the river and left my beard untouched; I plaited my hair and took the golden circlet upon my head; I donned the new clothes the tailors had crafted—black breeks and a blue jerkin with a gray horse stitched at the breast; I made sure the table in the hall was resplendent with wildflowers and polished pewter and that a lamb was slaughtered and a cask of our best ale was ready.

Then I waited for the Dermotts in the courtyard.

This was what I knew about the Dermott House: they were reclusive, avoiding the other noble families. They had no alliance; they had no open rivalry either. They were known for their minerals; their land was rich in salt mines and quarries. But perhaps more than any of this . . . they were a House of ruling women. I knew their noble lineage, and their firstborn was always a daughter. And in Maevana, the firstborn child was the one to inherit.

Needless to say, I was very curious to meet this Lady Grainne of Dermott and her lord consort.

She rode into Brígh's courtyard on a draft horse, dressed in leathers and dark red velvet emblazoned with her sigil—an osprey with a full sun crowning the tip of its wings. A baldric was buckled across her chest, hosting a broad sword sheathed at her back. Her long, black hair was curled beneath her circlet, and her eyes were bright yet cautious as she regarded me. For a moment, we merely stared at each other—I was surprised by how young she was, perhaps only a few years younger than me—and then her husband came to a stop at her side.

"So this is the lord of the Swift, returned from the dead," Grainne said, and she finally smiled, the last of the light gleaming on her teeth. "I must say, Lord Aodhan, I am grateful for your invitation."

"It is my pleasure to welcome you here to Castle Brígh," I said, almost bowing to her as I would have done in Valenia. But then Grainne dismounted and held out her hand, and I shook it, a proper Maevan greeting.

"My husband, Lord Rowan," she said, turning to the lord standing slightly behind her.

I extended my hand to him as well. "Please, come to the hall," I said, guiding them into the warmth and firelight.

Dinner began somewhat awkwardly. I did not want to ask too many personal questions of them, and it seemed they felt the same. But once Aileen set down a spice cake and hot tea, I overcame my politeness.

"How have your House and people fared lately?" I asked.

"Do you mean how did the Dermotts survive the past twenty-five years?" Grainne countered wryly. "I only just inherited the House from my late mother, who passed this spring. She was wise, and remained out of the Lannons' sight. Our people rarely left our borders, and my mother only attended court once a season, largely due to the fact that she was a woman, and she made Gilroy uneasy. She sent him salt and spices; he left us alone for the most part."

"Our positioning in the far north helped," Rowan added, glancing to his wife. "Lannon's stronghold was in the south, although we did have the Hallorans to deal with."

Grainne nodded. "Aye. The Hallorans were our greatest problem over the past few decades, not the Lannons."

"What did the Hallorans do?" I asked.

"Raids, mainly," she replied. "It was easy for them, since we share a territory border. They stole livestock from our paddocks and food from our storehouses. They would burn our villages if we resisted them. On a few occasions, they raped our women. There were quite a few winters when we were on the brink of starvation. We made it through such times because of the Mac-Careys, who shared their supplies with us."

"You are close with the MacCareys, then?" I asked, to which Grainne chuckled.

"Ah, Lord Aodhan, you might as well ask me outright."

"Do you have an alliance with them?"

"Yes," she answered. "An alliance of only five years. But one that is not going to be easily broken." I wondered if she was trying to tell me that it might be difficult for an alliance to be formed between us, since MacQuinn and MacCarey were still historically at odds.

I shifted in my chair, pushing my dessert plate aside. "I would not deign to ask you to break an alliance that has kept you and your people alive, Lady Grainne."

"Then what do you ask, Lord Aodhan?"

"That you would publicly swear allegiance to Isolde Kavanagh, that you would support her as the rightful queen of this realm."

Grainne merely stared at me for a moment, but a smile was at the corners of her lips. "Isolde Kavanagh. How I have longed to speak her name the past few years." She looked to her husband, who was carefully regarding her. They seemed to hold a conversation in their minds, in their gazes. "I cannot swear anything yet, Lord Aodhan." She directed her attention back to me. "What I ask for is a private conversation with Isolde Kavanagh. Then I will declare my support, should I grant it."

"Then I will see to it that you speak with the queen."

"You already call her such?" There was no mockery in her tone, only curiosity.

"I have always seen her as such," I replied. "Ever since we were children."

"And you trust her . . . and her magic?"

I was struck by Grainne's question. "I trust Isolde with my life," I replied honestly. "Although, may I ask what about her magic concerns you?"

Grainne was quiet. But she glanced to Rowan again.

The candlelight flickered although there was no draft. The shadows began to creep across the table, as if they were coming to life. From the corner of my eye, the light and darkness twined and moved, as if in a dance. And hair on my arms rose; I got the sudden feeling that the Dermotts were speaking, mind to mind. That there was an unseen current between them, and the only other experience I could liken it to was the moment Brienna had set the Stone of Eventide around Isolde's neck, the moment when magic had awakened.

"Perhaps you inquire about magic because you have noticed an odd occurrence in the past two weeks," I murmured, and Grainne's gaze narrowed on mine. "That when Isolde Kavanagh began wearing the Stone of Eventide . . . you felt something as well."

Grainne laughed, but I noticed that Rowan's hand went to the dagger at his belt.

"You presume an outlandish theory, Lord Aodhan," the lady said. "One that I would caution you against speaking so openly."

"What is there to caution against speaking of it?" I asked, my arms outstretched. "The Lannons are in prison."

"But the Lannons are not dead yet," Grainne corrected, which gave me a pause of apprehension. "And the Hallorans are still running amok. I heard that they were trying to get in bed with the MacQuinns."

She turned the conversation so rapidly that I could not shift it back to the topic of magic and my suspicions that the Dermotts might have a trace within them. But I knew exactly what she implied. Jourdain had written to me the previous day, describing Pierce Halloran's disastrous proposal to Brienna.

"The MacQuinns are *not* going to align with the Hallorans," I said, to ease her mind.

"Then what is to become of the Hallorans? Do they get to continue onward beneath a new queen, unpunished?"

I wanted to say to her, *you and I desire the same things.* We desired justice, we desired the protection of a queen, we desired answers concerning magic. And yet I could not promise her this; there was still too much uncertainty in the air.

"The Hallorans' fate, as well as the Carrans' and Allenachs', will be decided soon. After the Lannons' trial," I replied.

Grainne's eyes moved to the hall, to the Morgane banner above the hearth. She was silent for a beat, and then whispered, "I am sorry to know that your House has suffered so greatly."

I was quiet, inevitably thinking of my sister. I felt agony any time Ashling's fate came to mind. This castle, these lands, should have been hers. She would have been just like Grainne, a ruling Lady of Morgane.

Grainne sighed and looked at me, her hand reaching for

Rowan's beneath the table, to discreetly take his hand from his dagger. "I do hope that you and your people find full restoration." She stood before I could make a proper response. Rowan and I rose alongside her, the candlelight wavering. "Thank you for dinner, Lord Aodhan. I am rather exhausted from the journey. I think we shall retire."

"Of course."

Aileen stepped forward to escort the Dermotts to their chambers.

"We shall see you in the morning," Grainne said, taking Rowan's arm.

"Good night to you both." I waited a few moments before retiring to my own chambers, exhausted and feeling as if I had accomplished nothing.

Tomas was already there, sitting on his cot before the hearth, playing with a deck of cards. The lad had been insistent on sleeping in my room, no matter how adamant I was about him bunking with the other boys. He was not building friendships with the Morgane lads, which had me somewhat concerned.

"Is Mistress Brienna here?" he asked eagerly.

"No, lad," I replied, unlacing the draws of my jerkin. I collapsed in my chair, groaning as I removed my boots.

"Are you going to marry Mistress Brienna?"

I sat there for a moment, trying to decide how to answer this. Tomas, of course, was impatient.

"Are you, milord?"

"Perhaps. Now, in case you forgot, I am traveling to Lyonesse tomorrow. I do not know when I will return to Brígh, but Aileen said she would keep a close eye on you." I glanced up to see Tomas sitting on his cot, scowling at me.

"What is this look for?" I asked.

"You said I could go to Lyonesse with you, milord!"

"I never promised such, Tomas."

"Yes, you did! Three nights ago at dinner." To his credit, the lad could bluff well. I momentarily panicked, thinking maybe I *had* promised him such, and sorted through my memory.

But then I thought, of course I would not take a child on this trip, and I leveled my gaze at him. "No, I did not. I need you to remain here, with Aileen and the others, and—"

"But I'm your *runner*, milord!" Tomas protested. "You cannot leave without your runner."

My *self-appointed* runner. I sighed, feeling defeated on so many counts, and shifted to sit on the edge of my bed.

"One day, you will be my runner, my very best runner, no doubt," I told him gently. "But your foot needs to heal, Tomas. You cannot go running errands on it right now for me. I need you to stay here, where I know you will be safe."

The boy glared a moment longer before wrapping himself in his blanket and plopping down on his squeaky cot, angling his back to me.

Gods help me, I am not cut out for this, I thought as I lay down, drawing my quilts up to my chin. I watched the firelight dance on the ceiling, trying to quiet my mind.

"Is Mistress Brienna going to be in Lyonesse?" Tomas asked groggily.

"Yes."

Silence. There was only the lament of the wind beyond the boarded windows, the crackle of the fire, and then I heard Tomas wiggle around on the cot.

"She is supposed to finish telling me the story." He yawned. "About how she found the stone."

"I promise that she will tell you the ending, lad. But you will have to wait a little while longer."

"But when will I see her again?"

I closed my eyes, seeking the last scrap of my patience. "You'll see her again very soon, Tomas. Now go to sleep."

The boy grumbled but finally quieted. Soon, I could hear his snores filling the chamber. And surprisingly, I found a bit of comfort in the sound.

I was up early the next morning, preparing for my departure to Lyonesse. I packed my own bags, taking care to wrap the Morgane grievances in a sheet of waxed leather and binding it with twine before dressing for a brisk ride. It was just under a day's journey to the royal city, and I ensured enough provisions were packed for me and the Dermotts, who greeted me with polite smiles in the hall.

"Will you join us for breakfast, Lord Aodhan?" Grainne inquired as I approached them at the table. It looked as if they were halfway through eating, and I stood on the dais stairs, feeling as if I were the visitor, and she were the hostess.

"Of course I will," I said, even though my stomach was wound in a knot. "I trust you both slept well?"

But Grainne never had the opportunity to respond. I felt a sudden tug on my sleeve, and I watched Grainne's gaze slide from my face to my elbow, her smile waning.

I already knew who it was. I glanced down to find Tomas at my side, propped on the wooden crutch my carpenter had made for him, a small knapsack dangling from his shoulder.

"I'm going with you, milord," the boy insisted, his voice trembling. "You cannot leave me behind."

My heart softened, and I knelt so I could quietly address him. "Tomas. I'm giving you an important order. I need you to stay here at Brígh, to look after the castle while I'm away."

Before the words left my mouth, he was shaking his head, red hair tumbling into his eyes. "No. No, I cannot stay here."

"Why, lad? Why can't you stay?"

Tomas glanced up to Lady Grainne, finally noticing her. He grew very still before setting his eyes on me again. "Because I'm your runner."

I was growing irritated with his behavior, with his inability to heed me. I drew in a breath, wondering what could be at the root of this insistence, and asked, "Has someone been unkind to you here, Tomas? You can tell me if they have. I will set it right before I leave."

He shook his head again, but I noticed the tears in his eyes. "I need to go with you."

"For the love of the gods, Tomas," I whispered, my anger rising. "You cannot go with me this time. Do you understand?"

To my dismay, Tomas burst into tears. Embarrassed, he

shoved his crutch at me and darted off before I could stop him.

I knelt there a moment more, eventually taking up Tomas's crutch and walking to my chair at Grainne's side. I sighed and poured myself a cup of tea, trying to think of something light-hearted to say to the Dermotts, who were both staring at me.

"Lord Aodhan?" Grainne said, her voice so low I almost didn't hear her. "Don't you know who that lad is?"

I dumped far too much cream in my tea, still irked. "He's an orphan I found squatting in the castle. I apologize for his outburst."

She was quiet. Her silence made me look at her, at the shock and dread in her eyes.

"He's no orphan," Grainne murmured. "His name is Ewan. And he's Declan Lannon's son."

PART TWO

THE TRIAL

⟶ ELEVEN ⟵

HALF-MOONS

En Route to Lyonesse, MacQuinn-Morgane territory border

Brienna

"What is keeping Morgane?"

Jourdain's impatient breath turned into clouds, the morning frost still glittering on the ground as we waited for Cartier and the Dermotts. I sat on my mare between Luc and my father, our four guards also mounted on their horses, waiting a respectful distance behind us. We were packed and ready, our thoughts anxiously bent toward the journey, toward the trial that awaited us. And as the minutes dragged onward and we remained stationed beneath the trees at the MacQuinn-Morgane border, I began to feel my worries grow. Cartier was nearly half an hour late. And he was never late.

"We did agree to meet here, did we not?" Jourdain asked,

nudging his horse forward. He frowned at the road, which wound to Castle Brígh. He couldn't see far; the fog was still heavy, shimmering like a veil in the dawn.

"Do you think something went amiss last night?" Luc asked. "With the Dermotts?"

It was the only feasible explanation I could think of, and I tried to swallow the lump of fear in my throat.

My mare's ears pricked forward.

I set my eyes on the fog, waiting, my heart quickening as I finally heard the chorus of hooves pounding on the road. I had a sword sheathed at my back; my hand nearly went to the hilt, but Cartier broke through the fog first, the sunlight catching the golden circlet on his brow. For one moment, I did not recognize him.

His flaxen hair was braided. His face was unshaven. He was wearing leathers and a fur pelt instead of his passion cloak. He looked cold as stone, his face carefully guarded so that I had no idea what he was feeling, what he was thinking.

And then he looked at me, and I saw something in him ease just a bit, a knot coming unwound, as if he could finally breathe.

"I apologize for being late," he said, his gelding coming to a stop.

We didn't have a chance to respond, for the Dermotts were right behind him.

Grainne's gaze went straight to mine, as if a sightless channel was between us.

"I have been eager to meet the woman who found the stone," she said, smiling.

I returned her smile. "As I have been eager to meet the Lady of Dermott."

"Ride at my side, then?"

I nodded, my mare aligning with her impressive draft horse. Jourdain was saying something, but I didn't quite catch his words; I felt Cartier's gaze, and I looked up to meet it.

Why were you late? I wanted to ask him.

He must have seen the question in my eyes, because he glanced away from me, as if he did not want to answer.

We began our journey, Jourdain setting a rigorous pace. The good thing about riding fast was that it did not leave room for conversation, and I could wholly sink into my own thoughts.

I tried to come up with a reason for Cartier's coldness, and when that made my heart ache too much, I moved on to the next painful reverie. Neeve.

My sister. I have a sister.

I had hardly felt like myself since Dillon revealed who Neeve was.

I wanted to take her hand in mine, to look at her attentively, to listen to her voice. And yet I had not had the chance to speak with her since Dillon's revelation.

I wondered if that was somehow for the best, to give me time to adjust to the fact that I was linked to Neeve through Allenach, that Neeve was mine by half. And Dillon had insisted I not reveal anything to her.

When the time is right, we will tell her she is your sister. We will tell her who her father is.

Our pace eventually slowed, to let our horses rest at a walk, and I found myself riding alone with Lady Grainne, the men slightly ahead of us.

"Your cloak is beautiful," Grainne said, her eyes tracing my passion cloak.

"Thank you." I scrambled to think of a compliment to give in return, but ended up deciding it was best to wait and see what Grainne truly desired to talk about, because she had pitched her voice low, as if she did not want the men to overhear us.

"Perhaps you will start a House of passion here? In the north?" she asked when Cartier glanced over his shoulder, his gaze going directly to me.

"It is my hope to do such," I replied, my eyes meeting his again before he turned around in the saddle. He said something to Rowan Dermott, who was riding at his side.

"How long have you known Lord Aodhan?"

"Eight years," I replied.

"So you have known him for quite some time," Grainne commented. "Did he help you find the Stone of Eventide, then?"

"No." I was hesitant to give too much away; I still did not know if Grainne was going to unite with us or not, and it made me slightly nervous, as if any word I said might cast her one way or another.

She smiled, sensing my hesitation. "I am making you uncomfortable. It is not my intent. I am merely curious as to how all of you rebels fit together, to get to know you better."

I met her gaze with a smile. "You are not making me

uncomfortable, Lady." I shifted in the saddle, my legs already sore. "MacQuinn adopted me when he learned that I had knowledge of the stone's whereabouts. Luc became my brother, and it seems as if we have always been so. Lord Aodhan was my instructor for several years. I did not discover his true identity until a few weeks ago."

"That must have come as quite a shock," Grainne stated mirthfully.

I nearly laughed. "Yes."

We were quiet for a moment, Luc's voice drifting back to us as he dramatically told a story to the men.

"I just want you to know," Grainne murmured, "that any woman who scorns Pierce Halloran is an instant ally of mine."

Her confession surprised me. I met her gaze again, my heart soaking in the offer of comradery, and now I was the one swarming with questions.

"Ah, you've heard. You know him well, then?"

Grainne snorted. "Unfortunately, yes. He and his band of brigands have terrorized my people for the past couple of years."

"I hate to hear such a thing," I responded, sorrowful. I paused, remembering the last thing Pierce said to me—*You will regret this.* "May I ask you . . . Is he the sort of man to retaliate?"

Grainne was silent for a moment, but then she directed her attention to me, and I saw there were no guises or masks between us, that she was going to answer me honestly.

"He is a coward. He never strikes alone, only when he has numbers behind him. Many times, I thought of him as a puppet, and perhaps there was another man at the helm, giving him orders, pulling his strings. Because he is not the smartest beast I've come across, but all that being said . . . he never forgets a slight."

I mulled on her words, my dread deepening. "I noticed a mark on his inner wrist."

"Yes," Grainne said. "The half-moon mark. It is a sign of the Lannons' blessing. Those who took the mark permanently on their skin were ensured to remain in Gilroy's good favor no matter what House they hailed from. It was given to them after they took an oath of fealty. They are the king's staunchest of followers."

Which Pierce must be. My stomach roiled.

"And if you study the coat of arms of the Hallorans, the Carrans, and the Allenachs . . ." She paused a moment, and I surmised she knew I was Brendan Allenach's bastard. "They made a slight addition to their sigils. It is somewhat difficult to find, hidden in the embellishment, but I promise if you look closely, you will see the half-moon. Their way of proclaiming chief allegiance to the Lannons, even above their own House."

"So dissenters of the queen might be easily found," I murmured, "merely by pulling up their sleeves."

Grainne nodded, a gleam in her dark eyes. "Aye, Brienna MacQuinn. I would start with them, if it is opposition you fear for Isolde Kavanagh."

Our horses had nearly come to a halt in the road.

I owed her information in return. And I felt it in the air between us, the debt owed.

"Ask me anything," I whispered. "And I shall tell it to you."

Grainne didn't hesitate. "The Stone of Eventide. Has it burned any of you?"

She was referencing the legendary tale of how the stone burned those who lacked magic, the simplest way to test if one was a Kavanagh or not.

"I kept it in a locket as I bore it, and I still felt its heat at moments," I answered. "No one else attempted to touch it beyond Isolde, so I cannot answer that fully."

She wanted to say something more, but we were interrupted by Jourdain, who had trotted back to check on us.

"Ladies? Are we ready to press onward?"

"Of course we are, Lord MacQuinn," Grainne replied smoothly with a smile. "We will follow your lead."

My father nodded, glancing to me before turning his horse around.

"As far as Pierce Halloran goes," Grainne said, gathering her reins as our horses transitioned to a trot. I had to urge my mare faster, to keep stride with her gelding, to catch her final word of advice. . . . "Watch your back, Brienna."

⇥ TWELVE ↤

BITTER PORTIONS

The Royal Castle of Lyonesse, Lord Burke's Territory
Three Days Until the Trial

Cartier

Tomas was Declan's son. *I had Declan's son beneath my roof.* Which meant that I had been—inadvertently—harboring a Lannon.

When Grainne had told me who the boy truly was, I had bolted up from the table to call him back, unsure as to what I was going to do about it. About him. But Tomas—his real name *Ewan*—had vanished, darting off into castle shadows. I had been tempted to overturn every piece of furniture to find him, to speak to him. And then I had realized exactly who I was mimicking, as if this castle was cursed, and I had felt gravely ill.

Where are you, Ewan?

I let him remain hidden, and had gone to Aileen, wondering . . .

did she know? Did she know Declan's son was my runner? That Declan's son had attached himself to me?

"Will you watch over Tomas while I'm away?" I had asked her, trying to appear at ease.

"Of course, Lord Aodhan. I'll make sure he's taken care of," she had responded. "Don't worry about him."

Oh, I would certainly worry about him. Here I was protecting my enemy's son. Here I was forming a fondness for the lad, pretending that he was part of my own, a young Morgane orphan who needed me. Letting him sleep in my chambers and eat at my table, letting him follow me around like a shadow. Here I was caring for him when he was supposed to be in chains with the rest of his family, locked away in the castle dungeons.

My gods.

Aileen did not know who Ewan was. I could tell she didn't. And I do not think any of my people recognized him, most likely because all the Morganes had remained in Lord Burke's holding, and had never gone to the royal castle, where they would have caught a glimpse of the king's grandson.

But Grainne Dermott certainly had. And now that she knew of it, she held a dark secret over my head, one I didn't know if she would let drop to crush me.

I went straight to my office, to sit down in private for a moment. There was still a hole in the roof. I was sprawled on the dirty floor. And I remained there for as long as I could, sorting through my thoughts. I was bound by honor to protect a child who had come to me for help—who I had *promised* I would protect—and yet I was held by terrible responsibility, to hand Ewan over, to take him to the dungeons to join his family, to make him stand trial with them.

What was I to do?

I weighed the options, wondering if I should, indeed, take him to Lyonesse as he was so ardently begging, if I should place him in Isolde's hands and say, *Here he is. The missing Lannon prince no one is speaking of. Chain him up with his father.*

That is what I should do, what a Lord of Morgane would do.

And yet I could not.

If you cannot find him, you cannot take him.

I had summoned for the Dermotts to come into my office. No matter there was still no furniture for them to sit on, and no fire alight in the cracked hearth, and the sky was gazing in.

Grainne had taken note of all of the broken pieces of the chamber, those broken pieces I had striven to hide from her. Yet she said nothing of my disrepair or of Ewan. She stood next to Rowan and stared at me, waiting.

"I did not know it was him," I said, my voice strained.

"I know, Lord Aodhan." I thought she was pitying me until I relented to look at her and saw there was a measure of compassion in her eyes. "Rowan and I will not speak of this—we shall act as if we never saw him, if that is what you think is best for your House."

I wanted to believe her. And yet I knew she could very well be tucking my ominous secret away, to draw forth at a later date, to expose me.

"How can I trust you?" I rasped, knowing the morning was getting away, that we were supposed to be on the road, meeting the MacQuinns.

"How do any of us trust anyone these days?" she countered. "Let my word be enough for you."

Not the answer I was looking for. But then I remembered our conversation from the night before, how she had deflected my assumption that the Dermotts had recently discovered that their blood held a trace of magic. It was a wild hunch, and yet it was all that I held in terms of collateral.

Grainne knew it too. There was a stiffness in her posture, as she was daring me to bring it up again.

It made for a very long day of travel.

The weather had turned foul by the time we reached Lyonesse. A late-afternoon storm had rolled in from the west; we were all drenched and taciturn as we rode toward the castle, the thoroughfare nearly a swamp with all the rain and mud.

My eyes were on Brienna as we passed through the castle gates, coming to a final halt in the royal courtyard. Her passion cloak was speckled in mud, the braids in her long brown hair were dripping with rain, and yet she was smiling, laughing with Grainne.

Isolde was standing beneath the arch of the courtyard, defying the rain, dressed in a simple green dress with a woven belt of silver at her waist. The Stone of Eventide hung from her neck, luminous in the storm, and her red hair was pulled back in an array of little braids. I watched as she smiled, shaking Grainne's and Rowan's hands as if she were an old acquaintance and not a woman about to ascend the throne. There was a humility about her, as well as an air of mystery, which made me remember what she had been like when we were children, when she and I had learned who we truly were, that I was the heir of Morgane and she was destined to become the northern queen.

She had been quiet and gentle, the sort of child who observed far more than she let on. The sort of child no one suspects will draw her steel. Because of that, she and I had formed a quick friendship, and a tradition of eavesdropping on our fathers when they secretly met once a year, discussing strategies and plans to return home to Maevana.

"They want to make me queen, Theo," Isolde had whispered to me, terrified.

I was eleven, she was thirteen, and we sat in a closet, listening to our fathers' plans, their agony over our lost homeland. Luc had been with us, of course, bored to tears and complaining about the dust. But that was the moment we all realized . . . if our fathers succeeded, Isolde was going to be queen.

"It was supposed to be my sister," she had continued. "Not me. Shea was supposed to be queen."

Her older sister who had died beside her mother, during the first failed rising.

"You will be the greatest queen the north has ever seen," I'd said to her.

And here we were, fifteen years later, standing on royal ground, on the cusp of crowning her.

Isolde must have read my mind, because she met my gaze through the rain and smiled.

"It won't do us any good if you catch a chill from this rain, Lady," I said.

She laughed. The Stone of Eventide rippled with cerulean and gold, as if it felt the waves of her amusement. "You forget, Aodhan, that I have magic that favors healing."

"I forget nothing," I reminded, but I was smiling as I fell into stride beside her.

We followed the trail of the others, our boots clicking over the damp floor. "How have things been here?" I quietly asked, as we continued to walk deeper into the castle, toward the guest wing.

"It has been calm, although there has hardly been any time to rest," the queen replied, just as quietly so our voices would not carry. "I have news to share with all of you. I've called for a meeting, after you refresh yourselves."

We stopped when we reached a fork in the corridor, lanterns hanging from iron hooks in the wall. I could hear the MacQuinns and the Dermotts, their voices fading as they continued to walk to their appointed chambers.

"Lady Dermott has requested a private conversation with you," I murmured, listening to the rain drip from my clothes.

"I know," Isolde responded. "I could see it in her eyes. I'll ensure it happens on the morrow."

I wanted to say more but caught myself, remembering that there were many ears in this castle, that my thoughts should not be announced in the corridors.

"Go and tend to yourself, Lord Morgane," the queen said, and then drolly added, "Before you catch a chill and I am forced to heal you."

I snorted but granted her a bow of playful defeat, hurrying down the hall to my chambers.

She had been thoughtful; Isolde already had a bath drawn for me, and a plate of refreshments set out on the table. I stripped from my sopping clothes and sat in the warm water, trying to sort through the tangle of my thoughts. Ewan, unsurprisingly, was at the forefront. I still had not decided what I was to do about him, to tell Isolde or not that I was harboring him.

I had come up with a theory over the journey. Ewan had obviously escaped the day of rising, most likely when our battle broke out. He had gone north, seeking a safe place to hide. He had come across Brígh and squatted there for a day or two before I arrived and found him.

I did not believe Ewan was guilty of anything other than trying to survive.

And I struggled to imagine what it would be like to grow up as Declan's son, in such a terrible family. Had Ewan not been skin and bones, as if he had not been fed regularly? Had he not been fearful of me, expecting physical punishment from my hand?

Did I protect him? Did I defy his father and take him as my own? Could I honestly come to love my enemy's son?

I washed and emerged from the water feeling no better about my predicament, dressing in the blue and silver of the Morganes. I stood at the table and ate a few morsels of fruit and bread, and that was when it finally struck me. Somewhere beneath my feet, layers deep in this castle of old stone and mortar, the Lannons were sitting in darkened cells, chained, awaiting their fate. Somewhere beneath my feet sat Declan, breathing, waiting.

I could not eat anymore.

I stood before my fire and waited until Brienna knocked on my door.

Luc and Jourdain were with her, or else I would have drawn her into my chambers; I would have told her my troubles, all of them. I would have begged her to tell me what to do, bending myself to her as if she were fire and I were iron.

She regarded me with a strange gleam in her eyes as we began to walk the corridor together; I knew she had questions for me. And I did not even have a moment to whisper in her ear, to request that she come to me tonight, because Isolde and her father were waiting for us in the council chamber.

I had never been in this room before. It was an octagonal chamber void of windows, which made it feel dark until I noticed the walls were set with a shimmering mosaic. The little stones caught the firelight, making it seem as if the walls were breathing, as if they were the scales of a dragon. I could not see the ceiling, but the room felt endless, as if it continued upward into the stars.

The only furnishing in the room was a round table and a ring of chairs. And at the heart of the table burned a circle of fire, to cast light upon the faces of everyone who gathered.

I sat between Brienna and Jourdain. Luc was on her other side, followed by Isolde and her father, Braden Kavanagh. We were the queen's inner circle, her most trusted of advisers and support.

"I must say how good it is to be reunited with you, my beloved friends," Isolde began tenderly. "I hope that these past two weeks have been joyous ones, and that returning to your homes and gathering your people has been the beginning of your healing and restoration. Above all, I must express my gratitude for each of you returning to Lyonesse, for being my support and my eyes, for helping me prepare for this trial.

"Before I begin with my news, I wanted to give you the chance to share any concerns or thoughts."

Jourdain started, summarizing our plans to seal public fealty for Isolde, about our deliberation of alliances and rivalries. Which made a perfect transition for me to talk about the Dermotts.

"I do believe Lady Grainne will support you," I said, meeting Isolde's gaze over the flames. "But to prepare you for your talk with her tomorrow . . . the Dermotts have faced a great deal of persecution from the Hallorans."

"So I have feared," Isolde said with a sigh. "I confess that I am very uncertain as to how punishment needs to be given to Lannon supporters."

"Speaking of which," Brienna spoke up, "I made a discovery on the journey here, thanks to Lady Grainne."

My attention shifted to her. I had greatly wondered what the women had been discussing on the ride.

"Would it be possible to bring in the coats of arms for the Lannons, Carrans, Hallorans, and Allenachs?"

Isolde's brows rose, surprised. "Yes. They are hanging in the throne room."

We waited while Isolde asked a servant to bring the banners in. Once they were laid on the table, Brienna stood, her fingertip tracing the embroidered design. The House sigil was at the center—a lynx for Lannon, a leaping stag for Allenach, an ibex for Halloran, a sturgeon for the Carrans. Then came the shield patterns followed by the typical ring of flora interlinked with smaller fauna.

"Here it is," Brienna whispered, her finger stopping on something. The five of us rose and leaned over the table, to see what she was transfixed with. "All of them have the mark, as Lady Grainne said they would. A half-moon."

I finally saw it, hidden among the flowers of the Hallorans' sigil.

Brienna began to tell us about her conversation with Lady Grainne, and I merely stood and stared at her, marveling that she had come into this knowledge so seamlessly.

"This is incredible," the queen murmured, studying the Carran coat, finding the hidden half-moon. "I cannot even begin to express how vital this is going to be for us in the coming days."

"Have you faced any opposition, Lady?" I asked. It was the question all of us had been dreading to ask.

Brienna folded up the banners and dropped them unceremoniously to the floor. We then resumed our seats, waiting for the queen to speak.

"Not openly," Isolde said, and her father reached for her hand. She glanced at Braden, and I saw sadness in both of their eyes. "I have discovered that the Kavanagh House has been annihilated by Gilroy Lannon. I do not believe any other Kavanaghs remain alive."

The mood among us instantly dropped, deep into grief. From the corner of my eye, I saw Brienna lace her fingers in her lap, so tightly her fingers went white.

"Isolde . . . ," Jourdain whispered.

"It has been a difficult truth to come into," the queen said, briefly closing her eyes. "Gilroy kept a ledger of all the lives he took. There are so many names listed. Not long after the first failed rising, the king sent soldiers into Kavanagh territory, burning most of the cities and villages to the ground. I have been told that it is only ash and charred remains. There is nothing left there to return to. But my one hope is that perhaps there are other Kavanaghs still in hiding. And that maybe, once the Lannons are gone, they will come forward and reunite with me and my father."

I helplessly thought of the Dermotts, of my suspicions. That a spark of the Kavanaghs was within them, and yet I said nothing of it. That was for Grainne to share with the queen, not me. But it gave me hope that restoration could still be possible for Isolde and her father and their people.

"Now, on to the second matter of business," Isolde said. "One of the Lannons is missing."

Jourdain startled at my side. "Which one?"

"Declan's son, Ewan," Isolde replied. "We never recovered him after the overtaking."

"He's only a lad," Braden Kavanagh said when his daughter grew quiet. "We believe he is hiding somewhere in Lyonesse."

No, not even close, my blood pounded. I was beginning to

go numb, my thoughts circling around and around. *Speak*, one thought cried, which was swallowed by *Silence*. And so I sat there, unmoving, unyielding.

"Have there been any efforts to recover him?" Luc asked.

"We have searched, but very discreetly," Isolde replied. "When I realized we were missing a Lannon, I decided that it needed to be kept quiet. That is why I am just now sharing this with all of you, why I did not even trust sending you the news by letter. No one beyond us needs to know the grandson is missing, as it might give fuel to Gilroy's supporters."

"Do you trust the servants here?" Jourdain asked. "Has anyone here given you reason to doubt or worry?"

"I have established a very loyal guard in Lord Burke's men and women," Isolde said. "A vast portion of the servants in this castle have come forward and pledged allegiance to me. Many of them have also given their testimonies, and while I know some of this may not be wholly trustworthy, I feel as if the stories that are emerging all align. They all lend proof that Gilroy Lannon brutally oppressed the people here."

None of us spoke. And how the darkness seemed to creep upon us.

"All of this is to say," Isolde continued, looking to Brienna, as if her strength and courage was within her, "there is a vast list of grievances against the Lannons as a whole, not just isolated to the former king. His wife, Oona, also partook in tortures and beatings, as did their son, Prince Declan. My father and I have compiled the grievances, just as all you have done, and I have no doubt that this list will continue to grow as more people come forward. That there will be no hope for this family."

"Are you saying, Lady," Jourdain carefully interjected, "that there is no need to put the Lannons on trial?"

"No, my lord," Isolde responded. "They will go through the motions of a trial, for closure and for justice to be exemplified. We want to distinguish ourselves as coming out of Lannons' darkness, by becoming an era of light."

The chamber was quiet. It was Luc who broke the silence. "They will go 'through the motions'?"

"It is the people's voice that must be heard, not mine," the queen said. Her face had gone pale as bone. "And the people have already decided the fate of the Lannons."

And I knew what she was about to say. I knew what was coming, because this was history, this was the "bitter portions," as the old ballads called it, this was how it was done in Maevana. Had I not spoken such a sentiment to Jourdain, Luc, and Brienna nights ago, when we had begun planning the second leg of our revolution?

And yet I felt stricken, waiting for it.

There was a dark flame in Isolde's gaze; it was mercy meeting justice, twenty-five years of hiding and darkness and terror, twenty-five years of dead mothers and dead sisters, of destroyed Houses and people, of lives that could never be brought back.

But how things began to fragment when your enemy was no longer just a name, but a face, a voice, a little boy with red hair.

Isolde looked directly to me, as if she sensed I was inwardly conflicted, that I was crumbling between the desire to tell her and the desire to hide the boy. . . .

"The entire Lannon family must be executed."

─◆ THIRTEEN ◆─

LATE-NIGHT QUANDARIES

Three Days Until the Trial

Brienna

After our meeting came to a close, Isolde accompanied me back to my chambers. We sat before the fire in my hearth, listening to the storm lash the windows.

"I know you're weary from traveling all day so I will keep this brief," Isolde said. "But I have been eager to speak with you about a few things. Mainly about the coronation. I know all of our attention is on the trial, but the coronation is only a few weeks away, and I need help planning it."

"Of course." I reached for my satchel, bringing forth my writing utensils. As the queen spoke her ideas, I wrote them down, trying to organize them. Cartier had once told me that the queens of Maevana were always crowned in the forest, and I was about to share this when I heard a clatter beyond the window. Isolde stiffened. My quarters were divided into two chambers, one for visitors, where we sat, and one for a bedroom, where the noise was coming from.

"What was that?" I set aside my paper and quill and rose from my chair, the banging coming again, louder. It almost sounded as if someone was trying to open the bedchamber window. . . .

I reached for my broadsword, which sat sheathed on the divan, and Isolde withdrew a dirk from her boot. "Stay behind me," I whispered to Isolde as she stood.

The queen followed me into the darkness of my bedroom, our steel catching the flash of lightning.

I saw it at once—the window was banging open in the storm gust and rain was splattering the sill and the floor. Someone was in the chamber; I could hear their heavy pants as I stepped deeper into the darkness. When the lightning forked again, the silver limned a small figure crouching beside the bed, just before my feet. A boy with a tangle of red hair.

"Tomas?" I breathed, astonished.

"Mistress Brienna! Please . . . please don't kill me."

I sheathed my sword instantly, reaching for him. "Lady Isolde? Will you bring light to the room?"

She stepped out into the adjoining chamber, bringing back a candelabra, letting the light fall over the boy. She said nothing as I rushed to latch the window, nearly slipping on the floor. I took a moment to squint against the rain and peer down the castle wall before I shut the mullioned glass to the storm.

"By all the saints, Tomas. How did you crawl up here?" I asked, turning to regard him.

He was, not surprisingly, transfixed with Isolde, with the Stone of Eventide glimmering at her breast.

"Tomas?" I prompted, and he finally heard me, glancing back to look at me with wide, bloodshot eyes. "Does Lord Aodhan know you are here?"

He froze. For a moment, I thought he would bolt from the room.

I approached him slowly, reaching for his hand. He was so thin, so slight for a lad his age. I felt my throat close, but I smiled, to help ease his mind.

"Why don't we get you into some dry clothes? I'm afraid it will have to be one of my shirts for now. It will fit you like a tunic. Will that do?"

He studied his drenched, mud-splattered clothes. The clothes Cartier had given him, the blue of the Morganes. Hay and seed heads clung to him, as if he had hidden in the back of a wagon. "Yes, Mistress Brienna."

"Very good," I said, approaching my wardrobe. I had brought a few dresses, silk breeches, a pair of linen shirts, my cloak, and a fleece-lined leather jerkin. I selected one of the shirts and brought it to Tomas, laying it on my bed. "I want you to change into this. Lady Isolde and I will wait just outside this door."

Tomas looked as if he would rather wilt than wear my clothes. Thankfully, though, he gave me no fuss. He reluctantly nodded, knocking the hay from his soiled clothes.

"And I suppose you are hungry?" I asked. "How does a bowl of soup and a cup of cider sound?"

"I would like that, Mistress Brienna," Tomas said.

"Good. Come meet us in the next room when you are ready."

Isolde and I left the chamber. I quietly shut the door so he could change and was about to call for a servant to bring a tray of dinner when I felt Isolde's fingers close about my arm, holding me at her side.

"Brienna," the queen rasped. "Who is this boy?"

I stared at her, our faces only a breath apart. And that's when I saw it: the suspicion in her eyes, a marriage of disbelief and bitterness.

"No," I whispered in return. "No, it cannot be. . . ."

The pieces began to come together, interlocking. An orphan squatting in Brígh. Cartier having no inkling as to where the boy came from, as to who he truly was.

But Cartier would *not* have willingly sheltered a Lannon. He could not have known Tomas was Ewan, that he was Declan's son.

I drew in air to speak this, but the doorknob rattled, and the queen and I separated, schooling our faces into pleasant neutrality although both of our hearts were like thunder in our chests.

I rung for a servant, to request dinner for Tomas, and by the time I turned around from the main door, he had stepped into the receiving chamber, trying to conceal his limp.

"Are you hurt?" Isolde asked, noticing it too.

Tomas sat on the edge of the divan, making no response.

I wondered if Isolde would heal him. Would she willingly heal her enemy's child? The child that had frustratingly evaded her and caused her sleepless nights?

She knelt before him. "May I look at your foot, Tomas?"

He hesitated; he knew exactly who she was. How could he not? The queen who had overthrown his family was kneeling before him. I held my breath, held down the reassuring words I wanted to give to him to trust her, knowing he needed to make this decision on his own.

He eventually relented, nodding his consent.

I stood beside the fire and watched as Isolde eased off his boots, her hands gently accessing the cut on his foot. "Ah, it looks like you have pulled out your stitches," she said. "It's bleeding quite a bit. I can heal this for you, Tomas."

"You . . . how?" Tomas asked, his nose scrunching. "With more stitches?"

"Not with stitches. With my magic."

"No." He eased away from her. "No, no. My da . . . my da says magic is evil."

Isolde was still on her knees before him. But I knew she was feeling the shock of his words, as if he had thrown mud in her face.

"Does your da know much about magic?" she carefully asked.

Tomas crossed his arms, looking to me, like I was his way out of this. I stepped closer, sitting beside him on the divan, to take his cold hand in mine. I noticed his foot was dripping blood on the floor, had dripped blood on Isolde's dress.

"A few weeks ago," I began softly. "I was hurt too. I had a wound on my arm." Of course I did *not* mention this wound had come from an arrow Gilroy Lannon had ordered to be rained down on me, at the beginning of our rising battle. "Isolde used her magic to heal me. And you know what? It didn't hurt one bit. It felt like sunlight on my skin. And I was very grateful for it, or else my arm would still be weak, and I would be in pain."

Tomas stared down at his clothes, my shirt nearly reaching his knees. There were a few bruises on his legs, slowly healing, and a cross-hatching of scars on his skin. Isolde saw them too, and the resentment that had been in her eyes moments ago faded into sorrow.

"If the lady heals me," Tomas said, lifting his gaze to mine, "would I be tainted?"

"No, not at all," I responded, wondering what he meant by "tainted." "But if you are worried about that . . . look at me. Do you think I am tainted?"

Tomas shook his head. "No, Mistress. I like you."

I smiled. "And I like you, Tomas."

He chewed his lip, glancing back to Isolde. "I . . . I would like for you to heal me, Lady."

Isolde held out her hands, and Tomas carefully set his heel into her fingers. His grip on my hand tightened; I felt the tension in his body, his breaths skipping like a rock over water as he watched her lay her palm against the arch of his foot. He must have been expecting pain, because Isolde lowered her hands and he blinked at her, surprised.

"Did you do it?" he asked.

Isolde smiled at his wonder. "Yes. Your foot is healed."

He let go of me to grab his foot, to turn it inward so he could examine it. There was no trace of blood, no trace of his stitches. There was only the pink of a scar as evidence that it had once been there.

"But I didn't even feel anything!" he exclaimed.

"I told you it wouldn't hurt," I said, tucking a stray thread of his hair behind his ear.

The three of us fell quiet, Tomas and I still seated side by side, Isolde still kneeling before us, the storm still raging beyond the windows. While Tomas continued to touch his foot, amazed, I met Isolde's gaze.

I wanted to know what she was thinking, what she was going to do.

She looked down at the pattern of blood on her dress, betraying a moment of bewilderment.

We were not wholly certain this was Declan's son. Although something in my heart told me it was.

"Mistress Brienna?" Tomas broke the quiet. "Is that the stone you were telling me about? The one you dug out from beneath a tree?" He shyly pointed to the Stone of Eventide, and I was partly relieved for the distraction.

"Yes. That's the one," I replied just as a knock sounded on the door.

Isolde was up on her feet before I could even think of moving. "I bet that is your supper, Tomas," she said as cheerfully as she could manage, but I saw the warning in her eyes.

Do not let anyone see him, her glance said to me as she strode to the door.

"Here, let's take you to the bedroom," I murmured to Tomas. "You can eat in bed." I nonchalantly guided him into the next chamber, out of sight from the main door, pulling back a heap of quilts.

"But this is your bed," he objected.

"I'll sleep in the other room. Come now, Tomas. Into bed." I all but lifted him and plopped him on the mattress.

"I've never slept in a bed this big," he said, wiggling around. "It's so soft!"

His innocence about made me cry. I wanted to ask him what sort of beds he had been sleeping in. If he had been a prince, shouldn't he have had the very best?

Maybe we were wrong. Maybe he was truly just an orphan with no drop of Lannon in him.

I willed that it was so.

Isolde returned with a tray laden with soup, buttered bread, and a tin cup of cider. She set it carefully before him, and Tomas's eyes went wide at the generous portion of it. He began to stuff his mouth, too intent on eating to pay Isolde and me any heed.

I followed the queen to the receiving chamber, just out of Tomas's sight. We stood facing each other; she was like a flame with her auburn hair and gleaming stone, and I was like a shadow, with my dark braids and my rising dread.

"I need to know what he is doing here, if he is truly who we believe him to be," Isolde whispered. "Can you speak more with him, to get affirmation from him?"

"Yes, of course," I responded.

"You must keep him hidden, Brienna. If he is discovered . . . I will have no other choice but to chain him in the dungeons."

I nodded, but there was a catch in my thoughts. I took a moment to steady my voice before asking her, "What of Cartier?"

Isolde sighed, rubbing her brow. "What of Aodhan?"

"Cartier has been caring for him at Castle Brígh, thinking he was a Morgane orphan."

The queen was quiet for a moment, her hands on her waist, her posture beginning to stoop, like I had just laid a boulder on her shoulders. "Has he grown fond of the boy?"

"Yes."

"If you think Aodhan is going to struggle with my ultimate decision, then keep this from him."

I tried to imagine what the trial would be like, how it would unfold. I tried to imagine what Cartier would do if Tomas was unexpectedly brought forth on the scaffold, after all this time believing Tomas was safe at Brígh. That Cartier would have to weigh if Tomas deserved to live, and even then . . . it would not be enough if the people of Maevana wanted the boy executed.

"Am I asking too much of you, Brienna?" the queen whispered gently.

I met her gaze. "No, Lady."

She had to come first. And I had to support her, no matter her decision.

"Find out the lad's true identity," she said. "Tonight, if possible. And then bring me the truth tomorrow morning."

I nodded; I bowed to her, my hand over my heart, to show my utter submission.

But Isolde touched my face; she took my chin beneath her

fingertips, to lift my eyes back up to the light, to her. I wondered if the Stone of Eventide was reflecting in my gaze, reflecting in my expression. "I trust you, Brienna, more than I trust any other."

Her confession moved me, and yet I swallowed the emotion, let it settle somewhere deeper in me, where it would not grow into pride.

It was then I knew what she was shaping me into, that I was becoming her right hand, that I was becoming her counselor, a position Brendan Allenach had once held for Gilroy Lannon.

The irony of it all stole my breath.

Isolde's fingers fell away and she departed, quiet and swift as the last bit of sunlight at dusk.

It was just me and Tomas now, and a vast ocean of questions between us.

Tomas had scraped the bowl of soup dry, licking the butter from his fingers as I moved back into the bedroom, bringing a second candelabra with me. I sat beside him on the edge of the bed, mulling over questions.

"Are you going to tell Lord Aodhan that I'm here?" he asked somberly.

I smoothed the wrinkles from the quilt, tracing the threads with my fingertips. "I think I need to know *why* you are here, Tomas." I paused and stared at him, waiting for him to look at me. "I'm sure Lord Aodhan told you to stay at Brígh. So right now, I'm trying to understand why you came to Lyonesse regardless of what he said. Why you crawled up a castle wall and snuck in through a window."

He was silent, unable to hold my stare.

I began to feel sweat trickle down my back. But I did not look away from him; my eyes were on his face, slowly finding similarities with the Lannons in his features. . . . He had auburn hair, which was unusual, but his eyes were sky blue like all the Lannons I had ever confronted, and his features were aristocratic in shape.

Tomas was about to speak when I heard a distant knocking at my door. I knew who it was, and it filled me with such sorrow and desire that I felt like a battle was raging in my heart.

"Tomas?" I whispered. "I want you to stay here. Do not move. Do not make a sound, do you understand?"

He only nodded, his face blanching.

I rose from the mattress and pulled the bedroom door shut behind me. I was trembling as I walked, the hem of my dress dragging over the floor.

The door creaked beneath my hand; I only opened it a sliver, the cool air of the corridors rising to my face.

There stood Cartier, his shoulder leaning on my lintel, his gaze on mine, his face nearly concealed in shadows. But I saw the gleam in his eyes, like embers smoldering in darkness at the sight of me.

"May I come in?" he asked.

I should tell him to return later. I should tell him that I was exhausted. I should do everything to keep him from stepping into my chambers.

And yet the way he was standing, the way he was breathing . . . it was as if he had a wound beneath his clothes.

I opened the door wide, and he walked to the fire. He waited until I had closed and bolted the door, joining him in the light.

"Is everything well with the queen?" he asked, searching my face.

"Yes."

He stared at me a moment more, as if the truth would shift my expression.

Slowly, I reached up, tracing the gold of his beard with my knuckles, surprised by its roughness. "Are you angry with me?" I whispered.

He shut his eyes, as if my touch was hurting him. "How could you think such?"

"You scarcely looked at me the entire journey."

Cartier's eyes opened. My hand was about to drop, but he caught it with his own, holding my hand against his face. "Brienna. I could scarcely keep my eyes *from* you. Why do you think I forced myself to ride ahead of you?"

His hand moved away from holding mine. His fingers trailed the length of my arm, up to my shoulder, then down, down my back to rest on my waist; I could hear the silk of my dress whisper beneath his touch, and now I was the one to close my eyes.

"Although it seems as if you are averse to look at me now," he said.

"I am not averse," I responded, my voice nothing more than a rasp. But my eyes were still shut, and I was still trembling from the weight of this night. He could feel it; his fingers fanned over my waist, over my ribs.

"Brienna. Is something troubling you?"

"Why were you late this morning?" The question shot forth like an arrow, much sharper than I intended.

When he was silent, I opened my eyes.

"I was late," Cartier said, his hand falling away from me. "Because I finally discovered who Tomas belongs to. And that is why I have come to you tonight. Because I cannot bear this on my own."

I stood there gaping at him, my heart doing a somersault. This was the last thing I expected him to say.

I finally understood his coldness, the hollowness in his eyes. He knew Tomas was a Lannon, that he had been ignorantly hiding him. I didn't know if I should be relieved of this, that Cartier knew the brunt of the revelation.

"Who does he belong to?" I forced myself to ask, my hand rubbing my collar, as if I could calm the wildness of my pulse.

There was a clatter behind my bedroom door, the sound of a bowl overturning. Tomas must have been eavesdropping. I had to swallow a curse, the misfortunate quandary that this night had become.

Cartier stiffened, his eyes flickering to my door.

And I could only stand there, feeling as if I had just been caught in a web.

"Is the queen still here?" he asked carefully, his gaze returning to mine. He asked, but he knew it was not Isolde. And I could not lie to him.

"No."

"Who is in your bedroom?" Cartier whispered.

Fate must have decided this encounter needed to happen. I drew in a deep breath and laid my hands over his chest. I could feel his heart pounding just as wildly as mine. The wound that was within him—I understood it now, and I despised myself, that I was about to drive it deeper.

"You're going to be angry, Cartier," I began. "You must swear that you will not express it, that you will be calm."

His hands were like ice as he took hold of my fingers, drawing them away from his heart.

"Who is in your bedroom, Brienna?"

I could not answer with my voice. I laced my fingers with his and guided him to my bedroom, opening the door.

There was Tomas, crouched on the floor. He had been going for the window, his dinner tray overturned.

Cartier halted at the sight of him. *"Tomas?"*

"Milord, please don't be angry with me!" Tomas stammered. "I had to come. I tried to tell you I needed to come, and you wouldn't listen to me."

I widened my eyes at Tomas, to warn him. This was *not* the way to soften Cartier's heart. Tomas glanced from Cartier to me, and then back to Cartier, as if he wasn't sure which one of us would be his salvation.

And while I could feel the stiffness in Cartier, the shock and anger, he stepped forward with a sigh, sitting on the edge of my bed.

"Come here, lad."

Tomas shuffled back to the bedside, defeated as he sat next

to Cartier. I continued to stand on the threshold, like I was straddling two different worlds that were about to collide.

"Why did you need to come with me?" Cartier quietly asked.

Tomas hesitated and then said, "Because I'm your runner."

"Is there another reason, Tomas? One you are afraid to tell me?"

"Noooo."

Cartier shifted, and I knew he was agonizing over this. "Tomas, I want you to trust me. Please, lad. Tell me the truth so I know how to help you."

Tomas was quiet. He picked at the quilt and then mumbled, "But you won't like me anymore."

"Tomas," Cartier said, so gently that I knew the words hurt him, "there is nothing you could ever do to make me dislike you."

"Can I still be your runner if I tell you the truth?"

Cartier met my gaze. He didn't know that Isolde knew Tomas was here. And if Cartier said yes, he would be lying to Tomas. He was not the one to ensure Tomas's life, which was what Tomas was asking in a roundabout manner. But if Cartier said no, Tomas would most likely refuse to confide in him.

"I promise, Tomas," he said, looking to the boy. I could hardly breathe, listening to him make this vow. "You will always be my runner for however long you wish to be."

Cartier wanted Tomas to live, to slip through the trial.

And if he asked me to help conceal Tomas from the queen . . . I would have to oppose him. I felt torn betwixt the two of them, and I had to step deeper into the room and sit in a chair, unable to stand.

"I wanted to come with you because my sister is here," Tomas confessed in a whisper.

"Your sister?"

"Yes, milord. When the battle happened, he . . . I mean *I* tried to tell her, to get her to come with me. Because I knew that we might be in trouble. Our da and grandda."

"Who are your father and grandfather, Tomas?" Cartier asked.

I quietly braced myself, my hands on the armrests, my fingernails sinking into the wood.

"My grandda is—*was*—the king," Tomas replied, downcast. "My father is Prince Declan. And my name is not Tomas. It is Ewan."

I felt chilled, and I couldn't stifle the shiver. Ewan looked at me with large, mournful eyes.

"Do you hate me now, Mistress Brienna?"

I stood and moved to sit on his other side, taking his hand in mine. "No, not at all, Ewan. You are my friend, and I think you are a brave boy."

That seemed to console him, and he looked back to Cartier. "My sister is in the dungeons. I need to get her out."

Cartier rushed his hand through his hair. I knew he was struggling to keep his composure, to remain calm. His jaw was set, which meant he was sifting through his responses.

"What is your sister's name?" I gently asked, to give Cartier a little more time to craft his answer.

"Keela. She's two years older than me. And I bet you Tomas can help you, milord."

"And who is this true Tomas, Ewan?" Cartier asked.

"He's a thane of my grandda's, but he has always been kind to me," Ewan replied. "He was the one to help me escape during the battle. He gave me some coppers and told me where to go, to go north to Castle Brígh and say my name was his, so no one would know who I truly was."

"Where can I find Tomas, then?"

Ewan shrugged. "I don't know, milord. I suppose he could be dead, killed during the battle."

I exchanged a wary glance with Cartier. If Thane Tomas had fought against us, he was indeed either dead or in the dungeons.

"I can make you no promises, Ewan," Cartier said at last, his voice tight. "Your sister is being held in the dungeons with your family. I do not know how much I can do—"

"Please, milord!" Ewan cried. "Please help her! I don't want them to kill her!"

"Shh." I tried to calm him, but Ewan shoved away from my arms to kneel before Cartier.

"Please, Lord Aodhan," he begged. "*Please.* I will never disobey you ever again if you would save her."

Cartier reached for Ewan's arms, pulling him back to his feet. He must have realized that Ewan was no longer limping; he stared at Ewan's bare foot before forcing his gaze up to the boy's. "It is never good to make promises we cannot keep. And while I cannot make a vow, I give my word that I will do everything I can to save your sister. As long as you give your word that you will remain in my chambers, hidden and quiet, Ewan. No one must know that you are here."

Ewan nodded vehemently. "I give my word, milord. No one will know. I am good at hiding."

"Yes, I know." Cartier sighed. "Now, it's past your bedtime. You need to come with me, to my chambers." The three of us stood. And the questions must have been evident in my eyes, because Cartier asked Ewan to step out from the bedroom for a moment.

"You think it best that he remains in your chambers?" I whispered, trying to hide my worry. I wanted to trust Cartier, but what if he chose to hide Ewan? What would I say to Isolde?

"What do you think, Brienna?" He stepped close to me, so he could angle his lips and whisper directly into my ear. His voice warmed my hair as he asked, "The queen knows he is here, doesn't she?"

"She wants to speak with me about him tomorrow morning," I whispered in return. "To affirm who he is."

"Then let me do it, Brienna."

I leaned back, to meet his gaze.

"I can imagine Isolde is at war with her decision tonight," Cartier continued, his voice hardly more than a hum. "What to do with the child of her nemesis."

"And what would *you* do?"

He stared at me a moment, and then said, "I will do whatever she commands of me. She is my queen. But I want the chance to speak with her of it, to persuade her in the way I think best."

I could not fault him for this, to want the opportunity to speak privately with Isolde, to make the case for Ewan's life.

Nor could I stop the tears that filled my eyes. I didn't know where they came from, perhaps a hidden well in my heart, one that Ewan's predicament had just created within me.

I tried to turn away before Cartier noticed, but he took my face in his hands and held me before him.

A tear streaked down my cheek. Cartier kissed it, and the way his hands caressed my hair, the way my heart began to strike and spark . . . if not for Ewan being in the adjacent room, I don't know what would have unfolded between us, although I could imagine.

When he looked at me, I saw the same in his eyes, this insatiable desire to have nothing but the night between us, the stars above us, burning secrets into dawn.

Yet reality was like a splash of cold water in my face. For here we were with a Lannon child between us, with a trial bearing down on us, with uncertainty awaiting us.

I wondered if there would ever be time for me and him.

"Good night, Cartier," I whispered.

He left without another word once he was certain the corridor was empty, Ewan in his shadow.

And I was suddenly alone.

→ FOURTEEN →

ONCE A LANNON, ALWAYS A LANNON

Two Days Until the Trial

Cartier

I did not sleep that night. I gave Ewan the bed, and I stretched out on the divan and watched the fire die out to embers, thinking long into the night. Thinking of what I would say to Isolde, of how to convince her to let this child live. And then it was not merely Ewan anymore; it was now Keela.

And there were only two days remaining until the trial.

By the time dawn arrived, I knew I needed to speak to Isolde and then speak to Keela in the dungeons.

I called upon the queen midmorning, after ensuring Ewan was going to stay put in my chambers with a bowl of porridge and a book I had selected from the library.

"But I cannot read, milord," Ewan had complained at the sight of the massive book.

The lad might as well have shoved a dagger into my stomach, for all the pain his words caused me.

"Then look at the pictures," I had responded, and promptly left before I asked any more probing questions about Ewan's childhood.

Did you father beat you, Ewan? Did your grandfather starve you? Is that why you do not like to be alone in the dark? Why were you never taught to read?

I waited to meet with Isolde in the queen's solarium, a room that was still in the process of being stripped of Lannon's presence. The walls were now bare—they had been crowded with antlers and mounted animal heads before—and I wondered if the queen would commission Jourdain's weavers to create tapestries to grace the walls.

"You wanted to speak with me?"

I turned to see Isolde enter the chamber. "Yes, Lady."

"I actually just came from another private meeting," the queen said, taking a few steps closer. "With Lady Grainne."

"Oh? I trust it was a good meeting, then?"

Isolde smiled. "Aye."

"And did she agree to support you in full?"

"There was actually no talk of support or alliances between us."

"Really?" I could not hide my surprise. And while I wanted to know the details, it was not my right, and so I did not ask.

But when I looked at Isolde, at the light in her eyes, I saw the fire of secrets, the lustrous light of a dragon breathing flames over its hoard of gold. Perhaps I would learn the truth of it in the months to come.

"Please, tell me what is on your mind, Aodhan."

"I would like to request passage into the dungeons, to speak with several of the Lannons."

Her smile faded. "May I ask which Lannons you intend to speak with?"

"Keela."

"The princess? I fear that I have tried to speak to her myself, Aodhan. The lass will not talk."

"I still would like to try," I said. "I was also hoping to speak to a Lannon thane who goes by the name of Tomas. Is he in the dungeons?"

"Yes, he is being held."

I drew in a deep breath, rousing my courage to add, "And I need to speak to Declan."

The queen was quiet, glancing to the wall of windows. The storm had finally passed, leaving behind weak sunlight and soft earth, but soon the clouds would break and we would see the sky again.

Isolde slowly walked to the windows, the purple of her dress reflecting on the tilted panes as she stood and stared at the city of Lyonesse. Her hair was a deeper shade of red than Ewan's; she had it pulled back with a simple ribbon, her curls like a shield at her back.

"I do not want to behead Keela Lannon," the queen said. "She is but a girl, and she is terrified. I want her to live, to heal, to grow up to become a beautiful young woman. But the truth of the matter is . . . the people are going to demand *all* of the Lannon blood. And if I let the grandchildren live, then what happens if seeds of resentment grow in them, for being the last of their line? Will other Houses welcome them, or hate and shun them? Will they ever belong? Will the anger grow into something darker, dooming us to face another war decades from now?"

When she grew quiet, I moved to stand at her side.

"Your fears are justified, Lady," I said. "I feel them as you do. But Keela is just a child. She should not carry the weight of her father's and her grandparents' sins."

"But isn't this the way of Maevana? To extinguish entire families who oppose the queen?" Isolde asked. "The bitter portions?"

"And yet you said it yourself yesterday, that we want to emerge from an era of darkness; we want you to lead us into the light."

The queen remained silent.

"Isolde," I finally said, but still she would not look at me. Her eyes were on the city, and so I continued, "I have Ewan Lannon in my care. He is the lad who crawled in through Brienna's window last night."

"I knew it was him," she breathed. "I knew it when I looked at him, when I healed him." She closed her eyes. "I am weak, Aodhan."

"It is not weakness to want to heal a wounded child, to shelter children from the heavy cost of their family's wickedness, Isolde," I responded. "Keela and Ewan are innocent."

Her eyes fluttered open, fixating on me. "Keela Lannon is not innocent, Aodhan."

Her words struck me, made me momentarily pause.

"She has a list of grievances against her," the queen continued.

"They are sparse in comparison to her father's and her grandparents', and yet they are still there. Several of her chambermaids have come forward, saying she has ordered cruel punishments upon them."

"I would bet that she was coerced to do these things, Isolde," I rasped. But my doubt lingered like a bruise.

"I am not queen yet," she said, so softly I almost did not hear her. "And I do not desire to witness the trial with a crown, but as one of the people. I want to stand equal with them, shoulder to shoulder, when the verdict is given. I do not want it to seem that this is my justice. This is *our* justice." She began to pace, her hands pressed together like her heart was consumed with prayers. "Because of this, if the people demand Keela Lannon's head . . . I have no voice to override them. She is already in the dungeons; the people put her there, and I cannot raise her out of it."

I knew it would be so. I stood silent, waiting, watching her pace.

"Because of this," Isolde whispered, coming to a stop before me. "I want you to shelter and protect Ewan Lannon. Keep him hidden until after the trial. I want you to raise him up as one of your own, as a Morgane. I want you to raise him to be a good man."

"You are giving me your blessing?" I was not wholly surprised by this; I had imagined Isolde would decide upon mercy, and yet I could not deny the fact that I always felt humbled in her presence.

"I am giving you my blessing, Aodhan," she replied. "As the Queen of Maevana, I will find a way to pardon him. Until I am crowned, keep him hidden and safe."

"So I will, Lady," I murmured, laying my hand on my heart in submission.

"I will send word to the guards to grant you passage into the dungeon," she said. "You may speak to Keela and Tomas as well as to Declan, but just keep this in mind . . ." The queen accompanied me to the door, tilting her head, as if she was reliving a dark memory, one she wanted to dissolve. "Declan Lannon has a terrible way with words. Do not let him rile you."

An hour later, I was descending into the dark bowels of the castle.

The stone floor beneath me grew slick with every step, and I thought I could hear the distant roar of water.

"What is that noise?" I asked.

"A river runs beneath the castle," the master guard, Fechin, answered.

I drew in a deep breath, tasting a distant thread of salt and mist. "Where does it run to?"

"The ocean." Fechin glanced over his shoulder, to meet my gaze. "It was how the Lannons disposed of the dismembered bodies for years, by sending them 'on the current.'"

His words nearly bounced off me, they were so difficult to grapple with. But this manner of evil had been done here, in these tunnels, for *years*. I made myself dwell on that truth as I continued to draw nigh to the Lannons' cells.

We walked farther, until the hum of the river vanished, and the only sound was the water dripping from the cracks above. And then came another noise, one so odd I wondered if I was imagining it. It was the sound of sweeping, a persistent rushing, over and over.

I finally came upon the source, unexpectedly, as if it had blossomed from the stone before me. A figure draped in black veils from head to toe, their face concealed, was sweeping the floor. I nearly plowed into them, lurching to the side to avoid a collision.

They stopped, and a prickling sensation moved over my skin as my torch burned the darkness between me and them.

"The bone sweeper," Fechin explained nonchalantly. "They won't hurt you."

I resisted the temptation to glance at the sweeper one final time, my skin still rippling with gooseflesh. I had only been walking the tunnels for maybe half an hour, and yet how eager I was to ascend from here. I struggled to compose myself as the guard stopped before a narrow door with a crooked slash of a window lined with iron bars.

"The lady said you wanted to see Keela Lannon first?" Fechin set his torch into a sconce to fiddle with his ring of keys.

"Yes." I realized there was blood splattered on the limestone walls. That the glistening on the floor was indeed bones, and that the sweeper had a reason to be taking a broom to the tunnels.

Fechin unlocked the door, kicking it open with a rusty groan. "I'll wait here for you."

I nodded and stepped into the cell, my torch sputtering in tandem with my pulse.

It was not a big chamber, but there was a cot and plenty of blankets, and a narrow table graced with a stack of books and a line of candles. A girl stood against the wall, her fair hair and pale skin smudged into the darkness, her eyes glittering with terror at the sight of me entering her cell.

"Don't be afraid," I said, just as Fechin loudly clanged the door shut.

Keela rushed to her table to pry one of her half-melted candles from the wood, wielding the flame as a weapon. She was gasping in fear, and I stopped, my own heart pounding.

"Keela, please. I am here to help you."

She bared her teeth at me, but there were tears glistening on her cheeks.

"I am Aodhan Morgane, and I know your little brother, Ewan," I gently continued. "He asked me to come see you."

The sound of her brother's name softened her. I was hopeful this would be the meeting ground for us, and I kept speaking, keeping my voice low so my words wouldn't drift beyond the door.

"I found your brother at my castle. I think he left Lyonesse during the battle, searching for someplace safe to stay. He asked me to come and speak with you, Keela, to see what we can do to help you in the upcoming days." This was what I was most concerned about, after discovering Keela had grievances against her. I needed to think of a way to get her to talk about it, so I could help her form an answer when the grievances were read before an angry crowd. "Would you be willing to speak with me, Keela?"

She was quiet.

I thought she was considering my words when she let out a scream that rose the hair on my arms.

"You lie! My brother is dead! Get out!" She hurled the candle. I narrowly stepped out of the way as she continued to scream, "Get out! *Get out!*"

I had no choice.

I rapped on the door and Fechin opened it.

I stood outside of Keela's cell, leaning against the bloodstains on the wall, and listened to her weep. It tore my insides to hear it, to know this was Ewan's sister, that she was being held in the dark, that she was terrified at the mere sight of me.

"She acted the same way for the queen," the guard said. "Don't let it upset you."

I was not comforted by his words.

I felt ill as I continued to follow the guard down the tunnel, the air turning stale and putrid.

We arrived at Thane Tomas's cell next. Once again, Fechin unlocked the door and I stepped within the cell, uncertain as to what I would find.

This cell was relatively clean. An old man sat on his cot, his ankles and his wrists shackled, staring at me. Despite his years, he was still broad and powerfully built. There was no emotion in his face or eyes, only hardness, and he was difficult to look upon. His blond hair was almost completely gray, lank and tangled at his shoulders, and his face was haggard, as if he was more wraith than man.

"Thane Tomas?"

He said nothing. I sensed he would withhold his voice, that he would refuse to speak with me.

"I stumbled upon your namesake at my castle," I continued in a low tone. "A little red-haired lad."

As I expected, the mention of Ewan stirred something in him. His mouth was still downturned, but his eyes softened.

"I suppose you have him chained up now?" the thane grunted.

"On the contrary. I have him in hiding."

"And what do you want with me, then?"

"Are you loyal to Gilroy and Oona?"

The old thane chuckled. He spat on the floor between us and crossed his arms, the chains clanging. "They have ruined the name of Lannon. Utterly ruined it."

I had to hide my pleasure to hear his disdain. And I tucked his name into the back of my mind as a potential ally. He might be a Lannon we could swing to our favor, who could help us rebuild. If he cared for Keela and Ewan, enough so that he risked himself in battle to help Ewan escape, then he had to be worth more than any Lannon I had ever known.

I began to leave, but his voice rose again.

"You're Líle's son."

His statement stopped me cold. Slowly, I turned to look at him again, to find his gaze on mine.

"You have no idea who I am, do you?" Tomas continued.

I thought of my mother's letter, of how I was trying to suppress the truth of her revelation. But before I could respond, he spoke again.

"Sweet Líle Hayden. She was a light among us, a flower blooming in frost. I wasn't surprised when Kane Morgane swept her away to his lands, to crown her as Lady."

"And who are you to her?" I snapped. His words were wounding me; I did not want to imagine my parents, to dwell on my loss.

Tomas was grave as he whispered, "Her uncle."

I staggered back, unable to hide my shock.

"I am the last of the Haydens, the last of your family on the Lannon side," Tomas said, gentler now, as if he felt my agony.

And I wished he had not told me. I wished that I did not know he was a relation, that a great-uncle of mine was sitting in chains in the castle dungeons.

"I cannot liberate you," I said. But my mind was already seeking a way; my heart was a traitor, longing to set him free.

"All I ask is that you bring out a new chopping block and axe for me. That you won't stain my neck with their blood."

I nodded and departed, struggling to regain my composure as I waited for Fechin to lock the thane's cell before guiding me to my final stop. I considered returning to the light and forgetting about Declan. My clothes were drenched with sweat; I felt on the verge of illness. And then I heard my father's voice, as if he was standing behind me, saying, "You are Aodhan Morgane, the heir of the Morgane House and lands."

I had never been a Lannon.

This thought centered me, enabled me to continue onward.

There was more dried blood smeared on the walls, on the floors, as we came to Declan's cell. Fechin unlocked the door, and for a moment I stared at it, the gaping entrance. I was about to pass over a threshold and come face-to-face with the prince who had once been betrothed to my sister, the prince who had crushed her bones. Who had murdered her.

Aileen's voice came this time, a whisper in my mind. *I want you to look Declan Lannon in the eye and curse him and his House. I want you to be the beginning of his end, to be your mother's and your sister's vengeance.*

I stepped into the cell.

This chamber was bare, but the corners were scattered with bones and strung with cobwebs. There was a cot for the prisoner to lie down and sleep, one blanket and one bucket for refuse. A set of torches were pegged into the walls, hissing with light. And there, chained to the wall by both ankles and wrists, sat Declan Lannon, his tawny brown hair tangled and greasy on his brow, his large frame dwarfing the cot. A beard covered his lower face, and a wicked smile cut through it like a crescent moon when our eyes met.

My blood chilled; he recognized me, somehow. Just like Thane Tomas had. Declan knew exactly who I was.

I stood and stared at him; he sat and stared back, the darkness moving around us both like a wild, hungry creature, and the only power I had to ward it off was the torch in my hand and the fire that ignited in my chest.

"You look just like her," Declan said, breaking our silence.

I did not blink, did not move, did not breathe. I was a statue, a man carved of stone, who would not feel anything. Yet a voice told me, *He is speaking of your mother.*

"You have her hair, her eyes," the prince continued. "You inherited the best of her, then. But perhaps you already knew that? That you are half a Lannon."

I stared at him, the blue glint of ice in his eyes, the stray blond threads in his hair, the pale sheen of his skin. My voice was lost, and so he kept speaking.

"You and I could be brothers. I loved your mother when I was a boy. I loved her more than my own mother. And I once resented you, that you were Líle's son and I was not. That she loved you more than she loved me." Declan shifted, crossing his ankles. The chains scraped and clanged over the stone, but the prince did not seem the slightest bit uncomfortable. "Did you know that she was my teacher, Aodhan?"

Aodhan.

Now that he had spoken my name, had fully acknowledged me, I found my voice in my throat, lodged like a splinter.

"What did she teach you, Declan?"

His smile deepened, pleased that he had taunted me into a conversation. I despised myself for it, for longing to know more of her, and that I had resorted to asking *him* about it.

"Líle was a painter. It was the one thing I begged my father to let me learn. How to paint."

I thought back to my mother's letter. She mentioned she had been instructing Declan in something. . . .

My father had never once told me my mother had been a painter.

"What made your lessons cease, then?"

"Líle," Declan replied, and I hated the way her name sounded on his tongue. "She broke my betrothal to your sister. That was the beginning of the end. She no longer trusted me. She began to doubt me. I saw it in her eyes when she looked at me, when all I wanted to paint was death and blood." He paused, flicking his fingernails, over and over. The sound filled the chamber like the ticking of a clock, maddeningly. "And when the person you love more than anything in the world is afraid of you . . . it changes you. You do not forget it."

I did not know what to say to him. My jaw was clenched, anger pounding a dull ache at my temples.

"I tried to tell her, of course," Declan went on, his voice like smoke. I could not block it out; I could not resist breathing it in. "I told Líle that I was only painting what I saw day by day. Severed heads and sliced-out tongues. How my father chose to rule. And how my father was raising me in his mold. I thought your mother would understand; she was, after all, of the Lannon House. She knew our sensibilities.

"And my father trusted Líle. She was the daughter of his favorite thane, that old lump of a man, Darragh Hayden. Líle will not betray us, he said. But Gilroy forgot that when a woman marries a lord, she takes on a new name. She takes a new House and her allegiance shifts, almost as if she had never been fastened by blood at all. And how Kane of Morgane adored her! He would have given everything to keep her with him, I bet."

He finally quieted, long enough for me to process everything he had just spouted.

"I take it old Kane is dead?" Declan asked.

I decided to gloss over his inquiry by asking, "Where are the Haydens now?" I already knew where one Hayden was: several cells down.

He chuckled, a wet cough in his lungs. "Wouldn't you like to know. They're dead, of course, save for one. Old Faithful Tomas. His brother—your grandfather—rose up after he saw Líle rebel, after he saw a pretty blond head on a spike. He chose his daughter over his king. There's a special punishment for Lannons who turn on their own."

I needed to depart. Now. Before this conversation got any deeper, before I lost my composure. I began to turn my back to him, to leave him in the darkness.

"Where did your nursemaid hide you, Aodhan?"

My feet froze to the floor. I felt the blood drain from my face as I met his gaze, his smile like tarnished silver in the torchlight.

"I tore that castle apart trying to find you," Declan murmured. "I've oft wondered about it, where you hid that night. How a little child escaped me."

Where are you, Aodhan?

The voices aligned, sharpened. Young Declan and old Declan. The past and the present. The smell of burning herbs, the distant echo of screams, the cold scent of manure, the weeping of my father. The damp smell of this cell, the heap of bones, the stench of refuse in the bucket, the gleam of Declan's eyes.

"Wouldn't you like to know," I said.

He leaned his head back and laughed until I thought I would kill him. And the bloodlust must have been bright in my gaze, because he leveled his eyes at me and said, "It's a pity they didn't hide your sister as well as they hid you."

I reached for my hidden dirk before I could stop myself. The blade was waiting at my back, beneath my shirt. I drew it so swiftly that Declan was momentarily surprised, his brows arching, but then he smiled, watching the light flash on the steel.

"Go on, then. Go ahead and stab me until my blood fills this cell. I'm sure the people of Maevana will appreciate it, that they won't have to waste their time weighing my life."

I was trembling, my breath coming and going through my teeth.

"Go on, Aodhan," Declan taunted. "Kill me. I deserve to die at your hand."

I took a step, but it wasn't toward him; it was toward the wall. I had his attention now; I was moving and acting in an unexpected way.

He was quiet, watching as I approached the wall, just above his cot.

I took the point of my knife and began to carve my name into the stone.

Aodhan.

He would have to look at it at least for two more days. My name entrenched in the stone of his cell. Just above his reach.

Declan was amused. He must be remembering that night when he carved his name into the stone of my courtyard, thinking it would outlast the Morganes.

He was opening his mouth to speak again, but I turned and found myself crouching, to conceal how badly I was trembling. I looked at Declan, and this time I was the one to smile.

"I have your son, Declan."

He was not expecting that.

All that confidence, all that amusement, broke in his eyes. He stared at me, the one who was now turned into stone. "What are you going to do with him?"

"I plan to teach him to read and write," I began, my voice growing steadier. "I plan to teach him to wield words as he wields swords, to respect and honor women as he respects and honors his new queen. And then I will raise him up as my own. And he will curse the man he came from, the blood he descended from. He will be the one to blot your name out of the history ledgers, to turn your land into something good after it has been nothing but rot since you were born upon it. And you will become a distant mark in his mind, something he may think about from time to time, but he will not remember you as father, because you never were. When he thinks of his father, he will think of me."

I was done. I had the final word, the final carving.

I stood and began to walk to the door, tucking my dirk away, flexing my stiff fingers. I was almost to the cell door, to knock for it to open, to leave this cesspool, when Declan Lannon's voice split the darkness, chasing my heels.

"You forget something, Aodhan."

I halted, but I did not turn around.

"Once a Lannon . . . always a Lannon."

"Yes. My mother proved that, didn't she?"

I left the cell, but Declan's laughter, Declan's words, haunted me long after I returned to the light.

⟶ FIFTEEN ⟵

BROTHERS AND SISTERS

Two Days Until the Trial

Brienna

"I know I am not standing trial as the Lannons are," Sean Allenach said as he walked beside me in the castle gardens. "But that doesn't mean my House shouldn't pay for what it has done."

"I agree," I replied, savoring the morning light. "I know once this trial is over, Isolde will meet with you about reparations. I believe she hopes to see your House pay the MacQuinns over the next twenty-five years."

Sean nodded. "I will do whatever she believes is best."

We fell quiet, each of us lost in our own thoughts.

Sean was born three years before me. We shared Brendan Allenach as a father, but more than our name and our blood, I was beginning to realize that we shared hope for what our corrupted

House could become. That the House of Allenach could be redeemed.

I was relieved that Sean arrived in the royal city, just as he had promised the queen after she had healed him on the battlefield, seeking me out immediately upon his arrival.

"I wonder if the queen will see it fit to put the Allenachs on trial," Sean said, breaking my thoughts.

If Brendan Allenach had not been slayed by Jourdain on the battlefield, the House of Allenach would certainly face a trial similar to the Lannons': Brendan Allenach would have met the chopping block. And though Sean had thrown his support behind the queen, had urged his father to surrender in battle, I had no doubt that Isolde would call for another trial after her coronation, for the Allenachs, the Carrans, and the Hallorans.

I didn't want to mention this yet, though. I stopped, the garden around us withered from years of neglect beneath the Lannons.

"It's not just money and goods that will be required of you and your people, Sean. You were right when you wrote me last week: You will need to sow new thoughts in your House, beliefs that will grow to become goodness and charity, not fear and violence."

He met my gaze; he and I didn't look much alike, save for our tall and slender builds, but I acknowledged there was a draw between us, as brothers and sisters will always have. And that made me think of Neeve, who was Sean's as she was mine. Did he know of her? Part of me believed he had no inkling that he had another half sister, because Jourdain's weavers had vigilantly guarded her over the years. And part of me longed to tell him, that there was not just two of us but three.

"Yes, I wholeheartedly agree," Sean responded gently. "And what a task that will be, after my father's leadership."

He sounded overwhelmed, and I took his hand in mine.

"We will take this one step at a time. I think it will help you to find like-minded men and women in your House who you can trust and appoint as leaders," I said.

He smiled. "I suppose I cannot ask you to come back and help me?"

"I'm sorry, Sean. But it's best that I remain with my people now."

I didn't want to tell him that I needed as much distance as possible from the Allenach House and lands, that my utmost need, besides protecting and supporting the queen, was to remain with Jourdain and his people.

"I understand," he said softly.

I looked down to our hands, at the edge of his sleeves. He was wearing the maroon and white of the Allenachs, the leaping stag embroidered over his breast. And yet . . . his wrists. I hated to imagine it, but what if my brother was marked? What if he bore the half-moon tattoo on his wrist, just beneath his sleeve? Did I have the right to search for it?

"What are your thoughts on allegiance?" I quietly asked.

Sean lifted his eyes to mine. "I plan to swear my fealty to Isolde before her coronation."

"What about your thanes? Will they support you in this?"

"Four of them will. I am not so certain about the other three," he replied. "I am not oblivious to the fact that they murmur about me when my back is turned. That they no doubt believe I am weak; they think I would be easy to uproot and replace."

"Would they dare to plot against you, Sean?" I asked, a flare of anger in my voice.

"I don't know, Brienna. I cannot deny that their talk centers on you returning to the Allenachs."

I was speechless.

Sean gave me a sad smile, squeezing my hand. "I think they consider you above me, because you were Brendan's only daughter. And one daughter is worth ten sons. But more than that . . . while you plotted and overthrew a tyrant, I was sitting at home in Castle Damhan, doing nothing, letting my father trample his own people into the ground."

"Then you must do *something*, Sean," I said. "The first thing I would have you do is remove the half-moon from the Allenach sigil."

"What half-moon?" He merely blinked at me, perplexed, and I realized he had been in utter darkness of our father's involvement.

I took a deep breath. "After the trial, return to Castle Damhan," I said, letting go of Sean's hand so we could continue walking. "I want you to call your seven thanes together in the hall before all of your people. Have them pull up their sleeves and lay their hands on the table, palms to the sky. If they harbor a half-moon tattoo on their wrists, I want you to dismiss them. And if all seven of them bear the mark, find seven new thanes, seven men or women you trust and respect."

"I am not sure I understand," my brother said. "This half-moon mark . . . ?"

"Signifies allegiance to the Lannons."

He was quiet, drowning in all of the orders I was giving him.

"After you have weeded through your thanes," I continued, "I want you to once again summon every Allenach to your hall. Take down the coat of arms and cut out the half-moon mark. Burn it. Order a new sigil to be made with its omission. Tell your people you are going to swear fealty to Isolde before her coronation, and you expect them to follow your lead. If they have concerns about it, they should come and speak to you. You should listen to them, of course. But also be firm should they oppose the queen."

Sean snorted. At first, I thought he was mocking me, and I abruptly glanced up to him. He was smiling, shaking his head.

"I think my thanes are right, sister. You are far more capable of leading this House than I am."

"Beliefs such as that will not get you far, brother," I returned, and then softened my voice. "You will be more than Brendan Allenach ever was as lord."

I was just about to ask him more about his thanes when Cartier met us on the grass, his shirt smudged as if he had leaned against a dirty wall, his hair lank and tangled. I instantly was struck by worry; he must have had a long conversation with Isolde about Ewan, and it must have gone awry.

"Do you mind if I steal her away for now?" Cartier asked Sean.

"No, not at all. I have an audience with the queen anyway," my brother said with a bow of his head, leaving me and Cartier to the wind and clouds.

"Is something wrong?" I asked. "What did Isolde say?"

Cartier took my hand and began to lead me away from the openness of the gardens, to a private shadow. "Isolde has given Ewan's safekeeping to me. I must keep him hidden until the trial is over." He reached into his pocket, bringing forth a folded piece of paper. I watched as he opened it, revealing a beautiful illustration of a princess. "There is something I must ask of you, Brienna."

"What do you need me to do?"

Cartier looked down to the illustration, and then slowly passed it into my hands. "I need you to go talk to Keela Lannon in the dungeons. Ewan tore this page out of a book, saying it reminded him of the time Keela wanted to be 'princess of the mountain.' He thinks if you are the one to go to her with this message, she will trust and listen to you."

I studied the illustration. It was beautiful, depicting a princess mounted upon a horse with a falcon perched on her shoulder.

"Should I go now?" I asked, feeling Cartier's gaze on my face.

"Not yet. There is something else." He took my hand again, guiding me back to the guest wing of the castle. I let him lead me to his room, and that's where I first saw the list of grievances against Keela.

"I received this list from the queen," he said as we sat at the table, sharing a pot of tea, reading and strategizing over how to combat them.

They were serious offenses, with exact dates and names of the griever. A great majority of them spoke of how Keela had ordered her chambermaids to be scourged and then have their hair shorn. How she had withheld meals and made her servants do ridiculous, demeaning things, like lick milk up from the floor and crawl around the castle like dogs.

"Do you think Keela did these things?" I asked Cartier, my heart heavy.

Cartier was quiet, staring at the list. "No. I think Declan Lannon made her do these evils. And when she refused, he harmed her. So she began to acquiesce, to survive."

"So how do we go about this?"

"Brienna . . . that dungeon is perhaps the darkest place I have ever been. Keela was too terrified and angry to speak to me." He turned the grievances over and met my gaze. "If you can find a way to keep her calm, to reassure her that she can trust you, that there is the possibility of redemption for her . . . perhaps that will give her the confidence she needs to share her story, and the people will let her live. They need to know she is just like them, that she has greatly suffered her entire life because of her father and grandfather."

"I will go this afternoon," I said, even though I didn't know what to expect, even though I was struggling to grasp everything Cartier was trying to tell me.

A few hours later, I met the master guard, Fechin, to be led into the darkness of the dungeons. And I found myself standing in Keela Lannon's dim, cold cell, leagues of stone overhead, seeming to crush the air from my lungs, the hope from my heart. And I finally understood Cartier's words.

I couldn't help but shiver as I watched Keela rush to her little table and grab a candle, as if the tiny flame could protect her.

"Do you mind if I sit?" I asked, but didn't wait for her to respond. I lowered myself to the stone floor, crossing my legs, my dress spreading around me. I had the princess illustration in my pocket, with the words Ewan wanted me to say to her tucked in my memory.

"Get out," Keela whimpered.

"My name is Brienna MacQuinn," I spoke in a soothing tone, as if Keela and I were not in a cell beneath the earth, but sitting in a meadow. "But I haven't always been a MacQuinn. Before that, I belonged to another House. I was Brendan Allenach's daughter."

Keela froze. "Lord Allenach never had a daughter."

"Yes, so people thought, because I was illegitimate, born to a Valenian woman across the channel." I tilted my head, my hair falling over my shoulder. "Would you like to hear my story?"

Keela's mind was racing. I could tell by the darting of her eyes as she assessed me, and then the door, which was closed and locked, and then back to me, and then her nearby cot. I wanted her to know that I was just like her, born into an oppressive and cruel House, but that our names and our blood did not wholly define us. There were other things, deeper things, such as beliefs and choices, that were more powerful.

And if Keela had once loved the idea of becoming the princess of the mountain, then I knew she was a dreamer as well as a lover of stories.

"Fine," she relented, edging her way to her cot.

I began to tell her about my life: losing my mother when I was three, my grandfather sending me to an orphanage with a different last name because he was afraid of Lord Allenach finding me.

I told her about when I turned ten, I was accepted into Magnalia House, and how more than anything, I wanted to become a passion.

"How many passions are there?" Keela asked, slowly setting her candle aside.

"There are five," I answered with a smile. "Art. Dramatics. Music. Wit. Knowledge."

"Which one are you?"

"I'm a mistress of knowledge."

"Who taught you knowledge?" Keela pulled her knees up to her chest, propping her chin on them.

"That would be Master Cartier, who is better known as Aodhan of Morgane."

She fell quiet, studying the floor between us. "I think he tried to speak with me earlier today."

"Yes, that was him. He and I want to help you, Keela."

"How can you help me?" she whispered angrily. "My grandda is a horrible man. They say I favor him in the face, so if I am to live, how will other people bear to look at me?"

My heart beat faster as I listened to her. She had thought on the possibility of surviving the trial, had thought about how much she would be reviled. And I couldn't lie to her: it would take time for other Maevans to trust and accept her, just as it was taking time for Jourdain's people to fully welcome me.

"Let me tell you the rest of my story, Keela, and then we can try to answer such worries," I said.

I told her of the memories I had inherited from my ancestor, Tristan Allenach, about his treachery, how he hid the Stone of Eventide and forced magic to go dormant, how he assassinated the last queen of Maevana. I told her about the revolution, of how I crossed the channel to recover the stone, how Brendan Allenach had known I was his daughter and tried to tempt me to deny my friends and join him, to take the crown for myself with him at my side.

This hooked her attention, more than my history with the passions, because I could see how she was comparing us, me and her, two daughters trying to break away from their blood Houses.

"But I will always be a Lannon," she argued. "They will always hate me, whether I live or die."

"But Keela," I gently countered. "Is it only blood that makes a House? Or is it beliefs? What holds people together more? The red in their veins or the fire in their hearts?"

She was shaking her head, tears spilling from her eyes.

"Keela, I want you to live. So does your brother Ewan." I withdrew the illustration from my pocket and smoothed the wrinkles from it, setting it on the floor. "He wanted me to give this to you, because it reminded him of the time you desired to become the princess of the mountain."

She wept then, and while I wanted to comfort her, I stayed where I was, my legs numb from the hardness of the stone. I let her be the one to stand and crawl to where I had set the paper. She took it in her hands and dashed the tears from her eyes, returning to her cot to sit and admire it.

"He's not dead? My da told me he was," she said once she had calmed. "That the new queen cut him up in pieces."

"Ewan is very much alive," I answered, cursing the lies her father had purposely fed her. "Aodhan Morgane and I are protecting him, and we would protect you too."

"But the people hate me!" she cried. "They want my blood. They want all of our blood!"

"Is there a reason that they should want your blood, Keela?"

She looked like she wanted to cry again. "No. Yes. I don't know!"

"What was it like for you, living as a princess in the castle?"

She was quiet, but I sensed my question had found its mark.

"Did they beat you, Keela? Did they make you do cruel things?" I paused, but my heart was pounding. "Was your father the one to order you to hurt your chambermaids?"

Keela began to weep, hiding her face in the crook of her arm. I thought I had lost her until she raised her head and whispered, "Yes. My da . . . my da would hurt me if I didn't hurt them. He would lock me in my closet, where it was dark, and I would be hungry. It felt like I was in there for days. But he told me it would only make me stronger, that his da had done such things to him, to make him unbreakable. My da said he couldn't trust me unless I did exactly as he ordered."

Listening to her, I was torn between the hunger for justice, to see blood spilled after all the Lannons had done, and the painful desire for mercy when it came to Keela Lannon. Because I saw a shade of myself within her, and I had been given grace.

"This is what you need to tell the people when you stand trial, Keela," I murmured, aching for her. "You must tell them the truth. You must tell them what it was like for you as the granddaughter of King Lannon. And I promise they will listen, and some of them will realize you are just like them. That you want the same things for Maevana."

I stood, my feet prickling with pins and needles. Keela stared up at me with large, bloodshot eyes, eyes that were nearly identical to Ewan's.

"The trial will begin in two days," I said. "They will bring you out on the scaffold before the city, to answer the magistrate's questions, for the people to weigh whether you will live or die. I will be standing at the front, and if you feel afraid, I want you to look at me, and know that you are not alone."

→ SIXTEEN →

LET THEIR HEADS ROLL

Day of the Trial

Cartier

There was not a cloud in the sky the day of the trial.

I was the first lord to reach the scaffold that morning, a circlet of gold across my brow, the gray horse of Morgane stitched at my heart. I sat in my appointed chair, watching the castle green begin to flood with people.

I stared at the wooden stand at the center of the scaffold, at the shadows that already gathered about it, where Gilroy Lannon, Oona Lannon, Declan Lannon, and Keela Lannon would stand in a matter of hours. I tried to imagine Ewan standing among them, blood of their blood, bone of their bone.

Once a Lannon, always a Lannon.

I hated those words, the doubt Declan had planted in my mind.

Gradually, the other lords and ladies arrived, to take their places around me. Jourdain walked across the scaffold with a frown, taking the chair at my side, and the two of us sat in stilted silence, our hearts drumming as the trial grew closer.

"How are you?" Jourdain eventually murmured.

But my voice faded in that moment, until I caught sight of Brienna. She was standing beside Luc at the front of the crowd, wearing a lavender dress, the color of the MacQuinns, and her brown hair was captured in a braided crown. Her gaze found me as mine had found her.

"I am fine," I responded, and my gaze remained on her.

The castle green was overflowing with people by the time Isolde and her guards and the magistrate reached the scaffold. The lords and ladies stood for her—Lady Halloran and Lord Carran included—even though Isolde wore no crown, only a circlet of gold as the other nobles. She sat in the center of the arranged nobles as the Lady of Kavanagh, with a direct view of the stand. The Stone of Eventide rested against her heart, radiating a soft blue light.

The magistrate, an old man with a white beard that brushed his chest, stood before the crowd and held up his hands. The silence that fell over the people was thick; sweat began to bead on my brow as I shifted in my chair.

"My people of Maevana," the magistrate boomed, his voice carrying over the breeze. "Today we come to give justice to the man who once dared to call himself king."

Instantly, boos and shouts of anger kindled in the people. The magistrate held up his hands again, insisting on silence, and the crowd quieted.

"Each member of the Lannon family will be brought to the stand," he continued. "They will stand before you while I read the list of grievances against them. These grievances have come from those of you who were brave enough to share your stories. As such, some of your names will be read aloud beside each grievance as proof of witness. When I am finished, the Lannons will each have a turn to speak, and then you will have the power to weigh them. To raise a fist expresses execution. To not raise a fist equates mercy."

The magistrate glanced over his shoulder, to look at Isolde.

Isolde nodded, her face pale, her hair red as blood in the sunlight.

I could feel my heart throb deep in my chest. I thought of my father, my mother, my sister in that moment of silence.

The magistrate turned and cried, "Bring forth Gilroy Lannon."

The noise that came from the crowd was blistering. I could feel the sound tremble through the wood beneath me, through my teeth. I sat and watched as Gilroy Lannon was gracelessly dragged across the scaffold beneath endless links of chains.

The former king looked wretched. His lank blond hair was matted with old blood; it appeared that he had tried to bash his head against his cell wall and had failed. His clothes were dirty and reeked of his own filth, and he barely had the strength to remain upright as the guards set him on the stand to face the people.

The shouts, the curses, and the anger boiled in the crowd.

I momentarily feared they would rush the scaffold and violently break it to pieces. Until the magistrate frowned and held up his hands, and the people begrudgingly obeyed the call for silence.

"Gilroy Lannon, you stand before the people of Maevana with a vast list of grievances held against you," the magistrate said as a young boy brought forth a thick scroll.

I watched, stunned, as the seemingly never-ending scroll began to unwind, unspooling across the scaffold. The magistrate began to read, his voice carrying over the murmurs, over the wind, over the thrashing of my heart.

"Gilroy Lannon, on the twenty-fifth of May, in the year of 1541, you ordered Brendan Allenach to viciously cut down Lady Sive MacQuinn while she was unarmed. You then proceeded to burn MacQuinn fields and slayed three of MacQuinn's thanes and their families while they slept in the night. Seven of these lives were children. You gave your men orders to rape the women of MacQuinn, and to hang the men who fought back to defend their wives and daughters. You then proceeded to take MacQuinn's people and scatter them, giving them to Lord Brendan Allenach to ruthlessly rule. This grievance comes from Lord Davin Mac-Quinn."

I looked at Brienna who stood still with a stoic look on her face. But I could tell her anger was rising. "On the same day, you took Lady Líle Morgane and chopped off her hand. You dragged her . . ."

I forced myself to stare at Gilroy Lannon while my grievance was read. Lannon was shaking, but it was not from fear or repentance. He was chuckling as the magistrate said, "This grievance comes from Lord Aodhan Morgane."

"MacQuinn and Morgane defied *me*! They defied their king!" Lannon shouted, his chains clanging as he pounded his hand on the stand railing. "They rebelled against me! Their women deserved the punishment they received!"

I was on my feet before I realized what I was doing, that I was about to pull my concealed blade and lunge for Gilroy Lannon. But Jourdain was faster, and grasped my arm, holding me back while the crowd screamed in fury, every fist already raised in their verdict.

"Let his head roll!"

The chorus swelled over the people like a tide, breaking against the scaffold, against me.

Gilroy was still laughing when he turned to look over his shoulder, his eyes meeting mine.

"If only you knew, little Morgane," he hissed to me, "all that I did to your mother."

My face contorted in agony, in rage. There was more, then. More I did not know. I had been terrified of this possibility ever since I had met with Declan in the keep, his words still lodged in my mind. *There's a special punishment for Lannons who turn on their own.*

"Gag him!" the magistrate ordered, and two of the guards wrestled Gilroy Lannon back under control, stuffing his mouth with a dirty rag.

And all I could think . . . what more had he done to her? What more had he done to my mother?

"Sit, lad," Jourdain whispered into my ear, barely able to hold me back a moment longer. "You must not let this man own you."

I nodded, but I was trembling, unraveling. I knew Brienna was watching me; I could feel the draw of her gaze. Yet I could not bear to look at her.

I resumed my seat and closed my eyes. Jourdain's hand remained on my arm, like a father trying to comfort his son. Yet my father was dead. My entire family was gone.

I had never felt more alone and bewildered.

"On that same day," the magistrate continued to read. "You beheaded Lady Eilis and Shea Kavanagh, cutting their bodies up into pieces to be displayed on the castle parapets. You then proceeded to target and murder members of the Kavanagh House. . . ."

It took another hour for the magistrate to read all of Gilroy Lannon's grievances. But when he finally reached the end of the scroll, the people had already voted. Every lord and lady on the scaffold held up their fist. As did nearly every spectator in the crowd.

"Gilroy Lannon," the magistrate announced, passing the scroll back to the boy, "the people of Maevana have weighed you and found you wanting. You will be executed by the sword three days from now. May the gods have mercy on your soul."

The guards dragged Gilroy Lannon away. And he laughed the entire way off the scaffold.

His wife, Oona, was brought forth next.

She took the stand in chains with a haughty tilt of her chin, gray streaks in her long auburn hair. So that was where Ewan got the hair from.

Her list of grievances was not as long as her husband's, but it was still lengthy, filled with accounts of torture, beatings, and burning. She had nothing to say by the end of her record—it was evident she was too proud to stoop—and once again, the people and the nobles around me raised their fists.

She would die right after Gilroy, by the sword, in three days.

It was nearly noon by the time Declan Lannon was ushered to the stand.

I met his gaze as the prince walked in his chains across the scaffold. Declan smiled at me; he did not look at any of the other nobles, not even Isolde. Only me.

My dread deepened; I could see it in the prince's eyes that he had something planned.

"Declan Lannon, you stand before the people of Maevana with a vast list of grievances held against you," the magistrate began in a hoarse voice, taking up the prince's scroll.

It was a long record, a reflection of his parents'. As I listened, my beliefs were confirmed; Declan enjoyed tormenting and manipulating others. He had overseen the majority of the tortures that took place in the bowels of the castle. No wonder he had seemed at ease in the darkness of his prison cell; he was familiar with the dungeons.

"You now have the opportunity to speak, Declan of Lannon," the magistrate said, wiping the sweat from his brow. "To either beg for mercy or explain your cause."

Declan nodded, then spoke loudly and clearly.

"Good people of Maevana, there is only one thing I will say to you before you send me to my death." He paused, turning his palms upward. "Where is my son, Ewan? Have you lost him? Or maybe one of you has been sheltering him? Has one of your own lords betrayed your trust by protecting him?" And here, Declan looked over his shoulder, straight to me.

I was frozen in my chair, but I read the sneer, the triumph in Declan's face.

If I go down, you go with me, Morgane.

The crowd began to boo. The lords and ladies sitting around me started to furiously murmur. Isolde and Grainne sat unflinching, staring at Declan.

"Magistrate," Isolde finally said, her voice whetted like a blade. "Call this trial back to order."

The magistrate appeared flustered, glancing from me to Declan.

Declan was just opening his mouth, but the crowd was screaming, chanting, raising their fists.

"Let his head roll!"

The prince's shouts were drowned in the protest, and the magistrate rushed to recite Declan's fate, which mirrored his father's and his mother's. Death by sword, three days next.

My fist was still in the air when Declan was escorted from the scaffold. And when the prince's baleful gaze met mine, I did not gloat. But there was a promise to him in my eyes.

Your House will turn to dust.

And Declan understood it. He growled and tripped down the scaffold stairs, disappearing back into the castle with his armed escort.

My pulse was still spiking when Keela Lannon was brought forth.

The crowd was already exhausted and weary, their patience brittle. And the air swarmed with their boos as she walked the scaffold. She was not bearing chains, but she cowered all the same when the guards set her on the stand, her dress filthy, her pale blond hair matted.

From behind, her hair was the same shade as her grandfather's; I sensed this was not going to bode well for her. We should have brought her out first, before Gilroy, before the long list of her family's grievances could be transposed on her.

"Keela Lannon," the magistrate began, clearing his throat as he reached for the piece of paper. The one sheet of her grievances. "You stand before the people of Maevana with a list of grievances held against you."

Keela was trembling in terror, her shoulders caving as if she wanted nothing more than to dissolve.

I sought Brienna, my heart continuing to drop in alarm.

Brienna was still standing at the forefront, her eyes wide as she felt the tide of the crowd shift further and further from mercy.

"On the twentieth of December, in the year of 1563, you denied beggar children food in the streets, and instead of giving them bread, you gave them stones to eat."

"I didn't . . . He made me," Keela sobbed, covering her face with her hands as the people continued to boo her.

"Keela, you must remain quiet while I read your grievances," the magistrate reminded. "You will have your moment to speak after the list is finished."

She kept her face covered as the magistrate continued to read.

"On the fifth of February, in the year of 1564, you had your chambermaid flogged for brushing your hair too roughly. On the eighteenth of March . . ."

Keela wept, and the people only grew louder and angrier.

The magistrate finished reading, and then asked Keela if she wanted to address the people.

This was the moment Keela needed to speak the truth, to make her case.

Please, Keela, I silently begged. *Please tell them the truth.*

And yet she was cowering and crying, hardly able to raise her head and face the dissent of the crowd.

I looked for Brienna again. She had been swallowed in the shifting of the crowd, until she suddenly rose heads above the others, perched on Luc's shoulders. She held herself up so that Keela could look in the crowd to see her.

"Let her speak! Let her speak!" Brienna shouted, but her voice was drowned out among the protest.

I felt like shutting my eyes, like closing myself to the world, to block out what I knew was coming. Until I saw Keela finally straighten, until Keela finally found Brienna in the crowd.

"My grandda forced me to do these things," she said, but her voice was still too weak. "So did my da. They . . . they beat me if I disobeyed. They threatened to hurt my little brother! They wouldn't let us eat if we told them no. They would lock us in the darkness all night. . . ."

"Lies!" a woman in the crowd screamed, which roused the boos and shouts again.

"Let their heads roll!" the chorus rose with fists, as if the people could strike the sky.

One by one, the lords and ladies on the scaffold lifted their fists, in approval of her death. All save for four.

Morgane. MacQuinn. Kavanagh. Dermott.

How could it be that the four Houses that had greatly suffered beneath the Lannons would be the only four to give mercy to Keela?

Isolde, Grainne, Jourdain, and I all sat with our hands clenched in our laps. From the corner of my eye, I saw Isolde hang her head, saddened by the verdict. And in the crowd, amid a sea of fists, was Brienna, still on Luc's shoulders, tears in her eyes.

"Keela Lannon," the magistrate announced, and even his voice was heavy with disappointment. "The people of Maevana have weighed you and found you wanting. You will be executed by the sword three days from now. May the gods have mercy on your soul."

❖ SEVENTEEN ❖

DARK DISCOVERIES

Night Following the Trial

Brienna

We sat together in Jourdain's chambers that night—my father, my brother, Cartier, and me—all of us exhausted and quiet as we shared a bottle of wine, too upset to stomach food.

It was difficult to explain how I felt after hearing the grievances, especially those of MacQuinn and Morgane, which I had not known the exact details of. I do not think there were any words that could appropriately describe the pain I felt for them. And I could not imagine how it felt to write down such grievances and then to hear them read before hundreds of witnesses.

It was even more difficult to name what I felt after watching the people condemn Keela to die. I knew that I would have to witness her beheading, and I struggled to breathe whenever I imagined it.

"So the Lannons' reign has come to its bloody end," Jourdain said when our silence became too oppressive, when the wine had run dry.

"So they fall," Luc said with a salute of his empty cup, his knee pressed close to mine as we shared the divan.

I met Cartier's gaze through the firelight. We shared the same thought, the same emotion.

Not all of them will fall. We still had Ewan, who we would protect, who we would raise in defiance of his father and grandfather.

"Yet why do I feel like we have been defeated?" Luc whispered. "Why doesn't this feel like victory? I want them to die. I want to inflict as much pain on them as possible. Beheading is too swift for them. I want to see them suffer. But does that make me any better than them?"

"You are nothing like them, son," Jourdain murmured.

Cartier leaned his elbows on his knees, staring at the floor. But when he spoke, his voice was steady. "The Lannons stole my sister, my mother. I will never know the sound of my sister's voice. I will never know what it is like to be held and loved by my mother. I will always feel their loss, as if a portion of me is missing. And yet . . . my mother herself was a Lannon. She was Líle Hayden, daughter of a Lannon thane." He looked at Jourdain, at Luc, at me. I was surprised by this confession. "I do not think justice—in this moment—follows a clear, straight line. We have suffered with our losses, but so have the people here. For all the gods' sake . . . Keela Lannon, a *twelve*-year-old girl who has been abused by her father, is about to be beheaded right behind him, because the people will not hear her; they will not look at her; they cannot separate her from him."

Luc sniffed back his tears, but he was calm, listening to Cartier. So was Jourdain, who was watching Cartier with a gleam in his eyes.

"Do I think Declan deserves beheading?" Cartier asked, holding out his hands. "No. I would rather see every one of Declan's bones crushed, one by one, slowly, until he died, as he did to my sister. And I am not remorseful to confess this. But perhaps more than what *I* feel and what *I* want . . . I have to rest in knowing that justice has been served today. That the people spoke and decided the fate of a family who was finally held accountable. That we have all returned to our homeland. That in the days to come, Isolde Kavanagh is going to be crowned as the queen. The only thing we can do at this moment is keep moving forward. We will stand witness at the Lannon beheadings. We will crown Isolde. And then we will decide what to do with a people who are now without a lord and lady."

We fell quiet again, Cartier's words piercing us. He was half Lannon, and yet that did not change how I regarded him. For I was half Allenach. We had both come from treacherous blood. And if we looked closer into our hearts . . . we would all find darkness within us.

I went to bed shortly after midnight, kissing Jourdain and Luc on the cheeks, gently caressing Cartier's shoulder when I passed him in departure. My body demanded that I lie down and try to sleep, but more than that, I wanted to escape reality for just an hour of a blissful dream.

I was dozing when I heard the commotion in the corridor.

I sat upright, blinking into the darkness. I was struggling out of bed when my private door blew open, and Luc stood on my threshold.

"Quick, sister. The queen has called a meeting in Father's chambers," he said, rushing to light my candle.

I found my sword and my voice as I chased him out into the corridor, steel unsheathed in my hand, my chemise slipping off my shoulder. "What is it? What's happened?"

Jourdain and Cartier were standing in my father's chamber, waiting. I joined them with Luc, trying to calm my breaths.

Before I could muster another question, Isolde entered the room, still in the dress she had worn for the trial, a rush light in her hand, two of her guards flanking her. Her face was stark, her gaze hopelessly bleak.

"I'm sorry to wake you," she whispered to the four of us as we stood in cold shadows and flickering light.

"What has happened, Isolde?" Jourdain asked.

Isolde glanced down to her candle, as if she couldn't bear to look at us. "Declan and Keela Lannon have escaped the dungeons."

"*What?*" Luc cried, because the rest of us had lost our voices.

Isolde met our astonishment with bitterness in her eyes. "I believe they escaped an hour ago. They are still unaccounted for."

"How?" Jourdain demanded.

Isolde said nothing, but she looked to Cartier, who looked to me. Our thoughts aligned, like the moon eclipsing the sun, casting a long shadow between us.

Ewan.

Cartier turned and hurried down the corridor to his door. I followed him into his main quarters. I saw the blankets and the pillow rumpled on the divan, where Cartier had been sleeping. And my hands were cold as ice as I followed him into his bedchamber, into the room where Ewan was supposed to be hiding.

There he was, sleeping in the bed. Or so I thought, until Cartier viciously ripped the blankets away, exposing a pillow strategically placed where Ewan's body should have been.

And I walked to the window, which was open: Ewan's original route into the castle. I couldn't feel my hands, but I listened as the sword I held hit the floor with a metallic clatter. I stepped over the steel and stared into the night, into a sky dusted with stars, one of them my own constellation.

"No, *no.*"

Cartier's voice, Cartier's painful denial.

It was the beat to my own heart, my own denial. There must be an explanation. This must be a mistake.

But I came to the truth first.

I turned around. And when I saw Cartier sinking to his knees before me, clutching the tangle of blankets . . . I acknowledged what had happened.

I dropped to my knees too, next to my fallen sword, because I suddenly couldn't stand.

What have we done?

"Brienna, Brienna . . ."

My name was the only thing Cartier could whisper, over and over, as the truth overwhelmed us.

I met his gaze. He was frozen, but I was smoldering.

Ewan Lannon had played us.

PART THREE
THE SNARE

⇥ EIGHTEEN ⇤

RIDE THE CURRENTS

Cartier

There was no sleep to be had that night.

After I realized I had been fooled by a child, Luc and Brienna went to work poring over maps of the city, tracking potential escape routes, while I followed the queen and Jourdain down into the dungeons, bearing torches and steel, the queen's guards close behind us. My breath was ragged by the time we passed through all three levels; the cold on the lowest level of the keep was so bitter it was like stepping into ice water.

Isolde hastily led the way to Keela's cell. The door was wide open, the candles continuing to flicker on her table. I stared into the emptiness of her chamber, still unable to believe this had happened.

The queen led us forward without saying a word, where two guards lay in a pool of their blood, their throats cleanly sliced. There was no way Ewan had killed those men, I told myself, over and over. The door was also wide open, like a mouth trapped in a yawn. Two more guards lay dead at the threshold, their blood a black lake beneath them.

Isolde knelt, gently touching their pallid faces. That was when I heard it—the faint clatter of chains, the echo of movement coming from within Declan's cell.

The queen froze on her knees, also hearing it. I held up my hand, wordlessly bidding her to wait, and I took my torch and my sword and entered the cell.

I couldn't deny that I fervently hoped it was Ewan. Even after the sting of his betrayal, I longed for it to be him.

What I found was a person draped in black veils, their face completely hidden, their right wrist bound in one of Declan's shackles, holding them fast to the wall.

I stopped, regarding the bone sweeper with unfeigned surprise. Likewise, the bone sweeper ceased their struggle, drawing their knees close to their chest, as if they could curl up and vanish.

"Who is that?" Jourdain asked, arriving at my side.

I waited until Isolde had also stepped into the cell. The three of us stood in an arc, regarding the bone sweeper in silence.

"The bone sweeper," I said. "I saw you the other day, in the tunnels."

They did not move. But I could see the veil over their face rising and falling beneath their frantic breaths.

Isolde sheathed her sword and knelt. Her voice was gentle

when she asked, "Can you tell us what happened here? How Declan escaped?"

The bone sweeper was silent. They began to struggle against the shackle, pulling so hard on their right hand I saw the metal cuff slice them. There was a flash of pale skin as their sleeve fluttered; blood bloomed at their wrist. They were thin, like Ewan had been. Their hand was lean, coated in grime. The sight filled me with unspeakable anguish.

"Please. We need your help . . . ," Isolde began, but her voice faded. She glanced to me and Jourdain and said, "Ask my guards to find the key to this cell and to bring writing utensils."

Jourdain moved to carry out her order before I did, and while we waited, I looked to my name carved into the wall, glistening in the firelight.

Aodhan.

I had to cast my gaze away from it, as if my own name had spelled out this doom, as if I had precipitated it all.

And perhaps I had, by persuading Isolde to grant Ewan mercy.

One of the guards brought a key, a piece of parchment, a quill, and a small vial of ink. They gave it to the queen, and Isolde cautiously drew closer to the bone sweeper, still on her knees.

"I am going to set you free," the queen whispered. "And then I need you to help me. Can you write down what happened tonight?"

The bone sweeper gave a curt nod—it hit me like a blow, that they could not speak, that Isolde had known this from the moment she stepped into the cell.

Isolde closed the distance between them, sliding the key into the cuff. I noticed that Jourdain stiffened; I sensed he was about to step forward, mistrusting the bone sweeper. And if he so much as made a sudden movement in their direction, I knew this fragile extension of trust would snap. I discreetly held him back, willing him to wait, to let Isolde foster this. Jourdain glanced at me, curses in his eyes, but he remained silent and still.

The shackle fell off; the bone sweeper retreated slightly, as if Isolde's presence overwhelmed them.

"Did you see who set Declan free?" Isolde asked, opening the ink, dipping the quill into it.

The bone sweeper made no movement.

The queen held out the quill, gently set the paper before them.

They know nothing, I wanted to say. *We need to hurry; we have wasted too much time here.*

"Isolde . . ." Jourdain was one breath from saying my exact thoughts.

But Isolde did not acknowledge him. Her attention was consumed with the veiled person before us.

Finally, the bone sweeper took the quill. Their hand was dripping blood, trembling, as they began to write.

I waited, straining my eyes to try and decipher what they were writing. Their handwriting was wretched—we would never be able to read this account. And yet I found myself sheathing my sword; I found myself kneeling, moving to Isolde's side, where I could better see. One by one, I ate their words; I ate their words as if it was my last meal.

* * *

Ewan came for his sister. He asked me to distract the guards while he freed her from her cell. He already had the master key; I am uncertain as to how he obtained this. I did as he wanted; I distracted the guards, who were at Declan's cell, about to feed him dinner. But one of the guards grew suspicious. They heard a clanging down the tunnel—Keela's door. They left to investigate it. That's when I saw Fechin, the master guard. He unbolted Declan's cell and went into it. I did not know what he was doing until the two of them emerged. Fechin set Declan free, and that was when Declan saw me, in the shadows. I could not run from him. He dragged me into his cell and locked me in his place. I could only listen as he departed. I heard an altercation, the sound of bodies hitting the floor. I heard Ewan and Keela both screaming. I heard Ewan shout, "I'm a Morgane now!" And then it grew quiet. It was quiet for a while before the second round of guards came and found the prisoners gone.

My breaths were heavy as I finished reading the account. The relief almost bowed me over, melting my strength, to know that Ewan had only come for his sister. That Ewan had no hand in Declan's escape. That Ewan had chosen me over his own father.

"Do you have any idea how Declan and the children escaped the dungeons?" Isolde asked. "Because they did not pass through the gates."

The bone sweeper dipped the quill in the ink, painstakingly writing, *They rode the currents.*

"Rode the currents?" Isolde echoed. "What does that mean?"

"There's a river that flows beneath the castle, through the

dungeons," I explained, remembering how I had heard the distant churning of it. I looked to the bone sweeper and asked, "Can you lead us there?"

They nodded, slowly rising.

They led us down one corridor, then another, the passage growing narrow and shallow. And then it opened up into a cavern, so suddenly one might step from the ledge into the rapids. We stood and held our light to it; I could see the stone beneath me was stained black from years of accumulated blood. And beyond it was the river, raging through the darkness. It was not wide, but I could tell it was deep and powerful.

"They took the currents," Isolde said with disbelief. "Can anyone survive this?"

"If anyone could, it would be Declan." Jourdain stepped as close to the edge as he dared.

"The river will take them to the ocean," I stated, my heart beginning to hammer. "We should ride to the shore. Now."

I turned, looking for the bone sweeper, to thank them for their guidance.

But there was nothing but shadows and cold, empty air where they had once stood.

The stars were beginning to fade into dawn by the time Isolde, Jourdain, the guards, and I reached the Maevan coast. The city of Lyonesse was built on a summit, where the ocean met the earth. For hundreds of years, the waves had crashed upon the limestone walls of the shore, always reaching but never conquering the great wall that kept the elements divided, the wall that protected the city from the depths. But that underground river would take Declan straight to the bay, directly into the water. He was going to escape through a small divide in that natural wall. It almost seemed impossible, but this was a land built upon challenges and insurmountable odds. Nothing these days should take me by surprise.

My greatest fear was that Declan and the children had ridden the currents into the bay and then promptly boarded a ship in the harbor, and that we were too late to catch them. They could sail west, to the icy lands of Grimhildor. Or they could sail south, to either Valenia or Bandecca. We might never recover them.

I saw this same fear in Jourdain as we approached the harbor, the boats and ships quietly bobbing in their berths. For this was how he and Luc had escaped twenty-five years ago. This was how Braden Kavanagh and Isolde had escaped. How my father and I had escaped. A Burke captain had taken the six of us aboard his ship while Gilroy Lannon was busy hunting us north, in the heart of our own territories. All it took was one brave man and his ship to grant us freedom.

"Check the departure logs," Isolde rasped to Jourdain as we searched among the quay.

I came to a stop and stared at the horizon. The sun was rising, forging a trail of gold on the ocean. The water was calm, gentle this morning. There was no sign of a ship, no distant shadow of a mast or sails.

I shifted my gaze farther down the bay. The tide was out, exposing the sand, the foundation of the limestone walls.

I began to walk to it, faster, faster, until I was running. I heard Isolde shouting for me, but I could not break my gaze from that sand, from the footsteps sunk within it, because the tide was rising, beginning to fill them. I reached it, the prints unfolding before me. They were Ewan's footprints, I was almost sure of it. And then there was another set, coming alongside him. Keela's. And then there was Declan's, as if he had come out of the water last. The prince was a big man, and he had crushed the sand in a hurry. It looked as if he had taken hold of his children and dragged them along.

Their footprints did not lead to the harbor.

I stopped walking, my boots sinking into the sand, the tide beginning to wash around my ankles.

"Aodhan!" Isolde called for me. I could hear her running to me, through the swell of the waves.

My eyes followed the footprints to the wall. And then up, up the limestone, where the city lay above, just now awakening.

Isolde finally reached my side, panting, her hair snarled by the wind. "What is it? What do you see?"

I couldn't answer her. Not yet. My mind was swarming with possibilities, and I followed the footprints to the wall, the tide rushing in alarmingly quick now. I found a crack in the rock to hold to, and then another. I began to lift myself up, up the wall, my fingers and the tips of my boots forcing their way into nooks and crannies.

I didn't dare go any higher, but I clung to the wall and gazed upward at the daunting stretch of it, watching the clouds streak across the sky.

Was it even possible?

I let go, jumping back to the sand and water with a painful jar of my ankles. I waded my way to where Isolde and her guards waited, Jourdain rushing to rejoin us from the harbor.

"I checked the logs," Jourdain said. "No ships left or arrived last night, Lady."

"They didn't leave by ship," I stated.

"Then where are they?" Jourdain countered.

I looked back to the bay, the sand nearly swallowed by the incoming tide. "The currents emptied them out somewhere around here. Declan dragged the children from the water to the wall."

"The wall?" Jourdain's eyes swept it. His mouth hung open. "You cannot be serious."

But Isolde was staring at me, believing my every word.

And I lifted my eyes up again, to the sky, to the city of Lyonesse, to the castle that sat at the top of the summit like a sleeping dragon.

Where would your father take you, Ewan?

The light was strengthening; Declan would have found a place to hide by now. Until the darkness gave him the ability to move undetected. My one hope was that Ewan would somehow make a way to be found.

I'm a Morgane now. . . .

"Declan climbed the wall with the children on his back," I said, meeting Isolde's gaze. "He's in the city."

We didn't linger; we hurried back to the castle, my mind splintering in several directions. I was so distracted that I didn't notice the Hallorans standing in the courtyard until we were almost upon them.

Lady Halloran and Pierce were seemingly deep in conversation with each other until the lady caught sight of us. There was no hiding that we were rushing, that the queen and I were still half-drenched from searching along the shore.

"Lady Kavanagh!" Lady Halloran cried, moving to intercept us on the flagstones. She was dressed in her House colors, gold and navy, and her gown was so elaborate it could have rivaled the hyperbolic fashion of Valenia.

"Lady Halloran," Isolde returned politely, trying to maintain her quickened pace.

"Has something happened?"

Isolde slowed, but it wasn't to accommodate Lady Halloran; it was to shoot a glance at me and Jourdain.

"Why would you presume such, Lady?" Isolde asked. "Lord MacQuinn, Lord Morgane, and I were just taking some air before our council meeting."

She was prompting one of us to gather Luc, Brienna, and her father. And by the way Jourdain was standing at Isolde's side scowling at Lady Halloran, as if his feet had grown roots . . . I figured I should be the one to go and prepare the council.

Only Pierce sauntered up to join us. I could not hide my distaste for him, and I had to stand a moment more, to watch him. His eyes were fixated on Isolde, on the Stone of Eventide's light, but he must have felt my stare. His eyes shifted to me as he came to a stop beside his mother, and there his eyes remained, assessing how great of a threat I was. I must not have struck him as dangerous, because he snorted and smiled, and then elected to ignore me, ogling the queen once more.

"I wanted to request a private meeting with you, Lady," Lady Halloran was saying. "Perhaps later today? When you have time?"

"Yes, of course, Lady Halloran," Isolde replied. "I could meet with you sometime this afternoon, after my *council* meeting." She was prompting me again, her patience waning, and this time I moved, leaving them without another word.

The castle was alarmingly quiet. There were armored guards at every corner, but the silence sat heavy in the air, this attempt to maintain order and hide the fact that three Lannons had escaped. Eventually, though, this would leak, and I was not certain how the nobles would meet the news. Nor was I certain how Lannon supporters would respond.

It filled me with apprehension as I walked to Jourdain's chambers, where we had left Brienna and Luc studying maps of the city, tracing possible escape routes that Declan might have taken. They were no longer there; it felt like the room had been empty for some time, and so I went to her quarters, and then Luc's. Still, I could not find them, and I turned myself back into the corridor, heading to the dining hall, thinking that maybe they had gone to eat.

I ran into Isolde's father on the way there. He looked exhausted; purple shadows were smudged beneath his eyes, and his white hair was still bound by yesterday's braids. I knew he had been overseeing a covert search of the castle for Fechin, the master guard who had all but vanished, and several of the castle guards were in his shadow, awaiting his next order.

Braden Kavanagh cocked his brow at me, and I saw the

hopeful question in his expression. *Did you find them?*

I shook my head. "Council meeting at once. I'm trying to locate the MacQuinns."

"They're in the records chamber, one story below in the eastern wing."

I nodded and we continued on our separate ways, Braden to search the storerooms, me to the records chamber. I found Luc and Brienna sitting at a round table, ledgers and maps and papers spread out before them, as if a heavy snow had fallen. Brienna was still in her chemise, her hair unwinding from her braid, writing down something Luc was saying to her.

They both glanced up at my entry, that same hope in their eyes, that I had arrived to tell them good news. I shut the door and walked closer to them, and Brienna read my face. She set down her quill in defeat while Luc whispered, "Please tell me you recovered them."

"No." My gaze strayed beyond them to the open archway, a passage that led to a honeycomb of storage chambers; I could see portions of the records shelves, heavily laden with scrolls and tomes and tax records.

Brienna, again, read my thoughts. "This room is secure."

"Are you certain?"

She leveled her eyes at me. "Yes. Luc and I are the only ones in here."

I pulled out a chair and sat across from them, not realizing how exhausted I was. I took a moment to scrub my face with my hands; I could still smell the dungeons on my palms, that dank, moldy darkness.

I began to tell them everything, of the bone sweeper and their account, of the underground currents, of the search along the shore.

Brienna sat back in her chair, a smudge of ink on her chin, and said, "So Ewan did not double-cross you, as we thought."

"No, he did not," I replied, unable to hide my relief. "He disobeyed me, which is to be expected, to save his sister when I could not. And I think both he and Keela are in great peril right now."

"Do you think Declan would harm them?" Luc asked, aghast.

"Yes."

Brienna shifted in her chair, restless. I watched as she began to organize the papers before her, and my curiosity caught like a flame.

"What is that?"

"Well." She cleared her throat. "Luc and I began to think like a Lannon. We kept tracing over the maps, thinking . . . where would Declan go? If he is still in the city, where could he hide? Of course, we were not sure. But it made us think back on our own revolution plans."

"We had safe houses," Luc inputted. "Homes and shops that we knew would take us in unexpectedly if we ran into trouble."

"Exactly," Brienna said. "And since we know there are Lannon sympathizers—the half-moon clan—we figured we could strive to uncover their locations, thinking Declan will seek shelter from one of them."

"How have you uncovered their locations, though?" I asked.

"Scouring a map is not enough," she continued. "And we do

not have the time to go door to door and search every house in Lyonesse, pulling up sleeves. We need something to direct us. Luc and I decided to look through Gilroy Lannon's tax records, to see which people he went easy on. I think that will be the swiftest way to get started."

"Let me see," I rasped, reaching for her list.

There were eleven establishments listed, ranging from taverns to silversmiths to a butcher. All of them hailed from Lannon House, and four of them were located in the southern hold of the city, where I felt like Declan was at the moment. My heart began to pound.

"All of these places have gotten away with ridiculous tax pardons," Brienna said. "And I believe it is because they had some sort of agreement with Gilroy."

I looked up at her, at Luc. "This is incredible. We need to meet with Isolde, to tell her what you both have found."

"Maybe we should meet with her in here, so we can keep searching through the records?" Brienna suggested, standing with a groan. "Although I am ravenous. I do not know how much more I can plot without tea and food."

"Why don't the two of you clear the table, and I'll send for some breakfast?" Luc said, heading for the door. "And I'll tell the queen and Father to meet here."

"Very good," Brienna said before Luc departed. But she left the clearing of the table to me as she stretched and walked to stand before the one window in the entire room, a tiny sliver of glass. The sunlight caught the linen of her chemise, illuminating her. I forgot about the list in my hands as I looked at her; I forgot Declan Lannon even existed.

My silence made her turn around, to glance at me. And I do not know what sort of expression was on my face, but she walked to my side, to touch my hair.

"Are you all right?" she whispered.

I returned to my task, gathering up the papers and records, and her fingers fell away from me. "I'll be fine once we settle all of this."

She watched me for a moment, and then reached over the table to help, stacking the records. Her voice almost melded with the sound of the paper being gathered, but I heard her say, "We will find them, Cartier. Do not lose hope."

I sighed, longing for her optimism.

I leaned back in my chair and looked at her, standing before me. There was still a thread of sunlight passing through her shift, gilding her hair. She looked otherworldly, as if she did not belong here. It made me ache, and my eyes dropped, down to the floor, where she was barefoot on the stones.

"Aren't you cold, Brienna?" I whispered, only so that I could swallow the longings I dare not speak.

She smiled, amused. "I am now that you mention it. I didn't have time to think about it before."

She sat at my side, and I threw my fur-lined cloak over her legs, and we sat together in companionable quiet, waiting for the others.

Breakfast arrived first, and I settled for a cup of tea while

Brienna filled her plate with cheese, salted ham, and a biscuit. She was halfway done when Isolde, Jourdain, Luc, and Braden joined us, thankful for the repast. All of us were weary and ragged, but this shared meal gave us a moment to regain ourselves.

I listened as Brienna and Luc explained their list, which brightened the queen's demeanor. She read it over and we pulled forth a map, placing a copper on the eleven locations.

"We should start with the four southern establishments," I suggested. "If Declan did indeed scale the wall, then he would have dropped down into the city somewhere around that area."

"I agree," Brienna said. "I think the most likely of places is either this tavern, or this hostel." She pointed to them on the map. "I think two of us should venture inside as guests, take a temporary half-moon on our wrists just in case we are questioned. And it should probably be Luc and me, since the rest of you would be swiftly recognizable."

"No, absolutely not," Jourdain said, almost before Brienna could finish. He was pale with displeasure, but Brienna did not seem the slightest bit off put by his opposition. "I do not want you venturing into such dark places, Brienna."

"But have I not already ventured into dark places, Father?" she said.

Jourdain was quiet, as if he was weighing his answers, trying to find the one that would best dissuade her. Eventually, he murmured, "All of the old tragedies end the same way, Brienna. As soon as the heroine is one step away from victory, she is cut down. Every time. And here we are, one step away from setting Isolde on the throne. I do not want to be one moment from victory only to see one of us killed."

"Your father is right," I said, to which Brienna slid her eyes my way, half-closed with agitation. "But the worst of things *has* happened now, MacQuinn. Declan Lannon is loose in the streets, and he has support. This has the potential to grow rapidly out of our control. We must address this at once in the best way that we can."

"So we send my children into these corrupt places," Jourdain said, a touch sardonic. "Then what?"

"We scout them out, see if we can uncover Declan," Luc answered.

"And how are you to catch him, then?" Jourdain pressed, still angry. "The prince is a strong, powerful man. He scaled a wall with two children on his back, for gods' sake!"

Isolde set down her teacup, and we all glanced to her. "Mac-Quinn and Morgane, you will have forces waiting just beyond these places. If Lucas and Brienna find Declan, they will give you a signal, and you will descend, ready to capture him. I want him alive, and I want the children to be unharmed."

"What forces, Lady?" I asked. "Most of our fighting men and women are back home."

"I am going to approach Lord Burke," Isolde replied. "He fought with us on the rising day; he should have no shortage of capable men and women, and should hopefully keep his mouth shut about why I am requesting them."

"Another thought about taking Declan down," Braden Kavanagh said, who had been silent up to this point. "I think we should employ a poisoned arrow. Appoint an archer whose sole purpose is to shoot him in the thigh, to render him unconscious. It will give us the ability to bind and transport him."

"I think that is wise," the queen said. "Aodhan, can you locate a poison capable of this, to stun but not kill a man of Declan's size?"

I nodded, but I was wondering about the time frame for this plan. I had an incessant urge to move quickly, to don my armor and go now, before Declan had time to move.

"We're going to have to wait until nightfall," Isolde said, to my keen disappointment. "If our efforts prove futile tonight, I will make an announcement tomorrow that the executions have been postponed. Above all, I do not want the news to spread about Declan's escape, so we need to be as discreet as possible. Darkness will be our greatest ally. In the meantime, Jourdain and I will address Lord Burke for the warriors. Aodhan will locate the poison for the arrow. Brienna and Luc will prepare to infiltrate the tavern and the hostel. My father will continue the search for the traitorous dungeon guard. We will meet once more under the guise of having dinner in my private quarters, so the other nobles do not become suspicious."

We were quiet, soaking in her orders.

"Are we in agreement?" Isolde asked.

One by one, we laid our hands over our hearts, to express submission.

"Good," the queen said, draining the rest of her tea. She tucked a stray tangle of red hair from her eyes and set her palms on the table. "Then let us go and prepare for tonight, and hope that by moonrise, Declan Lannon is back in the dungeons."

⤺ NINETEEN ⤻

AT THE MARK
OF THE HALF-MOON

Brienna

I was nervous as Luc and I approached the tavern that night, a sagging brick building wedged in between two alehouses. The roof was overgrown with lichens and moss, and the windows were narrow, winking with leery candlelight as my brother and I drew close, black cloaks fastened at our collars with hoods drawn over our heads. We had inked a temporary half-moon on our inner wrists. We also had two concealed blades on us, per Isolde's order. We were not to enter the tavern or the hostel unarmed, nor were we supposed to draw our steel and cause commotion. If we could help it.

One street over, Jourdain and Cartier waited in a covered carriage, in sight of the tavern door. And one street behind them was a troop of Lord Burke's warriors. They would wait to see if

Jourdain gave them the sign to pursue, and Jourdain would wait to see if Luc and I gave the signal of Declan's presence, which we would indicate by lighting a bundle of firebelle.

Both Luc and I carried the small bouquet of herbs in our jerkin pockets. Cartier had chosen this particular plant since it was highly flammable and set off blue sparks once ignited. It would be difficult for the men to miss should we need to light it in the street.

I resisted the urge to glance behind at the coach, knowing my father and Cartier were watching my entrance. Luc took hold of my arm for solidarity, and we entered the tavern as one does a murky pond.

It was a low-lit place, the air reeking of unwashed men and spilled, cheap ale. Mismatched tables were scattered across the room, men gathered about them playing cards and nursing tankards. I was one of the few women in the room, and I sat beside Luc at a far-strung table, nervously laying my hands on the sticky tabletop before I shifted them into my lap.

We had drawn stares; we didn't belong here, and we appeared suspicious with our hoods still drawn.

"Lower your hood," I whispered to him, daring to draw mine back and expose my face. I had taken pains to kohl my eyes and rouge my cheeks. I also had chosen to unbraid my hair, to let it cascade over the right side of my face.

Luc slowly mimicked me, perching his chin in his palm, his eyes half-lidded as if he was bored. But I saw the way he studied every person in that tavern.

A young girl brought us some sour ale, and I pretended to

drink it, my eyes sweeping the place. There was a bear of a man behind the counter, leaning on the polished wood, staring at me with suspicion.

On the inside of his wrist was a dark tattoo. My heart skipped when I recognized it as the half-moon.

My assumptions had been correct. This was a lair of Gilroy's. But if Declan was here, where would he be? It was one great room with only one rounded door at the back, leading to what I assumed was the cellar.

The tavern keeper caught me staring at the back door. He turned, flicking his fingers in the air, as if in some sort of ominous signal.

"I think we should leave," I whispered to Luc.

"I think you're right," my brother whispered back just as a tall, lanky man with a jagged scar across his brow approached us.

"Houses?" the man asked, setting his fists on our table, rattling our full tankards.

"Lannon," Luc said without hesitation. "Same as you."

His eyes roamed both of us, but settled on me. "You don't look Lannon."

Luc and I were both dark-headed. But I had seen Lannons with all shades of hair, such as Ewan with his auburn tresses and Declan with his tawny-colored hair.

"We only wanted a drink," I said, reaching for my ale, so my sleeve would ride up my arm, just a bit. The beginning of my moon showed, and his eyes went to it, like a dog to a bone. "But we can leave, if that is what you want."

He smiled at me, his teeth yellow and rotting at the gums.

"Forgive my rudeness. We have never seen the two of you before. And I know most of our kind."

To my horror, he pulled out a chair and joined us at the table. Luc stiffened in response; I felt his foot touch mine in warning.

"Tell me . . . are you north or south?" he asked, waving for the servant girl to bring him a tankard.

It took everything within me not to look at Luc. "North, of course."

I couldn't tell if this pleased our Lannon companion or not. He continued to stare at me and completely ignore Luc. "I should have figured such. You have that look about you."

The girl brought his ale, which gave me a slight moment of reprieve from his gaze. But then he set his eyes on me again, even as he drank, and said, "Did the Red Horn send you, then?"

Red Horn . . . Red Horn . . .

I grappled with this strange code name, trying to come up with who he might mean. Oona Lannon had auburn hair, like Ewan. Did he speak of her? Was she conveying messages from the dungeons, somehow?

"Although he does like to keep the pretty ones close," he rambled on, disgruntled.

Red Horn was a he, then.

"He actually did not send us," I dared to say, sipping my ale to hide the tremble in my voice.

Luc's foot pressed harder against mine. He wanted us to leave, before we were exposed.

"Oh?" Our Lannon friend sniffed and scratched at his beard.

"That's surprising. We're expecting word from him. I thought you might be carrying it."

Surely the Red Horn wasn't Declan. . . .

But if it was, then Declan was not here.

Either way, my dramatics had nearly reached its full capacity. I could feel the trembling in my face, from trying to keep myself composed.

"I'm sorry to say that we bear no message. We only wanted to enjoy ale with our own kind," Luc said.

The Lannon gave Luc an annoyed glance before looking to me again. The shirt beneath my jerkin was nearly soaked in sweat by this point. I was trying to scheme a way out of this, a way that would not appear rude. . . .

The tavern keeper whistled, and the Lannon at our table turned. More hand motions between them, and then our revolting friend spun back around and said, "He wants to know your names."

Luc took a long draft of ale, to try to give him time to muster one up. Which meant I needed to speak. . . .

"Rose," I said on the fly, altering my mother's name of Rosalie. "And this is my husband, Kirk."

At the mention of "husband," the Lannon sagged a bit, his interest in me dimming.

"Well, take your time and enjoy your ale, Rose," he said. "This round is on me."

"Thank you," I said, thinking there would certainly *not* be a second round.

He raised his tankard to me, and I forced myself to lift mine, to clink it against his. He finally left us alone, and I made us sit there for another ten minutes.

"All right, let's go," I whispered to Luc after we had pretended to enjoy ourselves.

Luc followed my lead. We nodded to our Lannon friend who was playing a game of cards at one of the tables, and I went so far as to lift my hand to the tavern keeper, to flash my half-moon.

Luc and I stepped out into the blanket of night with shaking knees, and we didn't stop walking until the shadows had covered us.

"My gods," Luc panted, leaning against the closest building. "How did you get us out of that?"

"I studied the passion of dramatics for a year," I said, my own voice hoarse. I could not seem to catch my breath. "I had horrible stage fright at the time, but I will have to let Master Xavier and Abree know my skill has drastically improved."

Luc chuckled, a bit delirious.

I leaned into the wall beside him, to laugh into the stones, to let the tension ease from my bones.

"All right," my brother said after he had calmed. "Shall we move on to the next?"

The hostel was not far, just two streets over, and was even less inviting on the exterior. It seemed to sink into the ground, and Luc and I descended a string of worn stairs to the main door, which was guarded by a heavily armed man.

I flashed my wrist at him. My heart hammered as I waited, the guard lifting my hood to peer into my face.

"Any blades on you?" he asked me, his eyes roving my body.

I hesitated a beat too long. If I lied, he would know it. "Yes. Two dirks."

He held out his palm. I had the feeling that he only asked for weapons of those he did not recognize.

"Surely you will allow my wife to keep her blades," Luc said, his voice brushing my hair as he stood directly behind me.

I knew what he implied. I was a woman, about to step into a tavern most likely overflowing with drunken men. If anyone deserved to keep their blades, it was me. And the guard studied me a moment longer, but finally acquiesced. He jerked his head to the door, letting me in.

I tarried on the threshold, trying to drink in as much clean air as I could before I descended into smoke and ale fumes, watching as Luc flashed his wrist. But just before he could join me, the guard took his collar and held him back.

"Either she goes in with her blades, or with you. Not both, lad."

I met Luc's gaze. He was trying not to panic, because we both knew that Isolde had given us a strict order to carry concealed blades.

And I watched his worry rise when I said, "I'll be along shortly, love."

The guard chuckled, amused that I had chosen blades over a husband, and I entered the tavern before Luc could ruin our cover.

The hostel was bigger than I thought. From the main hall were offshoots of other rooms, some closed off with curtains of hanging beads and colored glass. There were clinks of pewter and laughter and smears of voices as I began to walk about the tables, trying to decide where to go, where to sit. There were also more women here, and I realized I was not dressed appropriately. I looked more like an assassin than the female patrons gathered about the tables, with their low-cut silks and black lace.

A few of them noticed me, but they only smiled, welcoming my presence.

I walked to the bar, to set down a copper for a tankard of more disgusting ale, and then meandered through the rooms, parting a curtain of beads. I finally chose a bench in a corner, where I had easy vantage of two different connecting rooms, leaning back to observe the occupants.

I didn't recognize him at first.

His back was to me, his brown hair loose to drag into his face as he stood from one of the tables. There was a leather satchel slung across his shoulder, and the only reason why it attracted my attention was because it made me think of Cartier. He had one very similar.

The man turned, eyes languidly coasting the room until they touched me. He had a narrow jaw, with a mole on the ridge of his cheekbone. Our gazes locked before I could shelter my face, before I could hide myself from him.

He stood frozen, staring at me through the curls of smoke, wide-eyed with horror. It was the guard who had led me into the dungeons a few days ago, when I went to speak to Keela Lannon. The master guard who had moved through the castle dungeons with ease and prowess.

The traitor who had set Declan loose.

Fechin.

I sat like a statue, white-knuckled as I returned his stare. I could think of nothing else to do but smile at him and lift my tankard, saluting him as if I were one of his own.

The guard all but vanished, he moved so quickly.

I lurched up in knee-jerk pursuit, spilling my entire tankard of ale as I wove around tables and chairs, from one room into another. I caught sight of his hair just as he bounded into the adjoining chamber, and I furiously cut through the beaded curtain, chasing him. I had attracted attention by this point, but all I could think of were my blades and the beat of my heart and the traitor I was chasing, deep into the veins of the tavern.

My reckless half insisted that I follow him before I lost his trail. My logical half begged me to adhere to the original plan, which would be to leave the tavern and light the firebelle in the street, to let Cartier and Lord Burke's men swarm.

In that split second, I chose the former, because I knew that Ewan and Keela were somewhere nearby.

I lost sight of Fechin just as the corridor narrowed, doors carved into the wall on either side, closed and dark. My breathing was heavy as I reached behind me to withdraw one of my dirks. My eyes traced every door; some had light flickering around their edges, seeping through to nibble the darkness.

I was trembling, anticipating, when I heard the crash.

I followed the sound to the room at the end of the corridor, kicking the door open.

It was a small chamber, empty. There was a narrow bed with rumpled blankets, a tray of half-eaten food. But more than anything . . . there was a torn piece of paper on the floor. I knelt and took it in my fingers. It was half of the princess illustration, the very one Ewan had asked me to give Keela in the dungeons.

They had just been here. Declan and the children. I could feel the lingering shadows that man had cast on the walls; I could smell the salt of the ocean and the filth of the dungeons.

There was one window, gaping open into the night, the candles flickering wildly in the sudden gust.

I rushed to it, slipping out into a narrow alley littered with trash, nearly twisting my ankles in my haste. My eyes peeled the darkness to the right, until I heard him.

"Mistress Brienna!" Ewan screamed, and I jerked my gaze to the left just in time to see Declan etched in moonlight a stone's throw away, bearing both Keela and Ewan in his arms.

My eyes locked with the prince's as he paused. He laughed, taunting me to chase him before vanishing into one of the branching alleys, into utter darkness, Ewan's muffled screams and Keela's sobs an echo for me to follow.

"Luc!" I shouted, hoping he could hear me from the front of the tavern as I broke into a run after Declan. The prince was a large, strong man—I was not fool enough to believe I could challenge him with my blades—but running with two children would inevitably slow him. My one and only desire was to recover Keela and Ewan. If Declan got away tonight, so be it.

But in the fray of my pursuit, I had forgotten about Fechin.

The guard loomed out of the darkness before me, his arm catching my neck. I landed on my back, my larynx stunned, the air snatched from my lungs.

He hovered over me. I rasped, desperate to breathe, unable to speak as he crouched low, to draw his grimy finger down my arm, exposing my now-melting half-moon.

"You're a shrewd one," he said. "We'll take better care with you next time."

He stood to leave me floundering in the alley. But he had forgotten that I was wielding a dirk.

I lunged for his retreating form, sinking my blade into his calf and dragging it down with a vicious cut, slicing his muscle to the bone. He screamed and spun, returning my favor with a boot to my face. I heard my nose crunch as I flew backward once again, pain exploding down my cheeks. I landed on cobblestones slick with dirt and refuse, and there I lay, unable to draw a full breath, choking on my blood.

"Brienna! *Brienna!*"

I didn't even realize I was fading into unconsciousness until Luc shook me so hard my teeth rattled and the pain in my nose sharpened my attention.

I cracked my eyes open, struggling to discern my brother's frantic face in the darkness. "Chil— The child—" My voice was nothing more than dust in my throat. Luc gathered me into his arms and began to carry me through the alley, to the coach where Jourdain and Cartier waited. The jump in his gait made my stomach rise up my throat, and I closed my eyes, fighting the urge to be sick on his shirt.

"Brienna? Brienna, what happened?" Jourdain murmured,

supporting me with his arms.

"I—" Again, my voice came out as a wheeze of painful air. I was slumped beside my father, and Cartier was kneeling between my knees in the cab, his eyes mercilessly dark as he stared up at me. My blood was on his hands.

"Did Declan do this?" Cartier murmured.

I shook my head.

"But you saw him?"

I nodded and took hold of the front of his shirt, to push him away, to urge him to go.

The coach wasn't in motion; we were still parked in the alley. And Cartier laid his hands over mine, because he understood what I was telling him. He was the one who was supposed to lead Burke's men, and I could hear them shouting and calling as they searched every winding street around us, searching for the prince who had gotten away, yet again.

"Take her back to the castle," Cartier ordered Jourdain, his voice smooth yet sharp. I had never heard him speak like that, and I shivered as I watched him slip from the coach, Luc taking his place.

As soon as the coach began its climb back to the castle, Jourdain snarled to Luc, "I thought you were given orders not to engage!"

And Luc looked to me, uncertain as to what he should say. Because *I* had been the one to defy the orders.

"I am sure Brienna has a good reason why," Luc insisted.

By the time we reached the castle courtyard, Jourdain was

stewing and Luc was fidgeting. My father and brother followed me to my bedchamber, and I wasted no time. My voice was still gone, my larynx seemingly crushed from Fechin's arm. So I grabbed my pot of ink and a sheet of paper and began to furiously scrawl my explanation.

"Brienna," Jourdain sighed as he finished reading. I knew he finally understood why I had chosen to upset the plans, but I could also tell he was going to simmer in his frustration for hours.

Isolde blew into my room before Jourdain could further his reprimand.

"Out," she barked at the men.

When her livid eyes fell upon me, I had my first moment of righteous fear of her. I watched the men swiftly depart and prepared myself to withstand any punishment from her.

But I quickly realized Isolde was not here to scold me. She was here to draw me a bath and heal my battered face.

I sat in the warm water, letting the queen wash the tavern grime from my skin, the dirt from my hair, and the blood from my face. It was humbling to have her care for me, searching for wounds as she cleansed me. Very gently, she took hold of my nose, and I winced at first, expecting pain. But her magic was gentle, like feeling sunlight warm my face . . . a brush of dragonfly wings . . . soaking the fragrance of a summer night. Her magic reset my nose, until all that was left was a small bump, barely perceptible to my fingers as I tentatively assessed it.

"Where else did he hurt you?" she asked, pouring water over my shoulders to wash away the lingering soap.

I pointed to my throat. Isolde drew her fingertips across it, and the painful egg that had been pressing on my voice box shrank, leaving behind a tingling aura in my larynx.

"Thank you, Lady," I said hoarsely.

"Your voice will be weak for a few days," Isolde responded, ushering me from the tub to wrap me in a towel. "Try not to use it too much."

I had to set my jaw, to keep my words tame and quiet, but to no avail. Because I wanted to tell her that I had found him, that Declan was running to safe houses, just as we predicted. That I had come face-to-face with Fechin.

I dressed into a fresh chemise and climbed into bed as I spoke of what had happened, telling her every detail, including the code name of Red Horn.

She was quiet after that, her fingertips tracing the patterns in my quilt.

"I'm sorry," I rasped. "I should not have deviated from the plan."

"I understand your intentions," Isolde responded, meeting my gaze. "In all honesty, I would have been tempted to do the same as you. But if we are going to catch Declan Lannon, we must be calculated. We must move in unity. You should have never been alone in that tavern. I know I gave you and Luc orders to remain armed, but it would have been better if you had declined entry. You should never have chased Declan on your own."

I took her correction with flushed cheeks and repentant eyes. My one consolation was the thought of the deep wound I had inflicted on Fechin. It was the only information I could offer her now. "I gave Fechin a permanent limp. You should search the surrounding physicians and healers, because he would have gone directly to one of them."

"I shall do that." Isolde smiled. She suddenly looked exhausted and peaked, and I wondered if her magic drained her, if by healing others, she made herself weak and vulnerable.

There was a knock on my outer door, and Jourdain emerged on my threshold like a thundercloud. I knew there would be no getting around him.

His eyes were sharp until I lowered myself back into my pillows. Isolde bid me farewell, and I thanked her as Jourdain took her place at my side, sitting on the edge of the bed, the mattress giving beneath his weight.

"Has Cartier returned?" I asked, struggling to hide the tremor in my voice.

"Yes."

And by the terseness of that "yes," I knew that they had not recovered Declan. I hung my head until he spoke again.

"I'm sending you home, Brienna."

I started, blinking at him. "I don't want to return home."

"I know. But I want you safe, daughter." He sensed my dismay and took hold of my hand. "And I need you to return and be Lady of MacQuinn for me."

This was the *last* thing I expected to hear from him.

"Father," I whispered. "I cannot do that for you. Your people . . ."

"My people will heed and follow you, Brienna. You are my daughter."

I didn't want to argue with him. But I also couldn't imagine returning to Castle Fionn and trying to exert leadership over a people who regarded me with perpetual wariness.

Jourdain sighed and rushed his hand through his auburn hair. "I received a letter from Thorn today. You remember him?"

"Your cranky chamberlain."

"That's the one. He writes and asks if Luc can return, to tend to some business he needs help overseeing. There has been trouble with one of the lasses, and Thorn is at an impasse. And I feel like Luc is not the one to send home. You are, Brienna."

"I do not know the first thing about being a Lady of Mac-Quinn," I softly protested.

"You'll learn." Such a simple, manlike answer. He could tell I chafed at it because he sighed and amended, "Sometimes, you have to be thrown into things, or else you'll never do them."

This was a very Maevan-inspired way of teaching, this thought of throwing yourself into a raging river to learn how to swim. In Valenia, we took our time to learn a new skill. Hence why each passion took an average of seven years to master.

"You are just trying to get me out of the way," I stated.

Jourdain's brow slanted in a frown. "When I ask for you to help me, daughter, I truly mean it. You overseeing this problem with the lass will take a tremendous burden off my shoulders. But more than that . . . I want you away from this mess; I want you to be safe. I cannot endure it if something should happen to you, Brienna. I lost my wife by the hand of the Lannons. I will not see the same done to my daughter."

There was nothing I could say to refute that.

This had been his fear from the very beginning of my involvement, and if he had had his way, I would never have crossed the channel into Maevana to recover the Stone of Eventide. He would have taken my knowledge and given it to Luc, if only to keep me away from the dangers of the revolt.

And I wanted to argue with him; I wanted to say this was not fair, to lock me up while Luc continued to chase down the Lannons. I wanted to say that he needed me; they all needed me. And the words rose, pressing against my teeth, desperate to come out sharp and angry until I saw his frown soften, until I saw the gleam in his eyes. He looked upon me as if he truly loved me; he looked upon me like I was his flesh-and-blood daughter, like I had been born a MacQuinn, like pieces of his wife were within me.

Wasn't this something I had longed for, something I had ached for my entire life?

And I chose in that moment to become that, to be his daughter, to let him protect me.

I chose in that moment to return as the Lady of MacQuinn, to do what he asked of me.

"Very well," I said quietly. "I will go."

The disappointment still stung, and I looked down until Jourdain lovingly took my chin, to draw my eyes back to his.

"I want you to know that I am proud of you, Brienna. There is no woman I trust more to lead my people while I'm away."

I nodded so he would believe I was at peace with this.

But within, I felt upset to be leaving Lyonesse, ashamed that

I had broken the plans for the night. I was honored that Jourdain trusted me enough to grace me with the power of Lady of Mac-Quinn, but I also felt dread to imagine the expressions that would meet me when Jourdain's people realized he had sent me back to lead.

Jourdain kissed my cheeks, and the simple act made me miss Valenia so fiercely that I had to close my eyes to quell the tears. He rose and was almost to my door when I cleared my throat to ask, "When do I leave, Father?"

I thought I would have at least another day or two here. Until he glanced over his shoulder to look at me with a gleam of sorrow in his eyes.

"You leave at dawn, Brienna."

✦ TWENTY ✦

A BLEEDING PRINCESS

Cartier

I was standing in the shadows of the corridor when Jourdain emerged from Brienna's room. I was exhausted now that my anger had ebbed, filthy and sweaty from combing the streets in search of Declan, a hunt that had proven fruitless.

We had been so close. So close to capturing the prince and regaining the children.

It was infuriating to think how he had slipped through our fingers.

I met Jourdain's gaze. He did not seem surprised to see me waiting here.

"What did she say?" I asked.

"She said she will go home, as I want. She'll leave at first light."

"How did you convince her?"

"My chamberlain needs assistance with one of the lasses back home," Jourdain answered. "Instead of sending Luc, I want to send her."

After watching this night go completely awry, Jourdain had outright told me he did not want Brienna in Lyonesse. He wanted to send Brienna home to Castle Fionn, where she would be safe. And while I had listened to him, I knew Brienna would be hurt by this, feel like we were shoving her out.

Furthermore, Brienna was the one in our circle who was a natural schemer. I had taught her everything I knew, from history to poetry to where all the vital blood flows were in the body. But I had not taught her how to scheme, how to move pawns across a board, how to strategize and outwit. It was her strength, the canon of her blood House, the blessing of the Allenachs that set them above the rest.

I could have made a strong case against Jourdain, told him that Brienna was the one who gathered up the safe house locations, the one who uncovered the meaning behind the half-moon. That Brienna was essentially the mind behind our revolution.

I could have reminded Jourdain about all of these things, and yet I resisted. Because deep within me, I wanted her as far away from Declan Lannon as possible. I did not want Declan Lannon to know her name, to look upon her face, to hear the sound of her voice. I did not want him to so much as know she existed.

And so I went along with Jourdain and Luc, because he certainly chimed in agreement to his father's will, even though it set a thorn in my heart to send Brienna away.

I remained standing against the wall, nearly dead on my feet; I had not slept more than a few hours at a time the past two nights.

"Go on to bed, lad," Jourdain said gently. "I'll make sure to wake you when it's time for her to leave."

I nodded. My feet were numb as I walked to my room and closed the door.

I sat on my bed, the bed I had not slept in one time since arriving. I leaned my head back until I found the pillow, descending into painful dreams of my mother, of my sister. I had never known what they looked like, because the only word my father had used to describe them was "beautiful." But I saw Líle and Ashling Morgane that night, walking through the meadows of Brígh, the mountain wind soaking in their laughter. I saw them as they should be now, my mother with silver in her blond hair, Ashling just shy of thirty, dark-haired as our father.

I woke at dawn with tears in my eyes, the fire given to ashes.

I changed my clothes and washed the dream from my eyes, raking my fingers through my hair as I sought Brienna.

She had already departed from her room, and I eventually found her in the courtyard with Jourdain's men-at-arms, waiting for her mare to be brought from the stables. As soon as I came up beside her, I could tell she had not slept much that night. Her eyes were bloodshot, and bruises were beginning to bloom on her face and neck, from her altercation with Fechin.

"I know," she said, realizing I had noticed her bruises. "But at least my nose is no longer crooked."

"Is it still hurting you?" I asked.

"No, thanks to Isolde."

I forced a smile to conceal how the sight of bruises on her upset me. I took her hand, drawing her close. She settled against me with a sigh; her arms came around me. I held to her and she held to me, my fingers tracing the loose silk of her hair, the range of her shoulders beneath her passion cloak, the graceful curve of her back.

I could feel her words warm my shirt as she said, "Do you agree with him? To send me away?"

My hand moved to her hair, to gently tug her head back, so she would look at me.

"No. I would not have sent you from my side."

"Then why are you letting me go?" she whispered, like she knew I had been complacent, like she knew I had the power to persuade Jourdain and I had withheld it. "When you know I should be here?"

I could not answer her, because to respond would be to uproot my deepest worry, to give my fear a shape, to let out the darkness in my heart that I did not want her to know.

She stared up at me, her eyes inscrutable.

And I wondered why this felt like such an ominous parting, as if a river were about to rise between us.

I lowered my head, my lips brushing the edge of hers. I should not kiss her here, in the courtyard, where anyone could see us. I should not, and yet she brought her mouth to mine. She gave me her breath as I gave her mine, until my heart was beating in her hands, until I felt like she had swallowed all of my secrets, all those nights when I lay awake with her on my mind, all those mornings when I walked through Brígh's meadows with my eyes set to the east, to that forest trail that bridged our lands, waiting for her to appear, waiting for that distance to close between us.

"Brienna."

Her father was calling her, his voice sharp, to wake us both.

She broke away from me, turned without speaking. But perhaps she and I no longer needed words. I stood and watched the morning catch the silver-threaded stars of her cloak. She mounted her mare in the center of the courtyard. Liam O'Brian, Jourdain's thane, and two MacQuinn men-at-arms would accompany her home.

Luc and Jourdain came up beside her, to bid their good-byes. Brienna smiled, but it didn't quite reach her eyes. She gathered her reins, and Jourdain patted her knee in farewell.

I was still standing in the same place as she trotted out of the courtyard. My eyes followed her, through the sunlight, through the shadows, until she disappeared beneath the stone arch.

Not once did she look back at me.

Hours later, I sat in the queen's council chamber, staring at the map of Lyonesse spread over the table. Six of us had gathered to plan the next raid—Isolde, her father Braden, Jourdain, Luc, Lord Derrick Burke, and myself. We had skipped breakfast to pore over additional Lannon ledgers, and by that afternoon, we had chosen four more potential safe houses for Declan, each of them located in the southeastern quadrant of town, each of them close to the tavern and hostel Brienna and Luc had scouted the night before.

The news had finally leaked; Declan Lannon had escaped the dungeons, and he was hiding in Lyonesse. And Isolde had been left with no choice but to call for a curfew, for shops and markets to suspend until he was recovered, for the city gates to be closed and heavily guarded, for the residents to remain in their homes with their doors locked and their windows shuttered. She had also made the request for citizens to be ready to have their homes searched.

In addition, we put forth a vast reward for Declan Lannon's recovery. The sum was doubled if the children were also safely brought to the queen. Surely, I thought, someone would betray Declan, unable to resist the promise of wealth. But as the hours continued to pass, it would seem that the half-moon clan was not tempted by riches.

I sat and stared at the map, drumming my fingers over the table as I regarded the places we were about to search. Declan had been at the hostel. But where would he slither next? Would he keep moving, or would he try to remain in one place? How long did he intend to hide with two children? What was he ultimately trying to do? Free his entire family from the dungeons? Incite a revolt against Isolde? Was he truly the "Red Horn"?

As if he had read my mind, Lord Burke asked from across the table, "What is it that he wants?"

"That is still uncertain," Isolde responded. "Declan has made no demands of us yet."

"But he will, sooner or later," Jourdain said. "Lannons always do."

"Whatever his demands are," Isolde said, clearing her throat, "we do not entertain them. I will not negotiate with a man who has sown terror and violence for years, who has been weighed by the people and judged to be executed."

"That makes him even more dangerous, Lady," I stated. "He has nothing to lose at the moment."

Braden Kavanagh shifted in his chair, concerned as he glanced to her. "I would not be surprised if Declan sets a snare to capture Isolde. I want her guarded at all times."

"Father," Isolde said, unable to hide her impatience. "I already have a dedicated guard. I rarely have a moment to myself."

"Yes, but can we trust your guard?" Jourdain dared to ask.

Lord Burke stirred. The queen's guard were men and women from his House. They had indeed proven themselves to us, but that did not fully quell our worry that some might be persuaded to turn.

"This master guard that betrayed you," Lord Burke said. "He was a Lannon, not a Burke. And I can swear that the men and women I have provided as your guard are trustworthy. None of them bear the half-moon mark."

"And I thank you for that, Lord Burke," Isolde was swift to say. "Your women and men have been a tremendous support and aid to us since we have returned."

There was a soft, hesitant rap on the council chamber door.

Isolde nodded to her father, who removed the markers of Lannon safe houses from the map before answering the door.

Sean Allenach stood awkwardly with a fold of paper in his hands.

"Ah, Sean. Please join us."

"Forgive me for interrupting," he said, walking into the room, "but I think I have something that may be of use to you, Lady." He extended the paper to her, and Isolde took it.

"Where did you come across this, Lord Sean?" She read the contents, then slowly set down what appeared to be a very brief letter with slanted penmanship.

"I am sorry to say it was in my manservant's possession. The letter is addressed to him. There is no indication as to who wrote it."

"What is this letter?" Jourdain asked, and by the terseness in his tone, I could tell he did not trust Sean Allenach any more than I did.

Isolde passed it around the table. One by one, we read it. I was the last one, and my interest didn't catch until the final sentence: *Depending on the weather today, we may have to postpone the meeting.*

The *D* was filled in with ink. It looked like a half-moon mark.

"Does your manservant know that you have his letter?" Isolde inquired.

"No, Lady."

"Where is your manservant . . . Daley Allenach was his name, wasn't it? Where is Daley presently?"

"He's in the castle kitchens, eating with the servants," Sean replied.

I exchanged a look with Jourdain. Another Lannon rat in the castle, moving about freely.

Luc took a sheet from the stack of paper at his elbow to copy the letter, word for word, and then handed the original back to Sean.

"I know that most of you do not trust me because of my

father," Sean said. "But when I say that I wholeheartedly desire to help, I mean it. On my honor and my name, which means little more than dirt these days. Whatever I can do to assist you in recovering the Lannons, I will do it."

Braden Kavanagh looked like he was about to say something snide, but Isolde spoke before her father could.

"Lord Sean, you would be of great assistance to us if you would return this letter to your manservant's possessions, before he realizes it is missing. If any more correspondence occurs, inform us at once. In the meantime, I would ask you to take detailed notes as to where Daley Allenach goes, even under your orders."

Sean nodded, set his hand over his heart, and departed, leaving the six of us to decode what the strange letter meant.

"Lannon's minions are corresponding," Luc said.

"And one of them is Lord Allenach's manservant," Braden added. "What does that say to us about trust?"

"Sean Allenach has proven himself to me," the queen stated. "He defied his father the day of our rising, to fight for me. He took a sword in his side to protect his sister. I would readily ask him to join this circle if I knew most of you wouldn't vehemently oppose it."

We were quiet.

"As I thought," the queen said dryly. "Now, if the half-moons are writing to one another, they may lead us directly to Declan's location. I do not want to spook Daley Allenach *yet*, but we may have to trail him if we do not uncover Declan at one of the safe houses today."

I reached for the copy of the letter again, and skimmed it, beginning to read beyond the words. "They're employing a rather simple code. 'The ale has run dry' is apparently a warning against the hostel and possibly the tavern, since we made ourselves known in one of them last night. 'Can you bring some to me in the morning with the mutton?' is clearly asking if Declan can be kept at a new safe house. As far as the weather . . . I do not know what that implies. It could be anything from our observation to the curfew to the time of day Declan intends to move."

"Which means Declan is not hiding in one place," Lord Burke said. "And he's going to have to move at night, due to the curfew."

"Which means he should be holed up this moment," Luc added urgently. "We need to strike. Now."

Isolde hesitated, and I knew she was missing Brienna's input.

"I do not want any deviations from the plan," she said, staring at each of us. "Lord MacQuinn, you will take five warriors to the tailor. Lord Burke, you will take your five to the blacksmith. Lord Lucas, you will take your five warriors to the cooper. And Lord Aodhan, you will take your five to the butcher. You ask for entry, you search the building, and you walk away if Declan is absent. If he is there, you have your appointed archer shoot the poisoned arrow to take him down. Ewan's and Keela's safety is paramount, so take extreme care with any call that you make. You do not want to be the one to return and tell me that the children were harmed beneath your call, even by a scratch."

I waited a moment, to let her instructions settle, before I lifted my voice. "Lady? I would ask if one of my five warriors could be a Lannon."

Everyone looked to me, incredulous. All save for Isolde, who stared at me with interest.

"Which Lannon do you speak of, Aodhan?"

"I would like to raise Thane Tomas Hayden from the dungeons, to aid me in this mission."

"Have you lost your mind, Morgane?" Lord Burke cried. "How could you ever trust him?"

I leaned on the table. "You see, that mind-set right there is going to break this country in two. And yes, I am not going to lie: I hate the Lannons. I hate them so much sometimes it feels as if my bones will turn to ash over it. But I have found that we cannot label every Lannon as a Gilroy or an Oona or a Declan. There are good people beneath this House, who have suffered greatly. And we need to alliance with them, to flush out the corrupt ones."

The room filled with uncomfortable silence.

"If I raise Tomas Hayden from the dungeons," Isolde began, "what assurance can you give me, Aodhan, that he will follow you, that he won't turn on you?"

"He cares greatly for Ewan Lannon," I replied. "He is the reason why Ewan escaped the day of our rising. I think Tomas would have no hesitation whatsoever if it came down to betraying Declan to save Ewan and Keela."

"You must have no doubt, lad," Jourdain said. "You cannot think that he will. You must know it."

I glanced to him, trying to subdue my annoyance. "Tomas Hayden is my mother's uncle. He is a blood relation of mine." That quieted Jourdain. When I looked to Isolde, I steadied myself and said, "Bring him up from the dungeons, and let me speak with him again. If I deem him too unpredictable, I will send him back to his cell."

Isolde nodded, and the other men rose, one by one, their chairs scraping over the stone floors. They departed until it was just the queen and me, waiting for the guards to bring up Tomas Hayden.

And the longer I sat there, the more I wondered if I was wrong, if I was about to commit an irrevocable mistake.

Tomas was brought into the chamber, grimy and squinting against the light. But he recognized me and Isolde and stood very quietly, his eyes upon her.

"Are you marked?" I asked him.

"You'll have to unchain me to see," he said.

I stood to request the keys from the guard and unlocked his shackles myself, my dirk ready at my belt should the thane try to overpower me. But when the chains fell away from him, he merely stood, waiting for my order.

"Show us your wrists."

He obeyed, pulling up tattered sleeves, turning his wrists over. He was clean. No sign of a half-moon, or even of the attempt of removing one from his skin.

"I know you must have heard the commotion in the dungeons yesterday," I said to him, and he set his milky blue eyes back upon me. "That Declan and Keela escaped. Declan is loose in Lyonesse, and he is all but holding his own children hostage. I am going to lead a group of five warriors to search and recover him, Ewan, and Keela. And I want to know if you will join me, if you will pledge yourself to help me find them."

"And what will you do with Keela and Ewan upon recovering them?" Tomas asked. "Chop off their heads, right after their father's?"

"Thane Tomas," Isolde said patiently. "I understand that you care deeply for the children. I promise to do all within my power to shelter and protect them, to find a way to pardon them."

"Why would you do that?" he questioned. "They are your enemy's offspring."

"They are innocent children," Isolde corrected. "And it fills me with great sadness that Maevana as a whole indicted Keela."

Tomas seemed to hesitate, caught within his thoughts.

"Yes, Gilroy, Oona, and Declan Lannon destroyed my House as well as the queen's," I said. "But I know that he also destroyed yours, Tomas. That it will take many years for the Lannon people to recover from this."

He met my gaze, and I saw the anger, the remorse in his eyes.

"Join me in hunting Declan," I invited. "Lend us whatever wisdom and insight you can. Help me find Ewan and Keela."

"What do you require in return?" he rasped, looking to Isolde.

"Swear your fealty to me, as your queen," Isolde replied. "And I shall let you go from the dungeons and assist Aodhan."

I thought he would need a moment to weigh his options. So I was surprised when he knelt immediately, laid his hand over his heart, and looked at Isolde.

"I swear my fealty to you, Isolde of Kavanagh. I shall bow to no other save for you as my queen."

It was a rather crude vow, but it sounded genuine. Isolde took his hands, guiding him to stand. Her voice was sharp when she said to Tomas, "If you betray us, I will not kill you but keep you locked in the dungeon for the remainder of your days. Do you understand, Tomas Hayden?"

Tomas met her gaze. "I understand, Lady. But you do not need to fear betrayal from me."

Isolde nodded. "Very well. The two of you may go and prepare for the mission."

I was eager. Too eager. All I could think about was capturing the man who had caused me so much turmoil. My pulse was throbbing when Isolde held up her hand, stopping us.

"One final word." The queen's eyes locked with mine, over the shadows and the candlelight. "I want Declan Lannon brought to me. Alive."

It took everything within me to lay my hand over my heart, in complete submission to her order. Because as I left the council chamber, Tomas at my side, I let my confession swell in my mind.

I wanted nothing more than to be the one to bring Declan Lannon to his bloody end.

My four men- and women-at-arms were waiting for me in my chambers. Their armor was in place, their swords and blades belted at their waists, their hair plaited back from their eyes. They were surprised when they saw Tomas Hayden with me, but obeyed when I told them to fetch him armor and a broadsword. I quickly donned my leather breastplate and vambraces, my fingers trembling as I knotted the leathers.

I appointed my archer and gathered my five into a circle, to explain the plan.

Within minutes, we were striding from the castle, into the deserted streets.

The afternoon sun was just sinking behind the roofs, casting bars of gold onto the cobblestones. A cold wind chased clouds across the sky, carrying the brine from the sea and the smoke of the forges. The breeze nipped at my face, stinging my eyes as I approached the designated butcher shop.

I stood before the storefront, assessing. Tomas stood slightly behind me, and I turned to him to ask, "Does this look familiar to you?"

He shook his head.

I set my eyes back to the building. It was closed, heeding the queen's order. Flies swirled around dried pools of blood on the ground, and the hanging hooks used to display shanks of meat tangled like chimes.

I stepped forward and rapped my knuckles upon the lintel, waiting.

The butcher cracked the door. In the sliver of shadows, he was a tall man with limp gray hair. His nose was crooked as were his eyes, which blinked at me like a rodent in the light.

"We're closed." He made to shut the door, but I set my foot down, catching the wood.

"May we come in? Surely you have heard that all good citizens of Lyonesse are willing to have their homes and shops searched today."

"Of course, but my wife is unwell. . . ." the butcher stammered, but I had forced my way in, my five warriors following.

The main room was dark; all the windows were shuttered and it smelled like blood and foul meat. I stepped on something that crunched, and I fought the urge to heave.

"Light this room," I ordered, listening as the butcher fumbled about for his shutters.

"Sire . . . I really do not wish to be bothered today. My wife is ill, as are my children, and you will only distress them with this needless search." He opened the shutters just a fraction, to spill some light into the shop.

There was a long table, blackened from butchering, and more hooks dangling from the rafters. A bowl of tepid water, a block studded with knives, buckets brimming with entrails, bones scattered along the floor.

I resisted the urge to cover my nose, forcing myself to breathe through my mouth. According to the ledgers, Gilroy Lannon had not drawn taxes from this place. And I did not understand why. It was as any butcher shop, nothing unique about it. In fact, it bordered on disgusting. I had been in much cleaner, more organized shops.

"As you can see, sire, I am only a humble butcher," the man rambled on, his hands fluttering nervously through the air. "Perhaps I might send some meat back to the castle, for the future queen? Would she like some mutton?"

Mutton.

My attention snagged on that word, the word that had been used in the letter Sean had delivered.

My heart quickened as I walked deeper into the room, to the back of the chamber. My warriors followed, their boots hardly making noise on the warped wooden floors, their breaths measured, prepared for anything. And then I saw something odd.

At first, I thought my eyes were fooling me, because something was gradually creeping across the ceiling. Vines with wilted leaves were slowly unfurling, as if they had a mind of their own, as if they were desperate to catch my attention, spreading over the brick and mortar.

"What is that?" one of my men whispered, perplexed.

They saw it too. I was not merely imagining it.

"Sire? What about a rack of ribs to go along with the mutton?" The butcher was rambling, desperate. "Look, here! You can have the pick of the lot!"

But I hardly heard his voice, because I was watching those vines, which grew toward an inner doorway I would have never noticed, whose passage was covered by a filthy blanket.

"It's an enchantment," I murmured, and I was momentarily hung between awe and fear of it, this tendril of magic that had come to life. Where had it come from? Who was directing it?

In that split moment, I decided to go with my gut, to trust it.

"Sire! Sire, look! I can also give you a ham as well!"

I yanked the blanket aside from the door, exposing a corridor that fed into a curling stairwell. There was a scuffle overhead, and those magical vines continued to unfurl, a path of umber and green for me to follow.

"Arrow ready," I rasped to my archer.

I could hear her quietly select the poisoned arrow from her quiver, the bowstring softly groaning in her hands.

I drew my sword first, my warriors in unison with me. We took the stairs; it was a storm of pounding boots, pounding hearts, and a frantically shouting butcher. The vines vanished, melting into the shadows. It filled me with unease to see them disappear.

The second floor was nothing but a narrow corridor with six different doors, all closed.

I took the first one, splintering it with one kick, archer ready at my back.

It was a poorly lit room, windowless. But there was a host of candles, and a girl quivering on a bed, dressed in rags. I was so surprised that I did not realize she was chained to the bedpost until she whimpered.

"Don't hurt me. Please . . ."

Stunned, I moved to the next room. Kick, splinter, open. Another girl, also chained. And then another. My mind was racing, my heart smoldering with a fury I had never felt before. This was not just a butcher shop. It was an underground brothel.

In the fourth room, the girl was crouching on her bed, ready to meet me. She did not whimper or cower; the relief was evident in her face when she met my eyes, as if she had been waiting for me to come and break down the door, to find her.

And then I noticed the vines again. They wove around her

bedposts, streamed across her floor as serpents, glimmering with golden scales. I stopped short before I stepped on one, and realized the vine was one moment away from wrapping itself around my ankle.

The magic, the enchantment, was coming from her.

She was a Kavanagh. And I could not breathe as I looked at her, tears in my eyes, as she looked at me.

"Aodhan Morgane?" she whispered.

I stood frozen on her threshold, taking in her dilapidated room. And despite the darkness here, I felt the first spark of light.

"You know me?" I asked.

"The lad said you would come." With a trembling hand, she held out a piece of paper. Again, her vines melted into the shadows, granting me entrance.

I meekly approached her, and reached across the space to take the parchment from her fingers. It unfolded in my hand, half of the princess illustration, now tattered and speckled with blood. The girl's blood. Her wrist was nothing but a gaping wound around the shackle, like she had been struggling for years to free herself.

"Prince Declan was here with the lass and the lad," she murmured. "He left this morning. At dawn. I do not know where he went. He would not tell me."

I felt like collapsing; my legs were trembling as I crumpled the princess illustration in my hand.

"My lord," the archer called from the corridor. "The butcher is running. Do you want us to pursue him?"

"*Please*," the girl whispered, drawing my attention back to her. "Please help us."

I swallowed, struggling to steady my voice as I vowed to her, "So I swear, you have my protection, as well as the queen's." I turned to my archer, who had returned her arrow to the quiver. "Free these women. I want a covered coach summoned to carry them back to the castle at once."

The archer nodded as I passed her. I met Tomas's eye in the corridor; he did not appear shocked by this, but there was deep sadness in his gaze, his shoulders slumped.

I descended the stairs, my jaw aching from clamping down on my ire.

The front door was wide open, the butcher nowhere to be found.

I sheathed my sword as I emerged back into the street, into the fading sunlight and the taunt of the wind. I could hear the scuffing of boots and I looked to the right, to see the butcher sprinting away.

I followed, taking my time. I needed that time to calm myself, or else I would kill him.

He tossed a frantic glance over his shoulder at me, proceeding to trip and fall face-first into the street. He was crawling and mewling by the time I reached him, holding his grubby hands up in surrender.

"Please, milord. I am only a humble butcher. I didn't know. . . . Those girls were given to me by the king."

If I had not been under orders, I would have beaten this man senseless. Instead, I crouched beside him. With one hand, I took him by the neck, a grip shy of choking him. With my other hand, I tore his sleeve.

There it was. An inked half-moon.

"What are you going to do with me?" he wheezed, his face mottling. I enjoyed the fear that glinted in his eyes as he regarded me.

And so I gave him a sharp, frightening smile. "What else would I do with rot like you? I am going to take you to stand before the queen."

⤙TWENTY-ONE⤚

LADY OF MacQUINN

Lord MacQuinn's Territory, Castle Fionn

Brienna

I arrived at Castle Fionn drenched from a late-afternoon storm with two black eyes, not at all ready to wield the power of Lady MacQuinn. I knew I looked horrible when my horse clattered into the courtyard, Liam barking orders to the servants gaping at the doors, to rouse a bath and a fire for the lord's daughter.

The groom, Dillon, hurried from the stables to take my horse, his eyes wide in surprise to see it was me, and only me, that had returned.

"Are your father and brother well, Mistress Brienna?" Dillon asked as the rain speckled his face, and I could hear the worry lurking beneath the words. A worry that Jourdain's people were bound to feel at the sight of me.

Has our lord already abandoned us? Is our lord well? Have we gained him only to lose him?

"Yes, they are well, Dillon. My father has sent me back in place of my brother," I responded, dismounting.

I thanked my escort and then proceeded to walk through puddles of muck and dirt, my passion cloak dragging through it behind me, all the way into the foyer. Thorn, grouchy as expected, was there to meet me.

"Mistress Brienna," he greeted, his salt-and-pepper eyebrows arched in shock. "We were not expecting you. Shall I have Lord Lucas's fire also lit this evening, or is it only to be yours?"

"Only mine, Thorn. Thank you."

"And when can I expect to light the lord's fire? Tomorrow, no doubt? Since I asked specifically for him to return to handle this . . . problem." He looked shocked by the bruises on my face; I could tell he was curious to know what had caused them.

"Not tomorrow. Or the day after that," I answered with a sigh, unraveling the draws of my cloak. "Do not expect him or my father any time soon. It will most likely be another week at the earliest."

I began to ascend the stairs, Thorn following me.

"We heard there was trouble in the royal city," he said, still trying to pry answers out of me. "That several Lannons escaped."

"Yes." I was almost to my room, eager to shake Thorn out of my shadow.

"Is Lord MacQuinn in danger?"

"No. And neither is Lord Lucas."

"Then why did my lord send you back here? Shouldn't you have stayed with him? I specifically asked for—"

"For Lord Lucas. Yes, I heard you the first time, Thorn," I wearily interrupted. I finally reached my door, my fingers on the iron handle. I paused, to meet the chamberlain's shrewd eyes. "Your lord sent me back instead of Luc. I know this comes as a shock to you, and that as the chamberlain you are familiar with castle dealings. I won't step on your toes or get in your way, but all the same, I am here because my father wills it, so if there is a problem while he is away, bring it directly to me."

Thorn pressed his lips together, bowed his head, and retreated, and I entered my room with a sigh.

The chambermaids were still frantically trying to spark a fire in my hearth and warm a bath for me. One of the girls gasped when she saw the bruises dappling my face, and I smiled as I draped my cloak over the back of a chair.

"It looks worse than it is," I stated, hoping to ease the worry in their expressions.

The girls didn't say anything; they only worked faster so they could slip from my chamber. Alone at last, I disrobed and sank into the warm water, shutting my eyes, listening to the rain tap on the windows. Time faded away, like the steam rising from my skin, and I thought about Ewan and Keela and Cartier until I felt like I was drowning.

I wondered what was happening in Lyonesse, if—at this very moment, as I was sitting in a bath—Cartier and Luc and Jourdain had recovered Declan and the children. I wondered about Isolde, about her safety and her coronation. I wondered about my place in this land, a lord's daughter who did not quite fit in anywhere. Where was my home? Was it here, at Castle Fionn, among the MacQuinns, who still did not trust me? Was it in Lyonesse, at the queen's side? Was it beyond the channel, in Valenia, where I could finally establish my House of Knowledge? I thought of Merei, wondering where she was, how she was doing, if I should go and visit her.

"Mistress Brienna!"

I startled, splashing in water that had gone lukewarm. Neeve stood several feet away, her mouth open in horror as she studied my bruises. I had not even heard her enter, so lost was I in my own mind. And my heart began to pound at the sight of her, my sister. I wondered if there would ever be a moment that I could tell her who I truly was to her; I longed for it as I feared it.

"Did none of the girls stay to help you bathe?" she asked, kneeling beside the tub.

"No, but I didn't need it." And I certainly did not want her to feel obligated to help me. I began to rise, but Neeve had taken the sponge and my hand, beginning to buff the dirt from my nails.

"You broke your nose, didn't you?" she murmured, meeting my gaze.

I held my breath, unsure how to respond. "It's all right," I whispered when she reached for my other hand. "I do not need you to help me."

"If you are to be treated as the Lady of MacQuinn, as Liam has informed all of us you shall be . . ." She began to vigorously scrub my nails, as if she was agitated. I wondered if it was at me, until she continued, "Then all of us should be offering to serve you in any way that we can."

I tried to relax, but my back was sore and I had a crick in my neck and I felt like weeping. Eventually, I asked, "Shouldn't you be at the loom house, Neeve?"

She dunked her sponge in the murky water, taking the cake of soap in her hands. "Yes, well, everything is out of sorts right now."

I frowned. "What do you mean?"

When Neeve was quiet, I turned in the tub, so I could level my gaze at her. I suddenly felt a strange weight in the pit of my stomach as I put the pieces together. Jourdain had claimed there was a problem with one of the lasses, which I had disregarded as a lie to usher me home. But then Dillon had looked shocked to see me, and Thorn especially had appeared upset, because he had asked for Luc to return and handle whatever it was. . . .

"What happened?"

Neeve sighed, focusing her attention on the damp snarls in my hair. "You'll hear about it soon enough."

"Why can't I hear it from you?"

"Because I dislike gossip."

I pursed my lips at her until she smiled at me. She looked beautiful, her hair falling loose from her braid, her eyes the color of dark amber. I hardly noticed the scars on her face, the scars down her neck, the scars on the backs of her hands as she washed me, the evidence that she had fought and won against an illness that should have claimed her life.

"Should I be worried?" I asked as she assisted me from the tub, wrapping a towel around me.

"No," Neeve responded, reaching for my comb. "But let me just say that the lass in question is relieved you have returned, instead of Lord Lucas."

Jourdain's intuition, I thought. And I silently marveled, to imagine how my father had innately known to send me instead of my brother.

"I've been practicing my letters while you were away," she announced proudly, changing the flow of conversation.

I smiled and asked her more about it, sitting on a stool to let her talk and brush out my tangles, until my damp hair was smooth and draped down my back like a cloak of silk.

Neeve helped me dress, drawing the laces at the back of my gown until I was confident it would hold me together long enough to get through the remainder of the day. She braided my hair and I donned my slippers and pulled a shawl around my shoulders, leaving my room to find Thorn.

I didn't have to search for long. I found him in Jourdain's office, waiting for me.

I sat in my father's chair, a small throne carved from oak and draped with a bolt of sheepskin.

"What do you need my help with, Thorn?"

The chamberlain sniffed, choosing not to sit. "I merely need guidance. We have not had a situation like this in a long while."

"Very well. What is the situation?"

He didn't have a chance to explain. The office doors banged

open and in strode Betha, the head weaver, red-faced and damp from the rain. She took one look at me, sitting in Jourdain's chair, and instantly began shaking her head.

"I thought Lord Lucas was returning," she said to Thorn.

"Lord MacQuinn sent his daughter instead."

Betha stared at me. I felt the heat rise in my face.

"What can I help you with, Betha?" I inquired.

"I don't want to talk to her about this," she said to Thorn.

Thorn appeared flustered. "I'm afraid you will either need to bring it to Mistress Brienna, or wait until Lord MacQuinn returns."

"Then I'll wait." Betha pivoted to leave. She was almost to the threshold when a young girl appeared from the shadows, standing in her path. "Come, Neeve."

I thought I had misheard at first, or that there was another Neeve. Until I saw the cream of my sister's hair, heard the dulcet cadence of her voice.

"No, Betha," Neeve said. "I want to bring this before Mistress Brienna."

My pulse quickened, to know that the lass in question was my sister. I tried to swallow my surprise as Neeve walked into the room, wringing her hands, coming to stand before me with a nervous flicker of a glance.

I wondered why she had not said something sooner when she came to my chamber. And I wondered if she had wanted to, and had simply lost her courage.

"Neeve," I said gently. "Tell me. What has happened?"

Again, the words seemed to fade, because she parted her lips, but no sound came forth.

"She's refusing to work," Betha said, the disappointment keen in her voice. "Neeve has always been one of my best spinners. She has a natural inclination to it; she leads the others with her skill. And she has refused to work the past week. And now some of the other lasses have joined her in this . . . resistance."

This was not at *all* what I was expecting. I looked to her, unable to conceal my surprise. "Is there a reason for this, Neeve?"

Betha made a grunt, but I ignored her, wholly focusing on my sister.

"Yes, Mistress Brienna. A good reason," my sister replied.

"You are simply being stubborn, lass," Betha retorted, but even through this conflict, I could hear how fond Betha was of Neeve in the tone of her voice. Even the way she looked at the young girl . . . Betha's hard edges seemed to soften. "You are making it more difficult for the other spinners, who must now work twice as much to make up the difference."

"The other spinners should not have to do this work either," Neeve said adamantly. She was not going to sway, not even when Betha brought her before the lord's daughter.

"Tell me what this work is," I requested.

"It is a tapestry commission," Neeve began, "by Pierce Halloran."

Just the sound of his name made me tense.

"And I refuse to contribute to it," my sister continued, a defiant gleam in her eyes. "I refuse to so much as touch it because of how he treated you last week, when he thought he was above you."

I was amazed by this, by her and her resistance, her devotion to me. And I wondered if she felt the kinship between us, even without knowing I was her half sister.

"And while I understand this, Neeve," Betha said sternly, "you are young, and you do not understand how your actions will impact the *entire* House of MacQuinn."

"Please explain your reasoning, Betha," I said.

Betha flashed a glare at me, as if she resented my ignorance. "If we refuse this tapestry that Lord Pierce has commissioned . . . it will make things very difficult for us. The past twenty-five years, the Hallorans were our greatest supporters."

"Supporters?" My dread began to grow. . . .

"Aye. They kept us alive with their patronage. If not for them, we would have starved beneath Brendan Allenach. You see, Lady Halloran has very extravagant taste, and will *only* purchase our wool and our linen for her wardrobe. She kept us busy the past few decades with her orders, and of course, her sons as well. To suddenly refuse them now . . . I think it will cause tremendous trouble for us down the road."

I took a moment to calm my heart, to sort through my response. "I understand your concerns, Betha. But Brendan Allenach is gone. Davin MacQuinn is your one true lord again. And we do not need to cower and acquiesce to people like the Hallorans. We hold no alliance with the Hallorans, so we do not need to feel obligated to please them."

Betha chuckled, but it was born out of spite. "Ah, see? How

would you understand? You have no inkling as to what life was like during the dark years, when I woke every morning uncertain if I would live to see sunset."

Her words humbled me; she was right. I did not know. But I also wanted her to trust me, to see that we were emerging from the dark years.

"May I speak to you alone, Betha?" I asked.

She looked at me with insolence—I thought she would refuse my request—but she surprised me when she nodded to Neeve.

Neeve and Thorn, who I had all but forgotten about, both departed, leaving me alone with Betha.

We were silent for a moment, both of us uncomfortable. I listened to the fire crackle in the hearth; I looked to its light, to find the hilt of my courage in its dance. But before I could utter a word, Betha spoke.

"Neeve is my granddaughter," she began, shocking me further with her confession. "She is my daughter Lara's only child. And so I will do everything within my power to protect Neeve, because in the end, I could not protect her mother. And if that means I force her to work on the Halloran tapestry, then I do it out of love, to keep her from harm. And I would ask you to admonish her to cast off this resistance, this foolishness."

I was quiet, reeling from her request.

"I do not want her to be like you," the weaver rasped, her words sharper than a blade in my side. "I do not want her to get grand ideas in her head, that she can go about and anger certain individuals."

"Lest you forget, Betha," I said, and thank the gods I sounded calm, "Pierce came to *me*. I did not go to him."

"And that is what you do not understand, Brienna!" She tossed up her hands. "I don't know where exactly you come from, but you obviously could do whatever you desired and faced no consequences. Here . . . it is much different."

"So you would have me give Neeve an order to go against her conscience?" I countered. "I do not believe that is right, Betha."

Betha huffed, but she remained silent, and I wondered if she was heeding me, just a little bit. I eventually stood from my father's chair to level my eyes at her.

"I understand your fears," I murmured. "I hate to hear that you once lived in a time when you faced such terrible evil. But your lord has returned. Your queen has returned. And she is a striking light in the darkness. And the Hallorans know this and tremble in such light, because it exposes them. They do not own you. Nor will they ever. And if you stand against them this time, I promise that I will stand with you if retaliation comes. So will my father, and so will my brother."

She was glaring at me. But I could see a sheen of tears in her eyes, as if she had breathed in my words, as if she felt them settle within her.

"I think that Pierce is testing you, by making his request so soon after one of your tapestries embarrassed him. I have no doubt that he is trying to express his power, even though he has none here," I whispered. "So will you choose him, or will you choose me?"

Betha said nothing.

She turned and departed the chamber, slamming the door in her wake.

But I remained there, sitting alone in my father's office until the fire began to die and the darkness bloomed across the floor.

I did not hear the news until noon the next day. But the murmurs began, sprouting from the loom house to the castle corridors, winding from one building to the next like a vine, until they reached me in the cellar, where I was helping the cook hang boughs of herbs to dry.

The Pierce tapestry had been suspended.

And I sat among the jars of pickled fruits, the baskets of onions and potatoes, herbs crinkled in my apron, and smiled my joy into the shadows.

~*·TWENTY-TWO·*~

ROSALIE

Royal City of Lyonesse, Lord Burke's Territory

Cartier

When night fell, I stood as close as I could to the stars, on the castle battlements, letting the wind beat me until my thoughts were smudged and my face burned from the cold. The city of Lyonesse unrolled beneath me, like a scroll written with dark secrets, the houses gleaming with candlelight.

I had not found Declan Lannon.

Nor had Jourdain. Or Luc. Or Lord Burke.

The prince had not been hiding in the four safe houses we had searched, and Tomas had no wisdom as to where Declan would go next.

He was constantly one step ahead of me.

I sighed, preparing to retreat to my room when I felt the

presence of another. In the darkness, Isolde was standing a few feet away, her eyes also taken with the beauty of the city beneath us. She stepped forward to stand shoulder to shoulder with me, her hands reaching out to rest on the parapet wall.

"How are the girls?" I asked.

"I have healed their bodies the best that I can," Isolde responded. "They are resting for now." She paused, and I knew there was something else. "Aodhan . . . all six of those young women are Kavanaghs."

I had suspected this was so. The one lass who had cast the illusion of the vines to lead me . . . I had known she was a Kavanagh, that she was one of Isolde's people. I had concluded the other five girls were also the same, and perhaps their magic was still hidden deep in their blood, that it had not come forth yet.

"Did they tell you such?" I quietly asked.

"No. They did not have to," the queen replied, sorrowful. "I knew it the moment I took their hands in mine. I felt the fire within them, fire that had almost died to ashes today. I felt my soul call out to them, and theirs answered in return. Five of them are innocent to it—I think their magic will come gradually to them, once they feel safe and can rest. Their parents and families are dead. Gilroy left the girls alive to be shackled in the brothel."

I felt ill as I remembered the sight of it, the smell of it, the darkness and the blood and the chains. How long had those girls been held captive? Did they witness what had happened to their families?

"Gods have mercy, Isolde."

She was quiet for a beat. And then she murmured, "I knew my House was nearly extinguished, that Lannon purposefully targeted them over the past twenty-five years. I expected it would take some time to find my people, if I found any still living. But what I didn't expect was to identify them by merely taking their hands, by touching them."

I thought on that, wishing I knew what to say to comfort her.

Isolde glanced to me. "I know you must think this all sounds strange, but my father and I continue to pass on theories to each other, frustrated that we do not have a manual to become better acquainted with the rules of magic."

"It is not strange, Isolde," I answered.

I could see that her thoughts were shifting as her brow lowered. "The butcher has told us everything but where Declan went this morning. He claims he doesn't know the next safe house for the prince, but that a wagon appeared in the butcher's storeroom to transport the Lannons. And while I desire nothing more than to beat and torture such a vile man . . . I will not become the very thing that I am trying to purge from this castle."

I remained silent, because if she asked for my advice in that moment, I would say beat the butcher until he talked. And I could hardly believe such a desire could be found in me, after being raised in Valenia, where justice was always measured and held accountable.

"Do you ever wonder," Isolde began, tremulous, "why you and I and Luc survived when we should have been killed, when our bones should be beneath the grass with our mothers and our sisters? Do you ever hate yourself," she continued, tears streaking down her cheeks, "for being raised in Valenia? For being cared for and sheltered and loved, for living in ignorant bliss while our people lived in fear and brutality? That while I was sleeping in a warm, safe bed, these girls were chained in captivity, abused every single night? That while I was complaining about learning to read and write and wield a sword, these girls were too afraid to utter a single word, for fear that they would be beaten and maimed?" Isolde wiped the tears away, her hair tangling across her face. "I do not deserve to be queen. I do not deserve to sit on a throne when I have no idea what these people have suffered. I should not have survived the day of darkness."

I gently took her shoulder to turn her to face me. "There was a moment in my life when I thought I would never cross the channel, when I thought I would remain in Valenia and pretend that I was Cartier Évariste, that I was a master of knowledge and there were no people, no House of Morgane, no mother and sister buried in a northern meadow." I paused, because I hated myself in that moment. I hated to acknowledge that I had tried to live my life as I wanted. "But I didn't. You didn't. We gathered what little strength we had and we crossed the channel, and we took back this land. We fought and we bled. Yes, I was ignorant and naïve too. I did not realize how dark and corrupt things were until today, when I discovered those girls. And if you and I step back now, if we decided that we will bow out of this fight, then more girls will be snatched from their families and chained, and more boys will be raised to be cruel."

She finally met my gaze.

"You and I must continue moving forward," I whispered. "We must continue uprooting darkness and corruption, and replacing it with goodness and light. It will take time. It will take our entire hearts and the breadth of our lives, Isolde. But we do not wish we were dead. We do not wish that we were different individuals, despite what the saints or the gods have ordained for us."

She closed her eyes, and whether she was inwardly cursing me or agreeing with me, I could only wonder. But when she looked at me again, there was a different light in her gaze, as if my words had renewed her.

I was the first to return to the warmth of the castle, leaving Isolde to lift her prayers to the stars. And I knew what was before me: another sleepless night. Another night for me to pore over Lannon ledgers, desperately seeking yet another place of corruption that would draw Declan.

Two days passed, filled with searches and chases that yielded nothing.

We had tracked wagon movements and healers, still trying to recover Fechin. But every path we took ended, leaving us with no further answers or leads.

And every day that passed was yet another day for Declan to gather his forces.

Isolde had no choice but to begin making arrests. Anyone harboring the half-moon mark was brought into the keep, to be questioned and detained until Declan could be recovered.

I was conducting such an interview, sitting in the dungeons

with one of the tavern keepers, who stubbornly refused to answer any of my questions, when Luc appeared.

"Quick, Morgane. We need you in the council."

I passed my paper and quill to one of Burke's men to resume the interview and followed Luc up the winding stairs. I noticed Luc was moving with unprecedented speed, that Luc's hair was sticking up at all angles, as if he had torn his fingers through it.

"Do we have a lead?" I asked, struggling to keep pace.

"Sean Allenach's manservant has another letter. Hurry, in here." Luc opened the door to the council, where the fire was burning at the heart of the table and the others were gathered.

There was a strange pallor in Sean's face when he looked at me. I thought it was the firelight, that the shadows were playing tricks on his face. Until I noticed Jourdain had his face buried in his hands, as if he had lost his resolve.

My first fear was that they had found Ewan's and Keela's bodies.

I looked directly to Isolde, who stood quiet as a statue, and I demanded of her, "What has happened? Is it the children?"

Lord Burke merely handed me a letter.

We encountered no trouble, but there has been a change of plans. The previously addressed chosen one will not be visiting this autumn. Rather, we will host Rosalie. Prepare to send plenty of wine and bread.

I shrugged, read it again. "All right. Why does this have everyone out of sorts?"

Jourdain still did not move, so I looked to Luc, but he had his back turned, facing the wall. Even Isolde would not meet my eyes, and neither would her father. Lord Burke gently took the letter from my stiff fingers, until I had no choice but to set my gaze on Sean Allenach.

"Sean?"

"I thought you knew," he rasped.

"Knew *what*?" I snapped impatiently.

"Who Rosalie was."

My mind instantly began to sort through names, faces, people I had known in Valenia. Because Rosalie was a Valenian name. Eventually, I held out my hands, annoyed, and conceded, "I have no idea. Who is she?"

Sean glanced to Jourdain, who was still immobile. Slowly, as if Sean was afraid of me, he cast his eyes to me and whispered, "Rosalie was the name of Brienna's mother."

At first, I wanted to deny such—Sean Allenach knew *nothing*—until I realized that *I* had not known the name of Brienna's mother. And I should have known such a name, should have known who had given her life, who she missed, who she longed to remember.

But how would Sean know this?

I was indignant, until the threads of Brienna's life began to weave together in my frantic mind.

Sean knew the name because Rosalie had once visited Castle Damhan. Sean knew because Rosalie had fallen in love with Brendan Allenach. Sean knew because Rosalie was the woman Brendan Allenach had wanted to marry, because she was carrying a daughter.

Rather, we will host Rosalie. . . .

Rosalie was the code name for Brienna.

"No." I reached out to steady myself on the table, my denial swift, painful. It felt like a bone was caught in my throat. "No, it cannot be. They cannot mean Brienna."

"Aodhan . . . ," Isolde said, and it was the sound of comfort, like someone had died and she was trying to express how sorry she was for my loss.

"MacQuinn sent her home to Fionn, to be safe," I rambled on, looking to Jourdain.

Jourdain finally dropped his hands from his face and stared at me with bloodshot eyes.

"MacQuinn . . . ," I whispered, but my voice faded, because I knew in that moment the reason why we could not find Declan Lannon. Because Declan Lannon was no longer in Lyonesse. Declan Lannon had slipped out of the city the same morning Brienna had. And now it seemed that the half-moons had plans to take her captive.

"Yes," Jourdain whispered. "I sent her home. To be safe."

Only she was not safe. If this stolen message held any truth . . . she was the new target. And if Declan and his half-moons did take her, then they would try to use her for leverage, to bargain with us for her life.

My thoughts spun wildly; what would Declan want in exchange for her? His family? His freedom? The queen?

"Where is Daley Allenach?" I asked, my focus sharpening over Sean.

"My manservant has fled, Lord Aodhan," Sean replied mournfully. "He knows I have his correspondence."

I could have smashed Sean's face into the wall to hear this.

"Have you heard from Brienna?" I turned to Jourdain. "Did she reach Fionn?"

"I heard from her yesterday," Jourdain replied. "She arrived home safely."

I let out a slow breath, believing if she was home, then she would, indeed, be safe. She was in a fortress that had withstood ancient raids and clashes between clans. She was surrounded by people who hated the Lannons. She was cunning, and she was strong.

And yet she did not know. She did not know Declan had escaped Lyonesse. She would be caught off guard by it; the half-moons would have to take her by surprise if they were to capture her.

And perhaps even more than that . . . the half-moons seemed to be spread out everywhere, not just limited to the Lannons and the Allenachs and the Hallorans and the Carrans. What if one of the MacQuinns was a half-moon, willing to betray her?

I stared at Jourdain; he stared back, and the space between us was rife with fear and anger and worry. In the back of my mind, all I could hear was Brienna's voice, her parting words to me . . . *Why are you letting me go when you know I should be here?*

Jourdain and I had made a grave error by sending her home.

If Declan managed to overtake her, he would have my very heart in his hands. He could destroy me; he could ask for anything and I would surrender it without hesitation.

I shoved away from the table, striding to the door, unable to speak, overwhelmed with the desire to hurry and ride to Fionn, to reach her before Declan did.

"Aodhan. Aodhan, wait," Isolde ordered.

I stopped upright, my hand on the iron rings of the doors, breathing against the wood.

"Brienna MacQuinn is one of the smartest women I know," she continued. "If anyone can slip out of Declan's grip, it is her. All the same, it is time for us to move."

I turned. The others had gathered close in a circle, waiting for me to join them. I stepped back into the firelight. On the exterior, I was composed and cold, but within, I was breaking. I was shattering into pieces.

"Declan Lannon plans to take Brienna, to no doubt use her as a bargaining pawn," Isolde said. "If he has taken her before we reach Castle Fionn . . . he will ask for my life in exchange for hers. I have sworn not to negotiate with such a man, so that means we need to discover where Lannon is hiding and recover her as swiftly as we can."

"He will not capture her at Fionn," Jourdain protested. "He won't get through my people."

Isolde nodded. "Of course, Lord MacQuinn." But the queen glanced to me, and the same thought crossed our minds. Brienna was a blood-born Allenach. The MacQuinns had yet to accept her as their own, no matter if she was the lord's daughter.

"Father, I would ask for you to remain here in Lyonesse with Lord Burke, to hold the city and guard the remaining Lannon prisoners," Isolde said. "Lord MacQuinn, Lord Aodhan, Lord Lucas, and Lord Sean will ride with me to Castle Fionn at once. From there, we will begin to uncover possible leads for Declan's whereabouts, but I have a suspicion he will be hiding in one of the half-moon territories."

The queen looked to each of us, to watch us set our hands on our hearts. When her gaze touched mine, I saw the fire stirring within her, ancient fire as if she were a dragon that had just been woken. A dragon that was about to rise, blot out the half-moon with her wings, and rain terror.

I laid my hand over my heart, felt its ragged beat against my palm, and let my fury quietly rise with hers.

TWENTY-THREE

THE BEAST

Lord MacQuinn's Territory, Castle Fionn

Brienna

"There's been an accident, Mistress!" Thorn cried, storming into the office.

I stiffened, looking up from the MacQuinn ledgers to see blood streaked across Thorn's jerkin. "What sort?"

"A hunting accident. I'm afraid two of the men have been killed, and another is—"

I was out of the chair and down the corridor before he could finish, following the commotion into the hall. I didn't know what to expect, but my resolve waned when I saw Liam being carried in and laid on a table, his face mangled, an arrow protruding from his right breast.

The men bearing him felt my presence, turning to look at

me with wide, blank eyes of panic. They stepped aside to let me approach, and I gently laid my fingers to Liam's neck, where a faint pulse still beat.

"Summon Isla for me," I rasped, knowing I was going to need the healer's assistance with this wound. While one of the women frantically rushed away to find the healer, I turned to the men and said, "Help me carry him into one of the bedchambers."

We lifted Liam in careful unison and moved into one of the corridors, heading to the closest spare bedroom. Once Liam was gently resting on the mattress, I worked to cut off his jerkin and shirt, to expose his trunk and assess the arrow's position. I gently touched his chest, feeling for his ribs. I believed the arrowhead was lodged in his fourth rib. Removing it was going to be difficult; I had studied arrow wounds with Cartier as a student, and while I had never had the opportunity to tend to one, I knew chest wounds were almost always fatal if the lung was affected. I also knew that it was extremely difficult to extract an arrowhead if it was embedded in bone.

I studied his face next, which looked to have been swiped by a row of talons. His flesh hung in ribbons from his cheek, exposing his teeth. I almost had to look away, my stomach roiling at the sight.

"I need clean water, rose honey, and plenty of bandages," I murmured, turning to address one of the women who had followed me into the chamber. "And have the girls rouse a fire in this hearth. Quickly, please."

As soon as the woman had departed, her urgent calls echoing

down the corridor, I set my attention on the man who had helped carry Liam in, whose dark eyes fixated on me, waiting for my next command.

"What happened?" I whispered.

"Mistress . . . we don't know. The other two men with Liam were killed."

"Which men?"

"Phillip and Eamon."

Phillip and Eamon. The two men-at-arms who had accompanied me back home from Lyonesse.

Isla entered the chamber, diverting my shock. I had seen her around the hall for meals but had never spoken with her before. She was an older woman with long white hair and eyes the color of the sea. She set down her satchel and studied Liam's wounds.

After a moment, she looked at me and asked, "Are you swayed by blood?"

"No," I responded. "And I know how to tend wounds."

Isla made no response, searching through her satchel. I watched as she began to set out small probes made of elder wood, of various lengths and widths. Next came the tongs, which were smooth and narrow, specifically designed to extract an arrowhead.

She motioned for two of the men to hold Liam down. I did not move, not yet, and merely watched as she tried to twist the arrow shaft. The shaft refused to rotate and unexpectedly broke in her hands.

"The arrowhead's in his bone," Isla said, throwing the shaft into the fire.

"I can find and extract it," I offered, stepping forward.

I worked beside her, wrapping the probes with linen, dipping the tips in rose honey. She requested for the two men who had remained in the room with us to continue holding Liam down, one at the shoulders, the other at the waist, and the healer and I began to gradually open the arrow wound with the probes. I was drenched in sweat by the time I found the arrowhead, a dark gleam of metal coated with blood, lodged in Liam's rib.

I took up the tongs and lowered their point down into his wound until I found the arrowhead. I braced myself, crawling up to the side of the bed beside him, and heaved. The metal came loose and I went flying, tumbling down to the floor, into the table with a crash. But I held up the tongs, and in their pincers was the arrowhead.

Ah, if only Cartier had been here to see me do this. He would be sad that he had missed it.

Isla nodded curtly to me, turning back to Liam to remove the probes and begin cleaning his wound. The two men still held Liam, but they bowed their heads to me with a respect I had never seen or felt here before.

I rose and set the tongs down, handing Isla the linen while I held the jar of honey.

"We'll have to wait and see if his lung is affected," Isla said, finishing with her healing poultice. "As for his face . . . I am going to have to try and bring it back together. Do you know your herbs, Mistress Brienna?"

"Yes. What do you need?"

"Star thistle," she replied. "It grows in patches in the eastern woods, by the river."

"I'll go and harvest some." I quickly strode from the room, down the corridor, into the hall.

I was not expecting there to be a crowd gathered, the men and women sitting quietly at the tables, somberly waiting for news about Liam. They all stood at my entrance, and I stopped short, feeling their gazes go to the blood on my hands, the blood smeared on my dress and my face. Thorn was the only one to approach me.

"Is he dead?" the chamberlain asked.

"No. The arrow has been removed." I continued to the foyer, the MacQuinns parting before me. Again, I began to sense their respect as I walked among them, as they moved to let me pass, as their eyes continued to follow me. I realized it, then, that they were awaiting orders from me.

I stopped on the threshold, wondering what sort of order I should give. I pivoted on my heel, one breath away from saying they should cease work for the day, that something was afoot on MacQuinn lands and I needed to try and sort through this, when Thorn stole the moment.

"Everyone back to your work," the chamberlain said gruffly. "No sense in wasting the remainder of a workday."

The men and women began to leave the hall. I stood beneath the archway until Thorn looked at me.

"I need to speak with you when I return, Thorn," I said.

He appeared flustered by my request but nodded and said, "Of course, Mistress Brienna."

I walked to the foyer, snagging a basket on my way out. It was early afternoon, and the sky was overcast. I took a moment to stand and brush the hair from my brow, my back beginning to ache.

"Mistress Brienna!"

I turned to see Neeve hurrying toward me, my hound, Nessie, a few steps behind with her tongue lolling out.

Neeve stopped short at the sight of the blood on me, her hands fluttering up to her mouth.

"It's all right," I said. "I'm going to gather some star thistle."

Neeve swallowed her fear, lowering her hands. "I know where that grows. Let me help you."

Together, we walked a good distance from sight of the castle, where the trees began to thicken along the riverbank. I gave Neeve my dirk, so she could cut the thistle without touching the barbs, and we worked in harried silence, filling the basket.

I was on my knees, struggling with a stubborn thistle, when I heard the snap of a branch in the thicket. And I would have thought nothing of it had Nessie not started to growl at my side, her hackles rising, her teeth bared.

"Nessie," I whispered, but I peered into the shadows of the thicket, into the thick tangle of bushes and trees. A cold warning washed down my spine as I felt the prickling stare of hidden eyes.

Someone was within that thicket, watching me.

Nessie began to bark, sharp and angry, taking another step closer to the thicket.

Every hair on my body rose, and I stumbled to my feet. "Neeve? *Neeve!*"

My sister rushed into the clearing, coming from my left. I shuddered with relief to see her, my dirk still in her fingers.

"What? What is it?" She panted, noticing how Nessie continued to growl and slink closer to the shadows. "Is it the beast?"

"Beast?" I echoed.

"The beast that attacked Liam?"

I looked back into the thicket. It was no beast, I wanted to tell her. It was a man.

I gathered the basket of thistle onto my arm and took my sister with the other. "Come, we need to return. Nessie? *Nessie!*"

The dog relented to obey, only when she was assured that I was moving away from the danger. The three of us all but ran from the trees into the open air, into the gray light and thin patches of sunlight. I was sore for breath by the time we reached the castle foyer.

"Do you have your own dirk, Neeve?" I asked when she tried to hand the little blade back to me.

"No," she responded. "Lord Allenach forbade us from having them."

"Well, this one is yours now." I lifted my skirts to unbuckle the scabbard bound at my leg. I handed it to her, waited until I was sure she had fastened it to her thigh, the dirk snugly in place, hidden beneath her dress. "Wear it always. And if someone should threaten you, I want you to cut them here or here." I pointed to her neck, to her underarm.

Her eyes went large, but she nodded, acquiescing to my order. "What about you, Mistress?"

"I'll get another blade." I touched her arm, squeezed gently to reassure her. "Do not wander anywhere alone, even when you walk from the loom house to the castle. Always ask for someone to accompany you. Please."

"Because of the beast?"

"Yes."

Neeve was doing her best to quell her fright, to appear brave. But I could see how pale and worried she was. Gently, I drew her forward to drop a kiss on her brow. She went still beneath the affection, and I scolded myself for being too forward. This is not how the Lady of MacQuinn would behave, and I could see that I was confusing her.

"Go along now," I whispered with a gentle nudge, and Neeve retreated down one of the corridors, glancing at me with a dark gleam in her eyes, as if she was beginning to feel the sightless threads that bound us.

I returned to Liam's room, handing the healer the basket of thistle. We worked together in silence, crushing the blooms into a fine dust that she mixed with the honey into salve. She had brought Liam's face back together while I was gone, and I helped her wipe the salve on the thane's cross-hatching of stitches. While I washed my hands, the healer gently wrapped his face with fresh strips of linen.

"No beast made these wounds, Mistress Brienna," the healer said gravely.

"Yes, I know." I struggled to breathe, remembering the creeping sensation that someone had been in the woods, watching me, only an hour ago. "Do you mind sitting with him for a while? I can come relieve you at sundown."

"Of course, Mistress." She nodded and I promptly left, calling for Thorn to meet me in Jourdain's office. I sat in my father's chair as the chamberlain stood before me, fidgeting.

"I am sure you gathered information as to what happened this morning while I was tending to Liam," I stated.

"Yes, Mistress. Liam went hunting with Phillip and Eamon," Thorn began. "This is not unusual. The three of them are close, and have hunted many times together the past three weeks. Liam came riding back to the castle, barely in the saddle, shot by an arrow with his face mangled. The men who helped carry Liam into the courtyard said all he could rasp was one word. *Beast.* He said it twice before losing consciousness, just before you arrived, Mistress. While you and Isla were tending to him, I sent out a scout to locate the other two men. They were found dead in the northern meadow, their faces also mangled, but they had suffered deep punctures to their abdomens. I fear that . . ." He hesitated.

I waited, brow arched. "You fear what, Thorn?"

He glanced to the bloodstains on me and sighed. "I fear their entrails were spilled out, all over the grass."

I was quiet for a moment, staring into the shadows of the room. I felt horror, to know these two men had died in such a brutal way. And while I wanted to sink into shock, I knew that I couldn't afford to. "Would not a beast eat the men, rather than play with their entrails?"

Thorn was silent, almost as if he had never thought this.

"Furthermore, what manner of beast shoots an arrow, Thorn?"

The chamberlain flushed, indignant. "Why are you asking me such things, Mistress? How am I to know? I am merely telling you what I have uncovered!"

"And I am merely engaging you in conversation, so we can solve this terrible mystery."

"Mystery? There is no mystery here," he countered. "This was a tragic accident! Most of the men believed that Eamon or Phillip tried to shoot the beast when it attacked, and their arrow glanced into Liam by mistake."

This could be, I thought. But again, something felt off. And I sat back, thinking that things had not felt right since I had departed Lyonesse.

"Do you have the arrow fletching?" Thorn surprised me by asking. "If you wanted to give it to me, I can tell you if it was one of our arrows, or if it is an arrow from another House."

My hope rose, and then swiftly fell when I remembered how the healer had thrown the shaft into the fire, irritated that she had accidentally broken it. "No. There is no fletching."

"Then I do not know what else to tell you, Mistress Brienna. Other than I am deeply sorry you are the one who must handle this. Your father should have sent Lord Lucas home."

I had to clamp down on my irritation.

"Where are Phillip's and Eamon's bodies now?" I questioned, rubbing my aching temples.

"They are being prepared for burial by their wives."

I needed to go to those wives, assist them with the preparations. Rising, I said, "I want you to send out a group of warriors to scout the surrounding land, all the way to the territory borders. Start in the eastern woods, where the star thistle grows."

He frowned at me. "But Mistress . . . why?"

"Why?" I nearly laughed. "Because there is a beast loose in the demesne, killing our people."

"So you would have me risk more of us to take it down? It's most likely a bear, and has run back to its cave. I've already scouted and told you that we found nothing but Phillip's and Eamon's bodies."

"Thorn. This beast is not a bear. It's a man. He's most likely a Halloran, and he's most likely got a group of cronies with him. Find them and bring them to me. Do you understand?"

"The Hallorans?" He gaped at me. "This is absurd! Are you trying to start a war?"

"If I were trying to start a war, you would not have to ask me. You would know it," I stated coldly. "Now go and do as I request of you, before you test the last bit of my patience."

He still had that shocked gleam in his eyes as he departed, like he could not believe my orders.

I waited until the door was closed, and then I sat once more, my legs trembling.

It had to be the Hallorans.

I thought of Pierce, of his humiliation, of how we were refusing to fulfill his tapestry. Was this retaliation for that?

Watch your back, Brienna.

Grainne's warning rang once more, and I thought about how she and the Dermotts had suffered the Hallorans' raids for years.

What would I do if Thorn brought back the Hallorans? What would I do to them?

I had no idea. And that, perhaps, frightened me more than anything else.

I was in Liam's room later that evening, boiling a pot of herbs over the fire to cleanse the air, when Thorn found me. The old man was splattered in mud and looked bone weary as he approached me.

"We found nothing, Mistress Brienna. Nothing but birds and squirrels and rabbits," he said tersely, as if to express, *Didn't I tell you so?*

I stood so that I could fully face him. It was only me and him and Liam in the room. I had sent Isla off to dinner for a little bit of respite.

Thorn glanced to where Liam continued to lie on the bed. "How is he?"

"He's still breathing," I replied, but my words were heavy. It was as Isla and I had feared: Liam had fallen unconscious, and his breathing had become labored. Isla was skeptical that he would survive the night.

But I did not tell Thorn this. I tossed another bough of peppermint into my boiling pot, praying the herbs would clean the thane's lungs, even as his breaths became weaker.

"Go to dinner, Thorn. You have done enough for the day."

He left with a sigh, and I sat at Liam's side until Isla returned to relieve me.

I didn't realize how exhausted I was until I walked out to the front courtyard and whistled for Nessie.

My wolfhound dutifully appeared, as if she had been waiting for me to summon her. I brought Nessie up to my room, invited her to sleep on the bed beside me.

While she wallowed in my quilts, I took my broadsword in my hands. I unsheathed the blade, admiring it before climbing into bed. I set the sword on mattress beside me, the hilt ready to be grabbed at a moment's notice.

And then I lay down, dog on one side, steel on the other, and watched the firelight cast shapes upon my ceiling.

I don't remember falling asleep. I must have drifted away gradually, because the next thing I knew, Nessie was growling.

My eyes opened wide to drink in the darkness, my fire burned to embers. I lay there frozen.

Nessie growled again, and that's when I heard it. A soft, hesitant rap on my door.

"Peace, Nessie," I ordered her, and she quieted.

I slipped from the bed, sword in hand, and began to creep to my door.

"Mistress Brienna?"

It was Thorn. I let out an annoyed sigh and cracked my door, to see the chamberlain standing with a candle, waiting for me to answer.

"What is it now, Thorn?"

"There's someone I think you need to see," he whispered. "Hurry, come with me. I think it has to do with . . . the attack." And then he looked beyond me, where Nessie continued to growl.

His eyes widened ever so slightly in apprehension.

"Give me a moment." I shut the door so I could slip on my boots and draw my passion cloak about my collar. I belted my sword's baldric across my chest, letting the sword settle comfortably between my shoulder blades, her hilt peeking up behind me, ready to be grabbed.

When I opened the door again, Thorn was waiting a few feet away.

"She'll be afraid of the dog," he muttered to me, and I paused on my threshold.

"She?"

"Yes. One of the lasses says she knows something about the attack. She wishes to speak with you about it."

That surprised me, but I relented to leave Nessie in my chamber, despite her whines.

I followed Thorn through the castle, the corridors dark and quiet. I expected that he would guide me into one of the storerooms, so when he led me out into the front courtyard, the stones and moss gilded in moonlight, I hesitated.

"Where is this lass?" I asked, my breath emerging as a cloud. "And who is she?"

Thorn turned to look at me. He looked frail and old in that moment. "She's in the loom house. I couldn't persuade her otherwise."

"The loom house?" I echoed. There was a moment of hesitation—this felt odd and strange—but then I thought of how much Jourdain trusted Thorn, trusted him enough to let him guide and oversee the castle affairs. And so I relented to follow him along the path down the hill, the grass long and lank beneath us, curling about our boots. The wind extinguished his candle, so we moved by the moon and the stars.

When the loom house came into view, an inky blot against the silk of night, I noticed there was no light within the windows. The building was sleeping, like all the others.

I paused, a thread of fear pulling my heart down to my stomach. "Thorn?"

The chamberlain stopped, turned to look at me. I could see it in his face that someone was now behind me, and before I could move to draw my sword, I felt the warning of a blade brush my neck.

"Don't move, Brienna," Pierce whispered in my ear.

I didn't. But my heart was breaking into pieces. "Why?" It was all I could say to Thorn, the betrayal tightening my throat.

"We wanted Lucas," Thorn said. "So I asked for Lucas to return. But your father was fool enough to send you instead. I'm sorry, Brienna. Truly, I am."

"How could you betray your own lord?" I rasped, but then the truth hit me like a blow to my chest. I knew exactly what Thorn was. And I wanted to laugh, angry at myself for not taking my own advice.

Had I not instructed Sean to pull up the sleeves of his seven thanes, to test for the mark?

I had believed no MacQuinn had joined the half-moons, but how foolish I had been, to think corruption only spread to certain Houses.

Pierce's arm came about my waist. I felt him unbuckle my baldric, my one and only weapon slipping off my body. I could hear the steel land in the grass, swept away from me.

"My father will kill you when he discovers this," I said, surprised by how calm I sounded.

Thorn only shook his head. "Lord MacQuinn will never know."

Pierce wrestled me to the ground, stuffing a rag in my mouth as he bound my wrists behind my back. I could still see Thorn, looming over me, the stars smoldering in the night behind him. I watched as Pierce passed him a purse of coins; I saw Thorn's sleeve shift as he reached for it, the inked half-moon stark at his wrist.

"You won't get the remainder until the exchange is successful," Pierce said. And then he yanked my passion cloak away; the cold rippled over me as Thorn reluctantly took my cloak in his hands, as if the blue fabric would bite him.

Pierce picked me up and tossed me over his shoulder like I was nothing more than a sack of grain. I screamed, but my voice was muffled from the gag; I kicked, trying to jar my knee into his stomach, and he tripped. We sprawled on the ground and I rushed to crawl away from him, cutting my knee on a rock. Pierce was on me before I could get to my feet, striking me across the face. My sight blurred, my cheek smarting in pain; I fought to breathe as he dragged me into the woods.

I was still dazed as I tried to gain my bearings. We were in a small clearing, and there was a wagon; four of Pierce's men were gathered about it, waiting, their eyes regarding me coldly. Two of them had old blood dried on their jerkins. Phillip's and Eamon's blood, I knew, and I felt bile rise up my throat.

I watched as Pierce pulled back the wagon tarp.

There were grain sacks in the back. But there was also something else: a compartment beneath the sacks of grain, cleverly hidden. My heart hammered when I saw it, when I realized Pierce was about to slide me into the coffin-inspired darkness. I stumbled to my feet, clumsy without the balance of my hands, and wildly began to run. I got through two briar patches before Pierce caught me, his fingers snaking into my hair, yanking me back into his arms.

"You're a shrewd one, all right," he sneered. "Fechin warned me that you were, that it would be difficult to catch you. But this time I've outwitted you, Brienna." He brought me back to the wagon and hefted me into the secret compartment, his men chuckling and cheering him on. Then he leaned against it, regarding me with a tilt to his head, as if he enjoyed seeing me cower in the small space. "The prince wanted MacQuinn blood, not Allenach. But I suppose you'll do well enough."

He fiddled with one of the grain sacks above me. I could hear the clink of glass, and before I could react, Pierce pressed a damp rag into my face, forcing me to breathe in the fumes of something acidic.

I resisted, drawing farther back into the compartment, but my fingers began to tingle, and the world began to slow. I had almost succumbed to the void when I heard Pierce speak.

"You know . . . if you hadn't humiliated me before your father's

House, if you had chosen to alliance with me . . . the Hallorans would have chosen your side. We would have cast off the Lannons like they were dirty laundry. You would be mine, and I would have protected you, Brienna. But now look at you. It's amusing how power shifts, isn't it?"

He ripped the gag from my mouth, and I tried to scream again. But my voice was fading. I only had the strength to rasp, "Where are you taking me?"

"I'm taking you home," he said with a smile. "To the prince."

He shut me in the darkness. I felt the wagon rumble into motion, and I struggled to remain coherent.

My last thought kindled, just before I slipped into unconscious.

I was about to be handed over to Declan Lannon.

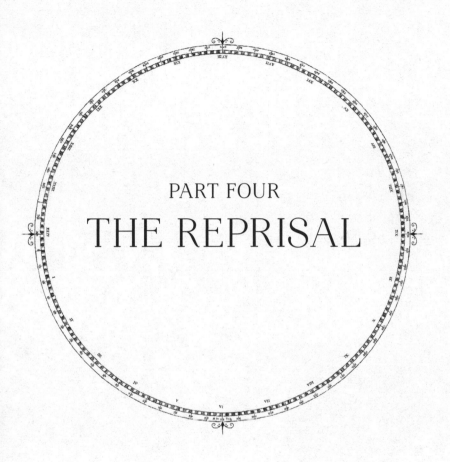

PART FOUR

THE REPRISAL

~•~ TWENTY-FOUR ~•~

ULTIMATUM

Lord MacQuinn's Territory, Castle Fionn

Cartier

I knew it the moment I saw Jourdain's castle appear through the storm fog. Brienna was gone.

I pulled my horse to a halt in the courtyard, just behind Jourdain. We were too late, and yet Jourdain did not realize it.

Isolde reined her horse beside mine; her face was streaked with mud and rain. We had ridden through the night, hardly stopping, to reach Castle Fionn. And yet we still had not arrived in time.

The queen looked to me, silently bidding me to follow Jourdain into the hall. And so I obeyed, my chest hollow as I dismounted, following Jourdain and Luc as they rushed into the foyer.

The remainder of our party—Sean, Isolde, and her guards— entered slowly, hesitantly.

"Brienna? *Brienna!*" Jourdain's voice boomed through the castle.

The MacQuinns were gathered, just finishing breakfast. The light even struggled here, where the fire was roaring in the hearth, casting a tepid glow on the MacQuinn banners. The people stood in clusters with pale faces, their eyes wide and solemn. There was one young girl with golden hair and scars on her face who was weeping, her sorrow the only sound to break the tense silence.

"Where is my daughter?" Jourdain asked, and his voice was frightening, the crack of a tree about to split through its heart.

At last, the chamberlain stepped forward. I watched him as he bowed his head, as he laid his hand over his heart.

"My lord MacQuinn . . . I fear to tell you . . ."

"Where is my daughter, Thorn?" Jourdain repeated.

Thorn held his hands out, palms upward, empty, and shook his head.

Jourdain nodded, but his jaw was clenched. I stood next to Luc and watched as Jourdain took hold of the nearest table, over-turning it. The pewter, the plates of food, the drinks all cascaded to the floor, spilling and clattering and breaking.

"I sent her here so she would be safe!" he shouted. "And you let Declan Lannon take her!" He overturned another table, and my reticence finally broke, to see Jourdain come unraveled, to see the agony on his people's faces.

I reached out and took Jourdain's arm, guiding him through the crowd up to the dais.

"Bring some wine and bread," I ordered the chamberlain,

who looked petrified as he scampered toward the kitchens. I then forced Jourdain down into his chair; he laid his head upon the table, his resolve gone as the shock settled in.

Luc sat beside his father, ashen, but he reached out to touch Jourdain's shoulder.

Isolde stepped into the hall at last. The silence returned as the MacQuinns looked upon her, drenched and storm battered. But she walked into the hall with grace, eventually coming to the dais steps.

She turned to look upon the men and women, and I wondered how she would address them, if she would ignite into fire as Jourdain had or if she would harden into ice, as I was.

"How long has Brienna MacQuinn been missing?" Isolde asked, and her voice was gentle, to coax out answers.

"She has been missing since this morning," one woman responded. She had a streak of gray in her hair and a hardness in her face, as if she had seen far too much. And her arm was wrapped around the weeping girl.

This morning.

We had been so close, then.

"So she was taken in the night?" Isolde asked. "Who was the one to last see her?"

The people began to murmur, their voices low and urgent.

"Perhaps her chambermaid? Who tended to her last night?" Isolde persisted.

Again, there was silence. I found my fingers were curling into my palms.

"Lady, I sent her to her bedchamber."

All of us looked to where an old woman stood off to the side of the crowd. There was blood on her apron, a gleam of remorse in her eyes.

Jourdain finally lifted his head to squint at the woman. "Isla?"

"My lord MacQuinn," Isla said, her voice hoarse. "Your daughter helped me tend to your thane yesterday. She pulled an arrow from his rib."

"Which thane?" Jourdain asked, trying to rise. I laid a heavy hand on his shoulder, keeping him down. That sour-faced chamberlain finally returned with the wine, and I poured a glass for Jourdain, wrapping his fingers around the stem of the goblet.

"Liam, milord. There was a hunting accident. . . ."

The story began to unfold. Jourdain did not drink his wine until I prodded him, and only when the color had returned to the lord's face did I let him up and our small party followed Isla to a bedchamber, where Liam was laboring to breathe, unconscious, his wounds draped in linen.

"Can you heal him, Isolde?" Jourdain asked.

The queen gently removed the linens, to assess Liam's wounds. "Yes. But it looks as if he has fever and infection. My magic will need to put him in a deep sleep for a few days, to purge it from his blood."

A few days? We didn't even have hours, I thought. I could tell Jourdain was thinking the very same, but he held back the words.

"Please, Lady. Heal him."

Isolde rolled up her sleeves and asked for Isla's assistance. While the women began to heal Liam, the rest of us proceeded to look upon the two men who had been killed in the accident. They were still being prepared for the burial, their wounds horrifyingly gruesome.

Luc swore, covering his nose and glancing away, but I stared at them, recognizing them. They were the two men-at-arms who had accompanied Brienna home. Along with Liam.

"I want to see her room," I said abruptly to Thorn, who startled at the harshness of my voice.

Jourdain nodded, and we followed the chamberlain up the stairs to Brienna's chamber.

The first thing I noticed was her bed. It was rumpled, as if she had been woken in the dead of night. And then I noticed the dog hair. She must have slept with her wolfhound. And that ice in my heart began to thaw, beating wildly as I continued to look upon her things, as I imagined her lying in the darkness with nothing more than a dog to protect her.

"Where is her dog?" I asked, glancing to Thorn.

"I'm afraid the dog is unaccounted for, milord. Although the hound tends to wander from time to time."

I had a terrible suspicion Brienna's hound might be dead.

"Did he come in through the window?" Sean asked.

Luc walked to one of the three windows, looking through the panes to the distant ground below. The storm light made him appear years older, drawn and worn. "That's highly unlikely. There's no way of climbing out safely from these windows."

I continued to walk around her room, feeling Jourdain's eyes follow me.

Brienna, Brienna, please . . . show me a sign. My heart ached. *Tell me how to find you.*

I approached her wardrobe, opening the doors. I could smell the essence of her, lavender and vanilla and meadow sunlight. My hands trembled as I looked through her clothes. . . .

"Her passion cloak is not here," I finally rasped. "That means she left her room with someone she knew. Someone she trusted." I turned to look upon the men. "She was betrayed, MacQuinn."

Jourdain blanched as he sat on the edge of Brienna's bed.

Sean was still studying the impossibility of the windows, and Luc continued to stand blankly in the center of the room. And there was Thorn, wringing his hands as he listened.

I ushered the chamberlain out of the room, rudely shutting the door in his face. Then I turned back around to the inner circle, the only people I trusted. And yes, that strangely included Sean now.

"Someone here is faithful to Lannon?" Luc whispered.

Jourdain was silent. I could tell he didn't know, nor did he want to toss out names.

"The healer?" Sean suggested.

"No," Jourdain was swift to deny. "Not Isla. She has suffered greatly beneath the hands of the Lannons."

"Then who, MacQuinn?" I pressed softly.

"Wait a moment," Sean said. "We continue to think of Declan coming *here*, of Brienna being betrayed directly into Declan's hands. But Declan is a fugitive right now. He has to be in hiding."

He was right. All of us had been thinking in one direction.

"Come," Jourdain said, motioning for us to follow. "Let's go to my office."

We followed him down the corridor, where he requested a fire to be sparked in the hearth and refreshments brought in to be set along the table. As soon as the servants departed, Jourdain ripped the map of Maevana down from the wall, to spread it out before us.

"Let's begin to think of where Declan would be hiding," he said, setting river stones on the four corners of the map.

The four of us gathered, beholding it. My eyes went to Mac-Quinn's territory first. His lands touched six others: the mountains of Kavanaghs, the meadows of Morgane, the valleys and hills of Allenach, the forests of Lannon, the orchards of Halloran, and the rivers of Burke.

"The first to come under suspicion," Jourdain said, pointing. "Lannon. Carran. Halloran. Allenach."

Sean was about to say something when Isolde finally joined us, her face noticeably pale and drawn, like she was in pain. I wondered if her magic weakened her, because she looked like her head was aching.

"I have healed Liam's wounds, but like I said earlier, he will most likely sleep for several more days because of the fever," she said, rubbing her temple as she looked to the map.

Jourdain filled her in on our suspicions of a traitorous Mac-Quinn, and her brow lowered, angry.

"We should obviously suspect the Lannon House," Isolde said, looking to the Lannon territory. "Declan could be hiding anywhere within his own borders. And it is not a far ride from here, MacQuinn."

"That feels too apparent," Luc protested. "What about the

Allenachs? No offense, Sean. But your manservant was a faithful half-moon."

Sean gravely nodded. "Yes. We are right to suspect my people."

"Do we suspect Burke?" Luc dared to ask.

I thought of Lord Burke, who had been ordered to stay behind with the queen's father, to guard the remaining Lannons and maintain order. How he had sheltered my people the best that he could the past twenty-five years, how he had risen to fight alongside us weeks ago.

"Lord Burke has fought and bled beside us," Jourdain murmured, and I was relieved that he felt the same as me. "He has also publicly sworn fealty to Isolde. I do not feel as if he would betray us."

That left the Hallorans.

I traced their territory with my gaze. "How far is it to Castle Lerah from here, MacQuinn?"

"A half day's ride," Jourdain answered. "You don't think . . ."

"It's a very good possibility," I said, reading the slant of Jourdain's thoughts.

We were interrupted by a knock on the door. Jourdain crossed the chamber to answer it, and I watched as Thorn placed a package into the lord's hands.

"This was just found in the stables, my lord, by one of the grooms."

Jourdain took the package, shut the door in Thorn's face, and wandered back to the table, ripping the paper open.

A brief letter fluttered loose first. It rested on the table, over the map.

I read the message, felt it strike my heart.

Brienna MacQuinn in exchange for the Stone of Eventide, delivered by Isolde Kavanagh alone, seven days from now, sundown, where the Mairenna Forest meets the Valley of Bones.

Declan's ultimatum. It had finally arrived.

But I didn't believe the words until I saw what was nestled within the package. Jourdain took it within his hands and lifted it to the light, and I finally let the shock devour me; I finally let my composure shatter.

"No," I whispered. I dropped to my knees, spilling the wine from my hands. It spread like blood along the floor.

I had chosen that shade of blue, chosen those stars for her.

And I knew in that moment the terrible danger she was in, that Declan Lannon would torture her regardless if we agreed to the exchange, all because I loved her. That he would break her little by little, just as he had done to my sister, all because of me.

I closed my eyes to the light, to the sight of Brienna's passion cloak in Jourdain's trembling hands.

⤛ TWENTY-FIVE ⤜

TO THWART AND TO HOPE

Brienna

I woke slowly. My head was splitting, and my mouth was painfully dry. I longed for water, for warmth.

I heard the slither of chains, cold and metallic, and then realized they were moving in response to me, that there was a weight about my wrists when I shifted them across my chest.

My eyes opened to shadows and weak light, to dark stone walls splattered with old blood.

Someone was breathing, heavily, close to me.

And I was lying down on something that felt narrow and sparse. A prison cot.

"At last, Brienna Allenach. You finally wake."

I knew it was Declan's voice, for it was deep and raspy. He

sounded amused, and I struggled to swallow, struggled to calm my heart as I turned my head to see him sitting on a stool next to my cot, smiling down at me.

His tawny hair was carelessly knotted back. His beard was thick across his face, and there were scabs on his fingers, a cut on his brow. He smelled of sweat and he looked haggard, half-wild.

I jerked upright, my chains dragging along the stone. I was shackled by both wrists, by both ankles. And then I realized that I was bound to the iron posters of the cot.

I didn't say anything, because I didn't want to sound afraid before him. So I edged as far as I could from him on my little bed, my eyes sharpening over his, my chains pulling along with me like the tendrils of a plant.

"My mentee gave you too strong a dose," Declan explained, stretching his burly arms. "I've been sitting here for hours, waiting for you to wake up."

Mentee? Pierce Halloran was Declan Lannon's mentee?

My skin crawled, to know I had been lying here unconscious with him watching me.

He read my thoughts, cut a smile at me. "Ah, yes. Don't worry. I haven't touched you."

"What do you want with me?" My voice was hoarse, weak.

Declan reached for a cup of water on a table beside my cot, extending it to me. I didn't accept it, and after a while he shrugged and drank it himself, the water running down his beard in veins.

"What do you think I want with you, Brienna *MacQuinn*?"

"Am I Allenach or MacQuinn to you?" I asked.

"You are both. Allenach by blood, but MacQuinn by choice. I confess, your decision is intriguing to me. Because no matter how far you run, you cannot escape from your blood, lass. In fact, I would be kinder to you if you embraced your true father's House. The Allenachs and the Lannons have a good history together."

"What do you want with me?" I repeated, impatient.

Declan set the empty cup aside and rubbed his large hands together. "Long ago, my father set out to punish the three Houses who tried to overthrow him. You know the story, of course, how the Kavanaghs and the Morganes and the MacQuinns tried to rise and failed. Despite their failure in the coup, three noble children escaped with their cowardly fathers . . . Isolde. Lucas. Aodhan. Three children who should have been killed."

I kept my jaw locked, forcing myself to listen to him. I clenched my hands into fists, willing myself to remain calm.

"Isolde would have been impossible to capture now with her constant guard. As would be Aodhan, after I realized how clever and angry he was. But Lucas? He would be easy to take. And I knew if I could take one of the three surviving children into my possession, I could barter for whatever I wanted."

He was still smiling, savoring the sight of me disheveled in chains.

"Do you know what I desire, Brienna?"

I waited, not willing to play his game.

"I want the very thing you once found, the very thing you uncovered," Declan said. "I want Isolde Kavanagh to surrender the Stone of Eventide to me. Is that too hard for you to believe?"

It was. I suddenly couldn't breathe.

"You see, Brienna, magic in this land eventually always descends into corruption," he continued. "Anyone who has studied the history of Maevana knows this. Magic grants the Kavanaghs a terrible advantage. It was a glorious day when the stone went missing, when the last queen was slain in battle back in 1430. It was a noble era for us, because it suddenly meant that we were no longer ruled by an unstable, tainted queen. That anyone could rise to take the throne, magic or no, queen or no."

He quieted, staring at me. I was trembling, trying to sort my response, to make sense of this.

"I must tell you," he went on, and I wanted to block out his voice. I wanted to cover my ears and shut my eyes, for his words began to sink into me like little hooks. "I was quite impressed by how you and your ragtag rebel group rallied and fought weeks ago. I am still quite impressed by you, for finding the stone, for fooling your own father so you could dig it up on his lands. My son can't cease speaking of it to his sister, the story as to how you found the Eventide, how it would burn someone like you or me should we touch it so you kept it tucked away in your dress pocket, the way it radiates around Isolde Kavanagh's neck."

I closed my eyes, unable to look at him a moment longer.

He chuckled. "And so I thought, Lucas is not the one for this exchange. It is Brienna. The lass who uncovered a stone, the lass who brought magic and a queen back to the land."

"What can the stone do for you, Declan?" I was relieved that my voice was steady, that I sounded calm. I opened my eyes to stare at him.

"Isn't it obvious, Brienna?" he countered. "Isolde Kavanagh loses her allure and her power without it. She and her father will become weak. But perhaps more than that . . . I will have the people behind me. Because your rebel group is too proud to see it, but the people are afraid of magic. They do not want it ruling us. And so I will be the one to quell their fears, to give them what they truly want."

"And what is that?"

"A king who listens to the people. A king who does not have an unfair advantage. A king who is one of them, who has a vision. And my vision is that of a new kingdom, a new Maevana where there is no magic and no Houses. There is simply one, one House, one ruling family, and one people."

Oh, there were so many things I wanted to say to that. I wanted to tell him that the only Maevans that feared Isolde were the half-moons, the Maevans who had been in bed with Declan's family for years. That magic had not corrupted this land; his family had. And that the only Maevans who would want him on the throne were those with darkened hearts and minds, who craved the sort of evil pleasures Declan was known for. But perhaps more than all of these angry thoughts was the one in retaliation to his vision of one House, one family. I knew exactly how he planned to execute such a vision, and that was to kill everyone who opposed him, to wipe out Houses just as Gilroy had done to the Kavanaghs.

I wanted to shout and rage at him, but I swallowed it all,

knowing that if I angered him, he would harm me. And I needed all my strength and all my wits to outmaneuver him.

Declan rose, his height intimidating, filling my small cell like a mountain. "I want Isolde Kavanagh to give me the stone in exchange for you. She is to come alone, to kneel before me and surrender it. And I know that she'll do it. It's just a stone, and your life is of more import to them than it. I know MacQuinn cares for you, as if you were his own flesh and blood. But it won't be MacQuinn who will press for your freedom. It will be Aodhan Morgane, the proud lord of the Swift, who thinks he knows everything. Because you have his heart in your hands. Because he has lost his mother and his sister, and so he will determine not to lose you."

I knew in that moment that Isolde would never agree to this exchange, no matter what Cartier wanted. There was no possible way that she would hand the stone over for me. She was not to negotiate with Declan Lannon. And I wouldn't want her to.

I drew in a long, slow breath. And I refused to speak, to reveal to him what I thought. Because I needed to give Isolde and Cartier as much time as possible to recover me, in their own efforts. Before Declan realized his plan was futile, and he had no other choice but to kill me.

"As long as they adhere to my desires, I won't hurt you," he promised. "But the moment they start trying to thwart me . . . let's just say you won't be leaving this cell the same way you entered it."

I couldn't hide my trembling as he left, clanging a door of iron bars behind him. I crawled to the foot of my cot and retched until

I was empty and my ears were ringing. My eyes were blurring as I lay facedown, struggling to remain calm.

My greatest challenge was trying to find a way to covertly send a message to Jourdain and Cartier, to reveal where I was. By now, they probably knew Declan had escaped Lyonesse and I was missing. But I wasn't even certain of my location. I believed I was being held in Castle Lerah's keep, in the Hallorans' clutches, but I wasn't certain.

I thought until I was weary, and I realized this was hopeless. And so I reflected on my fondest memories, the ones that had bloomed from my time at Magnalia House. I thought of Merei, of her music, of how she and I used to play cheques and marques and how she always beat me at the game. I remembered the summer solstice, when she and I had stood in our rooms, uncertain yet thrilled with how the night might unfold, that we were students becoming mistresses. I thought of all those afternoons I had sat with Cartier in the library, when he had seemed so cold and aloof and stern, and how I had finally challenged him to stand on a chair with a book on his head. I remembered the first time I had heard him laugh, how it had taken the room like sunlight.

I must have dozed off, but was awakened by sounds echoing below me. Voices, horses, clanging of iron.

I lifted my head to hear better, and I realized I was not in a dungeon, as I had once believed.

I was in a tower.

Something skittered over the floor of my cell. I thought it was a rat, until it came again, and I realized it was a pebble. And then came a small, beloved whisper.

"Mistress Brienna."

I sat up further, my heart in my throat when I saw Ewan on the other side of the bars.

"Ewan?" I rasped, climbing off my cot. The chains would only go so far, catching me in the center of the cell, even though I reached for him as he reached for me. The air between us was tender, our fingers just shy of touching.

"Ewan, are you all right?" I wept, unable to hold the emotion back.

"I'm all right," he said through his tears, scrubbing his face with his hand. "I'm so sorry, Mistress. I hate my father."

"Shh." I tried to calm him, to focus him. "Listen, Ewan. Can you tell me where we are?"

"Castle Lerah."

The Hallorans' holding.

"Keela is worried about you," Ewan whispered. "She wants to help set you free, like you tried to do for her. We think we can get the key from the guard tomorrow night."

There was the echo of voices below us again.

"I have to go," he said, and the tears began to pool in his eyes again.

"Whatever you and Keela do," I whispered, "you must be careful, Ewan. Please do not get caught."

"Don't worry about me, Mistress Brienna." He reached into his pocket to pull out an apple, rolling it on the floor toward me.

I bent down, my chains clanging as I caught the bright red fruit.

"I will set you free," Ewan promised, laying his hand over his heart. He smiled, revealing a missing tooth, and then he was gone.

I sat on my cot and held the apple to my nose, breathing in its promise.

And I dared to hope, despite the cold darkness and the chains and the rats that squeaked in the corner of my prison. Because Declan Lannon's children were going to defy him to set me free.

⇥ TWENTY-SIX ↤

HIDDEN THREADS

Lord MacQuinn's Territory, Castle Fionn

Cartier

Seven days.

We had seven days to find where Declan was holding Brienna. Because we were not going to hand over the Stone of Eventide.

I sat with Isolde's inner circle, and we argued deep into the night: to exchange the stone or not. But we eventually came to the same consensus: Declan could not be trusted. There was a great chance of him deceiving us, of taking the stone and slaying Isolde and Brienna regardless of what we chose. The location he had requested—where the Mairenna Forest met the Valley of Bones— was on Allenach territory, and I had no doubt that Declan would stand in the protection of the tree line, where he could tuck away a formidable force behind him.

We had determined not to negotiate with him from the beginning of our rising, and so we wouldn't now. Furthermore, to relinquish the stone to him was taking a huge step of defeat, one that would inevitably spell our own destruction.

Even so . . . I wanted to exchange the stone for Brienna. I wanted it so ardently that I had to sit with my mouth shut most of the night.

Eventually, we were too exhausted to plan any further.

Jourdain had arranged guest chambers for us, but no one stopped me from returning to Brienna's room. I removed my boots and my cloak, left them as a trail along her floor, and crawled into her cold blankets, pressing my body in the place where hers had been, breathing in the memory of her.

How do I find you?

I prayed this, over and over, until there was nothing but bones and dull heartache within me, and I drifted into dreams.

I saw her standing with my mother, with my sister in the meadows of Castle Brígh. There were flowers in her hair, laughter in her voice, the sun so bright behind her that I struggled to discern her face. But I knew it was Brienna, walking with Líle and Ashling Morgane. I knew it was her because I had memorized the way she walked, the way she moved.

"Do not give up hope, Cartier," she whispered to me, suddenly standing at my back, her arms coming around me. "Do not weep for me."

"Brienna." When I turned to embrace her, she became sunlight and dust, and I was left desperately trying to catch the wind, catch her shadow on the ground. *"Brienna."*

I spoke her name aloud, waking myself with a start.

It was still dark. And I could not lie here a moment longer and dwell on the dream that told me Brienna was closer to my mother and my sister than to me.

I rose and restlessly began to walk the castle corridors. It was quiet, and I eventually meandered to the dimly lit hall. The mess Jourdain had made had been cleaned up, the tables righted, the floors swept. I lingered by the hearth embers, to soak in the warmth, until I remembered Thane Liam.

We needed that man to fully recover, to awaken and tell us what he had seen.

I began to walk to Liam's recovery room, hiding in a shadow when I saw Thorn coming from the opposite end of the hall, a candle lighting his gruff face. I watched the chamberlain enter Liam's room, soundlessly closing the door behind him.

So the two of us shared the same thought.

I approached the door, my breath suspended as I set my ear to the wood.

There was a scuffle, a man's hissing.

I threw open the door to find the chamberlain had a pillow pressed to Liam's face, and the thane's feet were twitching as he almost succumbed to the suffocation.

"Thorn! What are you doing?" I cried, walking toward him.

Thorn jumped, his eyes bulging as he looked at me. He quickly drew a dirk and lunged for me, nearly catching me by surprise.

I reflexively blocked his cut with my forearm, shoving Thorn across the room. I watched him fly, crash into the side table, over-turning the healer's supplies. Jars of herbs shattered on the floor as Thorn scrambled, dirk still glittering in his fingers. He bared his crooked teeth at me, and I was amazed to see the man transform from a crotchety old chamberlain into a formidable opponent. I took his wrist in my grip, twisting his arm around until he let out a yelp of pain, his fingers helplessly dropping the blade. I took him all the way to the floor, straddling him.

"I don't know anything," he dared to sputter.

I tore his sleeve, exposing the half-moon mark. He shuddered with shock, that I had known to look for it, and he froze.

"Where is she?" I asked.

"I . . . I don't know."

"That is not the answer I am looking for." I proceeded to break his wrist.

He emitted a shout that was sure to wake the castle. And all I could think of was how I had just broken the brittle bones beneath this half-moon, how I would keep doing it until he told me where Brienna was.

"Where. Is. She?"

"I don't know where he took her!" he wailed, floundering. "Please, Lord Aodhan. I . . . I truly do not know!"

"*Who* took her?" I hissed. And when he sputtered, unable to form words, I bent back his broken wrist.

He screamed again, and this time I could hear calls in the corridor. Jourdain's voice, drawing near. He would stop me. He would drag me off the chamberlain. And so I reached for

Thorn's other wrist, preparing to break it next.

"*Who*. Took. Her?"

"The Red Horn!" Thorn cried. "The Red Horn took her. That's all . . . that's all I can tell you."

I felt the candlelight brighten the room, heard Jourdain's curse of surprise, felt the floor tremble as he approached me.

Thorn was weeping, "Lord MacQuinn! Lord MacQuinn!" as if I had attacked him, disgusting coward that he was.

"Aodhan! Aodhan, by the gods!" Jourdain declared, trying to pull me off the chamberlain.

But my mind was racing. The Red Horn. Who was the Red Horn?

"Who is the Red Horn, Thorn?" I pressed.

Jourdain's grip on my shoulder tightened. He blinked down at Thorn as if seeing him in a new light.

Luc came rushing into the room, Isolde on his heels. They gathered around me, regarding me with wide eyes until I turned Thorn's broken wrist upward to expose the half-moon.

"I just found our rat."

Jourdain stared at Thorn for a moment, a range of emotion crossing his face. Then he said in an even voice, "Bind him to a chair."

We stood around him, trying to coax out answers. I thought the old man would relent, especially when Jourdain offered him his life. But Thorn was stubborn. He had exposed that the Red Horn was involved, but that was as far as his revelations would go. The only way to get him to talk would be to continue beating him, and Jourdain would have none of that.

"I want you to assist Luc and Sean with solving the riddle of the Red Horn," he murmured to me. "They're in the office trying to hash it out."

I was quiet for a moment. Jourdain continued to look at me with worry in his eyes.

"I could get the answer out of him," I said. "If you would let me."

"I will not have you become that, Aodhan."

My irritation flared as I said, "Brienna's life depends on this, MacQuinn."

"Don't presume to tell me what my daughter's life depends on," Jourdain growled, his composure finally slipping. "Don't act as if you are the only one who is agonizing over her."

We were beginning to turn on each other, I thought as I watched Jourdain sneer at me. We were exhausted, devastated, clueless. We should give over the stone. We should not give over the stone. We should compromise with Thorn. We should beat Thorn. We should pull up everyone's sleeves. We should not invade others' privacy.

What was right, and what was wrong?

How were we to recover Brienna if we were too afraid to get our hands dirty?

I left Jourdain in the corridor, striding to the office, where Luc and Sean were sprawled over the map, half-eaten pastries on their breakfast plates, speaking what sounded like nonsense to me.

"Tell me all the reds," Luc said, dipping a quill in ink, preparing to write.

"Burke has red," Sean began, studying the map. "MacFinley

has red. Dermott, Kavanagh, and . . . the Fitzsimmons."

"What on earth are you speaking of?" I asked, and they paused to glance at me.

"Which Houses boast the color red," Luc replied.

I walked to the table to sit with them. "I think House colors are far too obvious."

"Then what do you presume?" Luc snapped.

"You are on the right path, Lucas," I said calmly. "The color red has significance. But it will be significant only to whatever House the Red Horn belongs to."

Luc tossed down the quill. "Then why are we doing this? We are wasting our time!"

Sean was silent, reaching for a stack of notes they had been compiling. I glanced over to read it, notes about horns, drawings of horns, the different meaning behind notes blown on the horns. Trumpets and bugles and sackbuts. All instruments. Which, of course Luc would hear the word horn and think instrument, since he was a musician.

But that is not what I envisioned.

I was about to share my thoughts when I heard a clatter in the courtyard, just beyond the office windows. Standing, I walked to peer beyond the panes.

"By the gods," I whispered, my breath fogging the glass.

"What is it, Aodhan?" Luc asked, forgetting his anger at me.

I turned to meet his gaze. "It's Grainne Dermott."

None of us knew what to expect when Grainne Dermott requested to speak with the queen and her inner circle in Jourdain's office.

She had obviously ridden here in a hurry, and she took no time to change out of her mud-splattered riding leathers before coming to meet us.

"Lady Grainne," Isolde greeted, unable to hide her surprise. "I trust all is well with you."

"Lady Isolde," Grainne said, sounding ragged. "Things are as they should be in Lyonesse, and I say such to ease your mind. Your father is well, and continues to hold the castle and the remaining Lannons in the keep. I have come because I heard troubling news."

"What have you heard?" Isolde asked.

"That Brienna MacQuinn has been taken captive."

Jourdain shifted. "Where did you hear such a thing, Lady Grainne?"

Grainne looked to Jourdain. "The royal city is teeming with constant rumors, Lord MacQuinn. I did not have to wander far in the streets and in the taverns to hear this."

We were silent, and I wondered if Isolde was going to hide the truth.

"The rumors appear to be true," Grainne said. "For Brienna MacQuinn is not among you."

"That does not mean my sister has been taken captive," Luc said, but hushed when Jourdain raised his hand.

"It is true, Lady Grainne. My daughter was taken in the night. She is not among us, nor do we know where she currently is being held."

Grainne was silent for a beat, and then her voice dropped. "I am sincerely sorry to hear this. I desired that it was not so." She sighed, rushing her fingers through the curls of her hair. "Have you stumbled across any leads?"

From the corner of my eye, I saw Jourdain regard Isolde. He was wondering if the queen was going to bring Grainne into the inner circle, and I already knew the answer before Isolde spoke.

"Come and sit with us, Grainne," Isolde said, indicating the chairs gathered about the table.

As Jourdain served everyone tea, she began to tell Grainne the chain of events that had occurred, bringing us to this moment. Grainne leaned forward as she listened, her elbows on the table, her fingertips absently tracing the rim of her cup.

"The Red Horn," she said, and then snorted. "Gods above. It has to be him."

"Who?" Jourdain demanded.

"Pierce Halloran," Grainne answered.

His name struck me like an arrow. And the more I contemplated it, the stronger I felt about it.

"Pierce Halloran?" Luc blurted. "That whelp?"

"He's not a whelp," Grainne corrected. "For the past few years, he has organized raids to terrorize my people. Brienna told me about how he tried to ally with the MacQuinns, and how she ended up mortifying him. That makes her a target; he will do whatever he can to demoralize her. But also, Pierce Halloran is a half-moon."

We merely gaped at her.

"Brienna did not tell you?" she asked, glancing to me. "She

told me on the ride to Lyonesse that she saw a half-moon tattoo on Pierce's wrist. And that is how the conversation began between us, why I told her what the symbol meant. Because I did not want her to be ignorant of what Pierce is capable of."

Brienna had not told us Pierce was marked. And whether that was an oversight or she was trying to deal with Pierce's threat on her own, I could not be sure.

"Why Red Horn, though?" Sean asked, frowning. "How did he acquire that name?"

Grainne smiled. "You know what the Hallorans' sigil is?"

"The ibex . . . ," Luc said, his voice trailing off as he realized, as we all finally realized, that the horn corresponded to the ram. "This whole time I thought it was a sackbut!"

She gave us a moment to draw it together, these pieces she had just given us. She waited until Isolde met her gaze and then said, "Lady Isolde. The House of Dermott will publicly support and ally with you. I will also bring the MacCareys into the alliance, which means the other two Mac Houses will be strongly influenced to join you. We will swear fealty to you as our queen. But all I ask is that you allow me to lead the assault on Castle Lerah."

Isolde looked ill. I hardly recognized her voice when she said, "To lead an assault on another House . . . I need to be absolutely certain—I must not have any doubts—that they are guilty."

"Can't you see, Lady?" Grainne fervently whispered. "They *are* guilty. They have been guilty for *years*, and they are plotting to overthrow you! They are holding Brienna MacQuinn captive, and most likely are harboring Declan."

Isolde began to pace. There was a strange current between the two women; it felt like the moment before a storm, hot and cold all at once, gathering into wind.

The queen finally stopped before the hearth and said, "Everyone, leave us. Please."

We all started filing out, but then Isolde added, "Aodhan, stay with us."

I halted just before the threshold. Luc gave me a nervous glance, and then closed the door.

I turned, remaining near the wall, and watched as the queen and Grainne stared at each other.

"If I let you lead the assault, Grainne . . . ," Isolde began, but she did not finish.

"I swear to you, Isolde. It would not come to that. It would only be by my sword."

I was utterly confounded by this conversation. And I had no idea why Isolde had asked for me to remain. It honestly seemed like the queen had forgotten my existence until she glanced to me, beckoning me closer.

The queen looked to Grainne, who said nothing, but I sensed they were speaking mind to mind. It raised the hair on my arms.

"Aodhan, Grainne is like me," Isolde said. "She has magic."

I looked to Grainne, and she pressed her lips together, as if she was hiding a smile. "He already knows. He sensed it when he hosted Rowan and me at Castle Brígh."

"Not much escapes him." Isolde sighed.

"I am still standing here," I reminded them, to break the

tension. "Although, I am unsure as to why you asked me to remain for this conversation."

The queen sat in her chair, crossing her legs. "Because I want your advice. About the assault." She took up her teacup, but she didn't drink. She merely stared into it, as if her answers might rise to the surface. "Grainne harbors magic of the mind. She can speak without words, thought to thought."

She is worried that my magic will go astray in the assault.

I startled when Grainne's voice entered my thoughts, as clearly as if she had spoken the words aloud. I stared at her, perspiration beginning to bead on my brow.

"Magic goes corrupt in battle," Isolde said. "We know this from our history, from the last queen who waged war by it and nearly sundered the world. And I'm concerned that it would get out of our control if we march on Castle Lerah bearing it."

"Lady," Grainne said, trying her best to sound patient. "I would take the fortress by sword and shield. Not by magic. I do not even know how to wield magic in battle. As we spoke before, we do not have the spells. What can go astray with it?"

Isolde was silent, but I could read her fears, her worries. It was right for her to feel so; I couldn't deny that I felt it as well. There was too much we still did not know about magic.

But if Brienna was truly at Castle Lerah, I would not hesitate to take up steel and armor and follow Grainne there.

"I find it so ironic," the queen whispered. "I nearly cannot believe this, that Declan wants to exchange Brienna for the stone. I asked Brienna weeks ago to hold me accountable, to take away the stone should I descend into darkness with it. And now she has been taken from us, and I must decide what to do with this stone."

Grainne and I were quiet, uncertain what to say.

"Do you want to give the stone to another to wear while we undergo the assault?" I asked. "I could bear it for you, just as Brienna did, within the wooden locket. Magic would go dormant for a while, until the conflict is over."

"Yes, I think that would be wise. But we still are not certain that the Hallorans are guilty," Isolde continued. "As much as I dislike them, I cannot lead an assault without proof. I cannot do it."

Aodhan, Grainne said to me. *Aodhan, reassure her. Or else we may never get this proof.*

I could not lift my eyes to Grainne, for fear that she and I would unite in our bloodlust.

The queen wearily sighed. "We need to wait for Liam to wake. Once he wakes from the healing, he can give us the confirmation we need."

Liam wasn't going to wake for several more days. And we were going to waste time.

But I consumed these words, let them sink as rocks into my stomach, taking my hope with them.

The next two days passed miserably. Thane Liam still slept, and even though his color and breathing improved with every dawn, we grew restless, resorting to pace the castle and study the map and conduct interviews among the MacQuinns, hoping someone had seen something that could give Isolde the confirmation she craved.

Our proof finally came late in the afternoon.

I was sitting with Thorn, trying to persuade him to speak, when Isolde appeared on the threshold.

"Aodhan."

I turned to look at her. When she remained silent, I stood, joining her in the corridor.

"Thane Liam has woken," she whispered. "It is as Grainne suspected. Pierce Halloran and four of his men are at fault."

"Then we have justification," I said.

The queen nodded, her eyes dark as obsidian. "Let us plan the assault."

We quickly summoned the others, gathering about Jourdain's table with vigor, with bowls of stew and a bottle of wine, and we began to plot our next steps.

Sean drew a diagram of Castle Lerah for us to study. He had been to the castle multiple times before with his father and had studied its design as a lad, because it was, unfortunately, one of the greatest and oldest holdings in all of Maevana.

I watched as he drew the four towers, the gatehouse, the middle ward, which was a strip of grass between the inner and the outer walls, and the moat that would be our greatest challenge. He then proceeded to label the towers—the southern one was the prison, where Brienna would be, the eastern was the armorer tower, and the northern and western towers were the family and guest chambers, where Declan and the children were most likely located.

"There are two gates that I know of," Sean explained. "The

outer gate and the north postern. I've only ever entered the fortress through the outer gate via the drawbridge. If we came from this direction, we would ride through the middle ward, past the gate-house, into the courtyard. Here there's a garden, the stables, the chapel, the bakery, and so forth. The great hall is here."

"What else can you tell us about the prison tower?" I asked, staring at its crooked rendition on the parchment. "How are we to get Brienna out?"

Sean sighed, staring at it. "If Brienna is in the prison tower . . . well, I think if you could get beyond the first string of guards, you could make it to the parapet wall. After recovering her, you could either descend the stairwell into the inner ward, which will be teeming with people, or you could scale down the wall into the middle ward and perhaps sneak your way to the north postern, or even to the armorer tower."

"Why the armorer tower?" Isolde asked.

"Because there is a string of forges here," Sean answered, drawing an inky line on his map. "They call it forge row. And forges need water, don't they? I could almost guarantee that there will be a door in the outer wall to reach the moat, so lazy appren-tice blacksmiths can draw water from there instead of coming all the way into the inner ward, to where the well is."

We were silent, mulling on his wisdom, when Sean suddenly laughed, raking his fingers through his hair, leaving a trail of ink on his temple.

"By the gods. Of course." He crossed his arms, nodding at his castle drawing. "Castle Lerah is built of red stone. The *Red* Horn."

Our planning then shifted to the most paramount of challenges: getting beyond the moat.

"We need a way to lower the drawbridge," Luc said.

"The weavers." Jourdain's sudden response drew our attention. "Every month, my weavers deliver wool and linen to Castle Lerah."

"Have they already delivered this month?" Isolde asked. "Would they be willing to drive the delivery wagon so we can smuggle ourselves in?"

"I'm not certain. Let me ask Betha." Jourdain swiftly left, and while he was gone, we continued to pore over the map and finish our dinner, refraining from planning any further until he returned.

He was back ten minutes later. "Betha has agreed to the delivery. She says she can smuggle four of us in the wagon bed."

"Which of us will go, then?" Luc asked.

"I think it should be Aodhan, Lucas, Sean, and me in the back of the wagon," the queen said. "Sean and Lucas will be responsible for the drawbridge. Aodhan will recover Declan, and I will recover Brienna. Grainne, you and your forces will be waiting here"—she pointed to a small forest on the map—"in the cover of these woods, where you have a direct view of the drawbridge. Jourdain will be waiting here with his thirty men- and women-at-arms"—she pointed to the orchards, to the northern demesne of the castle—"with a wagon to transport Brienna and the two Lannon children back to Fionn immediately."

I found her allocation strange, that she would go in to recover

Brienna while I was appointed Declan. I thought it would be the other way around, and I wondered if she was ordaining this moment for me, if she was granting me permission to slay Declan Lannon.

Her gaze met mine, but in that brief moment, our thoughts aligned. She was indeed giving me the chance to fulfill my vengeance. And perhaps there was something else, something to do with Brienna. If Brienna had been tortured, would I be able to get her out safely, or would I fall to pieces at the sight?

I was not certain; I honestly could not even entertain this thought.

"Lord MacQuinn," the queen continued, shifting her gaze to Jourdain. "I ask that you guard the Stone of Eventide for me during this assault, to wear it in the locket that Brienna once employed, and to hand it back over to me after the violence has ended."

She had already discussed this with Jourdain. I could tell because he did not appear the slightest bit surprised. He laid his hand over his heart in submission.

"Lady Grainne," Isolde said, now directing her orders to the woman at my side. "I am giving you this opportunity to take Castle Lerah, because I know your people have suffered greatly at the hands of the Hallorans. All this being said, I ask only one thing of you. If you shed blood, it would only be that of those who have directly harmed you. That you would protect the Halloran women and children and men who are innocent in this matter, who are going to find themselves in a sudden battle."

Grainne's eyes gleamed in the firelight. She laid her hand

over her heart and said, "So I swear to you, Lady. If any fall by my sword, it will be Pierce Halloran and his half-moons. No other."

The queen nodded. "Lord MacQuinn, do you think your weavers could quickly supply us with Halloran garb? This could be something as simple as navy-and-gold shawls, as I think the mere colors will help us blend in once Aodhan and I slip into the castle."

"Yes, Lady," Jourdain said. "I—" The office door blew open, startling all of us.

It was a young woman. I recognized her as the one who had been weeping in the hall when we had first arrived to Fionn.

Her cheeks were flushed, her eyes reddened. There was fury and wonder in her gaze as she looked to Jourdain.

"Neeve?" Jourdain stood, perplexed. "What is it, lass?"

"My lord," Neeve whispered, approaching Jourdain. Parchment was in her hands, crumpled to her heart. "I want to be one of the weavers who goes to Castle Lerah."

"Neeve, I cannot allow you to go," he said. "It is too dangerous."

Neeve was quiet, and then she cast her eyes to me.

"I am not *asking* to go to Lerah," she said tremulously. "I am *telling* you. I am going to Lerah, and I will be the one to bring Brienna out of the tower."

I held her gaze for a beat, but then my eyes drifted down to the papers in her hands. I recognized Brienna's handwriting on them. Just the sight of that made everything slow around me, as if time had stalled.

"Why must you go, Neeve?" I murmured and stood, stepping away from the table so I could draw close to her. I tried to read Brienna's words, words that Neeve had smeared with her tears.

She began to weep.

I did not know what to do, how to comfort her. Jourdain appeared baffled, and Isolde rose to approach the girl. But before the queen could reach her, Neeve wiped her eyes and looked at me again, resolved.

"Lord Aodhan." Neeve slowly extended the papers to me, knowing that I craved to read the words. "Brienna is my sister."

TWENTY-SEVEN

BLADES AND STONES

Lady Halloran's Territory, Castle Lerah

Brienna

I spent four days in dark solitude.

The guards brought me a bowl of soup and a cup of water in the morning and in the evening, and that's how I knew it was four days that passed. I spent the rest of my time wondering if Ewan and Keela had been caught trying to steal the key, wondering where Jourdain, Cartier, Isolde, and Luc were.

I woke to the clanging of my doors, to Declan Lannon entering my cell.

I shuffled as far away from him as I could on my cot.

Declan was quiet, dragging his stool closer, to perch his large frame upon it. He was looking down at the floor, absently stroking his beard, and that's when I knew that he had learned there would be no exchange. That he was about to hurt me in retaliation.

"My sources tell me that Isolde Kavanagh is at Castle Fionn, and has made no arrangements to meet me in the valley three days from now," he finally said. He appeared feverish, his anger gleaming like stars in his eyes. "That means your queen and your father plan to thwart me, Brienna."

My heart began to pound. I couldn't swallow, or hear much beyond his voice. Fear resonated through me. "You can't be sure of that."

"Oh, but I am. I gave them seven days to meet in the Valley of Bones. They should have already begun the arrangement to travel there." He shifted his weight, the stool groaning beneath him. "I told you I wouldn't harm you if they complied. But they are trying to outmaneuver me. The problem is, lass, that they will never find you here. And that means I can take my time, sending them one of your fingers here, a toe there, maybe even your tongue later on down the road, to help them make up their minds."

I shuddered.

"But maybe . . . maybe carving out your tongue would be a mistake. Maybe if you answer my questions, I will let you keep it."

I desperately wondered if answering him would gain me time, or if he was simply toying with me. But if it would truly save my tongue . . . I gave him a slight nod.

"How did you find the stone, lass?" he inquired. He sounded so gentle and polite, nothing like the demented man that he was.

I replied honestly, "My ancestor."

Declan's brow arched. "Which one?"

"Tristan Allenach. I . . . I inherited his memories." My mouth was so dry I could scarcely speak.

"How? How did this happen? Can you make more of them?"

Slowly, I told him about ancestral memories, about the bonds I had to forge between my time and Tristan's time. And how the only memories I had from him were about the Stone of Eventide.

Declan listened raptly, his hand continuing to stroke his beard. "Ah, Brienna, *Brienna* . . . how envious I am of you!"

I was shivering, unable to hide it from him. Fear had a deep hook in my heart; I could not tell if his excitement was good or bad for me. It was like I sat on the edge of a knife, waiting to see which way I would fall.

"You have descended from one of the greatest men in our history," he went on. "Tristan Allenach. The man who stole the Stone of Eventide and assassinated the last queen."

"He was a traitor and a coward," I replied.

Declan chuckled. "If only I could transform you, Brienna. To make you see life from the other side, to have you join me."

I stared coldly at him. "You would not want me on your side. I am an Allenach, after all. I would end up overthrowing you a second time."

He laughed at that. While he was distracted, I gathered the chains in my hands, readying to launch myself at him, to loop it about his neck. And yet he was faster. Before I could lunge, he had taken me by the neck and slammed me against the wall.

Stunned, I gasped for breath. I could feel my pulse throb hard, slowing beneath his iron grip.

He was still smiling at me as he said, "I think we are ready to begin."

He let me go and I slid down the wall, as if my bones had melted. My breaths wheezed, my throat still tingling from his choke hold.

Two guards entered my chamber. They unlocked the chains at my wrists, leaving the iron manacles in place, and dragged me to the center of the chamber. They forced each manacle onto a hook dangling from the ceiling. It was just high enough so that my toes could touch the stone floor, but not enough to offer me any relief. My shoulders began to ache and pop, fighting the pull of gravity, trying to remain in joint.

The two guards left, and I was, once again, alone with Declan. I thought about screaming, but my breaths were nothing more than shallow rasps.

I watched as he withdrew a gleaming blade from his belt. Cold sweat broke out along my skin as I stared at the steel, at how the light reflected off the dagger.

I struggled to breathe, my panic rising. Time. I needed to give Jourdain and Cartier more time.

"We'll start with something very simple, Brienna," Declan said. His voice echoed in my ears, as if my soul was already leaving my body, tumbling down a fathomless hole.

I gasped when he took a fistful of my hair. He began to shear me in painful jerks, and I watched as my long hair drifted away, down to the floor. He was rough, his blade nicking me a few times, and I felt the blood begin to trickle down my neck, seeping into my dirty chemise.

He has halfway done when we were interrupted by a shriek.

The sound pierced me. At first, I wondered if it had come from myself, until Declan whirled around. It was Keela, kneeling before the open cell door, sobbing hysterically.

"No! Da, please don't hurt her! Don't hurt her!"

Declan growled. "Keela. This woman is our enemy."

"No, no, she's not!" Keela wailed. "Please, *please* stop, Da! I will do anything if you would only leave her alone!"

Declan approached his daughter, knelt before her, and drew his large hand through her pale hair. She tried to lurch away, but he grabbed her tresses, just as he had done to mine. And my heart became wild within me, desperate, furious.

"Keela?" I called to her, my voice like steel in the forge, hammered into strength. "Keela, it will be all right. Your father is only cutting my hair so it doesn't get in the way. It will grow back."

Declan laughed, and the sound was like feeling serpents slither up my legs. "Yes, Keela. It will grow back. Run along now and stay in your room, like a good daughter. Or else I will cut your hair next."

Keela was still sobbing as she crawled away from him, stumbling to her feet. I watched her dart away, her cries eventually fading into the shadows, into the heavy silence of the tower.

Declan rose and wiped my blood from his blade. As he continued to cut my hair, he started telling me story after story of his childhood, about growing up in the royal castle, about choosing his wife because she was the most beautiful of all Maevan women. I didn't listen; I was trying to focus on a new plan, one that would aid my escape. Because I had no doubt that Declan Lannon would slowly kill me, sending pieces of my body to my family and my friends.

"I had my wife's hair shorn one time," he said, cutting the last of my hair. "For speaking back to me one night." And Declan took a step away, tilting his head as he admired his handiwork. He had not shaved me, but my hair was brutally cropped. It felt like it was uneven and sparse, and I had to fight my weeping, to resist looking at my hair, which was now brushing my toes on the floor.

"I know what you must think of me," he murmured. "You must think I am made of darkness, that there is nothing good in me. But I was not always like this. There is one person in my life who taught me how to love others. She is the *only* one I have ever truly loved in return, even though I must hold her captive, as I do to you now."

Why are you telling me this? My mind pounded. I looked away, but Declan took my face in his hand, forcing me to meet his eyes.

"You look nothing like her, and yet . . . why do I think of her now, when I look at you?" he whispered. "She is the only life I ever begged for."

He wanted me to ask who was this woman. As if by saying her name, he would no longer feel guilty about what he was about to do to me.

I clenched my jaw until I felt his fingers press harder into my cheek.

"Who?" I rasped.

"You should know," Declan said. "You love her son."

At first, I thought he must be thinking of another. Because

Cartier's mother was dead. "Líle Morgane died during the first rising, with Lady Kavanagh and Lady MacQuinn."

He watched my expression, reading the lines that creased my brow.

"I was eleven years old that day, that first rising," he said. "My father cut off Líle Morgane's hand during battle and then dragged her into the throne room, where he was to behead her at the footstool of his throne. But I could not bear it. I could not bear to see him kill her, to destroy the one good thing in my life. I did not care if she had rebelled, if she had betrayed us all. I threw myself over her and begged my father to let her live."

I was trembling, the weight of his words pressing down on me. I was going to be sick. . . .

"Why are you telling me this?" I whispered.

"Because Aodhan Morgane's mother is not dead. She is alive. She's been alive this whole time, because of *my* mercy, *my* goodness." He shook me, as if he could make me believe this.

But then I thought . . . what if he speaks truth? What if Líle Morgane is alive? What if she has been living this whole time?

Cartier. Just the thought of this, of his mother, made me come undone.

"You lie. *You lie*," I shouted, tears in my eyes.

"So my father dragged me off Líle," Declan continued, ignoring my defiance. "And he told me that if he let her live, I would have to keep her chained. I would have to silence her, or else the truth would spread like wildfire, and the Morganes would rise up again. He sent her to the dungeons and cut out her tongue, beheading another fair-headed woman in her place. Kane Morgane, that old fool, saw the blond hair on the spike and thought it was Líle."

You lie, you lie, you lie . . .

They were the only two words I could hold to. The only words I could believe.

Declan smiled at me, and I knew the end was coming. There had to be an end to this.

"You and Líle are similar. You both rebelled against my family. You both love Aodhan. You both try very hard not to be afraid of me."

I whimpered, struggling to hold the sob in my chest.

He blew upon his blade, let the steel fog before wiping it over his leather jerkin. "I'm not going to kill you, Brienna. Because I want Aodhan to have you, after all. But when he looks upon your face, he will see his mother in you. He will know where to find her."

I screamed when he took hold of my jaw, when I realized what he was about to do. I felt his blade cut into my forehead, at the hairline above my right temple. I felt him slowly drag the steel down, down, down to my jaw, opening my cheek. He spared my eye by only a hair. But I could no longer see from it, because the blood was rushing down my face, and the pain became a fire trapped beneath my skin, burning, burning, burning with my frantic pulse. Where was the end? There had to be an end to this. . . .

"Ah, you were such a pretty lass, weren't you? Shame."

I hung my head, watched my blood steadily drip into my shorn hair.

Declan was speaking, but the sound faded, as if it was being stretched over hundreds of years.

My ears popped. I wavered, trying to balance on my toes, and then came blistering pain in my face again. It felt like I had been punched. But Declan had not touched me; through the haze of my sight, I watched him wipe the blood from his blade and sheathe it, stepping back to look at me.

I met his gaze, my breath ragged, my gorge rising as I felt it again, pain so unbearable I screamed.

Declan frowned at me, confused by my reaction, and then came a voice, unfamiliar, distant, drawn from the past.

"Where did you hide the stone?"

Again, splintering pain, only this time in my arm. Someone was breaking my arm. Someone I couldn't see.

"Tell us where you hid the stone, Allenach."

More pain, climbing up my back, and I drew in a raspy breath, realizing what was happening.

I was shifting into Tristan's memory.

I surrendered to it because I was overcome, leaving one torture chamber for another.

My body became Tristan's body, and I saw the world through his eyes, let his skin ripple over mine as if he were a veil.

"Where is it, Allenach?" a young man asked, tall and powerfully built. He was standing before Tristan, blood splattered on his green doublet, a green doublet with a lynx pressed over the heart.

Lannon.

"Do you want me to break your other arm?"

Tristan groaned. He could only see out of one eye, and blood filled his mouth. His thumbs had been cut off, and his right arm was broken. He was confident half of his ribs were splintered as well.

"Speak, Allenach," the Lannon prince ground out, visibly irritated. How long had he been torturing him? "Speak, or else this will get much, much worse."

He chuckled, to know he had kept such a secret for so long, that the Lannon king and his sons had only now caught wind that Tristan Allenach knew where the Stone of Eventide was hidden.

"You're frightened, aren't you, lad?" Tristan struggled to say, spitting out blood and a few teeth. "You're frightened that the stone will surface, and your reign will end before it has even had a chance to begin."

The Lannon prince's face contorted in wrath and he punched Tristan again, until more teeth came loose.

"Enough, Fergus," the second Lannon son said from the shadows. "You'll kill the old gaffer before he talks."

"He's mocking me, Patrick!" Fergus Lannon screeched.

"What's more important to Father? Your pride, or the location of the stone?"

Fergus clenched his fists.

Patrick stood and approached. He was not nearly as built or powerful in stature as the heir, but there was a dark, wicked gleam in his eyes when he crouched down to meet Tristan's blurry gaze.

"I know you're an old man now," Patrick said. "There's nothing left for you here. You've had your share of plenty, and your wife is long dead, and your children await your death so they can take their inheritance from you." He paused, tilting his head to the side. "Why did you do it, anyway? What made you want to hide the stone?"

Ah, there were no simple answers to such a question. Once, Tristan believed he had done it for the good of the people, to prevent the devastation of a magical war. But these days, he honestly didn't know. Maybe he had resented the Kavanaghs and the magic they could wield. Maybe he wanted to do it simply to see if such a bold act could be done, if the legends of the Kavanaghs were true. To see if their magic would really die without the stone.

He smiled. "I know, you think I'm going to tell you. That if you break all of my bones I will tell you where I hid the stone. Well, you've about broken all of me. So come closer, lads. Come closer so I can tell you."

Prince Fergus instantly leaned down, but Patrick, the wiser one, took his brother's arm and held him back.

"You can tell us from here, Allenach," he said.

Tristan chuckled, choked on his blood. "You should be the heir, lad. Not Fergus."

Fergus took up a club and broke Tristan's other arm before Patrick could stop him.

The pain stole Tristan's breath, made his heart crack deep in his chest. But he gritted what little remained of his teeth and forced himself to remain conscious, for there was one more thing he needed to say to these Lannon scum.

"I am not the only one who knows where the stone is," he said, struggling to breathe.

"Who and where is this other man, then?" Fergus demanded.

Tristan smiled. "She is not a man."

Fergus grew still, shocked. But Patrick chuckled, not at all surprised.

"Where is this woman, then, Allenach? Tell us, and we might let you live, as well as her."

Tristan leaned his head back against the stone wall of his cell, the cell he had been living in the past week. His vision was about to go, and he fought for the last draw of breath.

"It's misfortunate for you. . . ." He lowered his chin to look at the Lannon boys one final time, to utter his last words. "Because she hasn't been born yet."

TWENTY-EIGHT

THE SOUTHERN TOWER

En Route to Castle Lerah, Lord MacQuinn's Territory

Cartier

When dawn arrived, I climbed into the back of the wagon with Luc and Sean. We lay down side by side, watching Neeve and Betha stack bolts of linen and wool upon us until we were hidden. It was cramped and uncomfortable and we had hours before us; I was already perspiring, my heart pounding an anxious beat. I drew deep breaths to calm my mind, to ease the tension in my body.

This was going to work. Our mission would not fail.

I listened as Neeve and Betha mounted the driving bench; the wagon began to rumble, rolling forward. Jourdain, Isolde, and a small force of MacQuinn warriors would trail us from a safe distance. And Lady Grainne had departed two days before, to rally her forces. By nightfall, we would all converge upon Castle Lerah.

None of us spoke, but I could hear the others' breaths as the wagon continued to jolt and bump throughout the morning. The silence gave me time to mull over the truth of who Neeve was. I retraced Brienna's words again, the account she had transcribed for the MacQuinn groom, the one that Neeve had brought to us in tears. *And when Allenach realized his daughter was not going to die, but wear her scars as a proud banner, he suddenly acted as if the child was not his, leaving her to the weavers to raise as their own.*

I could not believe that Brienna had a half sister. And yet when I looked at Neeve, I began to see similarities between the two. Both women had favored their mothers, and they had the same smile, the same cut of their jaw. They walked with the same languid grace.

And Sean . . . Sean had all but fainted when he had read the account. In the span of a turbulent month, he had lost his father and brother, gained the title of lordship, and then discovered he had two sisters. He had promptly wept when he and Neeve had embraced.

It was around midday when the wagon came to an unexpected halt. I looked to Luc, who was beside me. His eyes widened, sweat beading on his brow. We both waited to discover why Betha had stopped the wagon. . . .

"What's this?" a male voice sneered.

"We are MacQuinn weavers," Betha said calmly. "We have a delivery for Lady Halloran."

Another man spoke. I couldn't discern what he said, but I knew it wasn't good.

"Why must you search the wagon?" Neeve stated, her voice cutting through the textiles, clearly reiterating what the man had said to warn us. "We deliver wool and linen every month."

My hand moved slowly, down to my waist, where my dirk was sheathed. I nodded for Luc and Sean to do the same.

I could hear the crunch of boots coming closer. The bolts began to shift directly above me; a stream of sunlight found my face. I shot forward before the Halloran guard saw me, my dirk going directly to his throat. He fell backward, cursing, but I had taken hold of him, pinning him down while Luc and Sean confronted the other guard. There were only two of them, and the road around us was empty, but the hair on my arms rose; I felt exposed.

"Quickly," I said. "Drive the wagon into the trees, Betha. Sean, grab the Halloran horses."

I dragged my Halloran guard into the woods, Luc trailing me with the other.

Once we were sheltered by the trees, we gagged and bound the guards, wondering what we were to do with them.

But then I thought . . . why must we hide in the wagon when two of us could don their armor and ride their horses?

Luc shared the same thought, because he approached me and whispered, "We should just ride into Lerah."

Before I could respond, Sean had knocked both the guards unconscious. We worked to unbolt their armor, and then Luc and

I dressed ourselves. We looked just like Hallorans, in our navy tunics, yellow cloaks, and bronze armor with the ibex etched at the breast.

"Luc and I will act as your escort," I murmured to the women as I slid the guard's helm on my head. "As soon as we reach the castle courtyard, we'll help Sean exit from the wagon unnoticed."

Betha nodded, climbing back onto the wagon bench while Neeve hid Sean beneath the linen again. Luc and I tied the unconscious guards to the trees.

Our entourage emerged back into the sunlight, taking the road beneath us. All of this happened so quickly—within minutes. And while I now wanted to urge Betha to drive the wagon faster, I knew this slight delay was going to work in our favor.

We reached the iron drawbridge of Castle Lerah at sundown, the dusk like a protective veil around us as we came to a stop before the moat's roundhouse.

It was just as Sean had described: a formidable fortress on a summit, protected by a wide moat. My eyes traced the four towers, lingering at last on the southern one, the one gilded in sunset, the one that held Brienna.

And to the east, I could see the orchards in the distance, where Isolde and Jourdain and his forces would wait, and I could smell the forest at my back, a tangle of oak and moss and damp loam. I resisted the temptation to look behind at those woods, knowing Lady Grainne and her warriors were hiding within the shadows, watching, waiting.

A guard appeared on the roundhouse threshold, torch in his

hand, peering at us. Neeve and Betha were both wearing shawls over their hair, but a sudden flare of panic shot through me.

The guard stepped back into the roundhouse, giving the signal to the gatehouse.

I watched as the drawbridge was lowered, the iron chains clanging until the bridge was fully lowered, stretching before us with dark invitation. Betha snapped the reins, and the wagon began to rumble over the wood and the iron. Luc and I followed, our horses' hooves sounding hollow, the water dappled with starlight beneath us.

I did not dare to hope. Not yet. And not even when we cleared the portcullis, which hovered above us like the rusted teeth of a giant. Not even when we passed the grassy stretch of the middle ward, or passed the gatehouse. I did not hope yet, even as Betha brought the wagon into the inner ward, a vast courtyard alight with torches.

It was just as Sean described. I could faintly see the gardens ahead; I could smell the yeast of the bake house somewhere to my right. I could hear the pounding of a distant forge, most likely to the east, and the horses whickering from the stables. I could feel the height of the walls around us, red stone carved by arched doors and tiny slits of windows, glistening with mullioned glass.

I exchanged a glance with Luc, just barely able to discern his eyes in the firelight.

He dismounted first, just as the groom emerged from the stables to take our horses. The stables were behind us, nestled in the base of the southern tower. The prison tower. And I craned my neck to look at it once more, assessing it.

"I'll take your horse, sire."

I slid from my saddle, my knees throbbing from the impact, and handed my horse to the lad. Neeve had already jumped down from the wagon, preparing to shift the textiles so Sean could discreetly emerge. I walked to her side, holding one of the bolts up. Sean soundlessly dropped to the flagstones, wrapping a navy shawl about his head, to shadow his face.

"The southern tower is right here, at our backs," I whispered to Neeve.

She looked over my shoulder at it, suddenly sensing the impossibility of this. She was about to break into a tower and then escape with a prisoner.

"Can you do this?" I asked.

"Yes," she replied, almost harshly.

"Quick, take a bolt and let's walk in here," Sean rasped, interrupting us. He and Betha already had a bundle of wool in their arms. Neeve and I hurried to also take up the linen, and we followed Sean to an open archway, just to the edge of the stables.

It led us to a corridor that ran from the southern tower to the eastern one, the torchlights hissing in their iron sconces. I needed to work my way over to the other side of the castle, to the west–north corridors. And yet when Sean and Luc departed, heading to the gatehouse, I found that I could not abandon Neeve and Betha.

"You should go, milord," Neeve whispered.

"Let me at least help you get into the tower," I replied.

Neeve looked like she wanted to protest. "Hurry, someone is coming."

We fumbled for the closest door, slipping into the back door of the bake house. At first, I blanched, thinking we had just made a grave error, that the three of us would expose ourselves. But we had chanced upon an empty chamber. There was a long table dusted with flour, loaves rising on a heated stone, shelves of earthenware bowls, and sacks of flour. No one was here, even though I could hear the bakers laughing in the adjoining room.

There was a tray of rolls, just baked and buttered. I set down my linen and reached for a wooden trencher, setting three rolls upon it. I also grabbed a small honey pot and someone's forgotten cup of ale, placing it among the rolls.

"What are you doing?" Betha hissed.

"Trust me," I said, opening the door back into the corridor.

Betha huffed, grabbing my dropped bundle of linen, and the three of us began to walk south. The corridor eventually split, one-half rising in a curled stairwell.

I began to ascend, the women in my shadow, my plate of spontaneous dinner rattling in my hands.

We reached the landing, which opened up into the parapet walk, just as Sean had described. The door to the tower should be somewhere near, and I stepped into the open, the air reeking of the stables below. The smell of manure made me think of how I had once been hidden within it, how the muck pile had saved my life. I walked to the edge of the parapet, following the stench, and found the muckpile situated in the middle ward, the ground between walls.

"If you must jump from this wall," I said to Neeve. "Aim for that."

Neeve nodded. "And there is the door." She pointed to the tower, where a door latticed with iron was etched in the wall, draped in shadows. It was not guarded, which surprised me. Until I saw that there was a patrol walking along the parapet, and that he was about to chance upon us.

"Gods have mercy," Betha murmured, and I thought she spoke of the guard approaching us until I heard a trickle of loose pebbles.

I looked up the tower to see none other than Keela Lannon scaling the wall. She was following a vine that had cracked the mortar between stones, crawling from the battlements up to the one window in the wall of the prison tower. And I knew in that moment that Keela must be going to Brienna, that Keela was the beacon for us to follow.

"That is your way in," I said to Neeve. "Hurry and follow her."

Neeve didn't hesitate. She tossed her linen over the side of the parapet, down to the muck pile, and rushed to follow Keela's path. Betha was the one to make a sound of shock.

"I will not be able to scale that," the weaver stated, her ruddy face going pale as she watched Neeve struggle to gain her first foothold.

"No, so you must be waiting here, to offer a distraction," I said, handing her the tray of dinner rolls while taking her linen and her wool.

I dropped the textiles below to the muck pile, just as Neeve had done, and then watched as Betha relented to walk with the dinner toward the guard. And then I remained in a shadow, watching as Neeve continued to climb. Keela had already vanished into the window, unaware that we were here, that we were following her.

I waited until Neeve herself reached the stone casement, grappling to haul herself into the tower corridor. The window seemed to swallow her until I saw her face, pale as the moon, as she waved to me.

Only then did I hope, did I move.

I took the southern corridor, following it to the western quarter of the castle. When I heard the familiar clanging of the drawbridge being lowered, I broke into a run, my boots pounding over the stones, through the shadows. I could hear the first shouts of alarm, and I stopped long enough to look out the closest window, which afforded me a view of the drawbridge.

The drawbridge was fully down, and Grainne and her forces were coming, the moonlight glancing off their steel breastplates, the stars catching on their swords. They were quiet; they moved as one, like a serpent slithering over the bridge.

I reached the western tower just as the screams began to rise from the gatehouse. I could feel it in the stones—the shock, the tremble of the assault unfolding.

I drew my sword and began to ascend the tower stairs, seeking Declan Lannon.

TWENTY-NINE

TO HOLD FAST

Lady Halloran's Territory, Castle Lerah

Brienna

"Mistress? Mistress Brienna, wake up. Please, please wake up." A small, quivering voice that I wanted to cup in my hand, to cherish, to watch bloom into a rose. It was the voice of a frightened girl, her words like sunlight breaking a storm.

"I want to see her, Keela. *Keela!*"

An indignant, heated response, the voice of a determined and brave boy, his words like rain falling into a river.

"No, Ewan. Do not look. Stay. There."

"She's my lady, and I can do what I want."

I could hear the scuffing of boots, then silence, dark, painful silence, a void to drown in. The boy began to weep, weep, weep. . . .

"Shh, they will hear you, Ewan. I told you not to look!" But then she cried too.

"He killed her! He killed her!" the boy moaned, his voice smudged with fury.

"No, brother. She's alive. We have to get her down before Da returns. We have to hide her."

"But where? There's nowhere to hide!"

"I'll get the key, and you find a place to hide her."

Their voices dissipated, and all I could hear was a hum, a wheeze, the sound of something that wanted to melt into dusk.

When I opened my eyes, I realized that it was the sound of my breaths, shallow and labored.

I was still hanging by my wrists, by arms I could no longer feel.

I thought of Tristan, that final memory he had passed down to me still echoing in my heart, our pain linked over centuries of time. He had believed the curse that the last Kavanagh princess had set upon him—that a daughter would rise from his line and steal his memories; he had known I would descend from his blood, that I would right his wrongs.

My toes scraped the floor. A pile of hair. Whose hair was that? It was so pretty, they should never have cut it off like that.

And then the blood. I followed its trail in reverse, from the ground, up my leg, up my chemise, up to where it had dried in the hollow of my collarbone.

It was mine. My blood.

I shifted, desperate to feel my arms, only to brush the side of my face.

And I remembered. The sting of a blade. The words Declan had planted into my wound . . . *I want Aodhan to have you, after all. But when he looks upon your face, he will see his mother in you. He will know where to find her.*

I gasped, I flailed in the chains, until the pain in my face made the bitter stars return, as if I were spinning beneath a sky overwhelmed with constellations, blurred and dizzy. I wanted that dark mist again, the unconscious state of being.

Líle Morgane is dead. He is lying to me. She cannot be alive. . . .

And yet Líle Morgane was all I could think of.

I drifted, unsure of how much time had passed.

When I heard the iron door scraping open, I startled, bumping my face yet again. The pain shot through my bones until I choked and coughed, retching down the front of my dress.

I waited to hear Declan's menacing laugh, feel the hardness of his hands as he decided where to maim me next. But I was encircled by something delicate. I felt someone align themselves to me gently, lovingly. Hands moved up my arms, finding the hook.

"I'm here, sister."

I opened my eyes. *Neeve.* Neeve with her body pressed against mine to keep me steady, her hands working to set me free. There were tears streaming down her face, but she smiled at me.

I knew that I must be dreaming.

"Neeve?" I mumbled. "I've never dreamt of you before."

"You are not dreaming, sister."

She finally loosened my shackles from the hook. I collapsed, falling into her, and then there was Keela, her arms around us both. We stood in a circle, Neeve and Keela bearing my weight.

It was only then that I realized what Neeve had called me.

Sister.

"Who told you?" I rasped as Keela knelt to unbuckle the chains at my ankles.

"I will tell you as soon as we get home," Neeve promised. "Can you walk with me?" She laced her fingers with mine and tugged gently. I struggled to take a step.

"I think we need to hide her," Keela said, worried. "My father knows something is amiss. He'll come looking for her."

"We do not have time. We need to run," Neeve said. "Brienna, can you follow me?"

I tried to lift my hand, to feel the wound in my face. Neeve quickly caught my fingers.

"My face, Neeve," I whispered. It was difficult to speak, because every word tugged on my cheek. "How bad—?"

"Nothing Lady Isolde cannot heal," Neeve responded firmly. But I saw it: the horror, the sadness, the anger in her eyes.

"Sister," Neeve said, sensing my despair. She drew me close. "Sister, you must run with me. Lady Isolde waits for you beyond the orchard, to take you home. I will guide you to her."

"Isolde?"

"Yes. Are you ready?"

I nodded, squeezing tightly to her hand.

"Keela, take her other hand," Neeve beckoned, and I felt Keela's small, cold fingers weave with mine. "Hold fast to me, Brienna."

I let them draw me from the cell, out into the corridor. I was dizzy; the walls felt like they were beginning to narrow, to close in on us, as if they were a living creature, scaled as a dragon, inhaling, exhaling. We walked around and around, descending in a tight circle.

I could hear a distant shout. And then the shouts grew more urgent and louder, sounds of pain.

"I do not think we can leave by a window," Neeve said, stopping on the stairs, her breath ragged. "We will need to walk out the door."

"But someone might see us," Keela whispered.

We were quiet, listening to the sounds of a battle unfolding beyond the walls.

"I think there is enough bedlam for us to walk out," Neeve continued. "Can you hand me the keys, Keela?"

"What is happening?" Keela questioned, her voice trembling as she passed the ring of keys. "Is there about to be a battle? What about my brother? I don't know where he is. He was supposed to meet me back in our rooms, to hide her."

"Lord Aodhan will find him," Neeve replied. "We need to get out."

After a moment of tortured silence, she pulled me along with her, and I pulled Keela, still bound to both of their hands. We continued our descent, my legs trembling. I felt fever brush hot feathers down my face and neck. My teeth chattered as I tugged on Neeve.

"Neeve, I . . . I don't think I . . . can run."

"We're almost there," Neeve said, pulling me faster.

We reached the foyer of the tower, a room of simplicity. There was the Halloran sigil on the wall, the only color in this drab place, and a table and a chair. The guard who was supposed to be stationed here was gone, although his half-eaten supper was still on his plate.

"Listen, this is our plan," Neeve said, drawing Keela and me close. "We are going to take the stairs of the parapet, down to the middle ward. That will keep us away from the brunt of the battle. We'll run along the wall to the eastern tower, where the forges are. There should be a small entrance there for us to slip into the moat." She unwound the shawl she had tied about her waist, gently bringing it over my head. "All you must do is follow me, all right, sister?"

I nodded, even though I did not believe I had the strength for this.

"Then let us go."

She turned and approached the door, laboring to unbolt the locks. At last, she tossed open the door, and we were promptly greeted by a wash of night air and the clash of two men fighting on the battlement.

For a moment, the three of us merely stood on the threshold, watching the warriors cut and parry, one a Halloran, the other a Dermott. That's when I understood what was happening: Lady Grainne had led an assault on the castle.

No sooner did such hope bloom in my chest did the Halloran shove his sword into the Dermott's breast, nearly to the hilt.

"Hurry," Neeve said, as if the imminent death had woken her. She dragged me along before the Halloran could stop us, the chaos nipping at our heels as she tried to reach the parapet stairs. An entire slew of Hallorans were coming up them, rising from the shadows, swords drawn. They were coming in our direction, and Neeve abruptly halted, sending Keela crashing into my back.

"Quick. We must jump," my sister said tersely, backtracking to the wall.

I thought she could not be serious. She was about to have us fall to our deaths. But the Halloran warriors had spilled onto the parapet like ants emerging from a mound; they spotted us, two of them charging over.

I would rather jump than be taken by them again. My heart thundered in my chest as I stood on the edge of the battlement with Neeve, Keela resisting behind us.

"Trust me," Neeve said to the girl. "We must all jump together, and aim for the muck below."

I tugged Keela up beside me. She looked petrified, and I wanted to smile at her but found that my face had gone numb.

"*Now,*" Neeve breathed, and the three of us jumped as if we were nothing more than fledglings, casting our wings out to the wind.

The drop felt endless; the darkness seemed to howl at my face until I sank into the manure, all the way to my waist.

And yet my sister did not give me a moment to even catch my breath. She was scampering out of the muck, dragging me with her, and I dragged Keela.

"Stay in the shadow of the wall," she ordered, and I struggled to keep up with her. We were in the grassy canal of the middle ward, which was eerily empty and quiet, the brunt of the conflict happening in the heart of the holding.

We ran with the inner wall brushing our left shoulder, following the grass. I could hardly breathe, hardly feel my feet. My sister dragged me, kept me moving forward, or else I would have collapsed. We reached the eastern tower. Which seemed to be far busier than the prison tower.

We stood in the shadow, gazing up, listening as the Hallorans seemed to swarm above our heads on the battlement.

"Why are they all here?" I asked, fighting a sudden wave of nausea.

"Because this is the armorer tower," Neeve replied. "And I do not see forge row. I think Sean was mistaken. . . . It is within the castle, not in the middle ward."

She turned to me and Keela. "I want the two of you to stay here, in the shadows," Neeve said. "I am going to—"

Keela let out a startled cry. I didn't have the strength to turn and see what it was, but Neeve's eyes narrowed, her nostrils flared as she shifted her gaze. I heard it—the pounding of boots in the grass, the clink of armor, approaching us.

We had nowhere to hide. We would have to outrun them, and I could scarcely keep myself upright.

I braced myself against the wall, trembling. My sight began to blur and dim, but Neeve was like a pillar of light as she withdrew a dirk from beneath her dress. The dirk I had once given her. She stood before Keela and me, the blade in her hand, waiting.

But it wasn't Hallorans who were rushing along the middle ward. They were Dermotts.

Neeve recognized the sigil on the armor the same moment I did, and she called out to them, desperate. "Please, can you help us find a way beyond the outer wall?"

One of the Dermott warriors slowed, taking us in. I don't know if she knew who we were or not, but she pointed onward with her sword.

"Keep moving north. We've opened the north postern gate to let out the innocent."

Without a word, Neeve and Keela both grabbed my hands. I struggled to stand, to keep my eyes open.

"Neeve, I cannot—"

"Yes, you can, Brienna," Neeve ordered, not allowing me the chance to surrender. "Stay with me." Her grip was like iron as she dragged me in her wake, following the Dermotts. I forced my eyes open. The warriors took the stairs curling up to the armorer battlements, and we continued on the grass, trying to reach this elusive hope of an open gate.

But we found it, a small entrance carved into the outer wall. Several Dermott warriors had the gate wide open, yet there was no bridge. Only the dark lap of the moat water.

"You'll have to swim across," one of the Dermotts said after checking our wrists for the half-moon. And then his eyes rested on my face. "Although with her injury . . . she should not be in the water."

Neeve's anger flashed in her expression as she growled, "She is my sister and I am taking her to the queen to be healed. So stand aside."

The Dermott merely raised his brows but stepped out of the way.

But even now that we were here . . . we all three hesitated as we stared at the water. It felt as if we were jumping off another wall, only this time we could not see the bottom.

"Are you sure Lord Aodhan will find my brother?" Keela asked, wringing her hands.

"I am certain," Neeve responded, although there was a crack in her voice. "I shall jump in first, and then Keela will help Brienna."

My sister tried to gracefully enter the water, but she slipped in with a splash. I watched the darkness close over her fair hair; I watched her break the surface with a gasp, and I knew there was no way I was going to be able to keep my face out of the water.

I didn't even attempt to ease my way in. I jumped, letting the water rush over me. My face throbbed and burned in reply, and for a moment I seemed to sink, unable to find the surface until I kicked into Neeve. Her hands were strong as she drew me up, and I sputtered and choked and fought the incessant urge to touch my wound.

The three of us swam, the water dark and cold. It felt like leagues of secrets lay beneath us, secrets that could swiftly emerge from the depths and take hold of our ankles. I thought of Cartier as I struggled to swim. Neeve had said he was here, that he was going to find Ewan, and yet when I thought of Cartier, I thought of his mother, and so I had to push them both from my mind. Declan's words still weighed on me, so heavily they could have pulled me to the bottom of the moat.

We reached the other side and climbed out of the water, our fingers sinking into the soggy loam. Neeve and Keela both dragged me upward to the grass, because I could not do it on my own. I groaned as I crawled upon the ground; all I desired was to lie down and sleep.

"We are almost there, Brienna," Neeve whispered. "Hold fast to me, sister."

And before I could collapse, she had me up again, swaying on my feet. We ran together until the grass began to give way, surrendering to a hill. I found the dregs of my strength, willing myself to keep putting one foot in front of the other, willing myself to reach the end. We ran until I could no longer hear the chaos and the fury that brewed in the castle behind me, until the stars hid behind boughs of trees, and the stench that clung to me faded into the sweetness of an orchard. We ran until our breaths were broken and our lungs were heaving, until my fever settled into my joints and every step I took sent sharp pain up my back.

It felt like we ran for years, Neeve and Keela and I.

And I almost collapsed, refusing to go any farther, to insist my sister let me lie down and sleep, when I saw him in the distance.

He was standing in a field, the moonlight limning his armor. And I knew he was waiting for me. That he was waiting to take me home.

Neeve and Keela slowly let go of my fingers, fading away until

I wondered if they had even been real.

Jourdain ran to me as I ran to him.

He had not seen my face yet, I thought as he embraced me, his arms coming about me like an unbreakable chain, holding me up.

"I have you," my father whispered, and I knew he was crying as he stroked my shorn hair. "I have you now."

When he took a gentle hold of my chin to see why I was bleeding so badly, I jerked away. I fought him, flailing to get free of his arms, to hide myself.

"No, no," I panted, struggling even though he held me in love. I didn't want him to look at me.

"What is it? Is she wounded?" Another voice, one I didn't recognize.

"Brienna, Brienna, it's all right," Jourdain whispered, still trying to calm me, his fingers accidentally brushing my wound as I whirled away from him.

The pain was a star exploding in my mind. I dropped to my knees and retched.

"Find the queen!"

"Where is she wounded?"

"Call the wagon. Quickly!"

I could hear the words, circling me like vultures. I crawled a few paces, and then tried to lower myself into the grass. But Jourdain was there, kneeling before me. I had no choice but to tilt my face up, to the moonlight, to his gaze, to let the blood drip from my chin.

I watched him soak in the severity of my wound.

And before he could say anything, before his fury could devour him, I used the last of my strength to reach out, to take hold of his sleeve and give him a direct order.

"Father . . . Father, take me home."

—✦ THIRTY ✦—

WHERE ARE YOU, DECLAN?

Lady Halloran's Territory, Castle Lerah

Cartier

This would be the last time I hunted Declan Lannon.

I ascended the western tower with that promise clenched between my teeth. I opened every door I came upon—most were unlocked and yielded easily beneath my hand. And I knew that he must be somewhere in this western tower, because every chamber that I opened was dark but furnished, guest rooms draped with sheets to keep off the dust.

The higher I climbed, the more anxious I became, searching, searching. By now, the clamor in the inner ward was evident, even enclosed in tower stone. Declan must know something was amiss, and I predicted that he would run.

My only consolation was there was but one way down this

tower and I was claiming it, stair by stair. Eventually, Declan and I would chance upon each other.

Where are you, Declan?

I finally opened a door that exposed a lit room. A library. There was a host of candles to light the space, and I could see books were sprawled along one of the tables, a plate of scones nearby. Someone had just been here, I could sense it, and I wondered if it was Ewan. I was going to step deeper into the room when I heard a clatter overhead. A door being slammed. The distant murmur of voices.

I knew it was him. And I continued my ascent, soundless, following the curve of the stairs, stepping through darkness and torchlight, my breaths ragged by now. I could feel the burn in my legs, my muscles straining and taxed, and yet I pulled in deep breaths, keeping myself calm and sharp.

He would have the advantage of his strength, but I would have the advantage of the surprise.

The voices were growing louder. I was nearly upon them. Another door opening and slamming, a shudder in the stones.

I reached a landing. It was circular, the floor set with a mosaic that glistened in the firelight. There were three arched doors, all of them shut, but I could hear the hum of urgent voices. Which one was he hiding behind?

I made toward the one on the left, halfway there when the middle door unexpectedly blew open.

Declan saw me and stopped upright, narrowing his eyes at me.

Of course, he did not recognize me. I was wearing Halloran armor, and I still had the helm on my head.

"What do you want?" the prince barked at me. "Where is my escort?"

Slowly, I lifted my hand to remove my helm. I exposed my face, letting the brass helmet fall to the floor, a hollow clatter between us.

And Declan could only stare at me, as if I had just risen from the gleam of the mosaic, as if I had conjured myself here.

He recovered from his shock, chuckling. "Ah, Aodhan. You have finally caught up to me."

I took a step closer to him, my gaze locked on his. I saw the twitch in his cheek, the slight shift of his body. He was about to bolt.

"It was only a matter of time," I said, taking yet another step to him. "I had to merely follow the trail of stench you left behind." And here I stopped, because I needed to say this to him before he fled from me. "I want to break every bone in your body, Declan Lannon. I won't, however, because I am far more than you. But know this: when I pierce your heart with my sword, I do it for my sister. I do it for my mother. I do it for the Morganes."

Declan smiled. "Do you want to know what really happened that night, Aodhan? The night your sister died?"

Do not listen to him, my soul raged, and yet I continued to stand, waiting for him to continue.

"Yes, my father gave me an order," Declan said, his voice dropping low and hoarse. "He ordered me to begin breaking your sister's bones, beginning with her hands. I took up the mallet, and yet I could not do it. I could not follow his orders, because your sister was looking at me, sobbing. And so my father said to me, 'You already begged for one life, so you must now take one, to show yourself strong.' His hand encircled mine, and he broke your sister's bones through me. And it was the moment my soul fractured, watching her die."

He is lying, I thought, almost frantically. Aileen had told me something different. She had not said Gilroy took Declan's hand beneath his, controlling the blows.

"When I found your sister hiding in a cupboard," he went on, "I didn't think my father would torture her. So that is why I brought her to him. Because I thought we were going to take Ashling back to the castle, for her to live with us, to raise her as a Lannon. If I had known he would kill her, I would have left her hiding."

He was trying to confuse me. He was trying to weaken my resolve, and it was beginning to work. I felt the hilt of my sword slide in my hand, in my sweaty grip.

"Yes, I am the darkness to your light, Aodhan," Declan said, now the one fully in control of our interaction. "I am the evening to your dawn, the thorns to your roses. You and I are bound together as brothers through her. And she lives because of me. I want you to know that before you kill me. She lives because I love her."

Who did he speak of? Brienna?

I had endured enough. I would not listen to any more of his poison.

He lunged back into his chamber, trying to bring the door

between us. But I caught it with my foot, kicking it open, watching the wood swing and smack Declan in the face.

The prince stumbled back, the first blood drawn, dribbling from his lip. He reached out to restore his balance on a round marble table, where he had been eating dinner. The pewter rattled; a cup of wine spilled, but Declan's moment of surprise was over. He chuckled, and that sound woke the darkness in me.

I was so honed in on him that I almost missed it. From the corner of my eye came a blur of light on steel, a sword being thrust toward me.

I pivoted, angry that I had to divert my attention from the prince. I caught the blade with my own, just before it would have sunk into my lower abdomen, and I slung my new opposition back to the wall.

It was Fechin.

Fechin's eyes widened, to feel the brunt of my parry, to realize it was me. The guard struggled to regain his composure, scrambling, but I progressed on him, disarming him with fluid ease.

I took Fechin by the hair and said, "Do you know what I do to men who are foolish enough to break Brienna MacQuinn's nose?"

"My lord," he stammered, choking on his fear like they all did when caught. "It was not me."

I spat in his face and pierced his stomach with my sword. He shuddered, his eyes glazing as I withdrew my blade, letting him slump to the floor.

When I lifted my eyes, the room was empty.

The chamber was divided by a series of three steps; one side of the room led to the balcony, whose double doors were still locked, the glass fogged from the chill of the night. But the other side of the room possessed a wall carved with four arched doors, all yawning with darkness.

I took up a candelabra from the dinner table. Bearing sword and light, I moved toward the first door, my eyes straining in the darkness.

"Where are you, Declan?" I taunted, each of my steps measured, calculated. "Face me. Do not tell me that you are afraid of little Aodhan Morgane, the boy who slipped through your fingers by hiding in the muck pile."

I entered the first room despite its darkness, my sword ready, my light raised so it would not blur my vision.

It was a bedchamber, the floor scattered with husk dolls and a tangle of ribbons. Keela had been staying here. And it was empty.

I quietly retreated, progressing to the next door, stepping over the threshold.

The heavy silence was broken by a whimper, and my attention sharpened, my gaze cutting through the room to see Declan was sitting on a stool with Ewan before him, holding a dirk to the boy's throat.

Ewan was violently trembling, his eyes glittering with fear as he looked at me.

My heart all but broke in that moment. I had to fight to steady myself, to keep my composure. But a piece of my assurance broke away; I had the first taste of loss on my tongue, that I might not be able to get myself and Ewan safely out of this encounter.

"Not another step closer, Morgane," Declan warned.

I did not move. I only breathed, looking to Ewan, trying to reassure him with my gaze.

"Drop your light and sword, Aodhan," the prince said. "Or else I'll slit the lad's throat."

I swallowed, struggling to conceal my trembling. I had never imagined I would concede my weapons to him, that I would lay them down before him, that he would defeat me. But all I could think was I must keep Ewan safe and whole, and I did not doubt for a moment that Declan would slit his own child's throat.

"You would end your own flesh and blood?" I asked, only to try and buy myself more time.

"Oh, but he isn't mine anymore," Declan said sardonically. "Last I heard, Ewan was a Morgane. Isn't that right?" He tightened his grip on the boy, and Ewan flinched.

Please, *please*, I wanted to shout at Declan. *Let the child go.*

"I asked you a question, Ewan," Declan pressed. "Which House are you?"

"I . . . I am a . . . a . . . Lan . . . Lannon."

Declan smiled at me. "Oh. Did you hear that, Aodhan?"

"Ewan, did you know that my mother was a Lannon?" I spoke calmly, still trying to give him a morsel of courage, to ready himself to run. "I am half Lannon, and half Morgane. And you can be too, if you want."

"Don't speak of Líle," Declan snarled at me, the ire of his response taking me aback.

"Why don't you let Ewan go," I replied, "and you and I can finally end this rift, Declan?"

"Don't test me, Aodhan. Drop your sword and light and step back to the wall."

I had no choice. I lowered the candelabra and my sword to the floor. As I stepped back to the wall, I thought about how to proceed. I still had my dirk concealed at my back, but I didn't know how fast I could draw and successfully wield it against a long-sword in Declan's possession.

"Fetch his sword, lad," Declan said, shoving Ewan forward.

Ewan tripped, his left boot slipping off his foot. But he abandoned it, crawling to where I had surrendered my sword. More than anything, I wanted the boy to look at me, to see the order in my eyes.

Bring the sword to me, Ewan. Not to him.

But Ewan was whimpering as he took hold of the hilt; the sword was too heavy for him. The tip of the blade dragged as he walked it back to Declan, scattering a few marbles he must have been playing with hours ago.

"Ah, what a good lad," Declan said, taking my sword in his hand. "You truly are a Lannon, then, Ewan. Go sit on the bed now. I'm going to show you how to kill a man."

"Da, Da, please don't," Ewan sobbed.

"Quit crying! You're worse than your sister."

Ewan hurried to obey, sitting on the bed, covering his face with his hands.

I kept my breaths measured, drinking in as much air as I could to ready myself. But my eyes never left Declan's face.

"I tried to tell you, Aodhan," Declan continued, rising to his impressive height. He was taller than me by an entire head. "Once a Lannon, always a Lannon. And that includes your mother."

I did not respond; I let his derision slide off my back, knowing Declan was going to strike as soon as I talked, as soon as I let down my guard by speaking.

"How did you find me here?" the prince droned on.

Still, I did not speak. I began to count the steps it would take for me to reach that stool. . . .

"I wish I could witness it," Declan murmured, finally coming to a stop an arm's length away. The shadows crept over his face, twining like wraiths. "The moment you see what I did to Brienna."

He knew my weakness.

And my strength splintered. I could not breathe, the agony filling me like water as my greatest fear came to life. He had tortured Brienna.

I managed to lunge by reflex alone as Declan swung the sword. The prince caught me in the side, in the chink of my breastplate. But I didn't even feel the bite of the blade; my eyes were focused on what lay before me: the marbles on the floor, Ewan's discarded boot. The stool, the stool, *the stool* . . .

I took it in my hands and whirled, using it as a shield as Declan tried to cut me again. The sword sliced cleanly through the wood legs, and it fell into pieces. But I finally found my voice long enough to shout, "Run, Ewan!" Because even in this fray, I did not want Ewan to see me kill his father.

"Ewan, stay!" Declan countered, but the lad had already dashed out of the room.

I was filled with glee, to see the rage on Declan's face. I took a fragment of wood in my hand and drove it into Declan's thigh, trying to sever his artery. It gave me a moment to duck and run from the room, back into the main chamber.

I all but flew down the steps to where Fechin lay dead, my hands shaking as I took up the guard's long-sword. I turned just in time to miss the bottle Declan hurled at me. It shattered on the wall, raining glass and wine on the floor. It cracked under my boots as I answered, overturning the table, letting the food and the pewter scatter at Declan's feet.

He kicked it furiously out of his way, and we met in the center of the room, in a clash of blades.

I blocked blow after blow, the steel screeching. I was weakening, I could feel it, my exhaustion like a rope binding my ankles, slowing me down. I remained on the defense, trying to direct Declan backward to the steps. My hands went numb, and I finally felt the sting in my side, realizing I had left a trail of blood behind me.

Declan didn't forget about the stairs, as I was hoping. He walked up them, that splintered wood still lodged in his thigh. Our blood mixed on the floor as we continued to turn and strike, turn and block, orbiting like the earth around the sun. I finally claimed the offense, lashing him with a cut on the shoulder.

Declan bellowed, and I found myself on the defense again, struggling to guard myself against his quick and steady strikes. And I thought, *This realm cannot hold the both of us.* I could not live in a land where men like Declan thrived.

It will be me, or it will be him. And that vow kept me together, kept me moving, kept me blocking long enough to reach the moment I was waiting for.

It finally came: one slender gap when Declan stumbled, when Declan lowered his guard.

And I rose to fill that moment.

I pierced him, drove the steel deep into the prince's chest. There was a crack of bone and the thunder of a heart being divided, and Declan shouted, his sword glancing off my breastplate just before it tumbled from his fingers.

I wasn't done, though. I thought of my mother, the silver that should be in her hair, the laughter that should be in her eyes. I thought of my sister, the land she should have inherited, the smiles I should have shared with her. And I thought of Brienna, the other half of my soul. *Brienna.*

I took hold of Declan's shirt and hurled him through the balcony doors. The glass shattered into hundreds of iridescent pieces, broken stars and dreams and life that could never be because of this man and his family.

Declan sprawled on his back in the darkness, coated in glass and blood, wheezing.

I stood above him, watching his life begin to wane, until there was only a dim glimmer left in his hard eyes. The prince grimaced, the blood bubbling between his teeth as he tried to speak.

I spoke over him, my voice drowning his as I crouched at his side and claimed, "Here falls the House of Lannon. They are no longer fierce. In fact, they never were. Rather, they were cowards, and they will be turned into dust; they will be reviled. And Declan Lannon's children will become Morganes. Once a Lannon? Never again. Your offspring will become the very thing old Gilroy tried to destroy, and failed. Because the light always overcomes the darkness."

Declan sputtered. It sounded like he was trying to say, "Ask her," but the words crumbled in his mouth.

He died like that, with a sword in his heart, with his eyes on me, with half-spoken words in his throat.

I slowly rose. The wound in my side was throbbing; there was glass pressed into my knees. Every muscle ached as I stumbled back into the chamber.

I felt like collapsing, the excitement ebbing away from me, leaving behind a will of embers.

"Lord Aodhan."

I looked up to see Ewan standing amid the scattered pewter, amid the bones of their interrupted dinner.

"Ewan," I whispered, and the boy broke into a painful sob.

I knelt and opened my arms. Ewan ran to me, threw his thin arms around me, and buried his face in my neck.

"I will do anything, Lord Aodhan," he sobbed, his words hardly coherent. "Just please, *please* don't send me away! Let me stay with you."

I felt my eyes smart with tears, to hear Ewan's desperate plea. That Ewan believed he did not deserve to live with me, that he was worried I would not accept him. I held him until he had let out the worst of his tears, and then I stood, lifting Ewan with me.

"Ewan," I said, smiling at him through my own quiet tears. "You may stay with me for as long as you like. And I will pay you to be my runner."

Ewan wiped his cheeks and snotty nose on his sleeve. "Really, milord? And my sister?"

"Keela too."

He smiled at me, brilliant as the sun.

And I carried him, walking us both out of that bloodied chamber.

PART FIVE

THE LADY OF
MORGANE

—▪ THIRTY-ONE ▪—

REVELATIONS

Lord MacQuinn's Territory, Castle Fionn

Brienna

There were only a few moments of the journey home that I remembered.

I remembered Jourdain holding me in the back of a wagon, the sound of his breaths coming and going as he prayed.

I remembered Neeve beside me, the musical cadence of her voice as she hummed, keeping me awake.

I remembered Isolde's voice, sharp yet determined as she looked at my wound by candlelight. *This is going to take me some time. I need to have her in a calm, clean place where she can relax. We need to get her home swiftly.*

They were my three borders—father, sister, queen. At some point, I knew that I drifted into sleep in the crook of Jourdain's arm, the good side of my face pressed to his chest, to his heart, because the pain flared bright and unbearable again.

"She's falling asleep. Should I wake her?" Neeve asked worriedly. She sounded so far away, even though I still felt the loving trace of her fingers on my hand.

"No," Isolde responded. "Let her sleep."

When I fully woke again, I was lying in my bed, and sunlight was streaming through my windows. I was clean, the stench and the blood washed from my body, and I was covered with a soft quilt. But more than anything . . . I felt a bandage on my face.

I stirred—slowly, fearfully. I lifted my hand to graze the linen that covered my right cheek.

"Good morning."

I turned, surprised to see Isolde sitting beside me. The sunlight transformed her dark auburn hair into curls of tamed fire, and she smiled, her eyes crinkling at the corners.

"Are you thirsty?" She rose from her chair to pour me a cup of water. And then, very gently, she sat beside me on the bed and eased me up, propping several pillows behind my back.

I drank three cups of water before I felt like my voice could be found. "What happened at Castle Lerah?"

"Well, after I healed Liam, we planned an assault against the Hallorans." She told me the details—how their plans came together, how Lady Grainne led the assault, how Cartier, Sean, Luc, Neeve, and Betha snuck into the fortress under disguise. "The Halloran half-moons have been flushed out by the Dermotts' sword. Pierce has fallen. So have Fechin and Declan Lannon."

I took a moment to let this news fully sink into me. Pierce and

Declan both dead. I couldn't stifle the shudder that racked me at the mere thought of them, and Isolde laid her hand over mine.

"They cannot hurt you—or anyone else—anymore, Brienna."

I nodded, blinking back my tears. "What of Ewan and Keela?"

"The children are both safe. Keela has been staying here, at Castle Fionn with Neeve, and Ewan is with Aodhan at Brígh."

"And the MacQuinns have been kind to Keela?" I asked, worried over how they might receive her.

"Yes. Lord MacQuinn has been very adamant about how the children saved your life. By my word, Keela is now a ward of Mac-Quinn, and Ewan a ward of Morgane. There is enough evidence for me to seek a pardon for both children."

"And what about Thorn?" I rambled on. "He's a half-moon."

"So Aodhan discovered," Isolde replied. "Thorn is currently in the keep, but he will face death too."

We fell silent, and I could hear the sounds of the hall, the sounds of home. Of laughter and merry shouts and the clinking of dishes. And yet I could not seem to relax; I tried to lean deeper into my pillows, to bask in the sunlight, but there was a restless song in my blood, one that I could not ignore.

I knew what it was, this thorn in my spirit. I knew it was the doubt over Cartier's mother.

"Brienna? Is something hurting you?" Isolde asked, her brow wrinkling with concern.

"No, Lady." I thought about telling her. Perhaps the restlessness would ease if I shared the words Declan had said to me. Perhaps I could find confirmation; Isolde would tell me Declan had lied to distress me further, to cast a net of suspicion in my mind. That Declan had been playing a game with me, to inflict further pain upon Cartier. Because if I told Cartier . . . if I told him what Declan had said, Cartier would all but lose his mind. He would not rest until he had found Líle Morgane. And if Líle was truly dead, then he would be seeking a ghost.

"Well, if you come across any discomfort, even if it seems minor, you should tell me," the queen said gently. "It took three days for my magic to fully heal you. I can imagine you feel quite hungry."

I smiled, which instantly reminded me of my wound. My cheek tugged strangely, and I knew it must be the scar beneath the linen. "I am ravenous."

There was a sudden whine, and I frowned, leaning over to see Nessie was lying on the floor beside the bed, blinking up at me.

"Ah, yes," Isolde said. "We found her muzzled and locked up in one of the old storerooms."

I invited Nessie up on the bed, relieved that Thorn had not hurt her. She curled up in a ball at my side, demurely, as if she knew I was still recovering.

"Now, let me summon breakfast for you," Isolde said, rising. "Although I believe your brother already mentioned that he wanted to be the first to see you upon waking. I'll send him with some porridge and tea."

"Thank you," I whispered, and Isolde smiled at me before departing my chamber.

I waited a moment, my gaze somewhat blurry as it swept my room, my hand absently stroking Nessie's fur. But there on my bureau was my hand mirror.

I gingerly crawled out of bed, my legs tingling. It felt odd to walk, to feel the cold smoothness of the floor beneath my feet. I took my time, arriving at my bureau with a seed of worry in my stomach.

I wanted to look at myself, and yet I didn't.

Eventually, though, I unwound the bandage about my face and took the stem of my mirror in my hand, holding it up to my face.

Isolde had done her best to heal me, to bring my gaping face back together. But there was a scar, a line of silvery pink, running from my forehead down to my jawline. And my hair. It was gone, cut away in violent tufts.

I looked away. But my eyes were drawn to my new reflection, and I studied myself again.

I want Aodhan to have you, after all. But when he looks upon your face, he will see his mother in you. He will know where to find her.

I set the mirror down, my heart pounding.

What had Declan meant? Was he simply trying to cause me agony, to make me pull away from Cartier? Did he truly think that he could cut my face and make me cower, that all of my worth was based off of such things?

It filled me with rage that he had left his venom in my mind. And I took up my mirror and slammed it against the corner of my bureau. It shattered into fragments, pieces that caught the light as they fell, tumbling with prisms down to the floor.

It gave me some relief to break the mirror, as if it was merely the beginning of things I needed to break in order to see. Because I saw myself without it, not as a girl who had been chained and shorn and scarred, but as a woman who had survived.

I was calm as I picked up my bandage, rewrapping my face. And then I knelt and cleaned up the glass, hiding it in my drawer just as my brother knocked on the door.

I walked to answer it, greeting him with a smile, as if this were any other day. Because I did not want pity; I did not want weeping and sadness.

Luc was carrying a tray of tea and porridge, and I was grateful that he was not melancholy or worried or teary-eyed over me.

"Someone said you were ravenous and that war might break out if I don't feed you," he said mirthfully, and I waved him into my room with a laugh.

We sat in the chairs before my hearth, my stomach growling so loudly that he snickered as he poured me a cup of tea. While I ate honeyed porridge, trying to adjust to the odd pull of my scar every time I opened my mouth, my brother retold me everything. I noticed his storytelling was quite exaggerated, especially when he recounted the adventure of lowering Castle Lerah's drawbridge, but I did not care. I soaked it in.

"So you took out four Halloran guards with one mighty swing of your sword," I said passionately. "And then you stepped on the pile of bodies to reach the iron lever to lower the bridge. Extraordinary, Luc."

His face flushed, all the way to the tips of his ears. "All right, you are making me sound like a mighty warrior when I am only a humble musician."

"Why can't you be both, brother?"

Luc met my gaze, smiling. And there it was, the first gleam of emotion in his eyes as he regarded me.

Don't cry, I secretly begged him. *Please don't weep over me.*

Another rap on my door sounded, breaking the moment. Luc patted my knee and jumped up to answer it, sniffing back his tears. I heard Isolde's voice, a dark murmur, and Luc whispering in response.

I was pouring myself a third cup of tea by the time Luc returned to sit beside me.

"What was that about?" I asked.

"That was Isolde," Luc said. "Aodhan Morgane is here. He would like to see you."

I froze, uncertain. "Oh." I wanted to see Cartier so much that my heart began to ache. And yet I had not determined my mind. I had not decided what I would say to him, if I should say anything at all. I did not want to break his peace, to spread Declan's venom to him. I need another day, perhaps more, to find the path I needed to take. And so I said, "I feel like I need to rest today."

Luc was not expecting that. His brows rose, but he swiftly nodded. "Very well. I'll tell him to come back tomorrow."

My brother was up, out of his chair before I could stop him, before I could tell him that I would most likely avoid seeing Cartier tomorrow as well. I did not want him to come every morning, eager to see me, only to have me turn him away while I tried to determine what was best to tell him.

I stood and walked to my writing desk, finding my parchment, my quill, my ink. I kept the letter brief, and yet it seemed like my entire heart was breaking within those words I set down.

Cartier,
I feel as if I need to recover for a few more days. I will send for you when I am ready to see you.
—Brienna

I let four days pass before I finally sent for him.

It was midmorning, and Keela and Neeve were sitting with me in my chambers, the three of us gathered around a book of ancient Maevan legends, improving Neeve's reading skills. Isolde had been pleased with the progression of my healing and had returned to Lyonesse to prepare for the Lannon executions. I didn't expect Cartier to arrive so soon after I had sent my letter of invitation, that he would drop everything he was doing at Castle Brígh to come to me. But he did.

He caught me off guard, coming directly to my room, unannounced.

All three of us startled at his sudden appearance—the door uncharacteristically banged against the wall with his entry—and then Neeve and Keela both stood and wordlessly departed, closing the door behind them.

I was still sitting at the table, storybook spread beneath my fingers, my heart pounding at the sight of him.

Cartier stood in the sunlight of my bedroom, looking at me as if we had been apart for years, not weeks. His hair was loose and tangled—there were even a few stray leaves caught within it, as if he had torn through the forest dividing our lands, as if nothing could have kept him from me. His face was flushed from the cold, and his eyes . . . his eyes rested on mine, drinking me in.

I still wore my bandage. He could not see the scar yet, and I knew I needed to show him, that I needed to tell him everything Declan had said to me. That I could not withhold this from him, even if it was false.

I rose, trying to steady my breaths. But I felt like I was about to come undone, like I was about to take a dagger in my hands and plunge it into his heart.

"Cartier, I . . . I am sorry it has taken me so long to send for you."

"Brienna." He only spoke my name, but he expressed so much more than that.

I glanced down at the scattering of paper and books before me, trying to remember the speech I had planned for this. The exact words I wanted to say.

I could hear his footsteps as he drew closer. And I knew if he touched me, I truly would come unraveled.

"Declan said something to me, when he held me captive."

Those words stopped him, although his shadow was reaching for mine across the floor.

Look at him, my heart admonished. *You must look at him.*

I lifted my gaze to his.

Cartier's eyes were on mine; he had not looked away from me once. And for a moment, I rested in the blue of his eyes, a blue to rival the sky.

"Declan told me that your mother is alive, Cartier," I whispered, the revelation finally blooming from my voice, releasing me from its prison. "He told me that during the first failed rising, Gilroy Lannon cut off her hand and then dragged her into the throne room. And before the king could behead her, Declan threw himself upon Líle, to save her life. That he begged his father to let her live, because he . . . he loved your mother as if she were his own."

Cartier continued to stare at me with an intensity that could have brought me to my knees.

"So Gilroy let your mother live," I continued, my voice trembling. "He cast her in the dungeons, and beheaded another fair-headed woman, to put her head on the spike in the courtyard."

Still, he said nothing. It was like I had enchanted him, like I had cast him into stone.

"And Declan . . . Declan said to me . . ." I couldn't say it. The words melted, and I gripped the back of my chair.

"What more did he say to you?" Cartier said, his voice sharp.

I drew in a deep breath, as if I could keep the last of this revelation hidden deep in my lungs. But I could not hold this any longer.

"Just before Declan cut my face, he told me that he wanted you to have me. But when you look upon my face . . . you will see your mother in me. You will know where to find her."

I watched my words strike him, as if they were arrows. His

guard finally dropped; his face was etched with agony. And I thought, *This will destroy us. This will destroy him.* But then the lines in his brow eased, as if he were breathing for the first time, as if he was realizing something, coming into a light I could not see. . . .

"Brienna." He breathed my name again, as if it was a prayer, as if he was burning from within.

I watched, my heart breaking as he turned and strode for the door, as he stopped on the threshold. He came back to me, shoving the chair out of the way, until there was nothing between us.

He hadn't even given me time to remove my bandage, to show him my scar.

He gently cupped my face in his palms and kissed me, a soft brushing of our lips.

And then he was gone, striding from my room, leaving the door open. I listened to the beat of his footsteps, rushing, rushing down the stairs to the floor below. I walked to my window, looking through the glass to see him emerge in the courtyard, frantically requesting his horse.

I wanted to call him back to me, to ask him what he had realized.

It must be true, I thought, trembling. *Declan had not lied.*

And when Cartier mounted his horse, I watched him ride away. Not to the west, which would take him home. He rode south. To Lyonesse.

✦ THIRTY-TWO ✦

THE ACCOUNT

Lord Burke's Territory, the Royal Castle

Cartier

I rode deep into the night, my teeth cutting the wind, my heart matching the pounding of my horse's hooves. *This cannot be*, I thought, and yet I rode into Lyonesse with the stars and the moon watching above, guiding me with their silver light.

The castle gates were bolted shut. I hammered upon them, cracking my knuckles until the skin broke, bloodying the wood and the iron. But I did not cease my knocking, not until one of Burke's men looked down from the watchtower.

"What is it? Go to bed, you drunkard," the man snarled at me. "The gates remain bolted at night."

"It is Aodhan Morgane. Open the gates."

The Burke man was holding a torch, but I could see his face as he squinted down at me, trying to read my sigil in the moonlight. He disappeared back into the tower, and the gates cracked open, just enough for me and my horse to slip within them.

I rode all the way to the courtyard, dismounting and leaving my gelding to stand on the flagstones since the grooms were all asleep. And then I approached the main doors, which were also bolted shut, and I hammered upon them.

It felt like I pounded for an eternity before the peeping grate in the door slid open, and the castle chamberlain peered out at me, their eyes lit by a candle, their annoyance evident.

"What is it?"

"Open the doors," I ordered.

"We don't open the doors at—"

"Open the doors at once, or else I will have the queen dismiss you immediately."

The chamberlain blanched, suddenly recognizing me. "I apologize, Lord Morgane. One moment, please."

The doors unbolted, and I rushed into the castle, following the corridors that wound me to the dungeon entrance. It was guarded by two of Burke's men, and I spoke the same request for the third time.

"Open the doors and let me pass."

"We cannot do that, Lord Morgane," one of the men said. "All entrance into the dungeons must be granted by the queen alone."

They were right. We had established this rule after Declan had escaped, and so I turned and wound my way to the stairs, taking them two at a time, following the upper corridor until I approached the queen's quarters. Of course, her door was heavily guarded, and I could not even reach it to knock.

"Wake her," I requested, desperate. "Wake the queen for me."

"Lord Morgane," one of the women said to me, holding me back. "The queen is exhausted. Can this wait until morning?"

"No, no, this cannot wait. Wake Isolde." I was all but shouting, hoping she would hear me. "I have ridden through the night and I must see her."

"Lord Morgane, you must remain calm, or else we will need to escort you—"

"Let him pass."

Isolde's voice broke the commotion, and we all turned to regard her, standing on her threshold. She was holding a candle and a shawl was wrapped about her, and she did look exhausted. The guards parted, allowing me to approach the queen.

"Isolde, I need you to grant me entrance into the dungeons," I whispered.

This was not at all what she was expecting of me. She blinked, parted her lips to speak but then shut them. And I saw that she would not press me for answers. She trusted me, her oldest friend. The one who had once sat with her in a closet in a foreign land and had held her hand, telling her she would be the greatest queen of the north.

She nodded and walked with me back to the dungeon doors, the candlelight trickling over her face as she gave the guards the order.

"Let Aodhan pass into the dungeons, and wait for him to return to you."

The guard laid his hand over his heart before withdrawing his keys, beginning to unbolt the main doors.

I was suddenly trembling, unable to draw a smooth breath.

Isolde must have heard. She reached out and squeezed my hand—her fingers were so warm in mine. She released me, and I followed the guard into the mouth of the dungeons. We each took a torch from the foyer brackets and began our descent.

I felt the bitter coldness of the dungeons, the darkness rise up around me.

"I shall wait here for you, my lord," the guard said once we had reached the bottom of the stairs.

I nodded and began to pick my way through the tunnels, my torch throwing unsteady light upon the walls. I was bound to get lost; I did not know my way around, and yet I walked deeper into them.

Soon, I was so exhausted that I had to stop and lean against the wall. I closed my eyes and thought for the first time, maybe I am wrong. Maybe Declan had been lying, to wound me even further.

But then I heard it in the distance: the sweeping of a broom.

I pushed away from the wall and followed the sound. It grew faint, and then loud, echoing off the stone walls, and I struggled to locate it. When I thought that I was utterly turned around, that I was walking in circles, I saw light flickering from the mouth of one of the corridors.

I followed that light, coming to a tunnel that was lit by several torches in iron sconces.

And there was the bone sweeper.

I watched as they took their broom to a pile of rodent bones, sweeping them up. Their black veils fluttered in the movement; they had not seen me, not yet.

And so I spoke her name, as if I had summoned it out of the darkness of twenty-five years. "Líle."

The bone sweeper stopped, frozen. But then they straightened, turned to regard me.

I do not know what I was expecting, now that I had come into this moment.

But I did not expect the bone sweeper to turn, to begin to limp away.

It must not be her. Declan had fooled me, had finally shattered me. I could hear his words in my mind, spinning my thoughts. *You and I are bound together as brothers through her. And she lives because of me. I want you to know that before you kill me. She lives because I love her.*

And my heart began to beat wildly, rising up my throat as I spoke again. *"Mother."*

The bone sweeper halted. I watched that right hand, the one that had once been shackled in Declan's cell, reach to touch the wall, to find balance.

I approached her, whispering it again, again. "Mother."

A muffled sound emerged from her, beneath her veil. She was weeping.

I held out my hands, my arms, yearning for her to fill them. She remained against the wall, but her hand had risen now, to rest upon her veiled face.

"It is Aodhan," I whispered. "Your son."

And I will wait however long it takes with my arms open wide, I thought. *I will wait here until she is ready to step into them.*

The bone sweeper took that first step to me. She reached out her hand to mine, and our fingers laced, entwined. She stepped into my arms, and I held her to my heart. I could feel a hard mass of scars on her back through the veils. I could feel how thin she was. That is what made my tears rise.

She leaned back in my embrace, and I watched as her hand rose to take a fistful of her veils, to pull them away.

My father had been right. Líle Morgane was beautiful.

Her hair was like corn silk, falling to her collar, a few threads of silver shining within it. Her eyes were strikingly blue. Her skin was pale, almost translucent from years and years of being in the dungeons. There were long scars on her cheek, on her brow, and I knew Declan had given them to her.

Her hand rose again, gracefully forming motions. I realized they were letters. She was spelling my name.

Aodhan, she signed.

And I thought, *Declan might have kept her alive in captivity and Gilroy might have severed her left hand and beaten her, but neither of them have taken her voice or her strength.*

Aodhan, she said again, smiling up at me.

I pulled her close and wept into her hair.

It was like something spun from a dream, the day I brought my mother home to Morgane lands. I had written a letter to Aileen, the chamberlain, to tell her the news and request that she keep the people calm when I arrived. But of course, I should have known there would be a celebration awaiting us. The Morganes, who were not known to be the most sentimental of people, fell to their knees at the sight of her emerging from the coach. They wept and laughed and reached for her hand, which certainly startled her. I could see that my mother was one breath away from panic, and I had to corral the people into the hall, to request they sit quietly at the tables, that I would bring her to them. Even Ewan seemed very emotional, clinging to me until I told him to go with Derry and the stonemasons.

"Tell me if this is too much for you," I whispered to Líle, who was still standing in the courtyard, staring up at Castle Brígh. I wondered what was passing through her mind, if she was thinking of my father, my sister.

She spoke to me through her hand, a long graceful chain of movements that I could not yet understand. I thought she might be expressing how overwhelmed she was, that she did not want to see the people in the hall.

"I can take you to your rooms right away," I said gently, but she shook her head and formed the words again with her fingers. "You do desire to go to the hall, then?"

She nodded, but I felt that I was still missing the heart of what she was trying to say.

I took her hand and guided her into Brígh. Aileen was waiting for us in the foyer, hardly able to contain herself at the sight of Líle.

She bowed and said, "My lady." And I could tell she was trying her best not to sob.

Líle reached out, smiling fondly at Aileen, and the two women embraced. I cast my eyes away, giving them a private moment.

We entered the hall together, and the Morganes did their best to remain quiet and calm. But they still stood at the sight of her, their eyes following her all the way to the dais, where I gave her my chair at the table.

I sat at my mother's side and watched her carefully, looking for distress. But she only looked out to the hall, her face soft with affection as she recognized old friends.

She made the writing motion to me.

Aileen darted away for paper, quill, and ink before I could so much as rise from my chair to fetch them. The chamberlain promptly returned and set them before Líle, and my mother began to write. I now knew why her handwriting was so poor. She had been left-handed, the hand that Gilroy had severed. She took her time, writing out a paragraph before shifting the paper to me, beckoning me to read it for her.

I took the parchment and rose, willing my voice to remain steady.

"'To the Morganes. It fills me with joy to see you once more, and I want to express my admiration of you, that you have endured through a dark time, that you remained faithful to your lord. I cannot speak with my mouth, but I can speak with my hand, and I hope to speak with each of you in the coming days. But I only ask for one thing: that you do not address me as Lady. I am no longer the Lady of Morgane. I am only Líle.'"

I set down the paper, swallowing the lump in my throat. The Morganes lifted their cups to her, nodding in agreement although a few of them had puzzled looks on their faces, as if they could not break the title from her name.

And I realized with a pang that is what she had been trying to say to me, in the courtyard.

I am no longer the Lady of Morgane. I am only Líle.

The following week was one made of challenges and small victories.

I wanted to give my mother her chambers back—the ones that she had once shared with my father. But she would not even step within them.

She wanted Ashling's rooms. The walls that she had once painted a magical forest upon; the walls that had once held her daughter. Aileen and I worked to furnish the rooms, which had been swept clean and empty since we had repaired Brígh. I had my carpenter fashion a beautiful bed frame, and Aileen had the women quickly work to fill a mattress with feathers. We had clothes made for my mother, and hung drapes along the windows, and stretched rugs and sheepskin on the floors. I filled the shelves with books and stocked her desk with as much paper and ink and quills as she could want.

Líle was pleased with the rooms, and I could not explain how much this relieved me.

But then Aileen came to me one morning and said, "Lord

Aodhan, your mother is not sleeping on the bed. She is sleeping on the floor, before the hearth."

And I was humbled by this. Of course, Líle had been sleeping on the floor the past twenty-five years. "Let her sleep where she wants, Aileen."

"But, my lord, I cannot—"

I only took her arm and squeezed it, to remind her that we did not understand—we might not ever understand—all that my mother endured. That if Líle wanted to wear veils again and sleep on the floor, then that was what I wanted.

The next challenge was that Líle wanted to work. She wanted to sweep, she wanted to clean, she wanted to uproot weeds from the herb gardens, to knead dough with the bakers, to curry the horses with the grooms. She wore simple homespun and covered her hair with a shawl, shunning the finer dresses Aileen had tailored for her, and she worked alongside the Morganes. The first time this occurred, the women cleaning the hall had come to me in a panic.

"She wants to sweep and knock down cobwebs and clean the ash from the hearths," one of the women had said to me, wringing her hands. "We cannot allow this. She is our lady."

"She is Líle, and if she wants to work shoulder to shoulder with you, let her and welcome her," I replied, hoping my temper wasn't showing.

And then I watched my mother, to see that she began work as soon as she woke and labored until the sun went down, that she worked so hard that it seemed that she could outwork any of my people. I suspected that by working herself into exhaustion, she did not have the time or strength to dwell on certain things.

Again, she humbled me. She humbled all of us.

Perhaps what surprised me the most, though, was Ewan. He was drawn to her, and she to him, and the lad followed her about, learning her language of signals before any of us. My mother was going to teach him how to work, I thought wryly, watching Ewan follow her with the dustpan, follow her with a stack of freshly washed linens, follow her with flour streaked on his clothes.

Within that first week, she only wanted to eat bread and cheese. She did not want meat, or even much ale. She was most excited about having tea again, with honey and a drop of cream. I found that the time I was to have with her was forged in the evenings, when I brought a tray of tea to her in her bedchambers, and the two of us sat—on the floor, mind you—before her hearth, soaking in the fire, bonding over our tea. Because the reality was . . . she and I were as good as strangers to each other. I knew nothing of her, and she knew nothing of me.

It was on such a night that she brought some paper to me, filled with her words.

"Should I read this now?" I asked her.

No. Wait.

I nodded and set it aside, enjoying the rest of my tea with her. But in the back of my mind, I knew that I was supposed to be in Lyonesse that day, witnessing the Lannons' execution. That Gilroy and Oona had been brought to the chopping block before the queen and her nobles and the people that morning, to kneel and lose their heads.

I was the only lord that had been absent. Isolde had told me not to come, to remain home with my mother. And so I had, because I could not imagine leaving. But what concerned me was the fact that Ewan and Keela still needed to be pardoned, and that I was not there to testify in favor of the children.

Brienna will testify for them, Isolde had written to me. *She will testify that Ewan and Keela Lannon saved her life.*

I cleared the Lannons from my mind and said, "There is a reason why I knew where to find you, Mother. Her name is Brienna."

Líle laid her hand over my heart. Ah, she sensed it. Or perhaps heard it in the way I said Brienna's name.

"Yes, she has my heart. She is Davin MacQuinn's adopted daughter."

And his name woke tears in her eyes. She smiled and signed, *I want to see him and meet her.*

"They'll be at Isolde's coronation," I said. "Will you come with me and the Morganes, to celebrate with us?" I dwelled on the letters I had written to both Jourdain and Brienna, sharing the news with them, that my mother was alive. And as eager as they had been to come and see her, they had understood that she still needed time to reacquaint herself with the Morganes first.

Yes, I will go with you.

I smiled and kissed her cheek, thinking . . . how would I bear this, to see all the people of my heart together, meeting and reuniting?

I left my mother after we finished our tea, taking the papers she had given me. Ewan was already asleep in my chambers, snoring on his cot before the fire. He had worked hard that day, following Líle around with the stonemasons.

And so I quietly sat at my desk with Líle's papers. I knew this was her account, a portion of her story. I hesitated for a moment, the paper crinkling in my fingers, the candlelight washing over it. I almost felt afraid to read this, but then thought, *If Líle is ready to share this, then I must be ready to hear it.*

Aodhan,

I know you must be filled with questions, questions as to how I survived the rising battle and my time in captivity. I first want you to know that not a day passed when I did not think of you, your father, and Ashling. You and your sister were always in my heart, even when I was in the darkness, thinking I should never see you again.

Perhaps another night, I can write to you of happier things, such as the day you were born and how your sister loved to get you in trouble. But for now, let me take you back twenty-five years.

During the battle, your father and I were separated. I had a phalanx of warriors behind me, and a sea of Allenachs and Lannons about me, and Gilroy Lannon rode up and severed my hand. My sword went with it. He hauled me before him on his horse and then rode me back to the courtyard, dragging me into the throne room. I knew what he was going to do. Because I had been born a Lannon, he wanted to make an example of me, to behead me at the footstool of the throne.

I was in such great pain, and despite all of our efforts, I knew we were going to lose the battle. And yet even as I knelt, waiting for him to bring down his sword on my neck . . . I wanted to live. I wanted to live for you and Ashling, and yes, your father, whom I loved. But out from the darkness came Declan. Out from the darkness came his voice, screaming at his father for mercy, to let me live. And then he laid himself over me, claiming if Gilroy killed me, he would have to kill Declan as well.

But perhaps I need to tell you more about Declan.

When Declan was seven, he asked me to teach him how to paint. He had seen some of my art, and he wanted to learn. His father, of course, thought art was a waste of time. But I saw the value in this arrangement, that I could draw Declan away from the castle, where I knew a great evil was flourishing beneath Gilroy and Oona. I could try to protect the future king, to raise him up to be a good man, not like his father. But, of course, Gilroy wanted something in return for this. He wanted me to show my allegiance to the Lannons by betrothing Ashling to Declan. Ashling was only a year old, and I absolutely balked at this. Until your father said to me, "If you can teach Declan to paint, you can mold the future king. And our daughter will be Queen at his side."

And so I agreed to it.

Declan came and stayed with us many weeks out of the year, learning how to paint. And while I came to love him as a son, I began to see the darkness in him. Little by little, year by year, he grew harder and more violent, and I realized that I could not save him. I could not redeem him. It filled me with such despair, that I failed him in some way, and yet he still loved me. He was trying, for me, to be good.

But soon, I was not only afraid for him, I was afraid of him.

I broke the betrothal. And your father and I began to plot a coup, because we had witnessed enough of Gilroy and Oona. You already know the rest of the tale.

So in the throne room, Declan begged for my life.

Surprisingly, Gilroy agreed to it. He sent me to the lowest level of the dungeons, and there I was chained, in agony, for months. He waited until my wrist had healed, and then he cut out my tongue, so I could no longer speak. That first year was the hardest. The pain never seemed to ebb, and all I could wonder about was if your father had survived, if you and Ashling had been harmed. I knew nothing, and could not ask the guards what had happened.

But then, one of the guards took pity upon me. Yes,

he was a Lannon, but he cared for me. He brought me the best of the food, the cleanest of the water, and herbs to help me heal. He told me what had occurred after the failed coup. He said you and your father had escaped with Davin, Lucas, Braden, and Isolde. That the Morgane people had been given to Lord Burke. That my father, a Lannon thane, had tried to incite a second revolt and had failed, that Gilroy had destroyed all of my family because of it. And I wept to learn of this—the death of my family—but to also know you and your father had survived. That gave me the hope I needed to stay alive, to play my cards. I would defy the Lannons by living, and I would be ready when you and your father returned.

I was locked in the dungeon cell for five years. Declan would often come and visit me. I cannot even describe how sad and terrible these visits were, not because he was cruel to me, but because I knew he was drifting further and further away, that all the goodness and virtue I had tried to plant in him had withered and died. But he began to bring me paper and ink and a quill, so I could speak to him in writing. He kept telling me to drop Morgane from my name, to completely deny my House and your father, because if I did, he could bring me up from the dungeons. He could find me a place in the castle.

Nearly every day for a month, he came to my cell

and waited for me to write my denial.

And when I didn't, the more frustrated he grew with me. "Don't you desire to live, Lile?" he would shout at me. "Don't you want to live in comfort? I can protect you. I can give you a much better life than this."

And yet I refused to give up the Morgane name.

So he refused to visit me for what felt like a year. During that time, the Lannon guard tried to help me escape. He told me of the underground river, that it opened up into the bay. We plotted and planned, and then when the day came, he snuck me from my cell, leading me to the river. But it is difficult to escape a Lannon-run dungeon. We were discovered by none other than Oona herself. She had always hated me, because she knew Declan loved me more than he loved her. She had me whipped, and the guard tortured to death.

I was back in my cell, in utter agony, when Declan returned to visit me. He had not realized I had tried to escape, that his mother had nearly whipped me to death. "Do you want me to kill her?" he asked me, so calmly I at first thought he was teasing. But Declan was serious. He was only sixteen years old, and would have killed his own mother for me. That is how dark and corrupt their family was.

He brought me up from the dungeons to recover

in his private quarters. I think he was hoping that I would drop the Morgane name, now that I could recover in comfort. He was afraid—all of the Lannons were afraid—that you and your father, Kane, Davin and Lucas, Braden and Isolde would return with vengeance. And Declan wanted reassurance that I would choose him over you in the event that you did return.

I could not give him such reassurance, and that angered him. He scarred my face and sent me back to the dungeons. I did not speak to a human for five years. It was only myself in the darkness.

And I hate to write this, but those five years finally broke my spirit. I had been a captive for ten years total by this point. If you did return to Maevana, Aodhan, you would only be eleven years old. And I began to pray that Kane would keep you away from this darkness, that he would raise you up in a realm that was safe and good. And perhaps Kane had even remarried, for he believed I was dead, and so you would be raised by another woman who loved you. I thought of this so much that I began to believe it.

When Declan finally came back to visit me, he was now a man, and I was now crushed. I gave up the Morgane name. I wanted to take Hayden as my surname, but Declan said the Haydens were all dead and I needed to be a Lannon.

I became Lile Lannon.

Declan veiled me and brought me up to the castle to serve as his wife's chambermaid. No one but him and Gilroy and Oona knew who I truly was. And things were fine for a few years—I kept my head down and was silent so that they hardly noticed me anymore—but when Declan began to beat his wife, I confronted him, told him I knew he was better than this. And all Declan did was laugh at me, laugh as if I had lost my mind. It was even harder now, because Keela and Ewan had been born and were mere children. I could not protect all three of them—Declan's wife, his son, and his daughter. When his wife died, Declan sent me back to the dungeons. I think he believed I would try to run away with his children.

He kept me in a cell for a year, and then decided to let me loose, to sweep up the bones in the tunnels. I finally ceased keeping track of time. I didn't know the day, the year, or how old I was. When the coup finally happened and the Lannons were imprisoned . . . I didn't know what to do. I had been a captive for so long, I continued sweeping up the bones, too afraid to try and pass through the dungeon gate, up to the light.

And then I saw you, Aodhan. You and I nearly collided in the tunnels, and I thought my heart would burst. I knew it was you. And yet I was too afraid to reveal myself to you, even when Declan shackled me in his cell and you saw me yet again, with Davin and the queen. I was ashamed that I had given up my name. I did not know what was best for you, so I remained where I was, in those tunnels, in the darkness.

Until you returned for me. And I will always wonder what it was that brought you back, how you knew it was me.

One day, I want to hear your story, about all the years that I missed. I want to know where your father raised you; I want to know the places you have seen and the people you have known and loved. I want to listen as you tell me how you planned to return to Maevana, to put Isolde on the throne.

But for now, I think it is enough for me to say that I love you. I love you, Aodhan, my son, my heart. And I am so happy you came back for me in the darkness.

THIRTY-THREE

THE DRAGON AND THE FALCON

The Royal Castle at Lyonesse, Lord Burke's Territory
November 1566

Brienna

"Have you spoken to Aodhan?" Isolde's question brought my eyes to hers. We were sitting in her solarium at the castle with all the old records, planning her coronation for next week. And I did not desire to tell her how overwhelmed and distracted I was, because all of us were exhausted. But I could not deny that I was overcome with thoughts of Cartier and his mother, thoughts of Keela and Ewan, thoughts of my healing.

I no longer wore my bandage. I chose to formally cast it off the day before, at the Lannon executions. I had watched Gilroy and Oona both kneel and lose their heads on the scaffold with my face exposed. I had felt the sunlight and the wind and the gazes of hundreds, tracing my scar. But it had not stopped me from standing before the people of Lyonesse to make my case for Ewan's and Keela's pardons.

This was my face now. It testified for me, more than words, of what I had come through. And I was relieved when the people now saw it—saw *me*—that my brothers had seen it, my sister, my father, all the nobles of the realm. All save for Cartier, for he had not come to the executions.

I had not seen him since the day I had told him of his mother, nearly two weeks before. And I could not deny it, despite the courage I found day by day. He had not seen my scar.

"Only in letters," I replied. "He says his mother is doing well."

"I am happy to hear that," Isolde said, falling quiet. She had met Líle Morgane. The queen had been waiting for Cartier to return from the dungeons that night. Isolde had been one of the first to speak to her, to embrace her.

I wanted to ask more about Líle, but the words were too heavy to rise. And though it seemed that Isolde could read my mind—she knew I was worried about seeing Cartier again—I chose to cast my attention back to the coronation.

Isolde wanted her coronation to be as the queens before her—a celebration entwined with tradition—and yet she wanted it to also be illuminated with progression. Maevana was emerging from a very dark time, and so I tried to write down all of Isolde's desires, wondering how I was going to fulfill all of this for her in a mere seven days.

"What else do we want?" I asked, taking up my quill again.

"There should be music, of course," Isolde said. "Plenty of dancing and plenty of food."

"I believe everyone is to bring their own food to share," I said, sorting through the ancient papers that had miraculously survived Gilroy's reign. "Ah, yes. It says here that every House brings their best dish."

"Then that should be included on the invitation," the queen said.

Invitations. Right, I thought, scrambling through the ledgers to see if I could find an old sample of one.

"I want the invitations to be beautiful," Isolde said, almost dreamily. "They should be drawn by a calligrapher, with red and gold ink."

Saints above, I thought. How was I to execute all of this? Was there even a calligrapher in Maevana? Had Gilroy allowed for such beauty?

"Very well, Lady. I shall see what I can do," I replied. "Do you want to invite every House?"

Isolde slanted her eyes to me. "Do you mean do I want to invite the Lannons and Hallorans? Yes. They are part of this realm, no matter what the nobles of their Houses have done."

I finished adding to my vast list of things to accomplish, and when Isolde grew quiet, I glanced up to see she had set a small box before me.

"What is this?" I asked, wary of surprises. It was a small wooden box, handsomely carved. I gently opened it to find a silver brooch within, nestled on red velvet. It was crafted as a dragon and a falcon, one facing the west, one facing the east, their wings brushing. At first, I did not realize its significance, until I met Isolde's gaze, to see she was smiling at me.

"I want it to be known that I rise with a counselor," she said. "And that is you, Brienna, if you would choose it."

I was at a loss for words. All I could do was trace the beauty of it with my thumb. The dragon was her, the Kavanagh queen. But the falcon was me, the daughter of MacQuinn.

"Well, my friend," Isolde murmured. "What do you say?"

I pinned the brooch to my shirt, just over my heart. "I say, let us rise."

Isolde smiled, and I was surprised that she actually looked relieved. "Good. I know I have overwhelmed you enough for one day. But there is a surprise waiting for you in your room."

"Ah, Isolde. I dislike surprises."

"You will like this one," she said, taking the list out of my hands and guiding me to her door. "No more work for the day either."

I gave her a quizzical look but let her usher me out of the solarium.

My chambers were not far from hers, and I slowly walked toward them, wondering what she could surprise me with. I opened my door almost shyly, my eyes sweeping my receiving chamber.

"Brienna!" Merei was on me before I could so much as blink. She wrapped her arms around me and squeezed so tightly that I let out a burst of laughter, struggling to hold us upright.

"How did she sneak you past me?" I cried, pulling back so I could look at Merei's face, my hands tangling with her purple passion cloak.

"The queen has magic, doesn't she?" Merei said, her eyes glistening with tears. "Ah, Bri, I have missed you so! And you are going to make me cry."

"Don't cry," I rushed to say, but my own throat had grown narrow at the sight of her. She was taking me in as I was now—scarred, shorn, and yet I had never felt stronger than at that moment. "I know. I have looked better."

"You look beautiful, Brienna." She hugged me again, and for a moment we merely held each other, until her curls got in my mouth and I stepped on her toes. "But I'm not the only surprise for you."

"Mer," I said, half pleading, half warning as she gleefully approached my bedroom door. "You know that I *hate* being surprised."

"And that is why all of us decided to surprise you," Merei said, grinning. She paused, her hand on the door, purposefully drawing this moment out. "Are you ready?"

She didn't even wait for me to say yes or no. She opened the door and Oriana came bounding out. A cry of joy escaped me as I embraced her, and then all three of us stood in a circle, arms around one another, foreheads close together, sisters reunited. I had spent seven years of my life with them at Magnalia House. Merei had studied the passion of music, Oriana the passion of art, and I had studied the passion of knowledge. And seeing them now . . . I did cry. I held them and cried, to realize how much I had missed them. And then our tears transformed to laughter, and Oriana drew us over to my hearth, where a bottle of Valenian wine was waiting with three silver chalices.

"You must both tell me why you are here," I begged as Oriana poured us each a glass. "And how long I get to have with you."

"We are here to celebrate the rising of the queen," Merei replied.

"And," Oriana added, glancing to Merei, "someone said you needed to find a musician and a calligrapher for the coronation. We are here to help you, Brienna. We know that we are Valenian, but we want to share this moment with you and Maevana."

I could not hide my joy. It radiated from me as we toasted to the queen, as we toasted to our sisterhood and our passions. And then we sat before my fire and we talked for hours, time seeming to have no hold on us. Oriana told me of the passion House she was now instructing at, of how terrible and wonderful her pupils were, and Merei told me of her consort, where they had recently played, and all the beautiful cities she had seen.

The queen herself brought dinner to my chambers, and the four of us sat and talked of Valenia and our fondest memories and the exciting days to come. I could not have asked for a more exquisite night, sharing a meal with those I loved best, the friends of my girlhood and the queen of my future.

Isolde caught my eye from across the table. Discreetly, she lifted her chalice to me. And I knew she had reached out to Merei and Oriana for my sake, not for the coronation. She had brought my passion sisters here because she knew that I needed to see them, that my heart would be renewed by them.

I thought of the days before us, days we would carve with our hands and our minds and our words, days that would no doubt be uncertain and difficult and yet beautiful in the same breath.

Isolde drank to me, and I to her, the firelight glimmering between us, the dragon and the falcon.

—✦THIRTY-FOUR✦—

BETWEEN DARKNESS AND LIGHT

Mistwood, Territory of Lord Burke

Cartier

The day of Isolde Kavanagh's coronation arrived just as the last of the leaves fell, crimson and gold and umber.

I stood with my back to the wind, in the field that spread between the royal castle and Mistwood, the very ground we had waged war on the day of rising, mere weeks ago. I watched as the tables were arranged in the grass, in preparation for a great celebratory feast. The girls set the tables with polished pewter, rivers of white candles, and petals of autumn's final wildflowers. The boys had already marked off a designated stretch of green for games, and the women were bringing out their best dishes as the men tended to the roast pits, turning suckling pigs and freshly plucked fowl on skewers.

The air teemed with excitement, with fragrant smoke and crushed clover and harvested flowers. For Maevana was about to gain a queen after decades of darkness and decades of worthless kings.

And we all brought something, whether it was a loaf of bread or a wheel of cheese, a cask of ale or a bowl of plums. Everyone wore the colors or the sigils of their Houses, and so the field became a tapestry of color, woven together as the light began to wane.

I looked down to the doublet I wore, blue as the cornflower. For the thirtieth time, I brushed the wrinkles gathering in my garments, the wrinkles gathering in my heart, and I tried to distract myself with a group of lads who were attempting to out throw one another. And yet I could not help but search for her, for the MacQuinn lavender and golden falcon I knew she would be wearing.

"Milord! Milord, watch me!" Ewan shouted, and I smiled at the blessed distraction. I watched as Ewan hurled his three balls, not quite as far as the other lads, but still impressive for his small stature. "Did you see that, Lord Aodhan?"

I clapped and was promptly forgotten in Ewan's excitement to show off for a group of girls who had gathered to watch.

I merged back into the crowd, where most of my people were helping with last-minute food preparations. I saw Derry the stonemason chuckling, already tasting the ale and cider. And there were my mother and Aileen, sweeping a few wayward leaves off the plates that had been set. And Seamus, taking a turn at the roasting pit, dabbing the sweat from his brow. And Cook, fussing over where to set his herb potatoes and apple tarts.

I smiled at the sight of them.

From the corner of my eye, I saw Jourdain in his lavender and gold, standing off to the side, uncertain. He waited in the grass, regarding my mother. And I thought about how he had once planned a revolution with her, one that had failed, one that made him believe she had been dead for twenty-five years.

Líle felt his stare, glanced upward. I watched the joy brighten her face as she recognized him, as she walked to him. They embraced, laughing and weeping.

I turned away to grant them a private moment.

And then I thought, *If Jourdain is here, Brienna must be nearby.*

I had not seen her since that morning she had summoned me to Fionn, that morning she had told me of my mother. Brienna's hair had been shorn, her face had been bandaged, her skin pale and bruised. I had all but broken at the sight of her; what had she endured, and why had I not been able to reach her sooner?

I remembered how I had waited days for her to summon me, how I had paced the corridors and walked the meadows of Brígh, unable to think of anything but her, worried sick over why she did not want to see me. And then when she had called me to Fionn, how I moved toward her, aching to hold her, and how she had kept that distance between us with her voice and her eyes. She did not want me to touch her. And I still did not know if it was because of the news she was about to tell me, or if it was because she suddenly desired distance from me.

I walked to the forest, weaving through clusters of people, through the trees, looking for her. I knew it was almost time; it was dusk. And traditions were to be upheld; the queens were always crowned in Mistwood at dusk.

I was standing in a group of Burkes when the flutes began to play, to usher people into the woods, to prepare for the queen's coming.

And that is when I finally saw her.

Brienna stood beneath the great oak. She was wearing a dress the color of dawn, a purple that rested between darkness and light. The Stone of Eventide hung from its chain in her fingers, and a crown of wildflowers rested on her brow. She was not wearing her passion cloak, but neither was I, both of us choosing to represent Maevana alone that night.

I saw the scar that now claimed the right side of her face, a scar that I knew matched the one in my spirit. And yet it faded away the longer I looked upon her, for I was consumed by her entirely.

I willed her to look this way, to find me in the crowd.

And she almost did; her gaze was skimming the firelight when I felt Lord Burke touch my shoulder.

"Morgane! Thought you'd be with your people."

"Ah, yes, well." I glanced to him, hardly remembering where I was. He must have noticed that Brienna was all I could look at, because he smiled and said, "You must be very proud of her. Although she outranks you by far, lad."

And I wanted to ask what he meant, but then I noticed the

silver pin at Brienna's breast, gleaming like a fallen star, proclaiming who she was.

And that was when I realized it, my breath leaving in a quiet rush.

Brienna was the queen's counselor.

⊰ THIRTY-FIVE ⊱

THE QUEEN RISES

Mistwood, Territory of Lord Burke

Brienna

The light was beginning to fade, the shadows beginning to sweeten, and I knew the queen would soon arrive. I admired the forest around us, these old trees that had sheltered the queen's coronation centuries ago. There were lanterns hanging from the boughs, trickling warm light over our shoulders. The air smelled cool and sweet. Garlands of flowers were woven from tree to tree like gossamer.

I continued to wait for her, standing beneath the great oak, the magistrate at my side.

He would crown the queen. And I would grace her with the stone.

I closed my eyes for a moment, quieting my mind. In many

ways, this felt like the summer solstice five months ago, the night when I was to passion and gain a patron. And how that night had gone astray; nothing had gone according to plan.

Yet that night had inspired this one, for if I had not failed, I would not be standing here.

I opened my eyes, my gaze going straight to where my people were gathered. Neeve, Sean, Keela, Ewan, Oriana, Merei, and Luc. They were talking, laughing, enjoying this moment. And my heart swelled at the sight of them; I belonged to them, and they to me. And yet where was my father? Where was Cartier? I could not deny that I was anxious to see him. For him to see me.

No sooner had I thought such did I see Jourdain weaving through the crowd, a woman at his side. I knew it was her. It was Líle Morgane. Because Cartier was her very image, this wheat stalk grace and flaxen hair and eyes so blue they seemed to burn.

And yet I had no time to wonder over her, for the flutes began to play and Isolde and Braden finally arrived, as if the magic had brought them. Isolde had never looked so lovely, so radiant. I could not take my eyes from her as she and her father walked to stand before me and the magistrate.

"Isolde, daughter of Braden and Eilis Kavanagh, you stand before us to ascend the throne of Maevana," the magistrate said, and even though his voice was old and weathered, it carried through the woods. "Do you accept this title?"

"Yes, sire," Isolde replied, steady, unwavering.

"Upon receiving this crown"—I began to recite the ancient vows—"you recognize that your life is no longer your own, but that you are married to this land, to its people, that your sole responsibility is to protect them and serve them, to uphold and honor them, and above all else ensure that the magic you create is meant for good and not for harm. Can you accept this vow?"

"Yes, Lady."

"The lords and ladies of the Houses and the men and women of Maevana gather here this evening to witness your vow," the magistrate continued. "In return, we vow to serve you, honor you, kneel to none other but you, and trust that the decisions you make are for the good of the land. We vow to protect your life with ours and to guard the lives of your sons and daughters to come."

The magistrate paused, unable to hide his smile. "Come, daughter, and kneel before us."

Isolde let go of her father, planting her knees into the earth among the roots.

First came the stone.

I was careful as I lifted the necklace by the chain, to hold the Stone of Eventide up so all could see. And then I looped it over the queen's head, and I heard the whisper of it settling, watched as the Eventide came to rest above Isolde's heart. It did not burn her, for she held the fire within her blood. Rather, the stone shone for her, coming alive with iridescent colors. I could see the light of it on my hands, dancing crimson and turquoise and amber on my knuckles, reflecting on my dress, and I marveled at it, at her, the queen of the north, my friend.

Isolde's crown came next.

The magistrate held it up to let the candlelight kiss the

diamonds. And then he set it gently upon Isolde's head, the silver glittering like stars among her dark auburn curls.

Last came the cloak.

The captain of Isolde's guard brought it forward, the royal robes draped over his arm—red and gold velvet adorned with black threads, pearls, and sunstones. The warrior brought it about her shoulders, and I could smell the incense within it, clove and cardamom and vanilla, spicy yet sweet. The cloak was a beautiful display of the dragon for the queen to wear at court.

"Rise, Queen Isolde, House of Kavanagh," I said as I turned up my hands, palms to the sky.

Isolde stood, as if she was rising from shadows, rising from the mist.

The flutes and the drums began to play a joyful melody, and Braden Kavanagh stepped back, knowing Isolde was no longer his; she was ours.

Isolde looked directly at me. A smile illuminated her face; my own face mirrored hers. When she turned, we cheered for her, raising our voices with our hands, the boys and girls tossing flowers in her path. Isolde's six Kavanagh lasses—the girls Cartier had found in the butcher's shop—came about her dressed in red and black, the colors of their House. And it filled me with joy to see them grinning broadly, to see the flowers in their hair and the affection they held toward the queen. Isolde had claimed them as her sisters; they would always have a place in her castle, at her side. And I looked forward to seeing the girls' magic begin to awaken.

I stood among the oak's roots for a moment more, lingering

in the excitement, the splendor of the moment. Jourdain came to stand with me, his hands resting on my shoulders as Isolde wove through the trees, her long cloak dragging over the earth behind her.

"I never thought I would see this day," my father murmured, and I heard the emotion in his voice.

I thought he spoke only of Isolde, so he surprised me when he dropped a kiss in my hair and said, "I am proud of you, Brienna."

I laid my hand over his, thinking of that moment we had first met, when I had been suspicious of him, when he had been intrigued by my ancestral memories, when the two of us decided to trust each other and plot for the queen's return. I would never have dreamt that I would be the one to partake in her coronation, that I would speak the ancient vows to her, that I would be her right hand. I was filled with both awe and rapture.

"There is an old friend of mine that I would like you to meet," Jourdain whispered, squeezing my shoulders.

I turned to see Líle step forward. She smiled at me, and I thought I might weep, to finally come face-to-face with her.

I did not know what to say, and then I realized . . . there were no words for this. And so I embraced her; I let her hold me and for the first time in my life, I knew what it felt like to be held by a mother.

Gently, she drew back to lay her hand upon my scar, as if she knew that my pain had brought her joy. We were reflections of each other; I laughed and cried in the same breath. And when my tears fell, she wiped them away tenderly.

I do not know how long we stood there, but I suddenly became aware of the light fading. Jourdain was still at our side, but everyone else had already left the woods for the meadow, and I could hear the drums pounding in the distance.

"Come, dear ones. The celebration awaits," Jourdain said, his arms outstretched to escort us.

I let my fingers rest on his elbow, and Líle took his other arm. We walked together, my father, Cartier's mother, and me. Just before we reached the meadows, I looked at Jourdain and said, "This all feels like a dream, Father."

He only smiled at me and whispered in return, "Then let us never wake."

THIRTY-SIX

THE BEST OF YOUR HOUSE

Mistwood, Territory of Lord Burke

Cartier

The feast officially began, and there was a mad dash to the roast pit and food tables. I was still among the Burkes, and rather than fight the current, I walked with them to the meadow. The first stars had broken the dusk, and I stood for a moment, gazing up at them until I was jostled by a group of lads. I began to weave about the tables, slipping through knots of people who were all trying to fill their plates and catch a glimpse of Isolde.

I looked for Brienna; I sought a glimpse of her lavender dress, a glimpse of her grace among the revelry. But there was no sight of her. And the longer I searched, the more worried I became.

Gradually, I drifted into the heart of the field, feeling as if I was floating in a sea of strangers until I saw Brienna standing with Merei, both of them holding long ribbons in their hands. Merei felt my stare first, meeting my eyes over Brienna's shoulder. Her gaze flickered back to her friend, but it was apparent Merei was creating a reason to step away. She pointed to something and melted into the crowd, leaving Brienna alone. I moved forward, knowing this might be the only chance I had to speak with her.

Brienna stood quietly. But Merei must have told her I was coming, because Brienna didn't seem to be breathing as she felt me move closer. Nor did she turn to meet me as I hoped she would. She kept her back angled to me, and it only heightened my worries that she had been avoiding me.

"Brienna."

She finally pivoted, to stand face-to-face with me, her eyes luminous in the firelight. For a moment, she did not speak. Her gaze touched mine and then darted away, distracted by a nearby reveler. But I saw how she tilted her face so that her scar was partially hidden from me. As if she was anxious for me to see it.

My heart ached, and now I was the one who could not speak.

"Lord Morgane," she said, still distracted.

Lord Morgane. Not Cartier. Not even Aodhan.

She was putting that distance between us, and I tried not to reel from it.

"Did you see Isolde's coronation?" she quickly added, and I realized she was just as nervous as I was. "I looked for you."

"I was there. I saw you give the vows." I waited for her to meet my gaze again. Slowly, she lifted her eyes to mine. The silver brooch at her heart caught the light. I smiled at her, unable to conceal my pride, my awe. "Queen's Counselor."

A smile warmed her face. I could hardly bear it, the beauty of her.

"Ah, yes. I meant to write and tell you about that but . . . things have been quite busy here."

"I can imagine. Although I trust you have been able to enjoy your time in Lyonesse?"

We spoke of the past few days and weeks. Brienna told me of the executions, the pardons for Ewan and Keela, the planning. And I told her briefly of Líle's return. In some ways, it felt like Brienna and I had been apart for years. So much had occurred since the last time we had seen each other. But the more we conversed, the more relaxed she became, the more she smiled.

"And what is this?" I asked, indicating the ribbon she continued to hold in her hands.

"I was looking for a partner." She glanced away from me, into the crowd, like she was about to pick a random stranger to join her.

"A partner for what?"

"A game you would hate, Cartier." Her gaze returned to mine, but only to grant me a wry look, one that said she knew me well.

"Should we find out, then?" I challenged.

"Very well." Brienna began to walk, and I followed as if I was already tethered to her. She glanced over her shoulder at me and said, "But I warned you."

She brought me to the game lawn. And I saw with horror that this was one of those racing games, where two people were fastened together by the ankle, subjected to running around ale casks, and made to look like absolute fools.

Brienna had been right. I inwardly balked at the notion, but I did not stray, I did not move away from her. Even when she cocked her brow at me, expecting me to protest.

Merei appeared, flushed and smiling, her flower crown beginning to slip from her hair.

"Hurry, the two of you!" she urged before she ran across the green, where Luc was impatiently signaling her.

I took the ribbon and knelt. Brienna lifted her hem, so I could wind the ribbon about our ankles. I knotted it fiercely, so nothing could break it. And when I rose, she smiled at me, as if she knew my thoughts. She wrapped her arm about me, and we awkwardly walked together to the starting line.

We stood with Luc and Merei, Oriana and Neeve, Ewan and Keela, all who seemed to be thrilled about the prospect of three-legged racing. I stared at the casks we were supposed to charge about, disgruntled, until Brienna whispered, "What will you give me if we win?"

My eyes shifted to hers. And yet I had no time to answer her. The race began, and we were the last off the line, but Brienna and I were evenly matched. We gained on Ewan and Keela, chasing after Luc and Merei. Neeve and Oriana were in the lead, unsurprisingly. But some fool had placed the third cask on a slope, and my foot went into a burrow. I lost my balance, taking Brienna with me. We were a tangle of limbs, of blue and lavender, as we rolled down the hill into the shadows.

I heard something shred beneath my knees. I dug my hands

into the soil to stop us, Brienna beneath me, and I struggled to gain my breath, to discern her face in the starlight.

"Brienna?"

She was shaking. I thought she was hurt until I realized she was laughing. And I sagged against her, feeling her laughter spread from her chest to mine until I had tears in my eyes, and I couldn't remember the last time I had felt so happy.

"I think I ripped your dress."

"It'll be all right." She sighed, meeting my gaze.

For a moment, we didn't move, but I could feel her breathing against me. And then she tilted her face away again, to hide her scar in the shadows.

I gently took her chin to draw her eyes back to mine.

"Brienna, you are beautiful."

And I wanted to bow to her. I wanted to know her, explore her. I wanted to be loved by her. I wanted to hear her say my name in the dark.

But I waited. I waited for her to lift her hand, to touch me. Her fingers traced my face, slowly twining into my hair.

I kissed her, and her lips were cold and sweet beneath mine. She held me close to her, and somewhere in the distance I could hear the music and the laughter of the celebration. I could feel the tremble in the earth from the dancing and smell the fire and the wildflowers, and yet it was only her and me lying in the grass, gilded in starlight.

There was a sudden rumble.

I pulled back to look at her, to see she was trying not to laugh again. And I might have been mortified had I not realized her stomach was growling.

"I'm so sorry," she breathed. "But I haven't eaten since dawn."

I only smiled and stood, helping her up. Brienna brushed clumps of grass from her dress, and I saw that I had, indeed, torn her skirts. I unknotted our ribbon and we walked back into the firelight, where another round of races had begun.

Our friends were waiting for us by the ale station; Oriana and Neeve had won, and Ewan was pouting about it until I hefted him onto my back, and together we meandered to the food tables to fix our plates.

"I need to find Líle," I said to Brienna after we had gone through the line.

"She's with Jourdain," Brienna replied. And she led the way to a long table, where I found my mother was sitting beside Jourdain. And beside her was Thane Tomas. And on the other side of Tomas was Sean.

My eyes roamed the table, at the people gathered here. MacQuinns. Lannons. Morganes. Allenachs. Valenians. Even a few Dermotts. People who had once been enemies were breaking bread and giving toasts.

I sat across from my mother, sharing a smile with her, listening to the conversations and the laughter that graced the table. And I thought, *This is what I have longed for. This is what the queen brings to our land, to our people.*

Brienna was at my side, engrossed in conversation with Oriana and Merei, when Ewan tugged on her sleeve. And I could not scold him, not on a night like this. I watched from the corner of my eye as he asked, "Mistress Brienna? Will you dance with me?"

Brienna was up before I could breathe, rushing with Ewan to the dancing green. And then half the table followed them, unable to resist the siren call of the flutes and drums. I turned about on the bench so I could watch, and amid the blur of colors and movement, my eyes never left her.

"My sister is very beautiful, is she not?" Neeve said, sitting beside me.

"She is."

Neeve and I continued to watch in companionable quiet. And then she whispered, "A word of advice, Lord Aodhan."

I glanced to her, intrigued.

Neeve stood but met my gaze before she joined the dancing, mirth alight in her eyes. "You would do well to remember my sister is a MacQuinn."

And I didn't grasp her words, not until well after midnight, when I was in my castle chambers. I was preparing for bed when I found it in my pocket. Slowly, I withdrew it, the ribbon that had bound Brienna and me.

And that was when I understood.

I thought of the Morganes; I thought of the best of my House.

I thought of Brienna, a lord's only daughter.

She was a MacQuinn. And there was only one way to prove myself worthy of her.

THIRTY-SEVEN

TO MEET THE LIGHT

Lord MacQuinn's Territory, Castle Fionn

Brienna

A fortnight after Isolde's coronation, I decided that it was time for me to write my story down. Because there were some mornings when I rose at Castle Fionn and some evenings when I stood with Isolde in the throne room, and I wondered how this all came to be.

I sat in my chambers in glorious solitude, pushed my desk before my windows, and I began to give my past a shape, ink on paper, page after page, beginning with my grandfather, and then about the girls I had grown up with and loved as my sisters at Magnalia House.

I wrote about Master Cartier, and how afraid we used to be of him, because he never smiled until the day I coaxed him to stand on a chair with me, the day I first heard him laugh.

I was almost to the moment when I met Jourdain and learned of the revolution, the first snow beginning to fall beyond my window, when Luc knocked on my door.

"Dinner, sister."

And I realized that I had not eaten all day, and so I set down my quill, tried to wipe the ink from my fingers, and meandered down to the hall.

Jourdain smiled at the sight of me, and I sat at his left while Luc sat on his right. Keela was sitting with the weavers, tucked next to Neeve.

I thought about how much I loved this place and this people, and poured myself a cup of cider.

That was when the doors of the hall blew open, and Cartier rode in on the most beautiful horse I had ever seen.

I don't know what surprised me more: the fact that he boldly rode a *horse* into Jourdain's hall, or that he was looking at me and no one else.

I forgot that I was pouring cider; it overflowed from my cup.

He took us all by surprise. I knew it because my father was just as frozen as I was, and Luc's mouth was gaping. Neeve was the only one who did not look flustered. My sister was trying to hide a smile behind her fingers.

Cartier walked the horse all the way to the steps of the dais, and there he came to rest, his passion cloak draped down his back as if he had captured a piece of the sky, glistening with snow, his face flushed from his ride, his eyes fixed on me.

"Morgane?" Jourdain stammered, the first of us to recover.

Only then did Cartier look to my father. "I have come to present myself as a suitor for Brienna MacQuinn. I bring the best of my House, a Morgane horse, bred for endurance and speed, should she accept my offer."

My heart was dancing, pounding, aching.

Jourdain turned to me, wide-eyed. "Daughter?"

And I knew I must set the impossible challenge upon Cartier.

Slowly, I rose from my chair and looked at Cartier.

He returned my stare; I saw the fire burning within him, that he would do this my way because he wanted to, that he would search for however long it took to find the golden ribbon.

"Bring the tapestry, please," I said, and watched as the weavers departed to bring it forth. They returned to the hall with the infamous tapestry, and the men worked to string it up from its four corners, so both sides could be seen.

Dillon offered to lead the horse to the stables and Cartier stood, patiently waiting until the tapestry was up, every eye riveted to him.

He looked to me as I looked to him.

"Within every MacQuinn tapestry lies a golden ribbon that the weaver has hidden among the wefts," I said to him. "Bring me the golden ribbon that hides within this tapestry, and I will accept your horse."

Cartier bowed and then proceeded to stand before the tapestry, searching it methodically, beginning with the very bottom right corner.

Thirty minutes passed. Then an hour. But Cartier didn't rush. He took his time, and when Jourdain realized this, he sat back in his chair and motioned for his new chamberlain.

"Bring out some more ale and a batch of honey cakes. This is about to be a long night."

And it was a long night.

Eventually, Ewan appeared, bright eyed and flushed, and I knew he had run all the way here, terrified of missing the drama. He sat beside Keela and bit his nails, brother and sister quiet as they watched Cartier look for a ribbon that did not wish to be found.

MacQuinn's people were also fairly quiet. Every now and then a conversation would spark, but no one left the hall. Everyone watched the lord of the Swift. Some people laid their heads down on the table and fell asleep.

Eventually, I was so weary of standing that I resumed my seat, and I could only imagine what Cartier was feeling, standing and searching before a vast audience.

The eastern windows blushed with sunrise when Cartier finally found the ribbon.

My eyes had never left him that night, and I watched—hardly breathing—as his graceful fingers uncovered the ribbon's edge, as he gently tugged until it came free, a thin shimmer of gold.

He turned to me and knelt on the dais stairs, holding the ribbon between his hands.

"Before you decide anything," Cartier said, "let me say a few words."

Luc, who had been snoring in his chair, perked up. As did Jourdain, who linked his fingers and propped his chin on them, trying to hide the smile tugging at the corners of his mouth.

I nodded, my voice captive in my chest. But a song was rising in me, a song I knew Cartier heard as well, because his eyes gleamed as he looked at me.

"I remember the day you asked me to instruct you, like it was yesterday. You wanted to become a mistress of knowledge in only three years. And I thought, *This is a girl who will do something with her life, and I want to be the one who helps her reach those dreams.*"

He paused, and I worried he was about to cry, because I also felt the tears build in me.

"The day I left you at Magnalia, I wanted to tell you who I was, to bring you home with me to Maevana. And yet I was not the one to bring you. *You* brought *me* home, Brienna."

I was weeping now; I couldn't hold back the tears as I listened to him.

"I love the heart that is within you," Cartier said, smiling as his tears fell. "I love the spirit you are forged from, Brienna Mac-Quinn. If you were a storm, I would lie down and rest in your rain. If you were a river, I would drink from your currents. If you were a poem, I would never cease to read you. I adore the girl you once were, and I love the woman you have become. Marry me. Lead my lands and my people, and take me as yours."

I stood and wiped the tears from my eyes, laughing and crying and feeling like I was about to unravel from his words. But then I breathed, steadied myself, and looked at him, still kneeling in wait, still holding the golden ribbon.

I came to stand before him. The hall was quiet, so quiet I do not think anyone dared to move in that moment.

"Aodhan . . . *Aodhan*," I whispered his true name; I explored the rise and fall of it, and he smiled to hear it.

I reached down to accept the ribbon from him, to take his hands and bring him to his feet. I wove my fingers in his hair and I breathed against his lips, words only he would hear. "I love you, Aodhan Morgane. Take me, for I am yours."

I kissed him before my father, my brother, my sister, my people. I kissed him before every eye in that hall. Cheers swelled around us like a mist, until I felt the celebration move through my body, until I heard the pounding of cups on the tables, to usher a toast for MacQuinn and Morgane coming together, until I heard Keela shouting for joy and Ewan telling her, "I told you so! I told you it would happen!"

And when Aodhan's mouth opened beneath mine, when his hands pressed me to him, I forgot about all others save for him. The sounds and the voices and the laughter faded away until it was only me and Aodhan, sharing breaths and caresses and planting secret promises that would soon bloom between us.

Eventually, he drew back to whisper against my lips, so only I could hear:

"Lady Morgane."

I smiled, to hear the beauty of such a name. And I thought of the women who had worn it before me—mothers, wives, sisters.

I claimed it as my own.

ACKNOWLEDGMENTS

Writing this sequel was a magical but challenging experience, and it could not have happened without the love and support of so many people.

First, to my incredible agent, Suzie Townsend. Suzie, you changed my life with an email back in 2015. I sometimes can't even believe it: that I now have two books published because of you. Thank you for the love and passion you have given to my stories, for being there to lead me through the highs and the lows, and for helping me reach a childhood dream.

To the team at New Leaf Literary—Kathleen, Mia, Veronica, Cassandra, Joanna, Pouya, and Hilary. I am so blessed to have such an amazing group of people behind me! Thank you for all the magic you have created for *TQR*, here in the United States and overseas. Also, to Sara, for reading this sequel at its first draft, and to Jackie and Danielle, for warmly welcoming me into the New Leaf family.

To my wonderful editor, Karen Chaplin. You have brought my writing to the next level, and I am so grateful for the time and love that you have poured into my books. Thank you for fearlessly diving into my world and helping me polish it until it shined. Also, thank you for the suggestion to write Cartier in first person. I did not think I could do it until you believed I could.

Rosemary Brosnan, thank you for loving this story and believing in it from the very beginning. I am so honored to be a part of your incredible team, and I cannot thank you enough for your guidance and support. Many thanks to everyone at HarperTeen who have helped shape both of my books into beautiful things: Bria Ragin for your wonderful notes and insight, Gina Rizzo for all of the amazing opportunities you have given me in interviews and travel, Aurora Parlagreco for creating not one but TWO absolutely stunning covers that still bring tears to my eyes, my sales team (thank you for helping me title the first book!), my publicity team, my marketing team, my design team, and my production editors. I am so honored to have your expertise and support in bringing my books to life. Also, a huge hug and thank-you to Epic Reads, for all the love, pictures, and videos that you have created and shared with readers.

Thank you to Jonathan Barkat, for taking such beautiful photographs for my covers, and to Virginia Allyn, for the jacket illustration and for creating the exquisite map of my world.

Aly Hosch—where would I be without you? Thank you for taking my author photo and making me look good despite the drizzle. Your enthusiasm for my books has been a ray of light. Thank you for helping me spread the word about *TQR*, and for being at my side throughout this entire publishing adventure.

Deanna Washington—I made sure I put a few "candelabras" in this book just for you. But in all honesty . . . your friendship has inspired so many elements in my writing. Thank you for reading an early copy, for supporting me in spirit even when there's an ocean between us. You sharpen and strengthen me.

Bri Cavallaro and Alex Monir, my two Epic Reads tour buddies! I am so thankful that I got to tour with you both. Thank you for all the encouragement, friendship, and insight you gave to me in my debut year. Victoria Aveyard—thank you for letting me join you on two of your amazing *War Storm* tour stops, for befriending me and sharing in my debut excitement. You are an inspiration to me. Heather Lyons—I am so happy you reached out to me! Thank you for your friendship and encouragement in my writing.

There have been so many wonderful bloggers who have supported my books from the beginning. A warm thank-you to Bridget at Dark Faerie Tales and Kristen at My Friends Are Fiction. Your love for *TQR* and your gorgeous pictures are things that I cherish. Heather at Velaris Reads—my very first fan who I happened to bump into at YALLFest in 2017. Heather, I cannot thank you enough for all the love and support you have given me.

To my readers—thank you! I am so honored to have such amazing fans. Your sweet emails and messages, #bookstagrams, cosplay, tattoos, and fan art are the wind in my sails.

My family, above all, has been my rock throughout this endeavor. Mom and Dad—thank you for raising me with a love of stories and for encouraging me to dream and write from an early age. To my brothers and sisters, for reading early drafts and sharing in my excitement—Caleb, Gabe, Ruth, Mary, and Luke. A special thank-you to my in-laws, Ted and Joy, and to the Ross clan. To my grandparents, aunts, uncles, and cousins. All of you have supported me, and I cannot thank you enough.

To my Heavenly Father, for giving me the love of words and bringing these incredible people behind my books. My cup runneth over. *Soli Deo Gloria.*

To Sierra, for making sure I took breaks from drafting to go for much-needed walks. Also, for all the Frisbee throwing—the epiphany for this sequel happened while I was sitting on the back porch tossing a Frisbee to you. Of all things.

And to Ben. For dreaming alongside me, for believing in me, for carrying me through deadlines and launches, for reading my messy drafts, for building me a wall of bookshelves. I love you.